TRIASSIC 2 .

REVENANT

BY
JULIAN MICHAEL CARVER

SEVERED PRESS
HOBART TASMANIA

TRIASSIC 2

To Paul and Sharon Kelly.
Thanks to you both for years of creative motivation.

A MESSAGE FROM JULIAN MICHAEL CARVER

Hello! Thank you for buying a copy of *Triassic 2: Revenant*. After you finish reading this book, I would very much appreciate an honest review of the work on Amazon.com and Goodreads.com. Honest reviews help writers get noticed and, in turn, will help more readers become aware of my books. Likewise, if you have read any of my other works, such as *Triassic* or *Megacroc*, please leave an honest review for those books as well. Thank you, and enjoy the story.

-*J.M.C.*

PROLOGUE: 3545 A.D.

The sepia emergency lights inside the cockpit of *Harvester One* glowed through their glass enclosures as distress alarms roared out the recessed speaker ports. Around the command bridge, more Federation personnel scrambled to regain control of the ship's command features, such as communication functions and trajectory points, babbling out frequency codes to Captain Rupert Mason who shouted back, fighting to keep his crew organized amid the imminent disorder. But even more boisterous and overwhelming than the mechanized screeching and human shouting was the onslaught of the ruthless asteroids.

It was an asteroid field that appeared out of nowhere, in the deep space around the last known coordinates where the *Supernova* was last seen many years ago, long before the cultivation of Solis. As Corporal Adam Ross sat there behind his observation station, he wondered if this was the same dreadful asteroid field that knocked out much of Admiral Steve Perry's Federation fleet hundreds of years earlier. His instincts told him it was.

WHRRRR....CRACK!

To his surprise, Adam realized that he was suddenly airborne, spinning out of his wheeled chair and toppling to his left before smacking roughly off the bone-chilling cold floor of the *Harvester One* bridge. To his rear, he could hear a pair of female communication specialists careening from their seats as well, followed by violent, brash landings.

"*Aughhh!*" cried a female voice as her head hammered off the floor like a toppled appliance.

Adam turned, grabbing his throbbing head as he regained his footing, rearing around the desk to examine his injured comrades. The scream came from one of the women whom he met during the mission debriefing before *Harvester One* departed into the cosmos. To his surprise, he even remembered her name.

Sana.

"Are you all right?" he asked, leaning over her as he extended a helping hand.

"Yeah, thanks," Sana replied with a pause, as if unsure of the answer. "But she may not be."

The other communication specialist, or "Vira", as her brass embossed name-tag suggested, lay in a theatrical sideways pose on the ground, motionless. Sana crawled over to her, even as the captain roared from the background urging everyone to stay at their stations, no matter how dire the asteroid field had become.

WHRRRR....CRACK!

Another asteroid rocked the ship, sending tremors rippling over the internal rooms. The emergency indicator lights flickered on and off again, adding to the uncertainty of their survival.

"*Vira!*" Sana yelled at her unresponsive friend, cradling the specialist's solemn head from the frigid floor. "Damn, I think she's out cold!"

Adam stood watching in shock as the sounds of an approaching death echoed around the room. The fifty other crew members on the bridge began to fidget in their seats and disregard their duties. Rupert shouted resonant commands for them to hold their positions, rallying them to continue their jobs as the ship continued through the fierce swaths of space rocks.

Strapped to Captain Rupert's left arm was the *Harvester One* portal oscillator, a device enabling up to three portal jumps back to their home world. Adam was shocked none of the other personnel hadn't mutinied yet and stripped it from him. There were a few angry glares from the crew, but so far, none attempted to challenge the captain – despite the increasingly volatile situation.

Behind him, Adam felt a few defectors streaking past, their footfalls clacking down the hallway, heading presumably toward the escape pod bay.

"They better not launch unless they're ordered to," Sana remarked, trying in vain to wake her friend back to consciousness. "If the oscillator doesn't work, and that's if Rupert chooses to use it, we'll be stranded up here without any escape. We all know how shoddy that silly device can be."

"How many pods are there?" Adam asked.

"Hopefully enough," Sana answered, with a lack of confidence that made Adam regret coming on board this suicide mission in the first place. "You're not needed here now," Sana turned back to him, raising an eyebrow. "Don't you have that kid with you?"

"*Huh?*" Adam asked, rousing back to reality.

Nathan!

His nephew was still waiting obediently in his room six floors above the bridge, ever since the F80 surveillance craft spied a potential threat looming ahead.

"Why do you mention him?" Adam asked, a dreadful series of thoughts haunting his mind.

"Get him to the escape pod bay, and make sure he's in a hyper-sleep lockup pod. Any minute now, Rupert will order evacuation. I guarantee it. You better be on one when he does, in case the oscillator malfunctions again. Who knows how long the crew will wait before taking matters into their own hands, ejecting all the pods with them. Then we'll really be screwed."

"What are you saying?" Adam asked, still rubbing his head. He could feel a large goose-egg forming where his head met with the granite floor. A trickle of blood descended from his temple, meeting with his hand as he sought to quench the flow.

Sana looked up again from her deathly still friend, her eyebrows arched in a stern look. Her face static, the expression unforgivably grim and telling.

"I'm saying we're not gonna make it. *Harvester One* has failed. Now get the kid to an escape pod!"

WHRRRR....CRACK!

The next asteroid rocked into the ship, causing several computer terminals around to spark as the monitors switched to error screens before blacking out. Another pair of jagged rocks hurled themselves at the cockpit before the overhead pulse cannons wiped them away into space pebbles, buying the ship more time.

"Okay," Adam muttered, acknowledging the severity of her words.

"Be quick about it," she reinforced grimly. "We don't have much time."

Adam staggered backwards with an awkward nod, watching as Sana turned back to Vira and the rest of the remaining bridge personnel as they struggled to map out a last-ditch path through the asteroids. He started down the *Harvester One* main hallway in a full-on sprint.

I didn't sign up for this bullshit – that's for sure!

Adam ran down the corridor, his eyes trying not to focus on the maelstrom of asteroids rolling past the glass windows that Federation scientists claimed were structurally sound. Yet even as he bolted around another corner, he could see cracks forming from where the rocks avoided the cannon fire, connecting with the first layer of safety glass.

Passing a pair of Federation technicians who sought feverishly to repair a circuitry terminal, Adam turned to his left and bounded up a flight of stairs, beginning a six-story ascent to where Nathan's quarters were. The elevators had been deactivated when *Harvester One* entered the perimeter of the danger zone, otherwise that would've been his first stop.

First Nathan. Then I'll find Jade.

Nathan was his brother Andrew's only son. Nathan begged his father to let Adam take him aboard *Harvester One*, having recently taken up an interest in space exploration and colonization. His fascination with space travel began three years earlier, when the ancient and seemingly ghostly distress call from *Supernova* was discovered by Adam during his tenure in *Music Box*, a space station commissioned by the Federation Watch Force. Since the day the bureaucratic gridlock had finally been lowered to send a rescue team to investigate, Nathan somehow weaseled his way onto the rescue mission by means of educational opportunity, going as far as speaking with a contact at Central Command for permission. When a senior ranking official at Central Command sent a letter issuing Nathan a spot on board *Harvester One*, under the careful watch of his uncle Adam, Andrew reluctantly consented.

Now, as Adam Ross surged up the stairwell while asteroids pummeled *Harvester One* like an unfair boxing match, he realized he should've fought harder to keep Nathan back on their home world.

He also regretted bringing his girlfriend, Jade, whom he served with in the Watch Force at the *Music Box*. After the two left the service, they went their separate ways, until finally reuniting months earlier when Adam reached out to her, saying that he reserved a seat for her on *Harvester One*. He recalled saying that it was only right for her to come along, citing that she helped him discover the signal from *Supernova*, and that she should be there when they discovered who sent the distress call – a moment that would be remembered in the history books of Solis for centuries to come.

Adam had served as a lieutenant in the Watch Force, but since he was no longer enlisted, and since this mission could technically be classified as a potential combat mission headed by the Federation Galactic Marine Corps, Adam was demoted to corporal in exchange for the right to tag along.

Now he wished he would've stayed back on the planet, resuming his post military life of landscaping and sprucing up his new domicile. There he would be safe, and thus wouldn't be in this life or death situation right now with his nephew and recent girlfriend.

With a swift thrust, Adam pushed through the exterior stairwell doors to the sixth level, emerging into yet another chaotic scene.

Several *Harvester One* personnel were sprinting past, nearly running him over in their attempts to quicken their pace. They melted around him like a wave, their backpacks bouncing along as they hurried down the stairs, eager to get to an escape pod or within range of the captain's portal oscillator.

Assuming the old bastard actually gets that thing to work – if he chooses to use it!

In another group of uniformed Federation figures rushing toward him, he noticed an alluring familiar face.

Jade.

Adam hugged her as her colleagues streaked around the embracing couple. A few crew members grabbed at her sleeves in a vain attempt to herd her along. Eventually, they gave up and scurried down the stairs.

The doors slammed ominously behind them.

"What's going on?" Jade asked fearfully. "I thought this asteroid field was going to be brief. Now there's alarms going off and people rushing around. Adam, tell me what's happening! And don't sugar-coat it!"

"The ship won't make it," Adam replied, almost as sternly as Sana told him below on the bridge.

"*What?*"

"The bridge is in an uproar. People are defecting and rushing to the escape pods. I guess no one wants to challenge Rupert over the oscillator so they're jettisoning out in the E20s. I'm worried there won't be any pods left if we don't hurry."

"What are you –"

"Get to the escape pod bay. I'm going to get Nathan and I'll meet you there."

"You really think they're going to use up *all* the pods?"

"I'm hoping there will be some sentries left guarding them. Hopefully bots. They won't defect as easily as humans. Just get down there. I'll be there soon!"

Jade kissed him quickly and then spun back to the stairwell, descending out of view as the doors slammed shut once again. Adam sprinted down the apartments sector, encountering fewer people as he went. Many of the doors to the apartments were left ajar with belongings strewn about, signifying that the occupants left in a hurry. There were over 500 people on board *Harvester One*, and the lack of personnel on the apartments sector gave him a shuddering thought.

What if they all ejected out already, taking all the remaining E20s in the bay?

He brushed the thought aside, thankful when he reached his apartment where Nathan was staying. As the electric recessed door buzzed open, he saw his nephew quickly packing his backpack, cramming it full of whatever valuables a ten-year-old boy deemed worthy to grab in a volatile situation such as this.

"Hey," was all the kid had to say, cramming some water into the backpack.

"Hey," Adam repeated, surprised and relieved that Nathan was already packed to leave. The child must have sensed the impending danger of the ship, and was preparing in case his uncle dashed up to grab him.

Nathan threw his backpack over his shoulder, brushing his hair out of his eyes as he headed for the entrance. Adam was surprised to see the boy was wearing his favorite red jacket, anticipating its need wherever their escape pod landed – if it landed.

Or if there's any left!

"We going?" came the brief reply.

Adam sensed a trace of fear in the boy, but nothing more, even as he looked up with his icy blue eyes.

"Yeah, let's go. To be frank, I don't know how long we have."

That was all he needed to say before his nephew nearly bulldozed him over, and soon they were both running down the hallway, doubling back from where Adam had come.

"Why aren't we taking the main stairs?" Nathan asked as his uncle made an abrupt right turn.

"I know a faster way from here," Adam replied. "There's a utility stairwell around the main –"

Adam's forehead struck another man's head, adding another intense pain to his wound from falling on the bridge. Adam fell backwards, being propped up by his nephew who outstretched his arms in a quick reflex.

"I'm sorry, are you all right?"

Adam recognized his would-be assailant as Sergeant Wyatt Brolen, a marine known for his short temper and iron fist style of military stewardship. Wyatt had an angry scowl on his face as he palmed his forehead, trying in vain to soothe the bruise.

"*Dammit*, Corporal! Why aren't you on the bridge?"

"I was told the ship is going down, and that it might be best if I grabbed my nephew in anticipation of the escape pods ejection or, heaven forbid, we test out that clunky oscillator again."

"You *abandoned* your post?" Wyatt questioned angrily.

"I'm not the first to do so, Sergeant, but yes, I abandoned my station." Adam didn't feel like dealing with the sergeant's tirade right now, not during the theoretical demise of *Harvester One*. Even as he stared into Wyatt's judgmental gaze, he could feel the brutal swell of the asteroids as they continued to pound the ship's defenses. Time was running out.

"You're a defector! We brought you along because you begged us to be a part of this mission, and this is how you repay us? You're weak, Corporal!"

"I'm hardly a defector," Adam replied, countering Wyatt's verbal abuse. "My post on the bridge was useless from the beginning. Hell, my terminal hasn't been operational in weeks! The damn mainframe keeps overheating."

He could feel himself getting hot under the collar. Behind him, he could sense his nephew waiting for the argument to end so they could resume their flight for the escape pod bay.

"I'll see to it you're dealt with for this when we get back home," Wyatt barked.

"If we get back," came Adam's snarky reply.

"*If* we get back? What the *fu* –"

A large impact rocked the ship, sending the sergeant again falling backwards, knocking over a utility cart of toiletries that had been parked nonchalantly behind him.

Suddenly oxygen piping burst in the hallways, flooding the passageway with emergency air.

There's a breach in the ship somewhere!

Adam grabbed his nephew by the shoulder and rapidly resumed their sprint. Behind him, he could hear Wyatt about to give chase, before heading off in a different direction, abandoning the argument altogether in favor of evacuation preparation.

"I'll see to it that you're dealt with!" Wyatt called back, his voice fading as they put distance between him.

"We need to get to the escape pods now!" Adam urged.

When there was no reply from Nathan, Adam knew that the boy understood the stakes.

The door to the utility stairwell was already open. Adam knew that the ship's emergency powers were being directed elsewhere to reserve what depleting energy remained, now rendering all utility entrances open by default. The stairwell inside was laden with debris from previous fleeing civilians and soldiers.

One of the maintenance workers must've spilled a supply bag on the upper balcony, Adam judged, as he took note of the various wrenches, bolts, and mechanical tools scattered over the oncoming steps.

"Watch your step," Adam said, almost tripping over one of the chrome instruments.

"I see them," Nathan replied abruptly, clearly getting stressed by the escalating deadly situation.

About halfway down the stairwell, Adam was shocked to hear the captain's voice blaring through the loudspeaker. Through the static reception, Adam could hear the meteors pelting the glass of the bridge, followed by the muffled frantic voices and petrified questions of the crew nearest the captain's microphone.

"Attention Harvester One. Attention Harvester One," came the booming, digital voice from Rupert. *"Harvester One is going down. The Supernova rescue campaign is aborted. Given the circumstances, I doubt the ship will last much longer than a few minutes. I'm giving everyone two minutes to get to the bridge before I activate the oscillator and transport us back to our planet. That's two minutes before... what the... Lieutenant, is that what I think it is... All available units, please resp-p-p-p—"*

The captain's voice ceased ominously in mid-sentence, and the audio went dead.

"What was he talking about?" Nathan asked as they exited the stairwell and headed down the main hallway toward the command bridge. Ahead, Adam could see the entrance to the bridge where a majority of the personnel had already gathered, awaiting the captain's use of the portal oscillator.

7

"Who knows? Change of plans. The oscillator is the top priority. The escape pods won't guarantee that we'll ge –"

BSSRRRKK! HISSSSS!

The hallway ahead imploded, sending searing sparks showering over the reflective floor as metal crashed onto the ground. A hole out into space had opened up, sucking with it the metal debris that collapsed only seconds before. It would have sucked Adam and Nathan with it, had it not been for the fail-safe glass shield that slid down to sever his continuation down the hall to where the bridge remained.

"Oh hell," Adam remarked, his skin turning white.

Their escape path to the bridge was completely severed. It would take much longer than two minutes to navigate another safe route back to the front of the ship – and *Harvester One* wouldn't last two minutes according to the captain's cryptic final message.

"Uncle Adam. *Look!*"

Nathan pointed through the newly formed glass hallway barrier, which fed into a chasm to the side, allowing them to see into open space without obstruction.

No, it can't be!

Adam realized that he was staring at the business end of a black hole, gurgling asteroids into its expansive gullet as *Harvester One* was towed toward the dark cyclone. The ship would be swallowed in under a minute. Through the glass on the other side on the bridge, several onlookers waved to them dramatically as if telling Adam that his fate was sealed. Behind them, the blue aura of a portal opened up, and the people began filing rapidly toward it, turning away from him in a hurry.

"We'll never make it! *Quick* – the escape pod bay. There may still be units available!"

Adam herded his nephew down a narrow maintenance hallway. After a few sharp turns, the escape pod bay entrance loomed before them. As the doors to the bay opened, Adam's worst fears had been realized. All the E20 escape pods had vacated *Harvester One* – all but one.

At the end of the bay, a single bot, armed with an ECR-130 pulse rifle guarded the entrance to *Burrower*. The bot motioned Adam toward the pod.

"Why hasn't it deployed?" Adam asked.

"It's deploying in thirty seconds. Get inside, Corporal!"

Adam nodded and shuffled inside. Many of the other hyper-sleep pods were already filled, their occupants frozen subconsciously in deep sleep. He buckled Nathan into the first open chamber he saw and threw the glass dome over the capsule, before setting an external terminal to transport the boy to artificially induced slumber in twenty seconds.

Jumping into a conveniently placed pod beside Nathan's, Adam closed the glass facade over him and manually set the timer inside his chamber.

As he pressed down on the activate button, a horrific thought entered his mind.

Jade!

He hadn't seen his girlfriend in any of the hyper-sleep chambers in the *Burrower*. Outside the glass in front of him, he could see the military bot about to close the door to the escape pod, signifying that the time was now to deploy the craft – then he saw her.

From where Adam's hyper-sleep pod was located, he could see her running down the hallway toward the entrance to *Burrower*. The bot saw her and waved his metallic arms, urging her to increase her sprint speed.

CRRKKKK!

As Adam's artificial slumber began, his vision began to fog over, but he could discern what was happening. It was a vision that would most certainly haunt his dreams for years to come. A large asteroid ripped the *Burrower* from the escape pod bay. The darkness of space instantly replaced where the bay had once been, sucking Jade out into the nothingness beyond the *Burrower*.

Jade's face glazed over as she was swallowed by the darkness, locking with Adam's eyes as her soul left her body, rendering her corpse frozen in time and forever lost in the emptiness of deep space.

The last thing Adam saw before he slipped into sleep was the bot sealing the entrance while fighting the gravity shift. With the pod secured, the machine shuffled past to pilot the *Burrower* toward their uncertain future.

I

THUD! TH-THUD!

Adam's dreary dreams melted away into the darkness, replaced with a hazy fog. In front of him was a blurry figure, knocking on the glass with his tiny balled fists. As Adam's eyes adjusted, he was relieved to see it was Nathan. As his nephew appeared on the other side of the glass, Adam was shocked that the boy didn't have a scratch on him.

"Uncle Adam," came the muted voice on the other side. *"How do you open this thing?"*

Raising a weary finger, Adam pointed above to where the glass met with the metal frame of his hyper-sleep pod. His head throbbed from where he struck the floor of the bridge, and his nephew's pounding and screaming wasn't helping.

"Right there, kid."

HSSSS!

Adam's hyper-sleep pod brace unlatched, the door sliding open. He wearily stepped out of his capsule, helped by his nephew.

"Uncle Adam. We landed, but we don't know where."

"We... *landed?* But not on Solis?"

"Nope, somewhere else. Probably on the planet where the *Supernova* landed, if I had to guess."

Adam stretched out, leaning against the hyper-sleep chamber for support. The thought of landing somewhere other than Solis wasn't something that he had anticipated. He tried to remember what had happened in space and found he could easily piece together what happened, which meant he hadn't been in his pod for more than a few days. Normally gaps in memory would tend to happen the longer an occupant rode in a hyper-sleep pod.

He quickly sorted through the memories.

The *Harvester One* journeying through the endless depths of space. The discovery of a potential asteroid threat, which turned out to be what ended up destroying the ship. Rescuing Nathan. The argument with Wyatt. The black hole. The portal oscillator, that ended up surprisingly operating correctly on the bridge that had been sealed off due to an oxygen leak. And finally, the death of Jade, right before the *Burrower* departed from the escape pod bay.

"She's dead," Adam remarked, rubbing the mark on his head. The pain was manageable, but quick instances of sharp pain were enough to be annoying.

"*Who?*" Nathan asked.

"Jade."

"How do you know?"

"I saw it happen. Right after the bot launched us from the escape pod bay. The ship was fractured, and she was pulled out into open space – no helmet or space suit."

Should I be telling him this? Adam mentally debated, slowly coming back to the present.

He realized the boy was old enough to understand life and death. And with Jade gone, his nephew was the closest thing he had to a friend. He had to confide in someone.

Nathan nodded with a maturity that belied his age. He hadn't been exceptionally close to Jade, because he spent most of his time on *Harvester One* exploring the ship and talking with the marines. Jade was there for a humanitarian role, providing relief to any *Supernova* crash survivors. Nathan was more interested in pulse guns and detonators.

"How many survivors?" Adam asked, finding it hard to keep his mind off his girlfriend's demise.

"Just the *Burrower* that we know of," Nathan replied. "See for yourself."

The *Burrower* had been utterly decimated. Patches of the hull had been shredded in an apparent crash landing that the E20 escape pod had endured during a brutal entry into an unknown planet's atmosphere. Chunky dirt clods and leafy branches littered the floor of the room, spilling through the cockpit where the *Burrower* first met with the earth, forcing the glass barrier to implode inward. The room looked as if a violent earthquake had occurred.

"Where the hell are we?" came a familiar, disgruntled voice.

Sergeant Wyatt Brolen helped another marine out from his pod, before turning angrily to the bot.

"Unsure at the moment," the bot replied, trying to get some of the terminal ports to work. "My digital instincts tell me this is the planet where the *Supernova* landed many years ago. Right after we left *Harvester One*, we passed through a wormhole, which shot our pod out here. By the time I managed to get all of the *Burrower* functions online, we were already in the atmosphere. My sensors switched off three days ago, reactivating when some of the hyper-sleep pods began to open."

Adam studied the room, seeing who also survived the *Burrower* crash landing.

Other than the bothersome sergeant known as Wyatt and the bot named Alter, he noticed five other male marines, most of whom had either ECR-130 pulse rifles or ECSR-20 snipers. He only knew two of them by name, Alex Meras, who was a fellow corporal, and Bruce Lere, a rifleman. He saw that his friendly acquaintance from the *Harvester One* bridge, Sana Diazal had also survived. He also observed two women, one of whom he was relieved to see was a medical specialist.

Adam checked his suit, and realized he hadn't grabbed a firearm in the confusion from the starship's evacuation, feeling useless without an ECR-130. Even Nathan had grabbed a pocket knife; his own nephew was more on top of the unraveling situation than he was.

Hopefully, he prayed, *this unknown planet won't be potentially dangerous in which lethal pulse weaponry will have to be used.*

"Rice, give me a status report out there," Wyatt commanded as one of the men returned from the berm that had once been the cockpit. The volume of his voice made everyone in the *Burrower* cringe, even as they went about packing their gear to begin exploration of the new planet.

"Very tropical and arid," replied Rice, from behind his heavy five-o'clock shadow. "I scouted about fifty yards from where we wrecked. Didn't encounter any lifeforms. Alter, do your sensors detect anything nearby?"

"None currently," replied the bot, checking the safety on his ECR-130.

Alter was a bot built back on Solis to assist the rescue mission with short-range radar functions. Alter belonged to a series of bots known as CC – *Combat and Consciousness*. These CC bots contained combat-based features but were also programmed with personal learning capabilities like the ancient Federation logistics bots, giving them both a personality and a lethal trigger finger.

"Hey, we're in luck!" Sana called out, retrieving a Federation communication device from her hyper-sleep pod and switching it on.

After fiddling with the controls for a few seconds, a low-pitched whine followed by a series of digital bleeps began to emit from the small console speakers. On her little screen, a blue dot started to glow near the bottom right corner. Adam deduced that the central white dot in the middle of the screen was their current coordinates.

"What do you have?" Wyatt barked as the group of survivors congregated around her.

"Looks like *Harvester One*, or at least part of *Harvester One*, crashed several miles southeast. Another lovely tidbit of information; it looks like when Rupert and the crew abandoned ship, they left the portal oscillator on the bridge. I'm getting a reading that it is still there, operational with at least two active portal charges. They must've left it behind, assuming that one day, we'd come looking for it! If we can locate the *Supernova* crash survivors, we still may be able to complete the mission."

A flurry of cheers arose from the *Burrower* survivors, patting each other on the back as they began to speculate the praise they would receive back on Solis – until a certain degrading whistle broke through the pod, forcing the soldiers to cover their ears.

"Hold up, hold up," Wyatt grumbled. "Sana, how far is the crash site?"

"Hard to pinpoint from the reading," replied the communication specialist, studying the small view port monitor on her console device. "There is some interference in the topography. I'd say perhaps a two day walk at the most. If we hurry, maybe a day."

"All right, let's make for the portal oscillator and head home," Wyatt ordered.

Silence blanketed the crumbling interior of the *Burrower*. It was clear that most of the group disagreed with the sergeant's opinion. Finally, Corporal Alex Meras broke the silence.

"Sir, we can't just head for the portal and go back to Solis. Against all odds, we found where the *Supernova* landed. It's here somewhere. We need to find the wreckage and locate the survivors – then we can head home."

"No can do, Corporal," Wyatt returned. "We've lost over ninety percent of the *Harvester One* personnel needed to complete this mission. With only the twelve of us, we won't be able to do any good. We need to get back to Solis, regroup, and come back with more firepower and equipment to –"

"Sir, with all due respect," a marine known as Bruce began, "we're already here. It shouldn't be too hard to locate the survivors and herd them to the portal oscillator."

"On the contrary, Private, it will be incredibly hard," barked the irritated sergeant. "We've lost all of the planetary scouting ships to patrol the surface to locate the *Supernova* crash. What's the big plan now? The twelve of us are going to scan over the whole planet with very limited food, water, and ammunition, hoping we encounter the sender of that distress call? No, we're heading for the oscillator and returning home. That's final."

"The hell it is," Adam exclaimed, surprising everyone with his sudden boldness.

"What's that now?" Wyatt shot back. After seeing who it was, a look of disdain came over his face.

Adam was actually surprised he had challenged the sergeant in such a manner. He guessed that after the two had previously exchanged harsh words on board *Harvester One*, he had already crossed the line.

"*Ah*, the defector," Wyatt started. "Why should anyone here listen to you, after you abandoned your post back on the bridge?"

"I've already told you," Adam scowled. "My terminal was shot from the beginning. I was informed that *Harvester One* could function at optimal power without my station in operation. As far as the oscillator goes, yes, I think recovering the device is our top priority, but we're not leaving here until we find the *Supernova* crash survivors. That's what

Solis and Central Command sent us here for."

Several nods of agreement started among the group, despite Wyatt angrily turning and glaring at Adam's co-conspirators.

"Corporal, an order is an order. Don't make me smack you down."

Adam was out of ideas on how to respond, but was thankful when Corporal Alex Meras again came to his defense.

"Sergeant, Corporal Adam Ross is right. All of us vowed to sacrifice our lives for this rescue mission. The fact that most of the *Harvester One* crew has departed or have been killed changes nothing. I say we make for the oscillator and resume the mission."

"I think Alex is right," Brandy Dietrich, a translator and interpreter added. "Even so, if we have the portal oscillator with us, and continue searching, we'll be able to jump back to Solis if need be."

Several agreements followed throughout the ruined *Burrower*. Soon, all present were agreeing with Adam Ross' idea – which further agitated the sergeant.

"Have you all lost your minds?" Wyatt roared. "There's *twelve* of us! We don't know where we are or what's out there. We could soon become the rescue mission itself – don't you see that?"

"Look," Adam started. "We're all in agreement about one thing. Getting the oscillator in our possession. After that, if we need to take a new vote, we'll reassess then. Sorry, Sergeant, I think we're outvoting you on this one."

"I'm in command here!" Wyatt fired back, red in the face. "Corporal, you are out of line!"

"I was a lieutenant in the Watch Force," Adam replied. "I was brought on as a corporal under the confines of being a terminal operator on the bridge. Well that time has passed – this is a potentially dangerous situation unfolding, and as such, I invoke the Federation Rank Jump Act of 3480, and assume my previous rank, claiming this mission as a 'dire situation'."

"*What?*" Wyatt scoffed, visibly offended. "That's completely absurd!"

"It is ridiculous," the marine named Jonas Carte replied, shouldering his ECR-130. "But it is an official Federation Act, nonetheless. I remember thinking how ridiculous it was when I read about it the first time. But this situation does technically constitute as a rightful use of the Act."

Wyatt frowned, defeated for the moment. The sergeant could plainly see that the marines were already nodding in agreement, turning to Adam Ross for guidance. Adam sensed this ranking situation might not last long, but he savored the moment.

A man like Wyatt won't take this lying down.

"What do we do now, Lieutenant?" Ziven Wyke asked.

"Gather what we can and leave our *Burrower* transport behind. The vehicle's destroyed and lost its usefulness. We'll make for the oscillator. After we've safely retrieved it, we'll begin fanning through the nearby regions for any lingering *Supernova* survivors."

A flurry of agreement rang out among them as the marines went to work. Some grabbed their pulse weaponry and headed for the gash in the escape pod near the windshield. Others attempted to salvage supplies among the rubble before joining their cohorts. Wyatt shot Adam a wicked look before grumbling out of the open windshield, disappearing in the sunlight that was flooding into the opening.

Nathan prepared to follow the last of the marines out of the hole before Adam grabbed his arm gently. The boy turned, a look of annoyance and disapproval passing over his face.

"*Yeah?*" an impatient young voice uttered.

"I know you're not a little kid anymore, Nathan," Adam started. "I have no doubt that you can handle yourself in any situation. But my brother would never forgive me if I let anything happen to you. I know he'll be beside himself in anguish knowing that you weren't among the ones found with Rupert's portal evacuation that headed back to Solis. With the death of Jade, I'm the only adult supervision you've got left on this world. Having said that, I want you at my side at all times. This is a new planet that we're about to explore. With any luck, we'll be back home in no time."

Nathan smirked.

"Don't worry. I know the rules. I won't go saying some childish thing like 'you're not my real father' or anything like that. Just try not to treat me like a three-year-old, and we should be good."

Adam smiled.

"Deal," he said, shaking his nephew's little hand. "Now, let's see what the outside looks like."

With a gentle shove, Adam pushed open the remaining brackets folding the cockpit glass window in place, joining the ten other Federation operatives in the clearing. Adam's jaw dropped as he took in the surroundings, forgetting momentarily about his bruised head and the tragic loss of Jade.

Enveloped around the crash site of the *Burrower* was a wilderness that stretched out in all directions, dotted with tall pine trees that swayed rhythmically in the afternoon sunlight. Mulch chips and dirt patches littered the earth, appearing intermediately as the tall grass allowed. A few boulder patches sat nearby, moss laden and covered in dead foliage that the trees had shed over the years. Straight ahead, the forest had begun a gradual uphill climb, telling Adam they were at the base of either a large hill or a mountain – he couldn't tell. The pine canopy was so thick, that often times it blotted out the sky.

"*Wow!*" Adam gasped, in awe of this lush new world. "Nathan, are you seeing this?"

"*Araucaria* trees," Nathan stated, running his hand over a trunk of a tree nearest the *Burrower* crash.

"What?" Adam laughed, impressed by the boy's botanical knowledge.

"At least, that's what they look like to me," Nathan replied. "Very strange indeed. A lot of these other plants I don't think I can identify. Doesn't look at all like anything back on Solis, does it, Uncle Adam?"

"Certainly not," Adam replied, in awe of the lush planet.

"Can we contact Solis with that thing?" Wyatt broke through.

He was hovering over Sana, who was fiddling again with her communication portable device in the center of the clearing.

"No, unfortunately," she answered. "Short range signals only. There's no way of contacting Solis, not without *Harvester One* being operational. And I doubt when it crashed any of the terminals are in operation. We're very lucky the oscillator survived."

"And how far till the oscillator?"

"Like I said, several miles southeast."

Four of the marines were beginning to disperse throughout the grassy rim of the small clearing, disappearing and reappearing intermediately from behind the foliage. Adam observed that they were setting up a defensive perimeter. Several others lingered toward the middle, watching in awe as Sana operated her device and expertly configured the settings to calculate a more accurate reading. Alex Meras found a spot atop a boulder nearby, peering through the scope of his ESCR-20 as he scanned over the tall grass for signs of hostiles.

"Anything?" Adam asked him, feeling useless.

He had been grateful for Alex standing up for him against Wyatt in the *Burrower*, and now felt he had made one additional friend besides his nephew.

"Just swaths of greenery. Hard to see much of anything. Damn wind blowing everything around."

He took off his Federation armor helmet and wiped his brow. The heat was not excruciating but enough to be uncomfortable, even under the shade of the tall pines.

"So no signs of the *Supernova?* Or any additional escape pods from *Harvester One?*"

"In this jungle, we could be right on top of it and we'd never know it," replied Alex, shifting in his perch. "*Supernova* has been out here for how long? It's probably covered in vines and undergrowth by now – if it's still in one piece."

"Good point," Adam admitted.

In this arid landscape that encased them, he suddenly had doubts that they would be able to locate the *Supernova* survivors, but they had to try. Not only had it been a huge investment to build a ship like *Harvester*

One to traverse that amount of space in such a short duration, but now he felt bound to his mission. He had to know the truth – for Jade.

The sniper dropped off the rock, landing beside Adam and Nathan.

"Corporal Alex Meras," the soldier announced, shaking Adam's hand.

"Corporal Adam Ross, now acting Lieutenant," Adam laughed. "I remember you from the mission briefing awhile back. This is my nephew, Nathan. You'll find that he loves pulse weaponry. You must be pretty good with that thing, huh?"

"Never leave anywhere without it," Alex replied. "You were in the right about the oscillator. Wyatt is unfit to lead at the moment. I think we'll find this mission to be successful, and we should be able to return to Solis with our heads held high. Say, want to hold my sniper rifle, son?"

Nathan looked at Adam for approval.

Adam wasn't sure, until he saw Alex Meras eject the pulse magazine and switch his safety functions on, and then nodded in approval.

"Careful, it's pretty heavy," Alex smiled as the youth cradled the long rifle.

"Wow, it's incredible. Yeah, you're right. Real heavy, I'll say!"

WHHRRR!

A sudden blaring siren erupted from Alter's chrome chest cavity, causing the survivors of the *Burrower* crash to turn toward the robotic soldier. The bot turned a small dial on the armored shoulder pad, and the harsh wailing ceased abruptly.

"Lifeforms approaching, Lieutenant," Alter replied, reading his pulse rifle.

"Which way are they coming from?" Adam asked, running over to the bot with Nathan in tow.

A pair of the marines emerged from the greenery, running into the clearing.

"Are they human, or something else?" Rice asked, pushing through some of the tall grass blades.

"Non-human," Alter replied, pausing for a moment while his internal computers calculated the oncoming threat. "And closing fast, from the north side of the trees and also from the west. They'll be on us in a minute."

II

"Well, this is your time to shine, Lieutenant," Wyatt muttered under his breath, causing Adam's pounding headache to return. "What are you going to do now?"

Shutting you up should be my number one priority, Adam thought.

By now, all of the marines had returned to the wooded clearing in the jungle. They encircled Nathan and Adam who were unarmed as well as Sana as she continued to triangulate where *Harvester One* had crashed.

"How's it coming?" one of the marines asked her desperately.

"Loading topology," Sana replied. "Batteries running low – not good."

Suddenly a loud gawking shriek rippled through the jungle, sounding over the rescue party as they herded toward the center of the clearing. The marines kept to the outer edge, some choosing to hide among the long grasses for added camouflage.

"The hell was *that?*" Wyatt asked, switching the safety off on his pulse rifle and turning the weapon clockwise to pinpoint distant movement.

"If I had to guess, something reptilian by the sound of it," Ziven deduced.

The crunching of ground and mulch commenced through the trees, although nothing had appeared. The shrieking resumed, quietly at first and soon taunting the whole jungle. Flying animals previously unseen began to fidget above in the canopy, soaring to higher perches for a safer view of the impending battle.

FLAP! FLIP-FLAP! FLIP-FLIP!

Fifty yards ahead through the barrier of green waving fronds, the vegetation began to convulse, signifying that the brood of monsters was about to arrive. Alex was the first to see the elusive creatures.

"I have visual confirmation," the sniper announced, having snatched up his rifle back from Nathan and resuming his stance on the boulder. "Long green tails. Yellow blotted patterns. Skinny, worm-like bodies. Like walking snakes, if I had to label them."

"How soon now?" Adam asked, turning to Alter.

"We'll have contact in... fifteen seconds!"

Click! Click! Click...

A flurry of safety switching noises rang out as the soldiers adjusted to their surroundings and resumed combat stances, double checking their firing mechanisms. With one final horrid growl, the jungle was quiet once again, save for the subtle buzz of insects. Adam sensed something horrific was about to happen. The anticipation alone was eating him alive.

Where are they? Adam thought, wishing desperately that he was brandishing a firearm.

"Anyone got eyes?" asked Bruce.

"Oh God, where are they?" Brandy cried, huddling closer to Sana, eyes frantically scanning the foliage around the crash site.

Alter switched off the siren radar, knowing it would be better to remain in silent-mode as to not give away their positions – the trade-off being that the marines had lost track of their targets.

Come on, get it over with, Adam thought, vigilantly scanning the foliage for movement.

"I've got an exact fix on the ship!" Sana called. "It's approximately five miles southeast, nestled between a pair of mountainous valleys. The systems check confirms the oscillator is there and operational, if we make it out of –"

"*Augghh!*" a male voice yelled out.

Rice!

No one had seen what happened to Rice Lere other than Adam, who wasn't certain how to process the rapid event that just unfolded. From what he saw, the jungle came alive and sacked its target with such a force that the marine's body was bowled over backwards. Rice pressed down on the trigger of his ECR-130, sending a shower of pulse rounds all over the clearing, thankfully missing his human counterparts.

"Rice, shit!" Adam yelled, mortified by what he saw. "Somebody get over there and –"

There was no time to check on his fallen comrade. The marine's body had vanished from view after being dragged into the high grass by the bipedal serpents. As the last traces of the marine's boots slipped into the dense barrier of grass, the attackers hidden on the other side pressed the attack, announcing their power-play by a series of haunting yelps.

SHREAAAH! FLIP-FLAP! FLIP!

With speed and agility that could rival the fastest athletic runners on Solis, a massive herd of green reptiles sprung over the grassy wall and began to land with hard impacts on the mulch bed. The rescue party was shocked at what they saw. The magnificent creatures were unlike any animal known to have existed on Solis.

SHREAAAH!

A familiar horrifying cry from the alpha male reptile told Adam all he needed to know.

"*Light 'em up!*"

The clearing became ablaze with a tangled web of galloping carnivores and pulse weaponry fire. Adam grabbed Nathan and pulled him to the mulch bed as green scaly bodies began to drop over. The two began to crawl over the ground toward the last known location where

Rice was located, careful not to get hit with the torrent of cross-fire.

I have to get a weapon, Adam thought, his palms and knees pounding over the wood chips as he led his nephew through the skirmish. *Then I gotta get this kid up a tree!*

He pushed through the battle, moving around Ziven and Brandy, pulling his nephew over a lizard carcass and toward the foreboding wall of grass that lay ahead. At last, near the edge of the clearing, Adam caught the trace of metal shimmering through the foliage.

The ECR-130, previously operated by Rice, was covered in blood and lying several feet into the lush jungle, half buried by leaf fragments. A gruesome string of slash marks from the lizard's claws adorned the firearm, as well as blood from the presumed dead marine.

Adam plucked it out from the ground and checked the cartridge.

109 shots. Good enough!

There was little time to test or safety check the weapon. From within the jungle, a green lizard jumped out toward Adam, jaws open wide with the freshly drawn blood of Rice Lere. The primitive reptilian sailed through the air, forcing Adam to fall backwards, nearly knocking over his nephew in the process.

Adam could feel his heart palpitating wildly behind his Federation armor suit as the ECR-130 released three golden rounds, catching the serpent in the midsection. The creature gagged in mid-leap as the blasts ate away at the green chest. The beast rolled over on its side, landing beside Adam and Nathan, dead on impact.

Rising to his feet, Adam wasted no time.

"Come on, we need to get you somewhere safe!"

Adam spun around to briefly survey the clearing – a scene that had erupted into chaos and disarray. The majority of the rescue party was huddling around the crashed *Burrower*, using the escape pod itself for cover. A few of the marines started taking up positions further into the green, trying to draw some of the lizards over toward them and away from the other unarmed survivors. Pulse rounds were flying everywhere; some hitting lizards, others hitting nothing or vanishing into the forest. Many of the green lizards had already slumped over in the clearing, but nonetheless, the creatures continued to press the savage attack. Adam was relieved to see that no other survivors had been harmed.

Frantically, he searched the area for a tree easy enough to climb.

There!

At the southern end of the clearing, a small path had formed from where the *Burrower* tore through the trees several days earlier. At the end of the newly carved trail, a tall pine tree rose up from the earth. Thick branches lined the base of the giant trunk, capable of being climbed easily by a small child.

"Follow me!" Adam commanded, pulling Nathan along by the wrist.

He heard his nephew grumble something – Adam didn't care. Already as he led the boy toward the tall pine twenty yards away at the end of the *Burrower* crash trail, he could distinguish a slithering reptile turning from the clearing and darting toward him.

"See that tree?" Adam yelled to his nephew.

"Yeah," came the exhausted reply of the youth.

"Climb up there!"

"How high?"

"High enough! You've seen how high these spotted bastards can jump!"

Finally, they reached the base of the trunk. Adam helped Nathan up a few branches before dropping to the earth to pick off his oncoming targets. When he turned around, Adam was startled to see how close they already were.

SHREAAAH! FLIP-FLAP! FLIP!

His closest adversary was following him down the trail, threatening to cut off his return to the clearing where the survivors herded in their defensive positions. The animal jumped from its clawed feet and soared toward him, closing the gap from fifteen feet to five in a split second.

Die, alien-serpent!

Adam fired the pulse rifle as the discharge forced him back against the trunk, bringing his foe crashing above him, hitting the bark with a violent push as the carnivore fell onto the earth. There was no time to celebrate – two other reptilians were already converging on his position.

Damn pulse rifles!

Adam raised his firearm to shoot, but the weapon jammed.

Not now, dammit! Anytime but now!

He quickly knelt down and banged the weapon hard against his hand. The rifle answered in a short blip; a sign that it had to cool down. Raising the weapon in a last chance effort to save himself, he tried to press the trigger several times to no avail.

Shit! Faulty Federation weapons!

The reptiles quickly arrived at his position and prepared to deliver a final blow, if not for a pair of well-placed sniper blasts that fired from the clearing. The pair of monsters landed on either side of Adam, whose ECR-130 had finally returned to normal, operable condition.

"Thanks!" Adam called out.

Alex returned a friendly wave and continued picking off more reptiles that breached the clearing.

"Stay there until this is over," Adam commanded his nephew who he saw had already scampered a good twenty feet above him, partially hidden by a canopy of pine needles.

"I'm not going anywhere," Nathan assured him, turning away from his uncle to view the battle.

Adam turned and was about to return to the *Burrower* crash when something caught his eye – Sana, running full speed through the trees, screaming as she was pursued relentlessly by the lizards. She was either unarmed or out of ammunition and didn't dare look back – the lizards would have her soon if he didn't interfere.

Hang on, Sana! Keep going!

Sana passed out of view after slipping into a cluster of six-foot tall palm fronds, chased by the green lizards. Adam turned away from the battle in the clearing and took off after her, double checking that his weapon was officially operational this time.

#

Corporal Alex Meras reloaded another pulse crystal cartridge into the bottom of his ESCR-20. In the middle of the reload, one of the green reptiles landed beside him on his boulder. With a swift kick of his Federation steel boot, Alex sent the small creature tumbling back onto the ground. The carnivore growled in defeat before slinking back into the undergrowth.

Other creatures breaching the clearing did not give up so easily.

Brave little assholes, aren't they?

Taking a second to collect himself, the sniper glanced around, alarmed at what he saw.

The defensive perimeter had fallen apart. Many of the marines on the outskirts of the grass had fled into the jungle, attempting to lure more of the intruders after them. A few survivors still remained near the *Burrower* crash site, choosing instead to climb trees. Despite having piled up many carcasses of the green lizards in the clearing and in the grassy weeds that surrounded the wreckage, the reptiles pressed their attack, refusing to let up.

Several yards below him, he could see Brandy forcefully fending off a vicious attack from one of the mature serpents as she sought refuge in the ruins of the crash. The animal had her pinned against the left side of the fractured escape pod. She tried with one hand to open the side hatch entrance and swatted at the animal with a stick with her free hand. As a translator and interpreter on the mission, Alex realized she was unarmed – and very valuable.

Sumbitch!

He swiveled his weapon toward the horrific scene that might have been Brandy's last moments, placing a pulse blast through the creature's neck, decapitating the head and sending the oozing innards all over the shrieking, hysterical translator. Momentarily free from her attacker, Brandy opened the hatch and sealed herself inside, just as more lizards converged on her position.

Alex smiled, pleased at his timing and turned back to survey the clearing. He could see Wyatt and Ziven laying down fire toward the adjacent end. Alter was near the front of the *Burrower* cockpit, preventing the reptiles from entering the vehicle from the broken windshield. That kid, Nathan was in a tree.

What was that?

It was the lieutenant, Adam Ross, whom Alex had just saved, running into the trees.

For a moment he immediately thought of Wyatt's remarks, calling Adam Ross a defector, until Alex noticed another sight.

Sana, the communication specialist, running through the brush ahead of him, being chased by the long-tailed reptiles as they shrieked and slithered after her. Adam himself had a few chasing him as well, unbeknownst to the lieutenant. Alex counted three additional reptiles behind Adam.

He must be trying to save her, he thought, resting the sniper rifle down on its two-legged tripod and aiming through the jungle in the direction of the chase.

They don't pay me enough for this job...

There wasn't time for beautiful accuracy, only time to put the targets down. Soon the chase would be lost in the trees, continuing somewhere out of sniper range. Alex took a deep breath and began to spam the trigger into the greenery, accurately pinpointing the best points for maximum damage in a short period of time.

#

Shifting from the branch, Nathan had a front row seat at the excitement – and terror – unfolding below him around the ruins of the *Burrower*. The reptiles were gathering around in small packs, herding the survivors into isolated kill-zones. Most of the humans on foot had departed from the clearing, taking their chances hiding in the outlying shrubbery instead of the open field.

He took a particular interest in the sniper, Alex Meras, picking off the green reptiles with ease, using his elevated position to assist whichever of the humans needed him the most. Most recently, Nathan saw him pick off three of the reptiles that were chasing his uncle into the lush forest. Adam failed to notice that he was being pursued; the targets long dead before the reptiles could reach him. The sniper was extraordinarily talented.

What are these things?

At first, the answer seemed obvious, and a little too obvious at that. Lizard-like creatures that walked on two legs that were as tall as he was could only be one thing – dinosaurs.

But it can't be, can it?

He turned on the branch, still a good twenty feet from the ground and reached for his backpack. One of the creatures passed around the trunk and looked up at the boy, realizing the prey was too high for a jump attack and resumed its approach to the clearing.

Nathan cracked open the main pouch and retrieved an animal encyclopedia, which he knew included fauna thought to be long extinct, including dinosaurs.

Son of a gun, there it is!

The page revealed a black and white illustration of a slender carnivorous animal, followed by a brief synopsis.

Coelophysis.

Nathan read on, picking up more random facts about the animal, and pinpointing their exact time and location.

We crashed back on Earth, in the Triassic Period... in the Carnian stage?

The Triassic wasn't a period of Earth's prehistory that Nathan knew very well, but after brushing through the next few pages in the encyclopedia, he was able to quickly retain many useful facts about the Carnian stage of the Triassic, and what surprises may be awaiting the rescue team.

He wasn't sure what to make of this information or how it could be helpful, but he was grateful he discovered it before anyone else. Maybe his uncle would treat him more like an adult now that he could provide some useful information.

As he put the book away, Nathan almost slipped off the branch after what he saw gawking at him from below. An enormous Coelophysis was waiting on the mulch, leaping up at him with jaws spread wide. This creature was much larger than its first counterpart, coming terrifyingly close to Nathan's dangling foot.

The creature landed and immediately bounced back up after the boy, only to be brought down by a pulse blast to the head. The life fizzled out of the creature's eyes, and the beast fell back to the ground once more, tail slapping once on the mulch before lying still.

Nathan waved a thank you to Alex Meras, who returned the wave from his sniper perch before selecting his next targets.

#

When Kara Barnels felt water lapping against her cheek, she knew she had either blacked out or had been knocked unconscious. As she came to, she saw the slide marks that her body had left on the side of a ravine – a tell-tale sign of what happened.

Fatigued and fighting off numerous body aches, she pulled herself out of the shallow creek and rose to her hands and knees, the water stinging her bruises. Over her shoulder, she could hear the distant sounds of animal cries trading with the echo of pulse rounds, scorching into their assigned recipients. None of her comrades were in sight, but she heard them on the top of the hill, where she assumed the *Burrower* clearing remained just beyond the ridge.

Where are you?

She searched the undergrowth, woozy from waking up and wearily searching for her firearm – an ECP-30 pulse pistol, with hopefully enough ammo to survive the attack. She found it, writhed in mud and buried under wet palm fronds. Fortunately, the weapon was still operational, despite lying partially submerged in the creek.

Thank God!

She grabbed it and began the long climb back up the hill, scooting around the corpses of fallen lizards that had been cast down earlier in the battle. An ECP-30 was the only weapon she was granted to use – her chosen field as a medical specialist rarely permitted Federation operatives to carry firearms. Kara requested it when the mission on *Harvester One* launched, and today, she was glad that she did.

SHREAAAH!

Two lizards arrived at the top of the berm, spotting her immediately through the rows of ferns and raced to meet her – claws extended in delight. Kara whipped the pistol up and caught both of the animals before they had a chance to intercept her, killing them both and moving past their convulsing bodies.

She thanked her handiness with a pulse pistol to her shooting days as a child with her father; a former Federation marine.

As the conflict began to die down, her only comrades to remain in the clearing were Wyatt, Ziven and the bot, Alter, who was still guarding the entrance to *Burrower*, spraying the area with pulse fire. She noticed her handsome comrade, Corporal Alex Meras, still holding steadfast on top of the rock he had chosen as a sniper nest.

Whoa!

Three carnivores crashed through the grass, landing on the rock behind Alex. The sniper rolled over onto his back, dispatching the two lizards that landed closest to him. As he was about to put down the third animal, a look of uncertainty and dread fell over his face. The sniper rife had jammed.

SHREAAAH!

Rearing up high on its hind legs, the animal gave a victorious growl as Alex raised the sniper rifle as a self-defense shield. The beast bounded off the stone, jumping five feet in the air and toward the corporal, claws raised in a slashing position.

ZRRRR!

Kara's shot – the final shot in her current ECP-30 magazine – rang true as it dispatched the reptile. Alex proceeded to ram the dying beast with his rifle, pushing the carnivore to the earth ten feet below. With a thankful long breath, the corporal lumbered back to his feet, inserting another magazine into the rifle.

"I owe you one, Barnels," he yelled over the clearing.

Kara smiled, doing the same with her pistol.

"It won't be the last time before this is over," she called back.

#

Stumbling over an outstretched log, Adam tumbled forward, rolling expertly into a somersault and continuing the chase through the trees. He had already lost track of Sana, somewhere ahead in the brush, but he could hear her screaming in the distance, as if the murderous creatures had already cornered her and begun dissecting her organs.

He saw something metallic ahead and realized his goal was in reach. When he saw how much larger the object was than he previously anticipated, he knew it wasn't Sana.

The silvery glinting came from the brutalized armor suit of Rice Lere, whose body had been ravaged by the reptiles and then dumped there after they had finished.

"*Dammit!*" Adam cursed, bending forward and fighting to catch his breath.

Where did they go? Come on. Think, Adam! Think!

He paused, looking around in all directions. Thankfully, no other carnivores had followed him from the *Burrower* clearing. The sounds of the distant battle were for the most part nonexistent, save for the occasional faint burst from Alex Meras' sniper rattle. An amphibious croak told him there must be a water source nearby.

Then he heard it.

A feminine cry, so loud and agonizing that he knew the caller would soon be dead. The yell was frequently cut off and restarted, telling Adam that the victim was busy fending off an assault as she screamed. He knew as a communication specialist she was most likely unarmed and untrained in combat. The fight wouldn't last long.

Doesn't sound... far...

Adam resumed his chase, trying to gather his thoughts and regain control of his breathing. The headache had come back full force, amplified by the mark on his head sustained from the *Harvester One* bridge back in space.

Hang on...

The afternoon heat of the jungle was excruciating. He craved water, but knew thirst was an afterthought. His teammate's life was hanging in

26

the balance.

The path contoured around a boulder field before turning sharply through a grove of ferns. In the muck near his toes, Adam realized he could see Sana's fresh footprints imprinted into the dirt, and knew he was heading in the right direction. As he arrived at the foot of the creek, he was greeted by a ghastly sight.

No...

SHREAAAH!

Three of the lizards had pinned Sana thirty yards upstream. She was face down in the flowing river, motionless as they pecked away at the flesh at the back of her neck. To her right was her communication console, partially submerged by the rushing current. Shards of glass on the rocky beach nearby told Adam the screen had cracked, thus rendering the software utterly useless.

The leader of the reptilian pack turned and challenged Adam, the gawk summoning its companions and alerting them to the human's presence. When they stood frozen in a challenging stance, Adam knew they would be easy targets.

WHRRR! WHRRR! WHRRR!

The carnivores had little time to react before the blasts struck them. They spiraled down onto the creek, the water sweeping their lifeless carcasses downstream. Adam rushed over and grabbed Sana, turning her over before the current could carry her away.

"*Augh*, no..."

Adam jumped back in fright.

Sana's face had been shredded from ear to ear. Lacerations to her face covered her flesh with oozing, watery blood. The eyeballs were removed, the mouth ajar with a trace of a final scream that most likely occurred underwater.

Adam stepped back onto the shore, watching as the current swept her eviscerated body away into the deeper confines of the primitive, unpredictable wilderness.

III

Adam lumbered through the trees, fatigued and aching from thirst, relieved when he heard the voices of his team through the branches ahead.

The surrounding area around the escape pod resembled the scene of a horrific animal massacre. Dozens of reptilian figures were draped over the dirt, scorched from pulse rifle fire. Some of the creatures matted the flora on the outskirts, their blood saturating the grass, oozing into small pools. His human comrades looked exhausted, but grateful the attack had ended and that the reptile attackers dispersed back into the woodland.

"Think they'll come back?" Nathan asked as Adam guided him out of the tree.

"Doubt it," Adam answered. "We decimated their pack. I can't imagine there would be many of them left at this point. But who knows – I sure hope not. I'm glad you're all right."

"Me too, obviously," Nathan replied, dusting himself off as they continued up the short path to the grisly clearing.

Adam quickly did a head count, and realized everyone was present – everyone except Rice and Sana. They had lost two of their own in the attack, bringing the total number of *Burrower* survivors down to ten.

Not good, Adam thought. *Not good at all.*

"Lieutenant, glad you're safe," Alter said in a digital voice. "We were just about to send a scouting team out to find you."

"Thanks," Adam replied as the survivors gathered around. A discussion about what had happened and how to proceed was imminent, and he knew the burden would fall on his shoulders now that he had assumed command.

"Any sign of Sana?" Alex asked.

A few of the others nodded, wanting to know what happened.

Sana's zombified face replayed in his memory. He couldn't shake her final gaunt expression, even as her rigid body moved away with the current.

"She's dead," Adam answered with a frank head tilt. "So is Rice. I found his body just a few steps into the jungle from where we last saw him. And even more bad news – Sana's communication equipment was destroyed by the creek. We'll have to guess on where *Harvester One* crashed, based on the last known reading that she gave us."

An uncertain silence fell over the group. The situation was becoming increasingly grim by the minute. Adam felt their hopes of finding the *Supernova* survivors, or escaping this frightening new world themselves, was quickly slipping out of his grasp.

"You sure that thing's broken?" the marine called Jonas asked. "I used to be able to troubleshoot comm devices pretty consistently in training simulations."

"Looks pretty broken to me," Adam replied, showing him the fragments of the device he collected from Sana's death scene.

The communication console broke further apart as he showed the computerized remains to Jonas, who waved it away after seeing how irreparable the damage was.

"Damn," the marine cursed. "Never mind then."

Adam tossed the useless device aside, trying to come up with a new plan. From the corner of his eye, he could see Sergeant Wyatt Brolen stewing in the corner. Adam could tell the marine wanted to ream into him, but was harnessing whatever willpower he had left to hold back.

"Spit it out, Sergeant," Adam turned toward his disgruntled foe. "I can tell you want to say something. Give me what you got! Speak freely."

That was all it took. Wyatt erupted with a tirade of insults.

"Without a doubt, that had to have been the shoddiest performance of a commanding officer I've ever seen. Those creatures were on us so fast we didn't have time to blink. Not to mention they separated us easily and picked off two of our own. Now Rice and Sana are dead, plus our chances to accurately pinpoint the *Harvester One* wreck. It's your fault, Ross!"

"That's not completely true," Kara interjected, stepping forward. "Before Sana died, she told us *Harvester One* is approximately five miles southeast between two valleys. The ship probably crashed a few days ago, right?"

Jonas and Ziven nodded on either side of her.

"That means that when we're close to the site, we'll most likely encounter the charred remains of trees and wildlife. The wreck will be easy to find once we're in range, then we'll just follow the destruction right to the ship."

"That's beside the point, Barnels!" Wyatt snapped back, stepping in front of her. "The point is that Adam Ross is undeserving to lead this operation and, in turn, is going to get us all picked off one by one by those lizards and whatever else is waiting for us out there!"

"What would you have done differently, Wyatt?" Adam said, draining a bottle of water that he found in his backpack. With a final swig, he wiped his mouth and blurted, "I'll answer that – not shit! There was no way we could've been prepared for an attack by a pack of lizards that size. The result would've been the same, regardless of whoever was in charge!"

"Careful, Ross," Wyatt chided. "Given our circumstances, I'm not above striking an officer. Even a phony one like yourself!"

"I'm right here, Brolen," Adam challenged calmly, gesturing with his hand. "I'm right here."

Wyatt stepped forward to meet Adam halfway, but the scuffle was prevented by Ziven, Bruce and Alex.

"It doesn't matter," Alex stated. "All this he said, she said bullshit. What's done is done – Sana and Rice are dead, and now we're down to ten. The more we sit here arguing, the more we're wasting precious daylight when we could be going after the *Harvester One* wreck. Just because Sana said it was five miles, doesn't mean it's a straight shot. Five miles could be more like twelve air miles, depending on the geography. We already can see how mountainous this area is."

"He's right," Bruce admitted. "And the longer we dick around here, the longer we'll be sittin' ducks. Those lizards don't shit around – I'd rather not meet them again. Might want to expedite our trek to the portal oscillator. I've seen enough of these highlands."

"They're not *lizards*," Nathan interrupted.

The marines turned and stared him down, as if the boy had spoken out of turn.

"What's up, kid?" Ziven asked gruffly.

"They're known as *Coelophysis*, a carnivorous dinosaur from the Triassic Period," Nathan answered.

Wyatt broke out laughing, in a tone that was meant to sound degrading and insulting. Several other marines chuckled, but quickly lost their smiles when Adam scowled at them.

"How in the world did you come up with that bullshit?" Wyatt demanded.

"From this!" came the boy's snarky answer.

Nathan pulled out his animal encyclopedia from his backpack, flipping the pages to the prehistoric Earth pages until he finally landed on the desired specimen. The illustration was almost a mirror image to the many deceased lizard-like lifeforms that plagued the clearing. The marines and personnel gathered around, reading about the creature.

"That doesn't prove anything," Wyatt rebuffed the child. "Sorry, Slick."

"The hell it doesn't," Adam argued, defending his nephew. "It's a perfect match. That's exactly what these things are. What did you say this place was called, Nathan?"

"The Triassic Period," Nathan answered. "It's not a place but a time. The place is Earth, over 200 million years ago. And it's likely there will be more of these dinosaurs around, maybe even bigger, predatory ones too."

"That's unmistakably what the lizards are," Brandy concluded, backing up Nathan's theory while doing double-takes to the deceased reptilians on the mulch.

"So we're back on Earth?" Ziven asked. "That's very hard to believe, but based on what we're seeing, it's the only theory so far that holds merit."

"Have you all lost your minds?" Wyatt lambasted the survivors. "Dinosaurs? Earth? Listen to yourselves. Earth is dead, long gone. We've learned that since we were kids – that's elementary school material. Shit, kid, I admit these animals look similar, but there's no way you're right on this. Sorry."

"The kid's right," Alex argued back, shouldering his sniper rifle, ready to depart.

"How do you figure, Meras?" Wyatt asked, raising a bushy eyebrow in anger.

"Well other than the similarities are uncanny, I'd have to say that the black hole gives testament to Nathan's Triassic theory."

"The black hole?" Wyatt asked, confused.

"Yeah, the one that *Harvester One* and our escape pod entered at the end of the asteroid belt. Wormholes are known to involve teleportation – even time travel. If that's what happened, it's damn near possible that we're stuck in the past. And that means the *Supernova* might have suffered the same fate, which is where our mystery man Brett Ambrose sent out the distress call. My guess is he's somewhere nearby."

"Meras," Wyatt blinked. "That has to be one of the most convoluted theories I've ever heard."

"Don't take his word for it," Adam said. "Take Nathan's. As soon as another one of these Triassic monsters appears, we'll know for sure that we're on Earth. And it'll confirm the correct time period. I'm betting it's the Triassic."

"So what's the plan now?" Brandy asked, changing the subject. "Go back and retrieve Rice and Sana and properly bury them, right?"

"Negative," Ziven replied. "That'll take too much time to double back and locate them, plus the burial itself will be a bitch – we don't have any shovels. What do you say, Lieutenant?"

"Correct," Adam answered. "Not enough time. We're already wasting daylight."

"We're just going to leave them?" Brandy said. "I don't like that."

"It has to be done," Alex told her. "With the limited amount of food and water we have right now, burying the two of them in the middle of this rescue operation will expend too much energy. Which brings me to the next point; how much food and water did everyone grab?"

"Everyone open your packs," Adam ordered. "Let's see what we've got."

A cacophony of unzipping commenced as the survivors opened their backpacks, displaying the collective amount of food and water everyone had gathered when they departed from space.

"Twenty water bottles, ten Federation ready meals," Adam counted.

"There's a stream not far from here, where Sana was killed. We can fill up any spare bottles there. Then we can follow Sana's directions to the *Harvester One* crash, get our hands on the oscillator and properly begin the rescue operation. If we hurry, we can make it there by tomorrow at the latest. Before we head out, I say we take one last look at the *Burrower* for supplies. Something tells me we won't be coming back here. Ziven, why don't you survey the wreckage one final time?"

"Yes, Lieutenant," Ziven replied with a nod, heading into the wreckage with Bruce and Jonas.

"Alter?"

"Yes, Lieutenant?" the bot asked.

"Are there any other lifeforms remaining in the area?"

"There's a few small flyers in the trees, but nothing on the ground in the immediate vicinity. I'm picking up small traces of dissipating body heat, but my sensors indicate they are from the dinosaurs we brought down."

"Good," Adam told him. "Keep your eyes on your radar. You're the only hope we have of identifying what may be heading our way, now that we know how big the packs of dinosaurs are."

Dinosaurs. I can't believe I'm saying this.

"I'll keep an eye on them," Alter replied.

"Thank you." Adam turned to his nephew. "Good job in identifying what we're up against here. Because of what you've found in your book, we know what type of threats we may be running into. Can I give you a little homework assignment?"

Nathan looked up at him, his expression that of disdain.

"*Homework?*"

"Not typical homework," Adam laughed, trying to make light of the situation. "Just homework that you already did by yourself. Can you go through your book and see what other animals may be traversing these areas? That book looks pretty scientific. With any luck, you can help us figure out what exactly we're up against."

"Yeah, I guess," Nathan mumbled. "Just don't call it homework. It makes me feel like a five-year-old. It'd be like you telling Alex or one of the marines they have homework to do."

Adam mentally laughed, noting how ridiculous the boy's comparison was.

"I understand," Adam smiled. "Hey, go easy on me. I'm not used to this adult supervision thing, much less a Lieutenant in a Federation combat role. I've got a lot to learn, and I'll work on the no-childish-remarks thing, okay?"

"That's all I ask," Nathan nodded. "I'll do my best to see what other surprises we may be running into."

"Great, thanks, Nate."

Adam saw Ziven approaching from the pod wreckage, carrying additional salvaged items.

"Sir, we've found a few other pulse cartridges for the ECRs, and an extra two water canisters, but not much else. Unless you're looking for scrap metal and dino innards."

"Better than nothing, I guess," Adam said, waving everyone over to form another group huddle. "Okay. I think we're ready to get moving. Please use your weapons sparingly. What's in your backpack is all you've got. Same goes for food and water. We can replenish water at the stream ahead, then we'll head for *Harvester One* and get this shit-show on the road. Anyone got any last minute comments before we embark?"

Adam was surprised when Wyatt didn't have any additional belittling statements.

"Just one," Brandy said, raising her hand. "What happens if we run into another pack of those things? That wave took out two of us. If we happen on another group of dinosaurs, who's to say we won't suffer even more losses. Hey kid, is there anything else in that book about what other monsters might be prowling around here?"

"It's Nathan," the boy replied with an obvious agitation. "And I'm going to look through here as we walk and see what else may be around. I'd count on seeing larger predators than the Coelophysis, which may end up being the least of our worries."

"Like what?" Brandy asked, still traumatized from the Coelophysis raid.

"I don't know," Nathan replied. "Larger predators. I don't know much about the Triassic Period or its animals. It's not prominently written about, unlike the Jurassic and Cretaceous Periods. Hopefully by the end of the day I'll know more."

"And hopefully by the end of the day we'll all still be here," Wyatt cut in impatiently, starting toward the direction of the stream and shouldering his weapon. "Unless of course, our new lieutenant gets us all killed. Let's get a move on! I'd hate to be here when that reptile clan regroups and comes back down here for round two."

IV

By the time the ten survivors of the *Burrower* made it to the creek, the afternoon heat had amplified, drenching them in sweat. A few marines exhausted themselves temporarily of their Federation body armor, cooling their arms and necks off in the brook to minimize the effects of the burning sun. Any sign of Sana and her three reptilian assailants had long since vacated the area, except for a few remaining glass and metal fragments that dotted the rocky coast.

"Fill up," Adam commanded. "Wash up if you need to. We shouldn't linger here longer than a few minutes for rest. I'm sure if there's a water source here, there's bound to be predators stopping by."

"Sir, do you want me to scout downstream?" Alter asked as the band of rescuers dispersed. "Water is of no use for me. It can be disastrous as I'm sure you're aware."

"Are your sensors working at top performance?"

"Yes, Lieutenant."

"Then just stay put and keep an eye on the others."

"As you wish," came the digital response.

"Thank you, Alter."

Adam took two of the water canisters out and filled them up to the brim. Having drained all of his water earlier in the afternoon, especially after his full-on sprint in the scorching wilderness, he was due for a refill.

"You're not going to fill up?" he asked his nephew, who was casually sitting on a rock nearby, nose buried in the thick animal encyclopedia.

He's still trying to be of use, Adam thought proudly. *Maybe bringing him on this mission is more of a blessing than a curse. He's already identified where we are and at least one threat.*

"No thanks," Nathan replied, having taken off his jacket earlier on the adventure. "I still have plenty."

"Well, I'd still fill it up in case if you have any room. You never know when you'll need it."

Nathan didn't answer. Instead, he continued to scan the pages in the encyclopedia for insights on what else may be of danger. Adam was surprised Nathan was able to fit the entire compendium in his juvenile backpack.

"Anything yet?" Adam asked, taking a seat beside him, surveying the brook as it cascaded by.

"No," Nathan answered. "The book is kind of screwy how they have it set up. I have to jump around to find Triassic creatures. I've found a few herbivores so far, but no other carnivores yet in the Carnian."

"*Carnian?*" Adam asked, impressed by the boy's use of 'screwy' in a sentence.

"Yeah, the Carnian stage of the Triassic Period. I'm assuming it's the Carnian we're in, because that's when the Coelophysis flourished, according to the article."

Adam was about to ask another question, trying to show his nephew how interested he was in his work, when he noticed Wyatt shooting him a disapproving look from down the river. He was filling up his canteen, checking the ammunition counter on his gun, then looked away.

He's still trying to get a rise out of me.

"What an asshole," came a feminine voice to Adam's left.

It was Kara Barnels, coming over through a dense fern patch. Alex Meras was with her as well, cleaning the barrel of his beloved sniper rifle.

"Pardon my French," she corrected herself, addressing the remark to Nathan.

"I don't mind," the boy smiled, turning back to the book.

"What makes you say that?" Adam asked. "Although you're a hundred percent accurate."

"He's just an asshole," Kara smiled. "That's a tough question to summarize. Here's my best attempt. He's an arrogant, self-entitled, stick-up-his-ass sergeant who couldn't hack it in the Officer Candidate Program, so they kept him where he was – hoping he'd go away or drop out. Instead they just dumped the problem on our laps and now we have to deal with him. How he got the privilege of investigating the *Supernova* crash is beyond me."

"You know all this as a medical specialist?"

"Yeah well, the marines talk pretty loudly," she laughed.

"I'd keep an eye on him if I were you," Alex warned. "Especially when we get closer to *Harvester One.*"

"What makes you say that?" Adam said, mildly concerned.

"The portal oscillator device – I have a feeling once he's within its grasp, he'll try to sway us against the rescue mission – and try using it instead to transfer us back to Solis, aborting our objective."

"You think so, Meras?"

"Just a hunch, Lieutenant. Just a hunch."

"Lieutenant!" Alter's digital voice processors yelled from upstream, causing everyone in the area to freeze. "Come quick! Something you'll want to see!"

Adam rushed over. Everyone congregated behind him as he shuffled upstream, eager to glimpse what the bot was referring to. Alter pointed to a patch of grass at the base of the rocky shoreline, where a long strip of hardened mud had formed, rigid from the sun.

There, imprinted in the earth, was a lonely human footprint, aimed in the direction of the river.

"*Humans?*" Jonas asked. "We must be in the right place. Right?"

"The *Supernova* crash can't be far!" Bruce affirmed.

Yet something about the footprint rubbed Adam the wrong way. He bent forward and studied the track, trying to identify what disturbed him. For one, why was it a bare footprint impression and not a boot print? He was aware that most likely the original survivors of the *Supernova* were long dead, unless they lasted over three hundred years in hyper-sleep, but wouldn't boots still be readily available from the wreckage for their offspring?

Another unsettling fact startled him: the dried dark liquid forming near the edges of the imprint – a tell-tale sign of blood. Adam followed the blood trail over the rocky embankment, where it eventually withered away into the water and dissipated. The maker of the mark was undoubtedly fatally injured, and the body was swept downstream just like Sana's. The blood couldn't have been more than a few days old.

He could hear the group behind him fall silent as they discovered the hidden blood trail and its rapid descent into the watery edge.

"Let's get out of here," Adam said, concerned by Alter's discovery. "We've loitered around here for too long."

#

Nathan felt out of place walking in the center of the adult convoy. He felt helpless and a burden, but being treated like a child was what Nathan had grown to hate the most. He kept his face planted into the book, trying to learn more about the Triassic Period of Earth's ancient past, striving to become a more valuable contributor to the group.

If learning more about this place is what earns me respect, then dammit, I'm gonna learn everything I can about it!

He felt guilty about cussing in his mind, fantasizing that his father, Andrew, would appear out of nowhere to reprimand him.

The Coelophysis section he had read over and over. The species interested him the most, reminding him of the legendary velociraptor or deinonychus. He had toys of both dinosaurs growing up and had cherished them both. Some of his dinosaur toys were still waiting for him back on Solis, although he wouldn't admit that to all the battle-hardened Federation marines – especially Wyatt.

Nathan concluded that the sergeant had it out for both his uncle and him ever since Adam assumed command of the *Burrower* survivors at the wreckage site.

Walking a few bodies ahead of him, Nathan studied the sergeant, trying to learn as much about him as he did about the Coelophysis. For such a young boy, Nathan felt he had a good sense of judgment about people. In his short life, he had learned he could easily discern the good people from the bad ones. Wyatt was no exception, easily falling into the latter category.

Don't trust him, Nathan thought, spying on the marine from over the top of his animal encyclopedia.

His espionage left him vulnerable to a hidden rocky precipice – one that he may have tumbled down if a saving hand didn't latch onto the back of his shirt collar. The fall wouldn't have been deadly, but a broken leg would've been imminent.

"*Whoa*, thanks," Nathan said, embarrassed as he turned around.

It was Alex Meras, Nathan's favorite of the marines. Alex was completely different to Wyatt in every way: dedicated to the mission, a kinder personality, and probably even a better soldier and marksman.

"Hey, Meras," Kara prodded the sniper on his shoulder. "Pick up the pace. Stop showing off with your boyish charm by saving kids from cliff jumping."

Alex responded by tussling her hair, to which she playfully fended him off, countering with a pretend chop to his neck.

Nathan smiled and turned, continuing the trek and rolling his eyes. If he didn't know any better, he thought they may have been flirting. Now there was something, Nathan admitted, he knew nothing about nor did he have any interest in learning.

Their banter continued behind him while he resumed the study of the Triassic, ignoring the obvious mutual infatuation.

#

Damn, this heat is a death plague!

Adam staggered along the path, the second to the front. Alter outpaced him by only a few steps, using his elbow and forearm saws to chop away the overgrown bushy vegetation that contoured to the trail. The path out of the highlands had been a tricky one, filled with sudden turns and rocky drop-offs which frequently forced them to slow down and reevaluate their trajectory. According to Alter's internal compass, this was the correct direction that Sana had given them before her untimely demise.

WHHRRRR!

Alter's forearm saw sliced through another palm frond, sending the plant tumbling onto the trail with a dainty flop.

"You sure we're going the right way?" Wyatt grumbled a few steps behind.

"According to Sana's communication console," Alter replied. "This route is the safest and most straight-lined southeast passage that my sensors have laid out. Although I must admit, this course has been difficult to navigate."

Despite the confession, the bot showed little sign of slowing down. Instead, Alter continued his demolition of the plants ahead, creating a safer, less crowded road for the marines.

"Strange world we've got ourselves into, isn't it?" Adam observed, talking to the bot as the other marines conversed in the background.

"Certainly, Lieutenant," Alter replied, tearing through another tree branch. "This will certainly be an ideal world for trade and commerce, once we establish a safe way of arriving here, past the asteroids and wormholes. I foresee this planet becoming a viable source of agriculture for people back in Solis, and eventually, a second planet once we successfully terraform."

"I don't see how that's possible," Adam replied, swatting at an irksome insect. "Solis and Earth, assuming that my nephew is correct and this is Earth, are in two different places in time, separated by millions of years. The only reason we've ended up here is by passage of the wormhole. I foresee significant ramifications."

"Ramifications, you say?" the bot asked. "Like what?"

"Well, time discrepancies for one," Adam asked. "If we die in the past, will it affect our future generations back on Solis? Unless there really are parallel realities as the ancient Earth theories suggest. Not to mention our presence now, on a prehistoric Earth, is bound to have effects on the future Earth. Will we affect the natural order of things – disrupt the future with our environmental endeavors earlier than we did before, which eventually led to the Old War and other deteriorating effects to Earth?"

"You've lost me, Lieutenant," Alter admitted. "I'm not one for age-old history, but I think you're worrying too much about the what-ifs and not worrying enough about the present. If I were you, I'd be more concerned with the functionality of the portal oscillator. If it doesn't work, or if the charge crystals are broken or damaged, how in the devil are we getting out of here?"

Oh... shit.

That wasn't something Adam had thought of until now. The portal oscillator was a loose cannon, working sometimes and failing miserably at other times. Of course, the only true times it had been tested were during its early development on Solis through Federation technicians and scientists. Since the mission was potentially life threatening to the *Supernova* survivors, there wasn't much time to play around with perfecting the oscillator's capabilities. There were enough Federation escape pods on *Harvester One* for everyone to abort ship – thus the oscillator was brought on board in the stages of mid development, to be worked on throughout the space voyage.

The only confirmed record of the device working properly was when

Harvester One went down. Adam recalled visually seeing the glowing blue aura forming on the bridge, just before he abandoned ship in the *Burrower*.

It worked at least once! It has to work again... it has to!

"I saw it activate right before we crashed," Adam said. "Rupert must have gotten desperate and figured the escape pods wouldn't be enough – or the escape pod bay was too far – and activated it. I'm sure everyone who was on the bridge bailed out and are safe on Solis as we speak."

"Then let's hope they send rescue, this time with more ships and troops."

"If they don't assume we've all been killed, you mean?"

"Let's hope for all our sakes, they don't," Alter concluded, sawing through a tall watery plant and paving the way into a boulder patch. It was a shadowy stretch of terrain that fed out to the bottom of the highlands. A hundred yards downhill, the tree line ended abruptly, giving way to a large swatch of grassland that stretched on under the blazing sun, transitioning to the prairies.

"Let's take five, everyone," Adam announced as the others filed into the boulder field. "I don't feel like braving the sun yet. Let's get some shade while we can and rest up. Those insects will be on us as soon as we hit the meadow."

The group disbanded, some sitting on tree trunks, others squatting on the shady rocks, cracking open their canteens and relishing the savory drinks. If not for the barely audible animal cries several miles away, the forest would've been completely quiet.

"How far now?" Nathan complained, sipping on his water.

"Why?" Adam laughed. "Thirsty?"

"Yeah, but that's not the problem – my feet are killing me."

"You'll get a break soon," Adam assured him. "We are heading into late afternoon. Probably somewhere open in the grassland we'll set up the base camp. Ideally on a hill plateau, where we can see everything around us."

"Do you think the Coelophysis will follow?"

"Doubt it," Adam replied. "My hunch is that they keep to the jungle. What does your book say about them?"

"Nothing about how far they'll go to stalk humans, I can tell you that." Adam laughed.

"On another note, how are you holding up?" Adam asked. "I feel as your uncle it's my duty to make sure you're comfortable during this. I know your father didn't sign you up for a march through a jungle with a pack of dinosaurs chasing you. And if he did, he planned to have five hundred people guarding you – not twelve."

"Actually, it's really only eight people," Nathan corrected. "Two are dead, Alter is a bot, and I obviously don't count."

"Even so, I'm sorry this is happening," Adam apologized. "I think you're handling the situation very well, especially after what happened to Sana and Rice. If there's more than one charge left in that oscillator, I'll be sending you home before you know it. You're really making it easy on me as far as keeping an eye on you, and I appreciate that."

"I'm not a little kid anymore, Uncle Adam," Nathan smirked.

The hell you're not, Adam thought, keeping his insights to himself.

"You know what I mean."

"Hey, what's he doing?"

Nathan pointed over to the far end of the boulder field, beyond where the marines had parked themselves to cool off. Alter was standing far away from his comrades, operating dial switches on his metallic chest cavity, far from the congregated group.

"I don't know," Adam said, studying his machine. "I've never seen a bot do that before. He must be adjusting his internal controls or doing part maintenance. Let's go ask him."

They slid around the marines and specialists, who were too engulfed in their own side conversations to pay any attention to the bot. Alter saw Adam approaching and waved him over hurriedly, continuing to fiddle with his exterior chest components.

"What's the deal?" Adam asked. "Loose parts?"

"Not quite, Lieutenant," Alter replied, keeping his head turned downward at the metallic controls. "To be frank, I'm not sure what's going on. Ever since we stepped through that last patch of jungle, my sensors are going off the charts. I didn't want to say anything, because when I brought up the internal radar for hostiles, nothing came up on the scanner."

"What are you saying?" Adam asked, reaching for his ECR-130. "Is there something nearby?"

"Well, don't get all worked up just yet," Alter warned him. "I'm not detecting anything, and yet, my sensors won't quit going off internally. Thankfully my speakers were on mute, which prohibited my internal alarms from blaring."

"So it's not the coelos?" Nathan asked.

"I wouldn't bet on it," Alter replied, slowly adjusting a switch. "The dinosaurs showed up quite clearly on my radar, although I didn't accurately estimate the size of the pack."

"Do you suppose it's a bug?" Adam suggested.

"A bug? No. I haven't had any bugs or significant glitches since we flew out from Solis. My programs have all been running at top performance."

"Maybe it's something in your settings," Nathan suggested. "Something in your data bank that's turned off or lagging."

"*Ah!*" cried the machine. "You may be onto something there! Let me do a few minor adjustments, keeping my alarm turned off of course, and – *presto!* Oh dear..."

"What?" Adam demanded. "What is it?"

By now the marines had stopped their side conversations and military banter and were listening in. Adam could feel Brandy hovering close by, worried that they had discovered something treacherous. Even Wyatt had finally stopped talking, choosing instead to pick up his pulse rifle and trod over to catch a glimpse of the commotion.

"Well, my computer was set to pick up animal related frequencies since we encountered the dinosaur pack earlier this afternoon," Alter explained. "Nathan just reminded me – I forgot to set the calibration codes to include human signals. Now I'm picking up several in the area. That is, several *unknown* signals."

"*Unknown?*" Brandy asked, her voice faltering.

"Correct," Alter replied, scanning the surrounding forest.

"*Several?*" Wyatt asked. "How many is *several* in bot terms?"

"According to my computer, there are a good number of them – fifty or more right up the hill, watching us as we speak. If you want an exact number, I can't provide it. I'm certain however, they outnumber us greatly."

V

The jungle around them grew quiet again. Even the insect hum had died down, and the sounds of the distant animals faded away. Adam had heard the myth about stillness in the forest before, back on Solis. It meant only one thing – the presence of nearby predators.

After casting a glance at the forest ahead, Adam snapped into commander mode.

"Everybody, take up positions behind these trees," he ordered, before Wyatt could critique his lack of direction in yet another potentially disastrous situation. Everyone obeyed without question, already clicking off their weapon safety functions as they scanned the eerie wilderness.

Raising his own rifle, Adam surveyed the surroundings ahead, noticing how corroded his barrel had become from the firefight with the Coelophysis pack.

Hope this piece of garbage still works, he thought, praying that the barrel wouldn't degrade any further.

"Anyone got eyes on what's out there?" Ziven asked from behind a boulder, reloading a cartridge.

"Negative," Jonas answered. "Just a bunch of greenery."

"Alter, can you confirm they're actually *human* signals?" Wyatt asked impatiently.

"They're human," Alter replied abruptly, offended by the question. "According to the readings, they are within our eyesight. We should be seeing them."

"Alter, I think your sensors are mistaken," Wyatt said, critiquing the bot's computer capabilities. "If there's something up there, we'd be seeing it by now."

"They're all over the hillside," Alter corrected him. "Many humans are there – I assure you."

"Why aren't they advancing?" Bruce asked. "Aren't they from the *Supernova*? They must know who we are. Someone should call out to them. We can end this mission, get to the oscillator and get everyone to Solis."

"I don't think shouting out to them is a good –"

Adam was interrupted mid-sentence, and he wasn't surprised by the source of the disruption.

"*Hello!*" Wyatt called out. "Is anyone out there? We come in peace! We are a rescue party from Solis, a planet discovered three hundred years ago by Admiral Steve Perry's Starfleet. We can take you out of here!"

After a few seconds, Wyatt's spiel went unanswered.

"Alter, I think your sensors need adjusting," Wyatt decided, standing up from his hiding spot. "There's nothing up there!"

"*Wyatt!*" Adam whispered harshly. "Get down!"

"Quiet, Ross! I'm through with all this bullshit. Let's get on with the oscillator and get the *fu –*"

BRAWLLLL!

A deafening drone blared out from the trees ahead, causing the marines to tense up and crouch back down. The noise was so powerful, several unseen creatures jumped from their hidden orifices in the underbrush. Suddenly the horn ceased, rendering the jungle once again in the original state of false tranquility.

"No humans, *huh?*" Adam glared at Wyatt. "The hell do you call that, Brolen?"

"Sounds close," Kara judged, peering over a mossy boulder. "How are they so close and we can't see them?"

"Let me adjust my settings," Alter said, twisting a dial and stepping out from his tree cover to collect more signals – a mistake that the machine realized too late.

WHOOOSH! KA-THUNK!

Alter staggered backward, striking a large trunk which served as a blockade to save the bot from tumbling down the hill.

"*Ahhh*, I *se-e-em* to have encountered a *prob-b-lem*," Alter attempted a complete phrase, his speech processor damaged in the attack.

Adam heard several of the marines gasp as the team realized what had transpired.

The bot had a large arrow embedded in the center of the chest. The shaft was over two feet long, crafted from strong wood and durable enough to pierce Federation issued bot armor. A faint sparking had begun in the crack formed by the wound, and the bot's eyes began to glitch and glaze.

"What is *happen-en-ing*, Lieutenant?"

"Alter, hang tight and don't move!" Adam said, shocked by what he saw. "I'll pull it out!"

"No time," Alex warned. "*Heads up!* Volley Fire!"

"*Find cover!*" Ziven yelled.

WHOOOSH! WHOOOSH! WHOOOSH! KA-THUNK! THUNK! THUNK-UNK

A hailstorm of arrows began to shred through the greenery, passing through jungle hedges as if materializing from nowhere, sailing toward the *Burrower* survivors. They darted out with such agility and precision that the marines had to wait to return fire until the volley had ended – the archers had them pinned.

They're camouflaged! Adam thought, pushing his nephew behind a large rock. Over his head, Adam could discern the wind created from the shafts as several archers tried to pick him off.

THUNK! THUNK! THUNK! WHOOOSH! WHOOOSH! WHOOOSH!

Three more arrows hit Alter, who was now virtually stuck against the trunk where the machine landed initially. The bot began to shake intermittently as the damaged internal computers fought to regain control.

What the hell's happening?

In the carnage that ensued, Adam realized his spot against the rock was suicide. Soon the enemy would advance down the hill to select better shots and scout for more advantageous archer vantage points.

To his side, he could hear a few of his comrades shuffling around, ducking from the arrows and trying to find more appropriate hiding places. Down the hill, he could see Alex Meras running to the grassland where it would be easier for the sniper to pick off targets from a safe distance. Beside him, he could see Wyatt and Ziven trying to pinpoint the enemy, readying their weapons for the counterattack. Jonas and Bruce had advanced, apparently spotting the enemy and moving in to engage. Brandy was crawling on her hands and knees to Alter, trying to free him from the tree. She screamed from the splinters that plagued her hands as her attempt to help the bot proved futile.

"Why are they shooting at us?" Bruce yelled. "They're survivors from *Supernova,* aren't they?"

"Who cares?" Ziven yelled, his face lighting up from his weapon's blast. "Take them down! There –at the ridge! *Engage!*"

VRRR! VRRR! VRRR!

The familiar rattle of Federation weaponry began to sound off, making the hillside ablaze with orange beams. The amount of arrow shooting decreased, as the nearby howls and shrieks from the natives washed over the hillside. The marines had begun to find their targets.

#

Relieved when he was finally beyond the tree line and into the grassland, Alex found a rotting log to hide behind within the first ten feet of the savanna. The heat had amplified throughout the afternoon, causing him to take his helmet off and wipe his brow before he picked up his sniper rifle and scoped through the jungle above. The glare from the sun began to glance off the scope, making pinpointing the Neolithic terrorists burdensome.

Where are you, you tribal sons of bitches?

The Federation friendlies were easy to spot. Their chrome armor and sprays of amber blasts through the woods narrowed down their positions. Finally, he noticed shapes in the jungle that didn't belong – shapes that appeared to fade up from nowhere in the foliage.

There you are!

The hostiles began to materialize through the brush, saturated with a muddy green coating, which explained why the hunters were invisible at first before the battle started. They bobbed and weaved between the trees, far enough away from the marines to attack with their spears but close enough to engage with longbows. The bulk of the army stayed back, but a few brave ones with pikes pushed forward, only to be shredded to pieces by the marines' suppressive fire.

Alex selected a target nearest Adam and Nathan, both of which he had begun to enjoy. The native was about twelve yards away from them, walking stealthily among the leaves so as to not draw attention. The small dot in the center of the scope glowed red as Alex steadied his aim, indicating that the round would be lethal.

SHHRRR!

The ECSR-20 recoiled as the blast sailed from the grassland back into the trees, bringing the attacker to a painful face-plant before Adam and Nathan knew what transpired.

Nice!

Next, Alex selected an archer who had Bruce pinned behind a rock, unable to move. Through the scope, Alex could tell the native was a very gifted archer, being able to load arrows onto the string and send them flying in a matter of seconds. The scope sight turned blood red again – an indication of another clean shot.

SHHRRR!

The blast caught the young man in the head. The lifeless corpse dropped the bow and perished behind a bush. Through the scope, Alex could see Bruce return a wave as he left his position for a more lucrative one.

Crack!

A twig broke somewhere beside him, forcing Alex to drop the rifle and draw a knife, assuming a native had somehow made it through the battle to flank him. He relaxed when Kara appeared, brandishing her ECP-30 at her side.

"Mind if I join you?" she asked, crouching beside him behind the rotting log. "It's hell up there!"

"Sure," Alex replied. "Don't get comfortable though. We won't be here for long."

"What do you mean?"

"There's too many of them. Adam will have to order a retreat soon. These primitives are smart and brave. I fear that they may be all that's left from the *Supernova* – which means our mission might be over a little sooner than we thought. There's no way we can let this barbaric culture back to Solis – it'd be catastrophic!"

"What do you need me to do?"

"Scout ahead into the grassland," Alex ordered. "Make sure it's free of primitives or dinosaurs. We'll need a quick getaway once they get down the hill, and we don't want to be stuck between a rock and a hard place."

"Anything to get away from those buffoons in the woods."

She nodded and slipped into the golden grass. Alex turned back to the battle in the trees and continued dispatching his targets.

#

"Come on," Adam whispered to Nathan. "Let's get further out of their range. Down the hill – keep your head low!"

WHOOSH! WHOOSH! THUNK! KA-THUNK!

"What?" Nathan asked, careful not to poke his head high enough over his rocky hideout. "We can't abandon the marines? What about Alter?"

"Alter's toast," Adam yelled, trying to be heard over the cacophony created by the fusillade all around them. "The marines are buying us time to get out. Now, as your uncle, I'm not asking – I'm telling. Get down the hill. Stay low!"

"But –"

THUNK!

Nathan's rebuttal was cut short by an arrow that lodged itself in a trunk, missing Nathan's head by inches. The boy's eyes grew wide realizing how close he came to death. With a hard shove, Adam pushed him backwards, sending his nephew rolling down a small animal trail, completely concealed behind a rocky wall. When he rolled back over, Adam had already caught up with him and grabbed his shirt collar, pulling him down the hill and letting his pulse rifle fire off up the slope.

VRRR! VRRR! VRRR!

That ought to buy us some time!

Now an extra twenty yards away from the battle behind a massive mossy trunk, Adam relaxed, knowing that his nephew was far away from the fray. He popped his head out for a moment to see what was happening, and was astonished at the amount of carnage that plagued the highlands. His team wouldn't last long if they stayed.

VRRR! VRRR! VRRR! WHOOSH! THUNK! KA-THUNK!

BRAWLLLL!

More horn calls began to flood down the jungle, as the elusive natives sprang from fern patches and bushes, trying to make up ground that their predecessors had lost when the pulse blasts snuffed out their lives. Although Adam's team wiped out at least thirty of the savages, more warriors seemed to arrive by the minute. The army appeared to have an infinite number of disposable soldiers.

My God, we'll waste all our ammunition here just fending off this attack! There's too many of them! We have to get out of here! The grassland! Yes, the grassland!

"Hey! Let's go! Retreat! Retreat!"

KA-THUNK! VRRR! VRRR! WHOOSH! THUNK! KA-THUNK! VRRR! VRRR!

His cries were useless. The sound of the conflict had become too great to shout over. Explosions from the pulse blasts and ensuing fires caused by burning, falling branches would mean Adam would have to climb back up the hill to order his crew out of there.

"Listen, Nathan," Adam turned to him. "No buts. I need to get our people out of here. I want you to run as fast as you can down to where Alex is in the grassland. Stay there and do what he says. I have to get the others."

"I think that –"

"Do as you're told!"

Nathan scowled, but quickly obeyed, bolting down the hill at a speed that impressed Adam. His stress eased when he saw that no archers had selected him for target practice, and the lieutenant began his slow ascent back up the hill.

The natives were now very easy to spot, running out from their cover, hoping to bring the battle to a more melee based engagement. Four of them – a small squad armed with pikes and crudely composited bone hatchets – flanked from the left side, where Brandy was crouched still trying to help free Alter. They hadn't yet spotted Adam, but had already selected Brandy and Alter for termination.

I don't want to do this, but I must...

One native noticed that Adam had popped out behind a trunk, pointing and babbling on in an unknown tongue, but it was too late for the squad of hunters.

VRRR! VRRR! BRRR! BRRR!

Four shots – four good hits, and Adam had safely dispatched the squad, reuniting with Brandy and Alter. To his surprise, Brandy had somehow plucked out Alter's final arrow, allowing the machine to land forward, and return to the fray. The damage caused by the arrows would eventually prove fatal to the bot, but his software had generated enough power for a final, herculean last stand.

"Brandy, get to the grassland," Adam commanded, tapping her on the shoulder and startling her. Her hands were bloody from arrow splinters, and her expression bordered on insanity.

"*Huh?*"

KA-THUNK! VRRR! VRRR!

"Just get to the field," Adam ordered, getting impatient, shouting over the conflict. "Run fast! The marines are drawing their attention for the moment. You have enough time to get away, but the window's closing!"

She nodded frantically, crawling on her hands and knees down the slope, eventually picking up speed and transitioning into a run as she tumbled down to the field.

KA-THUNK!

"*Daugghh!*" came a manly yawp to the right of the battleground.

Jonas!

An arrow found its way into Jonas Carte's forearm, causing him to drop his ECR-130. He fell forward against the tree he was using for cover.

"Ah, shit! I can't pull it out!"

Through the bushes ahead of him, two natives approached rapidly, ready to deal the death blow with a pair of rock clubs. Jonas reached sluggishly for his sidearm – an ECP-30 – dispatching both threats before returning to deal with the arrow.

"Hey, Jonas, hang on, I'll –"

THUNK! SPLAATTTT!

Adam's words of comfort were cut off by an arrow that nearly decapitated Jonas, puncturing the side of the marine's head before popping violently out of the other. The marine's eyes rolled back into his head as he was flung backwards, remaining static against the mulch. No sooner was Adam a witness to Jonas' death than Wyatt turned and commenced one of his famous, ill-timed tirades.

"What's the plan now, *Shit-For-Brains?*"

"*Retreat!*" Adam answered in a yell, wanting desperately to deck the sergeant in the face. But dealing with Wyatt would have to wait until a later time. For now, he needed to get the rest of the marines to safety.

Adam, Nathan, Alex, and Kara are already down in the field. With Jonas down, that leaves Wyatt, Ziven, Bruce, myself, and Alter, who won't last very long. I reckon he won't make it out of the woods.

"Hey, get down to the field!" Adam yelled at Bruce and Ziven, who had advanced a few yards ahead, keeping the advancing primitive army at bay.

WHOOSH! THUNK! KA-THUNK! VRRR! VRRR!

"Sir?" Ziven asked.

"Get to the field, Private!" Adam returned.

"Negative," Bruce yelled. "If we give up our posts and flee, they'll stick us up the ass on the way down. Their arrows are well placed. You guys get down, Alter and I will cover you. Ziven, go!"

Ziven cursed at the thought of abandoning his post, but obeyed everyone's commands, falling back down the hill. He shot past Adam and Wyatt, who had engaged in a fierce stare down while Bruce and Alter held their positions a few steps ahead.

"You next, Sergeant," Adam replied angrily.

"You imbecile," Wyatt fired back. "You're gonna get us all killed out here! Now with Jonas gone, and Alter surely not surviving, we'll be down two more gunmen. Not to mention we won't have Alter's short-range radar anymore! We'll never make it to the portal oscillator alive!"

THUNK!

Another arrow rammed into Alter's shoulder. The bot ripped out the projectile and kept firing, although few of the rounds were accurate. His aiming scanner had deteriorated to the point where the machine was firing at every quivering blade of grass.

"*Go-o-o Lieutenant, can't ho-o-old them off forev-e-er!*"

WHOOSH! THUNK! KA-THUNK! VRRR! VRRR!

"Wyatt, if you don't proceed down that hill to the others, so help me God –"

CRACK! CRACK!

Footsteps behind him broke his concentration, ruining his critical speech. It was three ax wielding natives, only a few feet ahead – so close Adam could make out their crude tattoos and curious piercings. There was no time to stop and admire the artwork.

VRRR! VRRR!

Two of the natives went down. As Adam raised the weapon to fire at the third, the pulse rifle jammed. Adam brought the weapon down to examine the damage – a move he would immediately regret. The native was on him instantly, tackling Adam to the ground and pinning him against the uneven earth, straining his spine underneath the armor suit.

"*Augghhh!*" Adam gasped, fighting off panic.

The native's eyes were cold as ice, staring into Adam's soul as they wrestled over the ax. A total of four hands on the weapon, Adam could feel the barbarian on top of him using his body weight to push the ax further down, trying to split Adam's skull.

Ahh! You prehistoric cocksucker!

From lying on his back, Adam shot a look at Wyatt who was standing a few feet away, capable of ending the fight quickly but doing nothing to prevent Adam's death. Up the hill, he could see Alter and Bruce continuing to hold off the rest of the army, oblivious to Adam's deadly stalemate.

"Wyatt, *kill him!*" Adam pleaded, his arms shaking as he tried to hold back the ax.

Wyatt gave one last look at the skirmish, a faint glimmer of a smile crossing his face as he turned and fled down the hill, leaving Adam to die by the hands of the homicidal caveman.

You bastard!

"*Wyatt!*"

The sergeant was gone, darting downhill and soon out of view. Adam couldn't worry about Wyatt. The situation at hand demanded immediate resolution – and fast. He looked back at the native briefly and then around for a weapon. Naturally the ECR-130 was useless, jammed and lying neglected a foot away.

Something lighter... there!

A rock, the size of a human hand, lay a few inches away to Adam's left. With a quick snatch, he took one hand off the ax and grabbed the rock, smashing the native in the head once.

THRAK!

The native blinked, mouth opening in surprise and unsure how to proceed. Adam repeated the action three more times, trying to find a more permanent solution to the problem.

THRAK! THRAK! THRAK!

"Uggh!" came the barbaric plea.

The native tumbled off him, dropping the weapon as the nearly nude man in his mid-twenties hurried to quell the blood flow. Quickly, Adam rose up, grabbed the hatchet and brought it down to the caveman's skull, ending the brawl, but certainly not the battle.

THUNK!

Adam looked up, just in time to see an arrow find its way into Bruce's skull, killing him instantly. Another squad of tribesmen ran forward with pikes, impaling the marine and moving to take down Alter, who at this point was firing in all directions, even unknowingly at Adam.

"Run, *go-o-o*, get out of *he-e-e-e-ere!*"

Adam turned to crawl down the hill, but realized to his horror, the unthinkable had happened. The natives had already passed him up on the sides, swarming down the slope past his position. How they failed to notice him sitting there beside a pile of their dead brethren, he didn't know. A quick look at the savanna told him that his friends had fled. There were no remaining living Federation personnel in sight.

They think I'm dead...

Around him, Adam could hear more footsteps breaking through the brush as the army of *Supernova* primitive descendants trekked down to the grasslands, taking the battle to the prairie. With a quick roll, Adam dove under the body of the native he had slain half a minute earlier, using his body as a shield as he heard the footfalls run past him. With the hunter's blood dripping steadily onto his concealed face, Adam listened quietly as the last sounds of the hillside battle died around him.

"Lieutenant, head for the – Lieutenant, head f-o-o – Lieutenant, he –"

THWAK!

With an audible crack of a club, Adam heard Alter go down, the last casualty of the fight, and instantly he knew he was alone.

VI

BRAWWWLLL!

The native attack transcended the jungle and swept relentlessly into the meadow, made evident by the continuous horn calls. Although many of the forest dwellers were slain in the highlands, Alex Meras was impressed at how many there actually were, watching them empty out from the woods a half a mile away in the grassland. Now free of trees, many of the archers stopped and took aim, sending their arrows sailing over the waves of golden grasses with their sturdy longbows.

SHWEERRR. WHOOSH! WHOOSH! FLUMP! FLUMP!

A volley of arrows rained down. The barbed tips vanished into the droves of golden fields, unsuccessful at hitting a target.

But they might get lucky, Alex thought, running after his companions.

WHOOSH! FLUMP!

An arrow landed two feet to Alex's right, disappearing into the golden landscape. Alex was the last in line, with Kara leading the group somewhere ahead, followed by Nathan, Wyatt, Brandy and Ziven. He wasn't sure about the fates of Bruce, Alter or Adam.

SHWEERRR. WHOOSH!

Another narrow miss.

How far are they planning on chasing us? Alex wondered as he quickened his pace. Ahead through their footpath, he could barely see the armored backpack of Ziven twenty paces ahead of him, glinting in the fleeting traces of the afternoon sun. If he didn't pick up the pace, he would lose his comrades in the endless meadow – a thought that he grew more comfortable with as the chase went on.

We'll have to give these hunters the slip sooner or later. I should be able to link up with them. I won't be gone too long.

Alex turned and crouched in the blades of grass, poking the sniper rifle barrel through the golden blades. With a quick glance, he managed to lay down two natives that had closed the gap to a quarter of a mile.

He turned back to follow, shocked that the other Federation survivors had already slipped away into the grass out of view. The sounds of the oncoming tribe drew near, although the arrows no longer came – he assumed the enemy couldn't find any targets to shoot at.

I have to draw them off somewhere...

The thought of getting separated from the main group wasn't the most ideal situation, but it may be necessary in order to end this relentless pursuit. Now Alter, Bruce, Jonas, and Adam Ross were either dead or missing. If this madness continued, there would be no one left to get to the oscillator.

Except for the dinosaurs, of course.

As Alex struggled to formulate a plan, an idea entered his mind: draw the natives to the west, then double time it to the southeast and reunite with the Federation comrades, assuming he was able to locate them.

SHWEERRR. WHOOSH! FLUMP!

The archers had found him, sending four projectiles his way, missing by a few yards. Pike bearers near the front began to advance, shrieking obscenities in their harsh, unknown tongue. A few at the front began to yelp and point, spotting Alex waiting in the grass. The time had come – it was now or never. Draw them away or risk them catching up with the others.

SHHRRR! SHHRRR!

Quickly, he scoped two of his closest targets and pulled the trigger. After seeing the targets jolt backwards and the weapons fall from their hands, he took off to his left, popping off rounds when he knew the pulse blasts would be guaranteed hits.

SHWEERRR! SHWEERRR! FLUMP! FLUMP!

The arrow volley resumed, followed by chants as the native army turned to the west, following Alex through the savanna, leaving the remaining five *Burrower* survivors to escape safely into the unknown.

#

Nathan was certain that his feet had never hurt so much in his life. They had been running for what seemed like hours, though he knew it was little more than twenty minutes. The ground along the meadow was soggy and uneven – evidence that it had probably rained earlier that morning or the day before. It was then that Nathan realized how much he wished he had packed some athletic shoes in his backpack, instead of his over-sized animal encyclopedia. When the running finally ceased, Nathan collapsed on the grass, cracking open his water canister for relief.

"*Wait!*" Kara yelled near the back of the group. "Where's Alex?"

They turned back to the self-made path they had just traversed. Alex was nowhere to be seen. Better yet, the native chanting and calls from the rudimentary horns had vanished entirely. Far away over the prairie, they could see the rim of the jungle highlands. There were no traces of the primitive *Supernova* survivors anywhere, except for the marred earth where the Federation blasters scorched the scene.

"He's gone," Ziven replied, holding up the rear of the group. "I can't remember when I last saw him – maybe ten minutes ago, if I had to wager a guess."

"Who the hell are they?" Brandy asked, sitting down and pulling out the splinters from her hands.

"Isn't it obvious?" Wyatt replied, checking the remaining ammunition in his ECR-130. "They're from the *Supernova*. In the three hundred years that the ship has been here, the survivors' offspring have all turned to savagery. We need to get moving, get to the oscillator and get home. There's nothing for us here. I know it's not the answer you all want to hear, but it's what we're doing!"

"You don't know that for sure," Kara argued, turning toward the sergeant.

"What did you say, Barnels?" Wyatt replied angrily, but too exhausted to yell.

"We don't know that all the *Supernova* crash survivors are savages. Someone had to have knowledge of how to operate the ship's solar signal emitter and send the distress call. A savage would have no such knowledge of the *Supernova* ship functions – especially advanced ones like distress signal operation."

"Wake up, Barnels. Anything can happen out here – if this morning hasn't proved that to me already. Any sane *Supernova* survivor died centuries ago. A savage must have gotten lucky and somehow operated the ship's signal. Let's do a munitions check. We're really going to have to conserve our ammunition from here on out if we plan on making it to the emitter. How is everyone's supply? I have two more cartridges. Ziven? Kara?"

"Two clips," Ziven replied.

"Three," Kara answered, annoyed by Wyatt but willing to comply for the moment.

"When are we going to wait for them?" Nathan asked.

"Wait for who?" Wyatt replied, in a tone that signaled disdain.

"Uncle Adam. And Alex?"

"They're dead," Wyatt replied bluntly. "And we can't afford to wait. You're just going to have to keep up or we'll have to leave you behind."

Dead? Nathan thought. *Uncle Adam is dead?*

The words rang through his head like a bell. If his uncle was dead, that meant he had nobody to count on – suddenly the adventure wasn't sounding so fun anymore. He wanted to get home to Solis, fast. How would he do that if he couldn't keep up with the athletic prowess of the adults?

"Hey!" Kara yelled, stepping up from the grass. "Don't talk to him like that! He's just a child, and probably scared out of his mind!"

"These are just the facts," Wyatt replied. "I saw it happen – it was one of the younger hunters, who snuck up behind us with an ax. I couldn't help him – there were already a dozen others already bearing down on me. His last command was a retreat, which saved my life at the cost of his own. Now, I suggest you don't take that tone with me again, Barnels!"

"I'm a medical specialist, Wyatt," Kara returned. "I'd say you need me right now more than I need you."

Her words were cold. A prolonged silence fell over the group, precipitated by the standoff. It was as if a transfer of power had happened – the tyranny of Wyatt was suddenly being questioned by someone below him, creating confusion of the pecking order. Finally, Brandy broke the silence.

"Well we can't stay here," she whined. "Not with those dinosaurs and those *Supernova* crazies out there. They may still be coming this way. What do we do now?"

Wyatt turned to the skies. The sun was beginning to set over the western peaks, setting the horizon line ablaze in a beautiful, dazzling gold. Traces of flying reptiles far away swept past the sun, shading the group momentarily before soaring away to another valley.

"With Adam dead, I'm assuming command of this operation," he began, eyeing Kara. "As such, I'm officially turning this rescue mission into an evacuation plan. The *Supernova* is a lost cause. Our one and only priority now is following our compasses to a rough heading to the southeast. The *Harvester One* wreck will be in reach, hopefully by tomorrow if we don't shit around. We'll use the oscillator to get us back to Solis and report our findings. Anyone have a problem with that?"

He shot Kara a final, devilish look. She knew she couldn't take him in a one on one fight and remained silent, taking a seat next to Ziven.

"Okay, let's return to the sprint. Those prehistoric pricks could be ten feet away from us and we'd never know in all this grass. Let's keep going until darkness and then we'll decide where to make camp."

With that, he took off into the grass. Ziven helped Brandy up and followed him. Kara helped Nathan to his feet.

For a medical specialist, she's kind of a bad ass, Nathan thought, a brief severance from his grim visions of his uncle's supposed death in the highlands.

"Don't worry, I won't leave you behind," Kara told him. "I'm not a total heartless asshole like Wyatt."

"Thanks, but I don't need anyone's help," Nathan answered. "I can keep up, I promise."

"Everyone needs help every now and then," Kara smiled. "We're gonna get home, don't worry. Now hurry before we lose them."

#

Apart from the occasional distant shriek or mating call from the unseen wildlife, Kara Barnels noticed that the journey through the savanna became gradually less cumbersome. The meadow kept feeding south, eventually filtering to a large grassy knoll, that seemed to rise high above the flora in the fleeting angelic sunlight.

She was pleased at the agility of the ten-year-old boy, whom she had come to know as Nathan. For such a small fellow, the lad kept up with the adults. Although Nathan's panting signaled a strong need for thirst, his mind was elsewhere: probably on the death of his uncle, Lieutenant Adam Ross.

He must feel so... alone...

Wyatt stopped at the base of the hillside, looking over their soon-to-be sanctuary.

"This looks like a good spot to camp out for the night," he announced. "It will be dark soon, and we don't have the resources or the knowledge of these parts to continue on at night. If we bust ass tomorrow, I'm confident we'll arrive at *Harvester One* and get the hell off this rock in the same day."

"Almost there," Kara said to Nathan, silently looking him over for bruises. She couldn't control her medical instincts for a second. "You'll sleep well tonight."

"Doubt it," Nathan answered, walking mindlessly past her, following Wyatt and Brandy up the grassy mound.

"Poor kid," Ziven remarked when the boy passed out of earshot. "First having his life almost sucked out of him in space. Then getting stranded here with the dinos and the natives. Now losing his uncle. I've been through hell today – losing some of my military brothers out there, but I'd hate to be in his shoes."

"I'm not so certain his uncle is dead," Kara whispered.

"What do you mean?" asked the marine with a curious tone.

"Walk with me," she whispered, waving him on. "Slowly as to not arouse suspicion."

They began a slow jaunt up the grassy knoll, letting the others easily outpace them. Finally, when she was sure no one would overhear, Kara continued.

"It's no secret that Wyatt was less than enthusiastic about Adam's ascension to lieutenant. Hell, Ziven, you heard him groaning and bitching about it all afternoon. He wouldn't shut the hell up about it! And no one saw what happened. Naturally all the witnesses in the highlands are dead. I think there's more to Adam's death than Wyatt is letting on."

"What are you saying?" replied a gruff voice behind his facial stubble. "You think Wyatt killed the boy's uncle?"

"I'm not ruling it out," she answered. "But I can't prove it. I'll never be able to."

"But Adam Ross, a Federation Watch officer as a marine lieutenant? Now don't get me wrong. I'm no fan of Sergeant Wyatt Brolen, but at least he is a marine. I think Adam's lack of experience in combat situations was evident all morning. Just look around – half of us are already wiped out."

"Oh come on, that's bullshit!" Kara fought back, trying not to raise her voice too loudly.

"What would you have done in any of these situations that we ran into? None of us were prepared for the Triassic – no amount of training could've prevented the native attack or the Coelophysis ambush. Adam tried his hardest, but Wyatt couldn't have done any better – I promise you that!"

She had shut the marine up. Kara knew that Ziven had no comeback, nodding at her comments and finally seeing her point.

"So I take it you don't particularly trust our new leader?" he asked finally, more quietly as they approached the top of the hill.

"Not in the slightest," she answered under her breath. "My own theory: if Wyatt had to choose between saving one of us and deploying the portal oscillator to teleport his sorry ass back to Solis, he'd chose that option. And we'd be screwed, with our thumbs up our butts, stuck here forever!"

"All right, this is our camp," Wyatt's voice boomed over the knoll, cutting off their conversation. "We'll have to take shifts throughout the night for predatory species. Ziven, can you help me clear away some of this grass so we can lay down more comfortably?"

"Yes, sir," Ziven answered, leaving Kara alone with her thoughts.

She finally arrived at the top of the plateau, sluggishly casting aside her backpack that had been crammed with medical supplies. In all of the deaths thus far on the expedition, the victims had died before she could provide relief – Kara hoped if the time came again, she could put her Federation military nurse training to better use.

Okay, Alex. Where are you?

#

Hiking through an ungodly amount of dinosaur infested jungles and boundless humid grasslands crawling with native hunters was not what Alex Meras signed up for. As he trekked quickly and quietly through the savanna, he reflected on what made him enlist with the Federation in the first place.

For a just cause. The chance at doing something memorable. Defending Solis from an extraterrestrial invasion. Not sweating my ass of for this shit, millions of years in the past!

Apart from wrestling internally with his life choices, he'd spent the last hour on high alert. Behind him, Alex no longer heard the horn calls of shrieking natives, having sharply cut to the left an hour before, taking him presumably southeast, or so his compass read. After another half hour of silence, Alex assumed that he had successfully eluded the jungle hunters, throwing them off course and thus safely putting his remaining comrades out of harm's way.

Now, where the hell did they get to?

He tried to think of where Wyatt would take them, based on what he'd learned of his sergeant after months spent together traversing the cosmos.

High ground. Most likely a hill. Wyatt's not that creative – I'll find them.

Alex took the sniper rifle and placed his eye up to the scope, switching the setting to night-vision as he surveyed the shadowy fields ahead. It didn't take long to discern a lonely knoll, probably half a mile away in the distance. Through the digital scope reception and flickering holographic binary readings, he could tell there were humans on the summit. A closer inspection revealed several pulse weapons lying about where the grass had been matted down, confirming the location of the *Burrower* survivors.

What's left of them, Alex thought, thankful that he'd located the remainder of the rescue party.

After a brisk run to make up time, he was caught off guard as he approached the silent encampment by an ECP-30 pulse pistol drawn on his face. For such an expert marine, Alex cursed at the thought of a medical specialist getting the jump on him.

"Alex? Thank God!" Kara exclaimed quietly, realizing who the intruder was. "What happened?"

"The native army wasn't giving up pursuit," Alex replied, stripping off his backpack and casting it to the grass. "I'm impressed at the amount of survivors spawned from the *Supernova* descendants. But I'm still clueless as to how they've spiraled into the barbaric tribe we see today. Anyways, I've thrown them off for the time being."

"Do you suppose there may be other survivors?" Kara asked. "Ones that haven't succumbed to lunacy?"

"I don't know," Alex answered. "We've only been here half a day. The way it seems, there's plenty we have yet to learn about the Triassic."

"Wyatt seems to think it's a lost cause," Kara said, lowering her voice. "He's taken over command. Apparently, tomorrow we're going to recover the portal oscillator and abort the mission – if it works this time."

"*What?*" Alex grumbled. "We haven't even been here for a full day, and he wants to head back already? I know we've lost a lot of our crew, but there could still be people here worth saving. He's such a coward!"

"Tell me about it. Do you know what happened to Adam?"

"No, I lost visual of him once I saw the natives had already passed their position in the woods and had passed into the fields. Why?"

"Wyatt claims he was killed by one of the natives."

Alex thought for a moment. It was true that Adam Ross would've been relatively new to hand-to-hand combat scenarios, but he had fared against the Coelophysis very well. If he wasn't taken down by an archer, Alex decided that it was doubtful a native could take him down in a one-on-one fight, especially if Adam brandished a pulse rifle. Besides, Adam had been a very muscular man, much larger than the jungle army warriors that they clashed with earlier.

"How did Wyatt say he died?" Alex asked suspiciously.

"An ax attack," Kara said. "An ambush, basically."

"And you believe him?"

"Not at all."

"Me either."

"Well, what are we going to do about it?"

"Nothing for the moment. I need to rest. I can barely function at this point. But I'll tell you one thing – we're not leaving the Triassic until we do a thorough sweep of the area. There's plenty of prey we can use for food if we run out of our Federation rations. There's at least one person here that needs our help, according to Adam's report from three years ago at the *Music Box*. If we pull out now it will take years of navigating Solis congressional gridlock to come back, and I'll be damned if I let that happen."

#

ERRREEWAH! ERRREEWAH!

The cry of a distant animal – or dinosaur, more likely – woke Adam Ross from his impromptu nap. The nauseating smell of cadaver jerked him out of unconsciousness, forcing him to cast aside the dead native and breathe freely the night air of the jungle as the corpse rolled away.

Oh... what a stench! I'm still alive. What a miracle! Night? How much time has passed?

It had to have been hours since he had hidden under the dead caveman. The brightness of afternoon had transitioned into the dead of night. Shortly after Bruce and Alter were slain, he hid underneath the corpse, thinking that the hunters would pass through quickly.

When a half hour passed and there were still patrols from the Neolithic tribe perusing the highlands, Adam feared that his unlikely refuge may be more long term than expected. With nothing to do but wait, Adam was forced to stare into the lifeless eyes of the native until, apparently, he fell asleep. Grateful that the native tribe had finally left the area during his slumber, he scanned the woods for any trace of movement.

ERRREEWAH! ERRREEWAH!

What the hell is that?

Adam winced, unsure of what prehistoric foe he'd be facing off with this time.

A winged animal, only a dark silhouette against the moonlit backdrop of the jungle, ascended from the high perches of a tree and circled above, slipping away into the clouded sky. Adam relaxed when the unknown flier soared away from the area, surmising the creature was of little threat.

Now, where's that damn pulse rifle?

The ECR-130 sat two feet away, buried partially in dirt clods kicked up during the fierce battle. The ammunition counter at the top read *95*, the number glowing through a pair of leaves, making the firearm easy to spot.

Adam seized it and began padding the sides. With a swift chop to the stock, a small red light switched over to green. Now that he was thinking clearly and wasn't fending off a murder attempt, Adam realized this simple fix would've fixed the gun – a fix that would've made the brutal fight from earlier end a lot sooner.

Well, that's one problem solved.

Crunch...Crunch... Scrapp...Scrapp...Crunch...

A subtle rasping began – alarmingly close. Adam scanned the area through the sight, using the moonlight to help his eyes adjust to the night surroundings.

Now what is it?

He soon gleaned the answer.

Twenty feet up the slope, two juvenile Coelophysis specimens were beginning to pick apart the remains of Bruce Rison. With a turn of the head, the larger of the two dinosaurs dislodged Bruce's rifle, letting the weapon strike stone in a small crevice with an abrupt *clang*. The dinosaurs turned and spotted Adam, but were too little and scrawny to press an attack, choosing instead to devour the dead marine. Beside Bruce, Alter lay slumped against a severed log, ten arrows jutting out from his chrome chest and his head crushed inward – the wound that most likely did him in.

A further check of the area found that Jonas Carte's corpse had already been ravaged. The marine's helmet had been stripped off, exposing a skewered skull that the two coelos had devoured. Jonas' ECR-130 lay discarded at his side, and with it, his tattered backpack.

Adam walked over to the pack confidently and rooted through it, retrieving three additional ammunition cartridges for his pulse rifle.

Rest in peace, pal. I need these more than you do! I won't forget your sacrifice.

He debated on going for Bruce's backpack as well, but decided it wouldn't be a wise idea. With the two coelos munching down on the marine's remains and standing guard so close, he figured it might provoke them. Shooting them with the rifle was off the table as well. Pulse rounds may draw other coelos into the area – or worse, the mysterious human jungle dwellers. He would have to make do with Jonas' extra clips.

Okay, now what?

He would have to figure out which way the other survivors went. With any luck, Alex or Kara had looked after Nathan well enough to get him through the savanna. It was a thought he quickly tossed out, not wanting to speculate over whether his companions and nephew were alive or dead. The only thing left to do was pick up their trail.

Thanks, Dad!

As he made his way out of the trees and into the grassy field, he reflected on his younger years in Solis, when his father would take him on hunting trails in the countryside, where he quickly picked up the necessary skills in order to follow human trails under ideal situations. Over time, he became rather adept at it.

It took only a minute for Adam to find the series of human boot impressions made by Federation soles that impressed down on the grass. The footprints of the natives crunched through a large swath of the area, but not enough to completely wear away the evidence left from the marines. The hunters had clearly pursued the *Burrower* survivors out of the woods – not a good sign for the hope of survival for his dwindling peers.

What could have made these barbarians so violent? Adam thought, making sure his rifle was loaded as he hurried into the dark field.

Many questions floated through his mind – questions that needed addressing.

Why are these primitive hunters so determined to kill us? Why have they regressed so much from their ancestors that crashed here in the first place? They clearly don't have the intelligence to operate a solar signal emitter from the Supernova. After all, who in this prehistoric nightmarish landscape does?

These were the mysteries of the Triassic, and Adam assumed there would be many more to follow in the upcoming days, provided that he survived that long. Based on their track record so far, he didn't count on making it to the oscillator – but he'd commit to die trying.

But above all the questions, all the strife that came along from surviving agile dinosaurs and a relentless militia of primitive cave-dwelling psychopaths and finding the sender of the distress call, one word remained above the rest of the thoughts.

Wyatt.

A streak of anger fueled his accelerated run into the unpredictable night landscape, egged on by the potential opportunity for revenge. Getting even with Wyatt was now at the summit of his to-do list, followed by making sure his nephew was alive and safe, completing the mission, and returning home.

I'm coming for you, you son of a bitch!

VII

ERRREEWAH! ERRREEWAH!

Kara glanced up, perplexed by yet another foreign animal call that she didn't recognize. The flying chanter was far away. If the boy wasn't fast asleep, Kara might have asked him if he knew whether or not that the noise came from a dinosaur.

Dinosaurs. Ha! What a crazy world we've found ourselves in...

The thought of clashing with prehistoric animals that were long thought to be extinct was not something she anticipated when ejecting from *Harvester One*. Yet here they were, alive and well in Earth's distant past.

Wonder what else we'll bump into?

She took a sip from her canteen. When Kara heard loud sloshing from inside, she shined a utility flashlight into the container, revealing that only a few sips of water remained. During their flight from the highlands and the arduous hike through the humid fields, she had almost completely exhausted her water supply.

Damn. I'll have to fill up soon...

"Here, take some of mine," Alex Meras said a few feet away, handing over his canteen.

"You sure?" she paused.

"Go ahead. I'll be fine."

Kara had been on shift watching out for the camp for an hour. Alex had recently joined her, falling asleep for an hour and then arising suddenly, stating that his internal alarm clock wouldn't let him rest for long. She took a swig from the canteen and handed it back to him, wiping her lips with her forearm.

"So, what's your story?" she asked, trying to pass time by learning more about the mysterious warrior.

"My story?" Alex laughed. "There is no story. I was eager to make a difference in the world – save lives, searching for glory. You know, the stereotypical soldier thing. Was selected for a sniper rifle certification after proving myself in basic combat training in the Solis combat camps. That's about it. What about you?"

Kara smiled, turning away so the sniper wouldn't see. Something about him made her feel safe. She had discovered his gentle nature, despite how many lives the soldier had snuffed out earlier that afternoon. And now, he wanted to know more about her too.

"Well, my mother was the one who pushed me into being a nurse,"

Kara began. "After a few months in nursing school, I realized I liked it, but not enough to be a traditional nurse working in some mundane Solis hospital. I traveled a lot by subterranean transit. In the transit station, I saw a recruitment poster for the Federation, signing the next day in the medical division. I earned a few badges my first year, one of which qualified me to carry a sidearm and the chance to apply to missions such as this one. If I had known how this mission would've ended up, I'll be honest, I may not have applied."

"Well for the record, I'm glad you're stuck on this trip with us," Alex admitted. "Not only is it good to have an armed nurse with us, but you saved my ass back there near the *Burrower*. I wouldn't be here right now if it wasn't for you. I've got your back, Barnels."

"Please, call me Kara," she said, disgusted. "Barnels is what Wyatt calls me."

"Well, we wouldn't want that," Alex said, turning back to the grasslands. "*Whoa*, hang on here. I think I got something!"

"What?"

"Not sure, moving toward the camp at a quick pace. Looks like whatever it is, it's alone. I don't see other grasses around the source moving, indicating only one presence. Keep your head below the grass. I don't know if they've spotted us yet."

Shit. Not more coelos or Supernova natives! We aren't prepared for this right now!

She quietly unzipped her pack, placing her canteen inside gently and retrieving a pair of binoculars she'd grabbed back on board *Harvester One*, when everything had started to fall apart. Switching the mode to night-vision, her view mimicked that of Alex's sniper scope. Through the green visor, her camera began to pick up motion not far from the base of the knoll, moving toward them in a bee line.

"I see it," Kara added. "It's moving straight for us. My guess is that it's a human."

"Get your pistol out," Alex told her. "It could be a barbarian scout. This could be the start of round two – we'll need to evacuate quickly if it is."

They've found us! Kara thought, gripping the pistol tightly in one hand as she continued to trace the source of movement as it began an ascension up the hill.

Beside her, she could feel Alex doing the same, keeping the sniper barrel trained on the visitor.

Loud footsteps and crunching of grass began to emit as the newcomer approached, closing the distance rapidly, destined to breach the camp in seconds. Kara's heart raced, she could feel the sweat dripping down her hands. In the jungle earlier that afternoon, she was fortunate enough not to have directly faced any of the natives. She feared if this was indeed a scout, that there may be many unseen reinforcements just waiting below in the meadow.

Huh?

A sweaty, tired man in Federation armor materialized through the grass into their watch area. He collapsed to his knees from exhaustion, draining a large drink from his water canister and sluggishly dropping his backpack.

Adam!

"Hey, long time no see," Adam managed in between labored breaths.

"You look like shit, Lieutenant," Alex remarked, lowering the sniper rifle. "Jeez, happy to see you made it out alive. We thought you'd been killed. What the hell happened up there?"

"Shenanigans, that's what," Adam said, trying to stabilize his breathing. "Bruce, Alter, and Jonas kept most of them at bay from the front, but they began to flank us. One had me pinned, almost killed me. Wyatt did nothing, could've stopped it, ran off. They killed Jonas first, and Bruce and Alter died shortly after. I hid from the other natives who had already moved past my position. Then I was stuck waiting for hours for them to leave the area, before guessing on where you all went. Now, where is that asshole? We have unfinished business."

#

Fueled with an unpredictable rage, Adam marched past Alex and Kara's watch point. As Adam arrived at the top of the hill, he could faintly see four human forms – Ziven, Brandy, that bastard Wyatt, and thankfully, Nathan, fast asleep around the dim orange glow of a battery powered lantern.

Thank God you're okay, Adam thought as he watched his nephew sleep.

The shining from the lantern made his target easy to locate. Wyatt was turned away from the others, his snoring body facing the grassy wall. In the orange lantern illumination, Adam could tell that the buzz cut hairstyle belonged to the sergeant.

There you are – you son of a bitch!

"Lieutenant," Alex said, placing a hand on Adam's shoulder. "You sure you want to do this?"

"Relax," Adam replied. "I'm not a murderer, Alex. But this is long overdue. Here, hold my ECP-130."

Alex took the weapon without question and stepped back. By now, Brandy and Ziven were starting to stir, wondering what was about to take place on the hilltop. Woozily they roused from sleep, shocked to see Adam standing above them in the faint glimmer of lantern light.

WAH-FOOM!

With a swift kick to Wyatt's buttocks, Adam's boot delivered enough pain to jolt the sergeant from his rest. Cursing and blurting out obscenities, Wyatt regained his composure as he stood up and searched the clearing for the source of the attack. The color drained from his face when he saw Adam standing in the middle of the crowd who had gathered around. By now, everyone was awake.

"Oh Adam, you're alive!" Wyatt gasped, feigning interest and sincerity. His comical acting didn't come off well. "Oh, thank God. We thought you were shish kabob'd by one of those spears."

"Surprise, asshole," Adam raged, with an expression hellbent on revenge. "Weren't expecting to see me again, were you? You thought you took care of me."

Wyatt cocked his head, channeling an imaginary offended demeanor.

"I have no idea what you're *talk –*"

"Sergeant Wyatt wanted me dead," Adam cut in, turning around to the others who had latched onto the dramatic situation, eyes spread wide in disbelief.

"When the *Supernova* natives attacked, I climbed up the hill to order a retreat. With only Bruce and Alter there as witnesses, Wyatt made his move when a squad of natives attacked us from the side. One had me pinned, using his weight to crush me with an ax. Wyatt was only a few feet away and could've stopped it all; instead he left me to die. He knew that even if Bruce and Alter had seen what had happened, they wouldn't live long enough to tell – their positions were being overrun. They were both doomed to die."

Adam turned back to Wyatt, who mustered up a phony surprised face.

"I waited up in the jungle for hours for the natives to vacate the area. What did you tell the others, Wyatt? You told them that I was dead, didn't you? You told them that the native killed me!"

Adam could feel everyone's gazes shifting to Wyatt, expecting a rebuttal that would never come.

"That's what he said," Kara finally chimed in. "Wyatt wanted to be in charge again, but most of all, he wanted to abort the mission and get to the oscillator – but not just to recover it. All he wants is to get back to Solis where there's no dinosaurs!"

Another passage of silence fell over them as they turned back to Wyatt, who at first tried to ease the tension by deploying a look of surprise, but quickly realized his motives were uncovered.

"You got me," he said finally, letting his hands fall. "I think Adam Ross doesn't deserve a title of officer in the marines, and is going to get us all killed. You all saw it first hand! The *Supernova* survivors are brutes. We need to get out while we can! We can come back again with more supplies and soldiers in a few years, when –"

"Someone had to send that distress call, Wyatt," Alex interjected.

"We're staying."

"Well then," Wyatt said, slowly reaching for his backpack as if he was ready to depart. "Looks like I'm completely outnumbered. Maybe I'll just have to make for the portal oscillator myself, and leave you all here to fend off the wildlife without my guidance."

He made a subtle motion to unzip his backpack.

Zippp...

"Oh, and Adam? See you in hell!"

He reached in and pulled out a hidden ECP-30, setting the safety off and firing a round at Adam. The bolt missed, sailing past Adam and missing the others, scorching into the grasslands with a powerful, loud buzz.

Adam was relieved to see that Alex Meras was already acting on the situation. A swift shot from the ECSR-20 sent Wyatt's pulse pistol flying out from the sergeant's hand, the sidearm disintegrating as it landed on the matted grass, sparking into a useless pile of caustic scrap metal.

"Meras, you *fu –*"

PHHHHF!

Wyatt's words were cut short by Adam who rammed into the aggressor before the sergeant could reach his pulse rifle. They tumbled backwards over the adjacent side of the hill from which Adam ran up only minutes earlier. Adam struck his opponent with such force that the two bodies only clung together for seconds before spiraling out of control as they rolled out into the open. Ahead, another jungle loomed, issuing an end to the savanna and giving way to another lush wilderness. Wyatt attempted to run only to be knocked down again by Adam.

"I'm going to enjoy this, Wyatt," Adam replied, sending a furious balled fist into the sergeant's face. "Maybe after this, you'll start –"

KRRR!

Wyatt registered a sideways punch to Adam's jaw, sending the lieutenant rolling off his sparring partner, back into the grass. Up the slope, he could hear the others rushing down to put an end to the dangerous sparring duel.

The sergeant moved in to engage again, turning and spinning his leg into an expertly aimed sidekick. Adam blocked the attack, sacrificing his wrist for a blow to his head, and went for a jugular punch. Wyatt rolled back, pulling Adam with him, once again taking the fight to the ground. Adam was surprised at the level of skill Wyatt possessed with hand-to-hand combat. Although Adam was larger, the sergeant's marine reflexes had proven difficult to predict. With an abrupt sideways stroke to Adam's head, he saw stars, and knew the fight had been taken out of him.

"Now, Lieutenant Ross," Wyatt said, staring down at him with a devilish grin. "For your mutiny and because you've been a general pain in my ass, I'm going to have to kill you now."

"Wrong again," came Kara's stark voice from behind the scuffle, followed by the safety being switched off her pulse pistol.

She shoved the barrel to the back of his head. Wyatt released his grip on Adam and let him up. Wyatt turned dramatically back to the others who had descended the hill, trying to hide his frustration that he had officially been ousted. The group stood watching in disbelief at the events that had played out. Adam saw Nathan hiding behind Alex Meras, peering around the barrel of the marine's sniper rifle, scared but thankful for his uncle's survival.

"You're all making a grave mistake," Wyatt reprimanded them.

"Save it for the Solis penitentiaries," Ziven answered. "Two accounts of attempted murder. That will put you away for a long time, Sarge."

"Spare me the poetry," Wyatt spat at him. "I'm not going to any prison. Because under Adam's command, none of us are getting out of here alive. We'll all die here! It's only a matter of time."

#

Standing by the base of the hill where Adam and Wyatt's life or death struggle ended prematurely, Nathan stared out into the rim of the southern jungle that rose up around them. When Alex disarmed Wyatt with his sniper round, Nathan was sure the sound would've alerted any predatory species in the area to their destination.

A nearby guttural gurgling sound told him he was correct.

RUHUHUKUKUH...

The dreaded sound hovered over the darkened field.

Nathan's ears perked up, alarmed by what he heard. None of the adults were paying attention or staying alert, choosing instead to put an end to his uncle's fist fight. He couldn't yet discern what was making that awful rumbling noise and took a few steps into the prairie to investigate.

Is there just one? Or are we dealing with another pack? They don't sound at all like the Coelophysis, and they're definitely non-human... They sound... bigger...

RUHUHUKUKUH... RUHUHUKUKUH...

The rumbling continued, closer this time, making Nathan retreat until he was in range of the adults. Walking backward, he roughly struck Brandy's hip.

"Hey, watch it, kid," she joked amid the arguing of the other adults.

"I think something's here," Nathan choked out.

"What?" Kara said, eavesdropping on the boy. "What did you say, Nathan?"

"Something's here in the grass with us," Nathan repeated, pointing to the shadowed prairie. "Listen!"

Kara and Brandy turned, staring out into the moonlit fields of flowing grass. Among the dark blue blades, the rumbling had quieted to the point where Nathan assumed that the fauna had fled the area, until an orange tail shot through the weeds, followed by a horrible screech.

WREEEE! RUHUHUKUKUH...

"*Whoa*, did you hear that?" Ziven asked, shouldering his weapon.

"Yeah, it's close," Alex added.

"Something's here!" Brandy yelled. "Oh God, I think they have us surrounded!"

VIII

RUHUHUKUKUH... RUHUHUKUKUH...

Dealing with Wyatt will have to be put on the back burner, Adam deduced after assessing their latest predicament. The wretched calls were beginning to reverberate around the field, a telling sign that the creatures of the night were beginning to encircle them. Just as it had been with the native army, their stalkers kept themselves well camouflaged, using the high grass to mask their appearance.

"Someone give me a gun!" Wyatt demanded, turning angrily to the others who disregarded him.

"Kiss my ass, Wyatt!" Kara returned, casting a disgusted look over her shoulder at him.

"Barnels, I swear to God, if you don't give me your pistol right *n* –"

"Touch her and you're dead," Alex returned, stepping in front of Wyatt, who backed off. "Now stay down and shut your mouth, or I'll be obliged to shut it for you!"

Wyatt scowled, defeated for the moment, too distracted by the sounds of the predators to continue to argue.

RUHUHUKUKUH...

The creatures continued their taunting chants.

"What do we do?" Brandy whined, although it was more of an uncertain cry than a question.

"Stay put and form up," Adam replied, taking charge. "Everyone with guns, stick to the outside and form a protective circle for those without guns. Brandy, watch over my nephew, will you? Wyatt, don't move! I swear, I'll blow your pathetic head off if you try to take one of our guns!"

Adam, Ziven, Kara, and Alex moved to the outskirts of the group, each facing a different direction. Brandy and Nathan stayed directly behind Adam. Wyatt remained on his knees near the center, under the careful watch of everyone on the perimeter who shot him occasional glances.

RUHUHUKUKUH... RUHUHUKUKUH...

"What are they waiting for?" Brandy whimpered, clutching Adam's back with one hand and his nephew with the other.

"They're communicating to each other," Nathan told her. "They must be deciding on who should attack first. They probably aren't sure about our weapons either. We clearly look different than the other *Supernova* survivors, so they're making up their minds if we're worth the effort."

"Well I hope they decide that we're not worth it," Brandy lamented, her grimy hair blocking out her panicked, sweaty face.

RUHUHUKUKUH... RUHUHUKUKUH...

Come on already. We don't have all night! Do it!

Adam could feel himself tensing up, antsy in anticipation of the attack that would soon be commenced. His body ached from running all night, his feet throbbed, and the mark on his head was bringing on renewed bursts of agony.

He studied his direction carefully, moving his rifle sight slowly between the waving grass clusters. His chosen visual range was the dense, shadowy jungle that severed the grassland just fifty yards away. A few seconds into his search, he caught a glimpse of something rushing forward. The grass ahead began to part, giving way to the monster within.

WREEEE! RUHUHUKUKUH! RUHUHUKUKUH!

Shit me in the face! That thing's horrific!

"Hey, here they come! I got a confirmed visual. Engaging *now*!"

The beast tore through the last layer of flora, exposing itself as a more muscular, larger version of the Coelophysis. The dinosaur's scales were a mixture of brown and orange. As the carnivore spread its salivating jaws, Adam saw that the gaping mouth could swallow his entire face with ease.

You're an ugly one, aren't you?

BRRR! VRRR!

Adam's blasts jolted through the dinosaur's mid-section, spilling out a torrent of blood as the attacker slipped on the grassy bed. Convulsing and spiraling in agony, the dinosaur grew still as the blast effects took root.

"Target down," Adam confirmed, keeping the gun trained on the grasses ahead. When he saw the weeds beginning to shake again, he knew the conflict was far from over.

#

Nathan leaned around his uncle's form, trying to get a clearer view of the deceased carnivorous dinosaur. The happiness he felt at Adam's sudden resurrection was quickly cut short after the brutal fist fight. Coupled with the new dinosaur threat that surrounded them, Nathan once again found himself wondering if he would live or die.

But these new dinosaurs were smarter than the Coelophysis. These orange theropods would only attack in controlled spurts, whereas the coelos seemed to not mind getting mowed down for the communal good of their tribe.

"What are you doing?" Brandy asked, tapping his shoulder.

"Research," Nathan told her, unzipping the backpack quietly and retrieving his encyclopedia again. "I'm pretty sure I know what these things are!"

Finally, he landed on a large Triassic carnivore dubbed a *Herrerasaurus*.

"I've found it," Nathan announced, reciting excerpts from the book. "Herrerasaurus, a large Triassic predator from the Carnian stage. Known for a more boxy head than later day carnivores, Herrerasaurus was a prominent hunter in Triassic landscapes. Although not as fierce as some of the other carnivores at the time, Herrerasaurus was a dinosaur not to be trifled with."

"Is that supposed to make us feel more comfortable?" Brandy whispered in his ear.

"I guess not," Nathan admitted, "but hey, at least we know what they are."

"Why don't you both shut the hell up!" Wyatt hissed from his degrading kneeling position in the center of the defensive ring. "Your babbling will be the death of us."

"Wyatt, be quiet!" Adam returned sharply. "It's taking every muscle in my body right now not to blow your brains out. At least my nephew figured out what we're dealing with. All you do is bitch about shit."

Wyatt once again was quiet. Adam heard Kara choke back a laugh.

"Stay focused, team," Alex spoke up, training his scope over the savanna. "These orange bastards are clever, much cleverer than what we've faced so far. If we hold our positions long enough, and they attack one by one, we just might get ourselves out of this mess!"

RUHUHUKUKUH! RUHUHUKUKUH!

The guttural taunting continued, this time noticeably closer and more concentrated around the human position.

"I think they're moving in, Lieutenant!" Ziven yelled. "Anyone else see anything?"

"Other than the occasional movement of grass?" Kara replied. "No, not yet."

"We need to head for the jungle," Wyatt broke in. "We'll have better chances climbing a tree and waiting them out then staying here on the ground."

"It's a long way to the trees, dumbass," Adam replied. "They'll sack us before we get halfway there. Not to mention they're already over in that direction. Don't you see the grass moving?"

"Hey, Lieutenant," Ziven called. "I've got some movement over here. I think they may be gearing up for *anoth* –"

RUHUHUKUKUH!

"Auggghh! Help-p-p!"

CRUNCH! Splll...

With a perfectly executed jump, a herrera bounced out from the grassland to the left of Ziven, landing on the marine's shoulders and forcing him to the ground. The dinosaur's jaws stretched over his head as rows of teeth knifed their way into his skull. Ziven's woeful cry was ended a second after it began, and the dinosaur broke the man's neck while giving him a nasty brain hemorrhage.

Incredible! So quick, so smart. So deadly...

Nathan saw the attack happen, awestruck by the orange predator. He could feel his mouth fall open at the sheer speed and hunting knowledge that the herreras possessed. They reminded him of the more popular deinonychus of the early Cretaceous Period. His gaze froze when he saw the herrera eyeing him next, already selecting the boy as a next meal. In the glimmer of the dinosaur's eye, Nathan saw his life flash.

#

SHRRRR!

Alex Meras took down Ziven's attacker, just as the herrera prepared to use the marine's corpse as a trampoline to springboard itself to Nathan.

"Ziven's down!" Adam called. "Reconfigure the pattern into a triangle. Get closer together, or they'll break us *u –*"

RUHUHUKUKUH! RUHUHUKUKUH!

After Ziven's demise, the herreras sensed the vulnerability of the humans and began to make themselves seen. Adam watched in horror as the grassland around them began to quake and sway violently in the night air. He could feel the footsteps of the dinosaurs begin to vibrate the ground beneath him.

THRUSH! THRUSH!

Two herreras appeared on opposite sides, their reptilian heads poking through the grass as the marines began sending rounds into the field. The dinosaurs swiftly returned into the brush, snarling as they went. Another trio of herreras appeared near Kara's corner. She launched a few pulse blasts at them, assuming that at least one of the rounds struck a target when a primordial groan was heard from over the wall of grass.

"Guys, I'm almost out here!" Kara yelled. "I only have one clip left!"

"I think Ziven had an ECP-30 sidearm," Brandy replied, choking back panicked breaths. "If you can get to his pack, maybe *you'll –*"

"*Hey!*" Alex yelled. "Wyatt, get back down! Dammit! He's escaping!"

Adam turned, alarmed at the movement behind him. Wyatt had shot up from his kneeling position, cutting a path for Ziven's discarded ECR-130. Kara Barnels moved to intercept him midway.

"Get back down," Kara ordered him, raising her sidearm to his face.

But Wyatt was too quick – the sergeant knocked her weapon out of her hands and planted a firm chop to her shoulder, sending the medical specialist falling over and scrambling for her weapon – more terrified of the herreras than of Wyatt with a pulse rifle.

During the scuffle, the herreras took notice.

THRUSH! THRUSH! THRUSH!

Seizing the opportunity, three herreras exited the grassland and engaged the humans, roaring menacingly as they emerged to press the attack. Confusion flooded the perimeter, and the defense toppled like dominoes.

BRRR! BRRR!

Adam's ECR-130 popped off two rounds, killing an advancing herrera that broke from the direction of the jungle.

WHAM!

Suddenly from behind, Adam felt a sharp pain from his neck, catching himself below on the matted ground. When he turned, he saw Wyatt standing over him, aiming the barrel of Ziven's ECR-130 at his chest.

"I should've killed you when I had the chance," Wyatt snickered. "Oh well, this will have to do. What the – hey, *get off!*"

Brandy had grabbed onto his pulse rifle, delaying Adam's execution. The scuffle was over quickly – Wyatt backhanded the Federation translator to the ground, but not without Brandy achieving her goal. She fell to the ground, managing to disarm him, hanging onto the ECR-130 via a death grip. Nathan rushed to her defense, bravely grabbing a rotted log from the ground and using it as a blunt force object.

SFTT!

Wyatt effortlessly kicked Nathan's weapon aside, grabbed him, and threw him under his arm in an awkward carrying position.

"Let him go, *Wyatt!*" Adam roared, getting back on his feet.

"Oh, he's coming with me," Wyatt smiled. "Consider it an insurance policy so you don't get tempted to tail me. I mean it, Adam, I'll snap his neck like a twig!"

"Uncle Adam, don't let him take me!" Nathan screamed, kicking and screaming under Wyatt's arm.

"See you back at Solis," Wyatt laughed. "But probably not. *Ciao!*"

He turned and picked up Ziven's backpack, slipping into the grassy wall with his hostage in tow, giving Adam the middle finger salute as he fled.

#

"Wait! Where are you going?" Brandy cried as Adam pried the pulse rifle from her hands.

"I have to go after him," Adam replied. "He took Nathan. There's no way he'll put up with my nephew for long. He'll be dead long before Wyatt arrives at *Harvester One.*"

Before Brandy could respond, Adam was already gone, tearing through the shrubbery after his rival. Kara Barnels witnessed the entire encounter, unable to intervene due to the attack from the herreras that still raged around them like a hurricane.

With Adam and Nathan gone, Ziven dead, and Wyatt on the run, it's down to just us three, she thought. Their odds weren't looking that great.

"Are you okay?" Kara asked, looking at Brandy's bruise from Wyatt's attack.

"Yeah, but I won't be for long if those dinosaurs catch us!"

I should've shot that cocksucker myself, Kara thought, fantasizing about shooting Wyatt as she picked off another Herrerasaur that dared enter their defensive perimeter.

"We have to go after them," Brandy urged. "Adam said Wyatt will kill Nathan! We have to help. We have to –"

RUHUHUKUKUH!

CRUNCH!

A herrera had slipped through the void that Ziven left unguarded, latching onto Brandy's arm and grinding its teeth through her skin, shaking its head to and fro with violent outbursts.

"Aughh! Kara, get it off! Kill it! Kill it, please! Oh God, it hurts!"

BRRR!

Kara pressed the barrel up to the dinosaur's skull and pressed the trigger. The Herrerasaur shrieked in misery and let go of its dinner, crumpling lifelessly below Brandy who screamed, clenching her wound in agony. Blood oozed out from the tooth impressions, leaking over her Federation uniform onto her waist and thighs.

"Oh, Kara! Help me please..."

"Hang on!" Kara tried to calm her, trying not to lose her cool. "Put pressure on the wound! I'll bandage you up after I know we're in the clear!"

She pushed Brandy against the body of the dead dinosaur, using the reptile as a shield from the rear as she scanned the scene with her pistol. Several yards away, Alex Meras – the only other human remaining in the area – was busy fending off several herreras who scooted back and forth, trying to cut him off from the others and effectively removing him from helping the two women.

THRUSH!

Ahead, another bold Herrerasaur launched itself through the high grass and bounded toward her. With a final blast of her ECP-30, the round penetrated the reptile's eyes – another clean hit for Kara Barnels.

Click!

Kara checked her pistol. A red light glimmered from the back of the firearm.

Magazine's empty. That asshole Wyatt! He took Ziven's bag with him! Ziven had extra clips for my gun – I'm sure of it!

She turned back to Brandy. By now, the blood had completely soaked her other hand as the translator tried desperately to stop the bleeding. Kara knew that if Brandy lost any more blood, she would, in a best case scenario, lose consciousness – worst case scenario, become a savory snack for the prowling carnivores.

"Okay, crawl through the grass here. Let's get away from the dinos. I'll patch you up!"

"What about Alex?" Brandy asked sluggishly, the loss of blood already affecting her ambition to escape.

"Alex can take care of himself! Now, move your ass if you want my help!"

They crawled into the grassy hedge wall, the sounds of the hungry herreras roiling behind them.

#

"*Damn!*" Alex cursed, trying to figure out how to use his sniper rifle for combat that required fending off close range attacks.

Four herreras lay dead around him, yet still behind the grass, he continued to hear their horrific breaths as the dinosaurs amended their strategy. To make matters worse, when Alex turned around, he realized that he was the only one left in the original perimeter – all except Ziven's mutilated corpse.

Where had they got to now?

Realizing that defending the area was no longer needed, he crouched down and executed an expert roll, away from the area where the grass stems had been bent from the battle. From behind his shield of plant life, he looked around, hoping to formulate a plan.

Looking for the other survivors seemed like a logical place to start. The only problem was that there were no screams, pulse weaponry fire or other noises to make that decision. Heading for the jungle was also ruled out. With so many herreras in the area, he doubted that he'd ever reach the tree line alive.

Ziven's bag, Alex thought. *He may have supplies we'll need!*

Alex glanced over to where his comrade had once been, only to notice that both Ziven and his gear were gone, stripped away somehow in the conflict. Straight ahead, two adult herreras entered the clearing, drawn in by the lack of noise and the smell of scorched flesh coming from their fallen counterparts. From behind the veil of grass, they failed to notice Alex watching, allowing him to crawl away further into the undergrowth, leaving the gruesome scene behind.

He moved slowly, as to not arouse the interests of the Herrerasaur pack that he was confident was still patrolling the dark savanna. Crawling in the direction of the jungle, as quietly as possible, he tried to piece together what happened that might lead him to the others.

He recalled Ziven being taken down, which essentially began the shootout. He recalled the boy, Nathan, identifying the carnivorous species as Herrerasaurus. Then he couldn't remember anything more, other than another argument prompted by Wyatt, shortly after the herreras pressed the attack.

Finally, ahead, he noticed something among the grass.

Movement. Non-dinosaur.

The glint of Federation armor accompanied by a white medical cross symbol confirmed it was Kara. She was with Brandy, who looked badly wounded from a nasty dinosaur bite to her arm.

"Thanks for leaving me in the dust," Alex said, announcing his presence as he crawled up to them.

"Shit, Alex!" Kara yelped as she turned toward him. "I almost punched you in the face! Do you have any pistol clips? I'm out."

"Yeah, here. I have two spares."

"Thanks."

She ejected her magazine, inserted the next clip and put the spare in her pocket.

"Where did everyone go?"

"Wyatt kidnapped Nathan and took off toward the trees. Adam followed. I had to get Brandy out of sight before the herreras returned. One caught her on the arm pretty badly. I didn't have any ammunition left to fend them off any longer."

"That asshole's gonna get what's coming to him," Brandy remarked as Kara finished bandaging her up. "We need to go after him!"

"It'll be difficult with the carnivores still in the vicinity," Alex stated. "But we don't have a choice – we can't stay here. Let's start crawling toward the trees. If we move slow and don't make a lot of noise, we should put enough distance between us and the dinosaurs. Then we can run when we get to the jungle."

#

Adam bolted through the moonlit prairie, keeping his head low, trying to decipher which way his enemy went. Wyatt had been shrewd in his escape – zigzagging through the grass. Adam's tracking skills were put to the test once again, only now it was a time sensitive situation.

Would Wyatt kill Nathan? Adam debated, trying to keep his mind occupied from the crunching of Herrerasaur footsteps he heard not far away.

Of course he'd kill Nathan. The past few hours have proven that Wyatt is a murderous opportunist who will stop at nothing to get home! And he's a coward, abandoning the mission for safety back at Solis.

RUHUHUKUKUH! RUHUHUKUKUH!

The herreras called out to one another in the field behind him, their vocalized rants sending signals to one another.

Just stay off me long enough so I can save my nephew. After that, you prehistoric shits can feed on Wyatt's corpse. Where are you, Wyatt? Where are you?

Nathan's delicate voice broke his concentration.

"Uncle Adam! *Hel –*"

The boy's voice was cut off abruptly. Adam stopped running, pausing to gauge where the shriek had originated. It sounded close, probably thirty yards or so. Wyatt's trail had begun to dissipate in the darkness, and Adam found it more likely he'd have to locate his enemy through his natural hunter instincts.

Hang on, Nathan. I'm coming! Thank God that Andrew isn't here right now...

He turned to his left, gambling on the direction that Wyatt had taken. Behind him, he could hear the herreras gaining ground, sniffing through the vegetation for his scent.

Come on, Wyatt. Where did you –

BRRR!

The distinctive whine of an ECP-30 blaster bolt whizzed past his head. Adam hit the dirt, face planting in the moistened grass bed as an orange rectangular bolt sailed over his head, striking a tree near the oncoming jungle.

To his rear, he could hear the herreras adjusting their course, moving now to intercept Wyatt instead of Adam.

Just wait till I save my nephew. Then you wretched bastards can take him down!

"I told you to leave me alone, Adam," Wyatt ranted, appearing in the weeds twenty steps straight ahead. Nathan was still alive, kicking and contorting frantically beneath his captor's arms.

"I told you I'd kill him if you came after me," he continued, his words cold and sarcastic. "Trust me that I'll be true to my word, only I'll kill you first and leave you for the dinosaurs. Oh, I found a little gift in Ziven's backpack."

Adam rolled to the side as another blast from the pulse pistol flew at him, sparking into the earth where he had landed and kicking up fizzling water droplets in its wake. Wyatt cackled happily at the thought of making Adam dance around the blasts before he took more careful aim, prolonging Adam's death in favor of twisted entertainment.

RUHUHUKUKUH!

A herrera rushed at Wyatt from the side, forcing him to pivot sharply and fire at the dinosaur. In the process, his arm opened and he dropped Nathan into the earth. Two more herreras closed in from his other side, causing him to neglect his hostage in exchange for fending off the relentless assault from the carnivores.

Adam motioned for Nathan to crawl toward him as he once again checked his pulse rifle.

Jammed! Dammit, not again!

He fiddled with the gun as Nathan arrived by his side, only this time, the indicator light remained red. He clicked the trigger, aiming it at the distracted Wyatt, only the trigger refused to budge.

Shit! Perfect timing. I'll have to take him one on one...

BRR! BRR!

Wyatt successfully brought down the remaining two dinosaurs before they could reach him – just in time to see Adam Ross running at him full speed from his grassy hiding place. That wicked smile cracked across the sergeant's face as he raised his pistol for the final blow.

Click...

Wyatt's smile transitioned into a frown as he realized his ECP-30 was officially spent of ammunition. Before he could reach into Ziven's blood-soaked backpack and retrieve another clip, Adam crashed into his front, this time with the advantage of battling Wyatt on level ground.

"You wanted to come back for more," Wyatt said, pushing Adam off and rising to his feet. "You got it!"

The sergeant's attack came at Adam full force – a mixture of jabs and low blow punches, which kept Adam moving backwards to keep out of his opponent's striking distance. Five feet away in the weeds, he saw Nathan watching him, eager to help but unsure of how.

Just stay there, kid! I won't lose this time. Now that I know how this asshole fights.

Finally, Wyatt went for a neck chop – a move Adam had been anticipating. Blocking with his forearm, Adam executed a fast uppercut. Wyatt's eyes widened as he dropped backwards, bewildered that Adam landed the first successful hit. He landed roughly on his back, a trickle of blood spurting from his nose.

"Oh, you – you've done it now!" Wyatt laughed, stuttering as he rose back up for round two. "I'll kill you and your nephew."

Damn you, Wyatt!

Adam realized to his horror the sergeant had outwitted him again. Wyatt landed right near Ziven's backpack, retrieving another full pulse crystal clip while ejecting the old one. Before Adam could engage him again, Wyatt had his weapon ready to fire from a safe distance, leaving Adam exposed, beaten again.

RUHUHUKUKUH!

Another herrera, previously unseen during the night ambush, surged out of the grass behind Wyatt, leaping high above on top of his head, forcing the sergeant to the ground.

"*Augghhh!* What the *fu* –"

Adam realized his chance for escape had come, brought on by Wyatt's demise. He grabbed his traumatized nephew by the wrist and pulled him swiftly through the grass, leaving his malfunctioned rifle behind.

"Where are we going?" Nathan asked as they fled.

"We're getting the hell out of here," Adam answered as they reached the first row of trees, leaving the savanna behind and entering the dark forest.

"What about the others? Alex? Kara?"

"I'm not sure," Adam admitted, already growing agitated from the boy's questions. "I've had a long rough night full of running and near-death experiences, Nathan. I can't afford to think about the others right now! My main objective at this point is getting you to a safe —"

The ground dropped away beneath their feet, and the jungle dipped down into a massive unseen cliff face. Adam felt his knees give out as the gravity shifted, pulling both Nathan and himself into the darkness of the shadowed ravine.

IX

Water...The rush of water...

That's what Adam Ross felt tickling his face, cascading onto his chin before splashing back downward. It was the cool sensation that woke him, yet he didn't want to move. The water temperature was soothing to his facial wounds sustained from the night's traumatic events.

He opened his eyes to see a school of primitive looking fish swimming just under his nose. No larger than two inches in length, the aquatic wildlife swam away as Adam moved his head, surveying the swirling underwater world in front of his face.

A tilt of his head revealed that he had been swept far downstream. The ravine that he and Nathan had slipped down was nowhere to be seen, instead replaced by a thunderous river that raged around him, surrounded on both sides by dense pine trees that formed yet another Triassic jungle.

His palms ached as he gripped the rocky basin on the beach. The disturbing events of the night before replayed themselves in his mind.

Herreras...Wyatt's demise... Nathan! Where is he? Oh no, did I lose him again?

Adam's aches returned to him as he realized he was still chaperoning his brother's child when, suddenly, he felt his nephew reach around and grab his arm, helping Adam to his feet. Adam turned and hugged him, smiling when he felt his nephew return the favor. He checked over the boy's face and shoulders for bruising. Miraculously, there was hardly a scratch on the child.

"*Jeez*, kid. Thank God I found you! I thought for sure we were goners after that cliff dive. How the hell did we survive that anyway? Why aren't you talking?"

"*Uh*, we have company," Nathan replied, gesturing behind Adam.

"*What?*" Adam replied, turning. "Who is it?"

There, sitting on a piece of driftwood lodged on the side of the river, was a woman, clad in a crude rain slicker, facing away from them. Over her head she adorned the shroud of a dark cloak, behind which flowed long reddish-brown hair, knotted in some areas but otherwise straight. A longbow was slung over her shoulder, which Adam assumed she stole from one of the other natives. The heavily dented and scratched chrome boots she wore told Adam she was a survivor from the *Supernova*, wearing footwear that had long since been deemed archaic.

"*Uh,* hello there?" Adam started, keeping Nathan guarded behind him.

What have we here? he thought, wondering who their savior was behind her cowled, intimidating appearance.

The woman stood almost nearly as tall as Adam. With a turn, she removed her hood, revealing a surprisingly pleasant, yet timid face. With her trim face and shapely features, she reminded him of Jade. This woman was a true survivalist of the Triassic. A weapon gleamed from her utility belt, one that Adam wasn't familiar with. He chose to ask her about it, hoping to begin a dialogue with the warrior.

"Nice piece," he started, pointing toward the firearm. "Never quite seen anything like it before. What type is it?"

She smirked, looking down at the pistol which lay writhed in mud, tucked partially behind her tattered cloak.

"It's an X2-20 pulse pistol," she answered, eyeing him over, checking him for irregularities and unseen weapons. "Don't tell me three hundred years on this planet was enough for the Federation to make the X-series weaponry obsolete."

"It's nice," Adam replied. "I've never seen a sidearm like that. Not in all my years in the Federation Watch Force. I take it that you saved us from the rapids?"

The mysterious woman hid her weapon entirely behind her garbs. Adam thought for a second he also saw a pair of long machetes tucked under her cloak, but he wasn't sure.

"I was hunting near the ravine when you broke through the upper cliff face. You and your son plunged over the edge. The current pushed you downstream but kept you both afloat face up, so thankfully, you didn't drown. I pulled you out probably two miles from where you plunged in. Now, explain yourselves or I'll leave you behind."

Leave us behind? We're your freakin' rescue party!

"Well, first, this isn't my son. This is my nephew, Nathan. He's quite a dinosaur admirer, as I've found out today. I'm Adam Ross, an emissary from Solis – a world you probably know nothing about. Three years ago, I received a distress call from a passenger named Brett Ambrose from the *Supernova* ship, long thought to be destroyed. It took the following years to get the political support to investigate the signal and put a crew together, thanks to Solis politicians and gridlock from Central Command. We're here to get you and any other sane *Supernova* survivors out of here."

The huntress looked him over suspiciously.

"How do you intend to do that?" she replied, eyeing him again for concealed weapons.

"A portal oscillator device. It's in our ship, *Harvester One*, which crashed here maybe a few days ago. We've developed the device as a means of teleportation. It's sort of finicky, but I've seen it work at least once. It will take us instantly back to Solis, but it only has a few functions remaining, probably only two. Do you know of any other survivors – ones that haven't become headhunters? Do you know of Brett Ambrose? Can you take me to him?"

"Brett Ambrose is dead," she winced. "He died years ago in an explosion – a direct result of a conflict that ended in the transmission of the signal that you acquired. As far as sane *Supernova* survivors, you're looking at her. Well, there is one more. You'll meet him soon enough."

"He's *dead*? You're the last survivor? Who are those hunters that my team ran into in the woods?"

"Descendants of another clan of *Supernova* survivors," the female warrior told him. "Shortly after the crash, they resorted to lunacy and soon had become something else entirely, becoming shameless killers who've forgotten how to speak our language. You're lucky you made it out alive. How many of your team are left?"

"Just myself and Nathan, as far as I know," Adam admitted. "With any luck, there may be three or four others, but that's it."

"Will they come looking for you?" the woman asked.

"Doubtful," Adam answered. "After the ordeal we went through last night, with the orange and brown dinosaurs, I'd be surprised if they made it out alive."

"*Herrerasaurus*," Nathan enunciated. "That's what they're called, I think."

"Herreras are one of the deadlier hunters in this region," the woman said, confirming the species. "I've had a few run ins with them myself over the years that I've spent waiting for you people to show up. I think I'd rather have run into the Neolithic hunters than run into a herrera. If your friends ran into a pack of herreras, it's unlikely that they're still alive."

"Did you see where our ship crashed?" Adam asked, trying to brush off the idea of his team's alleged demise.

"No," she replied. "A few nights back there was a tremendous earthquake. I was asleep when I felt it – the quake knocked over several items in my shelter. I didn't think much of it then, because quakes happen here all the time. I'm assuming now that it was probably your ship going down. When I awoke, I saw no such trace of any ship wreck. No flames or smoke. Do you have any bots with you that can help you identify the region where it might have landed?"

"We did have one bot," Adam said. "He passed away yesterday during the Neolithic attack, as you refer to them. But our main coordinates on our ship came from our communication specialist, Sana. She too passed, but before she did, she gave us a rough reading of where the ship had landed, roughly fifteen miles southeast of our position. She said something about the ship being between two valleys."

"Two valleys?" the woman asked, thinking. "I know where you're talking about. Several miles eastbound from here. It's a partially aquatic region, prone to marsh flooding. The area empties to a small sea to the south. If you think you've seen some mean dinosaurs up here, just wait till you get into marsh country. They're twice the size of the herreras. If that's where your oscillator is, we're in for a real treat."

"Can you take us there?" Adam begged.

"Yes, but first, let's head back to my shelter. The journey to the area which your comm specialist described is only a few miles from my camp, but it won't be an easy one. We'll have to deal with the dinosaur threats, plus whatever else may be lurking in the marshes."

"There's more to worry about than the dinosaurs and the hunters?" Nathan shivered.

The woman turned away, gathering her supply pack that lay slumped nearby, and a quiver full of self-constructed arrows.

"Oh yes," she muttered. "There's lots more to fear than the dinosaurs – let's pray we don't meet them."

Them? Adam thought.

The woman began to follow the river downstream, when Adam shouted out to her.

"Wait! We don't even know your name?"

She paused, turned around for dramatic effect, locking her alluring but deadly eyes with his. "Corporal Severine Solens, soldier of the Federation and the last human survivor of the original *Supernova* crew. Now pick up the pace and let's get moving. Those herreras get thirsty and this is their primary water source for miles."

#

Kara's eyes cracked open. The calamity and violence of the prior night had faded away, replaced with the tranquility of a beautiful, golden morning. The distant calls of birds – if they were birds – rippled over the grassland and surrounding countryside. Through her small shelter in the jungle, she could see a flock of them a mile or so away, soaring over the savanna in search for breakfast.

Sometime during the night, the herreras had departed from the area. She was unsure if they managed to kill most of them or, like the Coelophysis, if the pack was only the tip of the iceberg. It took a long, arduous half-hour of crawling and sneaking around for Alex Meras to lead her and Brandy to the tree line, where he quickly erected a small shelter of bramble for them to sleep on at the summit of the ravine.

She looked around, checked to confirm that she had her medical pack as well as her operational ECP-30 with two clips. Not far away, Alex was already awake, watching the sun rise through the canopy as it flooded the woodland trails with golden light. Brandy was awake too, checking over her gauze bandaging on her arm that Kara repaired only a few hours earlier.

"Oh good, you're awake," Alex smiled. "Hungry?"

"Not particularly," she admitted, stretching and rising to her feet. "I'd rather put as much distance between this area and myself as possible, knowing what dinosaurs hunt in this territory."

"Good. Let's scout through these trees and see what we find. After the skirmish near the grassy hill last night, I thought I heard a few pulse blasts around here. It's likely that Adam or Wyatt might have been responsible. Maybe we can find them."

"Adam, yes," Brandy began. "Wyatt – leave that prick where we find him."

She grumbled, expressing her disdain for the traitorous sergeant.

"I know he's a scumbag, but if everything that happened is true, he'll likely be required to go to trial on Solis, which I know will make Adam happy, seeing his rival at a court-marshal."

"What if we don't find anything?" Brandy asked. "What if Adam and Nathan are dead?"

"If we can confirm they're dead, then the only logical thing to do would be to head for the portal oscillator, retrieve it, patrol the immediate area around the crash for any logical thinking survivors from *Supernova*, and head back to Solis. At this point, with only three of us left, and only two of us armed, we won't last very long out here."

They nodded in agreement.

"Where did you hear those pulse rounds?" Kara asked.

"This way," Alex smiled, gesturing with his rifle barrel.

The sniper led them a short distance out of the jungle into the prairie. After a short walk, they pinpointed the marred scene of the attack. Alex bent down to examine the scorched ground.

Several pulse blasts had burned the grass blades. A few dead herreras were found in the grass nearby, followed by an area where the weeds had been flattened, indicating a scuffle had broken out. To the right was a large pool of blood, splattered over a large section of grass, but no victim was found. Lastly, Alex located a discarded ECR-130, lying neglected in the shrubs.

"Does it work?" Kara asked.

Alex toyed with the weapon, before tossing it aside.

"It has a jamming round security flaw," he replied. "Eventually, it has the potential to explode on impact, potentially dangerous to the user if the chamber gets overheated. I'd leave it."

"Look," Brandy pointed. "Footprints in the blood."

A trail of boot impressions saturated in red ran from the matted grassy section back to the tree line. The footprints led them back into the jungle to the foot of the ravine, a hundred yards from where they had camped out. There, at the base of the ravine, was an adult male covered in Federation armor, lying near the base of a river. From their vantage point high above, it was impossible to discern who the body was, but it was evident that he was the creator of the bloody trail.

After descending the cliff side, Alex arrived at the body, waiting for the women to catch up before he made the big reveal.

"Sorry, Brandy," Alex lamented, turning the adult male over with a nudge to the body's shoulder.

It was Wyatt Brolen, bloodied and wounded, but alive. Claw impressions from a herrera lacerated his neck and arms in several areas, but his armor suit protected the majority of his back and chest. He spat up red goop as he awakened, astonished to see the three *Burrower* survivors standing over him, scowls on their faces.

"Hey, you're all alive," Wyatt cheered, coming into consciousness.

"Save it, asshole," Brandy scolded, unhappy that the sergeant had survived the night.

"Where's Adam and Nathan?" Kara asked.

"Dead, evidently," Wyatt said.

"Did you kill them?"

"No. They fell down the cliff. I heard part of the ravine give out when they came out of the jungle. Their bodies are probably with Sana's, somewhere down the river."

Clink-clink...

Wyatt frowned as Alex Meras retrieved a pair of dazzling handcuffs from his backpack, dangling them in front of their new wearer.

"From now on, I'm in charge of this outfit," the sniper barked sternly. "Now put these on, and let's get a move on to that portal oscillator! I want to make it back alive with you by my side, so I can see you locked behind bars for the rest of your life!"

X

Adam was surprised at Severine's expertise and knowledge of the Triassic wilderness. It was evident that the *Supernova* survivor had mastered these lands, having hunted here for years and explored all of the nooks and crannies that the primitive jungle had to offer.

They lingered about ten paces behind her; the speed at which she walked outpaced them easily, making it difficult for Adam to keep up with his nephew in tow.

She must be very eager to get out of here, Adam thought, stepping over a small watery inlet as she took them around a river bend.

"Where do you think she's taking us?" Nathan asked. "The *Supernova?*"

"The *Supernova* is unlivable," Severine replied, overhearing them. "Over the years, it's become a festering place for all things vile and murderous. The last time I was there was when the last of my team activated the solar signal emitter. And, I'll be honest, after three years, I was beginning to think that the signal had failed."

"If you didn't pull us out of the river when you did, it may have failed," Adam admitted, stepping around a large mossy log. "I can't thank you enough for saving our lives. When we get back to Solis, I'll see to it you're well taken care of. You have my word on that, Severine."

"Let's just wait until we get to this oscillator of yours," she called back over the thunderous current beside them. "That will be a test in itself, if I'm correct as to where your ship's located."

At another bend in the river, she turned and began to cross the stream. The river arced over a small ten-foot tall waterfall. At the apex, smooth rocks formed a natural land bridge that Severine used to cross with ease. Adam and Nathan followed skittishly, not wanting to take any more falls than they already had endured. Adam walked with one hand out for balance and the other grabbing his nephew's arm, ready to snag him back up if the boy lost his balance. He relaxed when they both safely crossed over to the other side.

A series of rigid hills that formed a natural barrier loomed ahead. Severine walked up to the base and pushed aside an entangled mess of vines and dried ferns, revealing a small cleft between the rocks. The secret narrow valley appeared large enough for humans to move through in a single file line.

"You're full of surprises, aren't you, Severine?" Adam smiled.

"You can never be too careful," the huntress answered vaguely, beginning the trek through the cavern.

The journey was a brief one. A minute later, they exited out the other side of the rocky corridor, arriving into a swath of fields encircled on all sides by natural land barriers. A few clusters of herbaceous dinosaurs and animals roamed the fields in several areas, which Severine identified as *Pisanosaurus* and *Exaeretodon*. Nathan confirmed these findings in his Triassic encyclopedia, awestruck by the animals' graceful movements.

Near the back of the beautiful countryside, farther to the south, rose a blackened spire that Adam knew had to have been a Federation vehicle at one point in time. The obelisk protruded up through the troposphere like a giant spear head, covered with moss and rust. Adam noticed the top bore what remained of a glass cockpit, and identified the ancient shrine as an old Federation E5 escape pod.

"Your shelter, I presume?" Adam asked, gesturing to the corroded object. "I'm impressed!"

"*Mudskipper* is the pod's name. Brett Ambrose was responsible for finding it. He lived here for many years before I found him. Come on, there's someone you need to meet."

#

"Wow, cool place!" Nathan said as Severine led them down the trench at the base of the pod and through the narrow opening into the inside.

Severine smiled at the boy's remark.

"Oh really? You like it, huh?" she smiled, setting her supplies and gear down as they entered the interior of *Mudskipper*. "If I had more ideal things to decorate with, I might be able to make it look more appealing, but I work with what I've got."

Interesting rescue party I've stumbled upon, Severine thought as she watched them take in the sights of the escape pod's deteriorating interior hull.

Over the past three years that she was marooned in the Triassic, Severine recalled returning to *Mudskipper* shortly after the solar signal emitter had been activated, using the escape pod as a new shelter to wait until help arrived. The region around the pod had ideal natural barriers that acted as defenses, as Brett Ambrose described to her when she found him there.

To pass the time waiting in isolation, she reorganized the place from the bachelor pad that Brett had   designed into what she thought was a very organized dwelling. For starters, she leveled out the floor to make walking around less awkward, erected a more proportional firepit near the center, and tried to clean up all the lose wires and circuitry that plagued the interior. In her boredom, she searched the ship for additional supplies and munitions, eventually finding a hidden compartment with an X2-20 pulse pistol. Now, three years after the weapon's discovery, she only had six rounds remaining.

She watched the boy sit down on a chair she had crafted from rock and wood around the base of the firepit.

"How have you survived this long against the Herrerasaurus and the Coelophysis?" he asked.

"You certainly know a lot about your dinosaurs," Severine observed.

"I have an animal encyclopedia with me," Nathan replied, tapping on his backpack.

Severine smiled.

"I used to have one of those myself actually. It belonged to one of my colleagues. Unfortunately when times got tough, I had to use the pages to keep a fire going. I still kick myself for that sometimes – the book would've come in handy in identifying some of the other dinosaurs I've come across. And as far as avoiding the carnivores, that's easy. I have help."

"Help?" Adam asked. "Like what?"

"See for yourself," Severine smiled, turning her head toward a darkened corner of the pod. "His lights are dimmed for the moment. He does that sometimes when he's nervous – he's got a hell of a personality programmed in him. Hey Jord, come out and greet our guests. Keep them busy while I pack some supplies we'll be needing. We're getting out of here today, pal!"

Severine watched the boy's face light up as Jordy lumbered from the shadowed nook, his chest utility lights sparking to life as he approached the firepit. Time hadn't been kind to the bot. Rust plagued his exterior parts and continued to accumulate over the years, spreading as far as his metallic eye sockets. One of his eyelids had a splotch of mold growing behind the glass that Severine couldn't seem to get rid of, because Jordy's eyes were factory sealed in a way that prohibited easy maintenance.

"*Ple-e-eased* to meet you all," the bot said, his digital voice glitching.

"Holy shit," Adam exclaimed, apologizing to his nephew after swearing. "Is this a Federation programmed logistics bot from Steven Perry's Starfleet? I've only seen these in Solis museums, although obviously, none of them work. It's remarkable to see one of these up close in person, even in his condition!"

"This is Jordy," Severine said, introducing the bot. "He's been with me now for two years. We were together early on when we crashed, but shortly after we awoke from hyper-sleep, Jordy was damaged in a water incident. A year after my isolation here, I found a manual inside an old desk about how to troubleshoot water problems in bots. The manual suggested that most likely the computer would be unable to be revived, but I'd figured there was no harm in trying. After I dragged him back here, I made some makeshift tools from the *Mudskipper* wreckage and cracked open his internal components, replacing them with other unused pieces that I salvaged from the pod. Sure enough, after a long reboot, I was able to resurrect him. His short-range radar capabilities, although damaged and sometimes faulty, are a big help!"

"What's up with the glitch?" Nathan asked.

"An unfortunate side effect from the water damage," Severine answered, "as well as a year of lying in the Triassic wilderness. His vocal processor has become slightly degraded."

"*Ye-e-eah*, thanks for that, Sev," Jordy prodded at her. "Leaving me up there *i-i-n* the jungle for months like some pile of junk."

"You'll never let me live that down, will you, Jord?" Severine laughed. "Like I've told you a thousand times, I thought you were a pile of scrap at that point. Julius even said that it was impossible to bring you back without the proper equipment. Hey, when I found the repair manual, I came right back, didn't I?"

"Because you *mi-s-s-sed* me?" Jordy joked.

"I did," Severine smiled, patting the rusted robotic intelligence on the head.

"So who are *the-e-ese* jokers?" Jordy asked, wobbling toward Adam and Nathan. "Don't tell me this is the rescue party I *sa-a-crificed* my life to make contact with."

He shot Severine a look as she avoided his eye contact.

"It is, isn't it?" Jordy asked. "One man and one kid. *Gre-e-eat*. Sounds like typical Federation logical thinking, as I remember it. They haven't improved much."

"I'm Adam Ross and this is my nephew, Nathan," Adam began. "Well, unfortunately we're all that's left of the original *Harvester One* rescue party. I'll be honest to say that I believe Nathan and I are the only survivors. We need to get to the portal oscillator and get you both out of here – fast."

"Portal *o-s-scillator*?" Jordy asked with a tilt of his rusty scalp.

"Yes. It's a device that's currently on board the bridge of our wrecked ship, just east of here. It acts as teleportation transmitter – when it works correctly – and should send us back to Solis. It operates through charge crystals, the same as pulse weapons do."

"Well, that's *a-a-a* neat trick," Jordy smirked. "Would've been nice to have one of those on board the *Supernova*, right, *S-e-ev-v*?"

"Tell me about it," Severine yelled, packing some supplies in the corner of the room.

"*So-o-o* I take it you don't have any female vocalized *bo-o-ots* with you?" Jordy asked Adam with a crooked wink.

"Sadly, no," Adam laughed. "We had one male marine bot with us earlier, but he died. Shame, we could've used his radar many times yesterday. But back on Solis, yes, there are plenty of feminine based bots that would love to hear about your adventures."

"Tell us about Solis," Severine said, stuffing more arrows into her quiver. "What's it like? I want to have some motivation for the walk ahead."

"*Uh*, well," Adam replied. "You've been gone a long time for starters. There's a lot that happened after Steven Perry's fleet was obliterated in space. His remaining starships eventually found a beautiful planet in their voyage, naming it *Solis*. The planet bore a striking similarity to Earth, before Earth became a hell-hole, or so I'm told. Anyways, in the following years, mining operations and colonization began, and soon the planet was a budding metropolis."

"The buildings are huge," Nathan interrupted. "They're probably even bigger than the mountains we've seen here. You'll love it!"

"It certainly sounds like everything we've hoped and prayed for, doesn't it, Jord?" Severine said.

"It *s-s-ure* does," Jordy replied. "I *could-d* get used to a world where I don't have to worry about getting eaten by *din-n-n-osaurs* everywhere I go. Or left to rot in the jungle by *some* people."

"You just won't let it go, will you?" Severine returned, tossing a small pebble at the bot which bounced harmlessly off the machine's head.

"*Tr-r-y* it again," Jordy turned, raising a comical, corroded fist.

"So there were other, how do I say this, *normal* survivors at one time?" Adam asked.

"You mean sane humans?" Severine asked. "Yeah, there were a handful of them. They all died shortly after we were released from our hyper-sleep pods. As far as the hunters are concerned, I thought I dealt with them years ago, during the activation of the solar signal emitter. My team killed many in the ship, which as it turns out they were using as their base. I saw or heard nothing from their tribe until about a year ago, when they had me cornered near the savanna where you found me. I barely made it out alive, diving into the river and letting it take me back downstream. That was the only other time I've encountered them. They know nothing of this place, thankfully."

"What happened to them?" Nathan asked. "What made them revert back to such a primitive way of life?"

"There's a long story," Severine said, sorting through some water canisters. "Jordy, I don't know if I ever fully told you that story either."

How do I even begin to explain the Davenport story? Severine thought.

"If it *happ-p-pened* after you left me to die, then *probabl-l-ly* not," the bot snickered.

"Yeah, yeah," Severine jabbed back. "Basically, shortly after *Supernova* crashed, from what I've surmised, there was a lot of unrest with the survivors. Eventually the conflicts were resolved when a singular sect seized control, inflicting harsh punishments on those who tried to learn our native language as well as use our weapons. In turn, the survivors reverted back to a more prehistoric approach to life, forgetting their origins altogether. Thankfully, that happened centuries before I awoke from hyper-sleep. I only knew what happened because of the aftermath. I'm not sure how many of them are left. From the sounds of it, your rescue team may have killed a few yourselves?"

"Between all of us," Adam replied, "we probably took down at least fifty of them in the jungle where we crashed, back to the north. But we barely made a dent in their numbers. I'd speculate there may still be a couple hundred out there. Are they after you?"

"I'd have to guess so," Severine replied. "I was the one who invaded their home, after all. But after we get the hell out of this forsaken world, we'll be leaving them behind for good, won't we, Jord?"

"*S-s-s-ounds* like it, Sev," the bot smiled.

"Well I'm all packed and ready for the final departure," Severine concluded, beaming in excitement as she slung her backpack and supplies over her shoulder. "Let's leave this miserable pod behind and get going. Jordy, don't you need to go pack a few items?"

"*Li-i-ike* what?"

"Oh I don't know, how about your rain-dome shield I made you? The last thing I want to do is be stuck up another tree with herreras hunting for me because your radar gave out due to a flash monsoon!"

"*Psshh*, you *on-nly* use me for my radar," the bot laughed, bumping into her playfully as he walked away to retrieve some items. "Give *me-e-e* a few minutes."

"I didn't know logistics bots were so sarcastic," Adam chuckled as he watched the machine lumber into a different compartment of the *Mudskipper*.

"Neither did I until I met him," Severine replied, checking the sturdiness of her longbow string. "He's grown to be quite the little comedian – and a smart ass. Now, while we're waiting for him to pack, Nathan, are you armed?"

"No, why?"

"If your uncle allows it, I suggest you carry something on you for defense, in case we run into trouble between here and your downed ship. I have a spare dagger if you want it. It should fit nicely in your hands."

Nathan turned to his uncle, sporting a look of impatience. Severine knew no matter what Adam said, the boy needed some form of personal protection.

"Yes, you can have it," Adam said finally after a dramatic pause.

"*Sweet!*" Nathan exclaimed.

Severine produced a rough looking dagger carved from stone and bone, held together with twine and dried organic residue. Nathan cradled the object in his hands, paying special attention to the sharpness of the blade.

"Thanks so much!" he said, hugging Severine.

"You're welcome," she smiled. "I think it's better if you at least have one form of protection. The Triassic wilderness is very unforgiving toward the defenseless."

"From what we've run into so far, I think it's an excellent idea," Adam added. "Now I don't want you playing around with that thing. It's not a toy – it's a tool, a tool used for very –"

"Yeah I know, Uncle Adam," Nathan waved him off. "Not a toy, yeah yeah, got it!"

Must be at that temperamental age, Severine thought.

"The best case scenario is that you'll never have to use it," she went on. "Adam, do you have a weapon?"

"I had a pretty handy pulse rifle, one that you might have admired. During one of the many scuffles, I left it back in the grassland."

"Here," Severine said. "Take this."

She handed him one of her machetes, which he gladly accepted, tucking the weapon into his utility belt.

"Thanks, I'm sure I'll –"

WHRRR! WHRRR WHR–

A loud whine pierced the *Mudskipper* interior, amplified by the tight acoustics of the escape pod, generating a tumultuous echo. Severine covered her ears, dropping to her knees in agony. She saw her visitors do the same, confused and alarmed.

Damn, Jordy! What now?

The bot came running back out to them, his metallic ancient legs creaking from the swift movements. A chaotic light show beckoned from his chest, a clear sign that something significant was happening with his radar software scan.

"Don't tell me it's another faulty scan?" Severine asked, slightly annoyed.

"Afraid not, Sev," Jordy answered, running an interior computer systems check. "I *know-w-w* sometimes the signals come in and out when they *feel-l-l* like it. My parts aren't what they used to be, but this time the *signals-s* seem fairly precise. My *c-c-c-calculations* indicate several hot spots converging on our location."

"The pisanosaur herds again? They do that from time to time, remember? It's probably them."

"Nope, I don't think it's dinosaur or *animal-l-l* related. The traces seem to be strategically placed, with a large contingent of them already encircling our position. It seems the *bulk-k-k* of the *ss-ignals* came from the gap in the hills, down near the sauro marshes."

Severine felt her mouth drop open, her bottom lip quivering with fright and anxiety.

No! It can't be! I killed him! He's dead... He has to be dead!

Even as she contemplated the meaning of Jordy's signal, she could hear the sand above the *Mudskipper* begin to shift as the unseen army moved in, converging on the obelisk in the center. As if auto programmed deep within her, she drew her X2-20, anticipating one of the attackers to appear in the entrance at any moment.

"Jordy, do you have all your shit packed?"

"Yeah, Sev. Don't tell *me-e-e* it's –"

"You bet your sweet ass it is! Who else can it be? Adam, Nathan, pick up your shit! We're going to have to bolt in a hurry."

"Who is it?" Adam asked. "The natives?"

"Much worse," she answered. "These guys make the natives look like infants. I'll explain everything later, when we're far away from this asshole. We'll have to give these shitheads the slip."

"How are we going to do that if they already have us surrounded?" Nathan asked, gripping his dagger tightly with trembling hands.

"Don't worry, I have a backup plan in case of this event. Now just –"

An automatic loudspeaker blared from outside the *Mudskipper* hull, causing Severine to stop and listen. Her eyes opened wide when she confirmed the gruff voice on the other end was in fact the voice of the man whom she thought was dead.

No!

"Hey, Severine! Long time no see. As you may have guessed, I brought some friends with me."

XI

The haunting voice of the ghost Severine thought that she dispatched long ago had returned to torment her. Her instincts told her that her enemy had her trapped for a reason, keeping her encircled from all sides but refusing to enter the *Mudskipper*, possibly fearing a firefight.

"Who the hell is this?" Adam asked, guarding his nephew.

"Be quiet," Severine cut him off with an impatient hand wave. "They may not know that we're here yet! Jordy, deactivate all your computer components that emit noises and lights. The radar too, now that we know what we're dealing with."

"*Go-o-od* idea," the bot whispered, manipulating his exterior switches with his rickety hands.

How did he survive? How did he find us? How many are out there?

She crouched low to the ground, traveling around the perimeter of the *Mudskipper* interior, where various metal gashes formed narrow window slits that faced in all directions. A swift look behind her revealed that Adam and Nathan were following her every move. The boy looked terrified, holding the dagger in a death grip.

"Don't worry," Severine whispered. "I've planned for an event like this."

"Oh really?" Adam critiqued. "How so? Severine, they have us *completely* surrounded! What's the plan? Fight them down here until they finally break in and gun us down?"

"No, they're too smart for that. Most likely, they'll try to smoke us out."

"*What!*"

"Just hang on, *dammit!* We'll be safe in a moment. I just want to know how many Exiles we're up against."

"*Exiles?*"

"Yes. Now hush!"

The devilish voice resumed somewhere outside.

"Come now, Severine. Don't be shy. We can do this the easy way or the hard way. Your choice. Either way, you and your friends will be dead soon. That's a clever passage you have leading past the northern barrier. The cavern. I'm impressed. If my scouts hadn't spotted it, this entire valley would've gone unnoticed."

Finally, on the side nearest the southern border, she saw him.

Delios Deckard – leader of the Exiles.

I should've made sure you were dead...

The Exile tyrant was standing between a pair of his armed thugs. One of which she knew was named Tanner. Delios Deckard was masked in the attire that she last saw him wearing – a garbed dark cloak blanketing ancient Federation male armor that mirrored her own. His trademark weapon, a battle worn XR-90, was strapped over his back. Where his right hand had been, courtesy of his last encounter with Severine, was a crudely made sword, crafted from shrapnel. Behind his middle length hair, Severine could see that his face was still scarred from where her nails dug into his skin, leaving a lasting impression of their mutual disdain.

"*Wow!*" Adam gasped. "And I thought that you and the natives were the only humans here!"

"Yes, this would be the third group," Severine said, fitting an arrow onto her drawstring. "Jordy, do you think I can range him from here?"

"I wouldn't try, Sev," Jordy whispered. "If you miss, it might *p-p-p-provoke* his army. Or worse, if you hit him, it *m-m-ight* provoke them *f-f-further-r-r*. We're *o-o-outnumbered* and outgunned."

"So, you want to drag this out? Okay. Fine, I can wait a few more minutes for my revenge. Doesn't matter to me – I'll get what I desire one way or the other. How about a few questions to pass the time?"

Through her narrow window, she could see the warlord snickering with several of his armed thugs. She could see other warriors too, patrolling the perimeter of the *Mudskipper*, presumably cutting off all the assumed escape routes.

"The others you brought back with you. My sources say it was a man and a boy. Who are they? They were in Federation uniforms were they not? That means they can't be from the Neolithic tribe. Either they've awakened from Supernova pods – unlikely, seeing as how by now most of the pods would have failed and the occupants suffocated from within, or they're survivors from another unknown ship. Any thoughts you'd like to share?"

Severine observed the goons staring down at her shelter, waiting for an answer that she refused to give.

"Are they from the sky, sent to finally rescue all of us who were trapped here so long ago? Or, perhaps, are they from another Federation ship that crashed here and are just now entering this prehistoric arena?"

"Severine, I think they're trying to send people down," Adam whispered, tapping her on the shoulder.

"*Huh?*"

"Look – to your left!"

Peering through the narrow crevice, Severine saw one of Deckard's henchmen, a man in his mid-twenties, sliding down the *Mudskipper* trench and preparing to breach the main opening. At the top of the trench, three more vigilant warriors waited, carrying spears and self-made shrapnel swords. They had pulse weapons with them as well, but kept them strapped over their backs, choosing to save the ammunition for a more appropriate situation.

A grave mistake, Severine thought.

Adam and Nathan took a step back as she carefully loaded an arrow onto her longbow string, pressing the tip of the arrow toward the nearly invisible window gash through which they were watching. In front of her, the intruder slowly came into view, keeping his sword in front of him as a precaution.

No matter. This will just take a second...

PHHHHHR!

The arrow sailed out from the slit in the wall, lodging itself fiercely into the young man's exposed neck. A volcano of blood erupted out from his throat as the mercenary attempted to plead for help to his trio of reinforcements. After failing to quell the blood, he died seconds later, leaving his conspirators falling back from the entrance above the defensive trench, unsure of where the arrow was launched from.

"Still playing hard to get I see," Deckard went on sarcastically. *"I just couldn't resist sending in someone to toy with you."*

"This guy is sick!" Adam whispered, scanning the *Mudskipper* frantically for an exit.

"He's the devil," Severine acknowledged. "Needless to say, I'd recommend not bringing him back to Solis with you."

"We're in agreement there," Nathan added.

"So, since you insist on playing these games, let's make this interesting. This command is addressed to the adult male you brought back with you. I don't know who you are or where you're from, but I have a proposition for you. Kill Severine or bring her outside to me, and I'll let you live. And your son. You have my word on that – no harm will come to either of you if you help me with just this one favor. That's not such a bad deal, is it?"

It was then that Severine felt her skin turn cold. Instantly, she regretted giving her new friends a pair of knives. She turned to them, relieved when Adam dismissed the option.

"You have nothing to worry about," he assured her. "I came here to rescue you, not kill you. This madman will have to come in here and kill us himself – so clearly, if you can't tell, I'd really like to get out of here."

"It's almost time – I promise," Severine said in a calm voice. "Soon he'll smoke us out. The scouts are just to keep me guessing."

Deckard's devious proposal continued on the outside.

"I'm sure you are curious about me, who I am, and why I have unfinished business with Severine. If you bring her out here to me or kill her first, I'll offer you a spot in the Exiles. You know what that means out here? It means safety, security. Not just for you, but for your son as well.

This is a very unforgiving world we've found ourselves in. There's safety in numbers! You understand that? Right?"

"Here comes another one," Adam said, pointing to the right. Severine scooted over to him quietly. Sure enough, another assassin – this time a female – had slid down into the *Mudskipper* impact trench, moving slowly up to the entrance.

"Thanks," Sev whispered. "I'll handle it. Jordy, start removing the debris on top of the left wing. It's high time we start moving our asses out of here. This isn't fun anymore."

"It wasn't fun to begin with," Adam remarked, keeping his eyes on the approaching assassin.

She snapped up another arrow with expert precision, slid it onto her bowstring, pulled back the shaft and sent another dart out through Adam's window with the same lethal result. The woman, caught completely off guard, clasped her throat in terror as she collapsed, her regretful last look of fear frozen on her face as she passed on.

"Hahaha! Very good, Severine. Very good. I see you've really adapted well to that Neolithic bow I chastised you about before. As I've said, those sticks and stones weapons are good. We use them too from time to time – but they're no match for Federation firepower!"

Oh, hell no!

"Jordy, how's it going with that debris?" Severine asked quickly, a trace of fear in her voice.

"Slow," the bot admitted. "It *would-d-d* go a lot faster if I had some help. What's the *k-k-kid* doing? He could lend a hand."

"It's Nathan," the boy replied. "And what do you want me to do? Move some old deep freeze boxes? Why are we doing that?"

"You want to live, don't you?" Severine scolded him.

"Yeah, obviously."

"Then help Jordy move those crates!"

The boy grumbled and hurried over to the bot, unsure of why he was reorganizing items in the middle of a siege.

"And nothing says Federation firepower like a good old Federation detonator, does it, Severine. Well, by now I can safely assume that you and your cohorts have chosen not to come out, regardless of my kind offers to ease your suffering. Tanner, bring me the detonators, will you? And the fire bombs we made earlier this week. Bring those up here too, if you please."

Oh shit!

Severine jumped up from her position at the window and tore over to where Jordy and Nathan were removing a large stack of deep freeze boxes that she stored there in the event that her shelter was ever besieged. Today, she was glad that she did.

"What?" Adam demanded, confused about the madman's command.

"What's about to happen?"

"Are you deaf?" Severine replied, pointing to her ear. "They're about to firebomb the living shit out of us if we don't move! They have enough manpower to bomb every side of the pod. The explosions from the detonators will bring down the structure. We'll be crushed!"

"And what's your plan? Hide in a bunch of old Federation deep freeze cases? Those things might be good for fruit preservation, but hiding from a ship implosion? I'll take my chances out there with your friend, the neighborhood psychopath."

"Did it ever occur to you, Mr. Ross," Severine went on, "that I may have another way out of the escape pod?"

"*Huh?*"

With a final push, Severine and Jordy pushed off the last of the deep freeze crates. Wedged in the sand, sat a large square plate of metal. Adam recognized it as an old door to the fueling compartment.

"Your plan is to hide in the pod's fuel tank? Severine, I think you've been out here too long."

Severine opened the hatch, revealing a dark tunnel that dropped down five feet before turning sharply to the right, heading east from underneath the *Mudskipper*.

"Cool!" Nathan said, examining the dark hole. "A secret tunnel!"

"Dug out by my predecessor, Brett Ambrose, in all his boredom during his twenty year tenure here alone. I happened upon it by accident one day when I was snooping around the place."

"You're full of surprises, aren't you?" Adam asked, admiring the resilience of the warrior vixen.

VRRRR! BOOOOOOOOM!

The cockpit above them exploded, sending shards of glass dropping down into Severine's living quarters. Sparking explosions above near the driving controls ensued, destroying all the hard work put forth by Brett Ambrose to keep the *Mudskipper* partially operational.

Detonators!

"Okay, no more time to dick around here," Severine urged. "Nathan, you first! Then Jordy. Then you, Adam. I'll bring up the rear."

"Where does this lead out?" Adam asked. "When was the last time you were down there? With all the commotion up here, there could be a cave-in. We could be in even more of a world of shit down there than we are up here!"

"Would you care to take that chance?" she asked, raising a challenging eyebrow.

Adam couldn't help but smile, even amid the uncertain gloom that clouded around them. He was impressed by her spunky attitude, and, for a moment, unaware of their present danger.

"Absolutely not," he smirked. "Nathan, you heard the woman! Get down that shaft! Our escape time table just increased exponentially. We're going to the oscillator now!"

Severine let a laugh slip.

"That's what I thought."

#

Staring at a bunch of rusty brown spring coils that comprised Jordy's metallic ass wasn't what Adam Ross pictured himself doing during the course of the day. But if it meant getting away from the mercenaries up on the surface, he would gladly accept it as the situation.

"Jordy, turn more of your lights back on," Severine ordered. "Might help us see a little better down here, don't you think?"

"*Oo-o-ops*, I forgot. Good thinking!"

The bot's shoulder plates and knee-pads exploded with brightness, casting white and golden light throughout the tunnel, discoloring slightly due to the dust. The lights revealed the tunnel was surprisingly spacious, traveling in a straight line and reinforced with metal girders salvaged from the *Mudskipper* to support the walls.

Brmmmm. Brrmm! Krshhh...

The muffled sounds of the *Mudskipper* siege raged on somewhere above them. Wisps of dirt brought on from the vibrations above trickled down like sand from the tunnel's roof. Adam guessed that most likely, had they stayed, they would be dead by now.

"Keep throwing! Don't stop until – krsshhh... All broken up, Tanner, check the – krshhh...Burn in hell, Severine! Burn in hell!"

Deckard's voice continued to shout above them, barking orders to his grunts. Gradually, the farther they crawled, the sounds began to die down. Adam knew they had put a considerable amount of space between their position and the war above.

"This Brett Ambrose fellow had time to dig all this?" Nathan asked from the front.

"Apparently," Severine replied. "Who knows. He may have run into an old animal burrow and just continued with it. Keep moving. The end shouldn't be far now!"

"Throw more up to the cockpit – krsshhh... That's it, bring it... - krshhh. Ah, watch it burn!"

"I should've stuck him with an arrow before we dropped down here," Severine lamented.

"They would've dragged us *o-o-out* and clubbed us alive," Jordy corrected her. "You know how the Exiles play – brutal. We did the right *th-th-thing*. Only now, I have no *i-i-dea* where we're going to live!"

"Solis," Adam said with a hopeful tone. "Soon as we're out, were making for the *Harvester One* wreck and activating the oscillator."

"So you don't intend to save Deckard and his *b-b-band* of ruffians with your *p-p-portal* device?" Jordy laughed ahead of him.

"As far as I'm concerned, although they might be from the Federation, there's no proof that they came from *Supernova*. My mission was to rescue survivors of that ship. They might have had a chance, but that ended when they tried to kill us."

"They're not from *Supernova*, trust me," Severine replied behind him. "I don't know where they're from. They just showed up one night and never left. Their armor, although Federation, doesn't have the *Supernova* insignia. Besides, from the way they rule these parts, I don't think they'd want to go back anyway. I'd say you're making the right call."

"The decision was an easy one," Adam laughed nervously. "Those thugs have no place at Solis. Hopefully they don't know anything about *Harvester One* or the oscillator – I'd hate for them to make it back somehow."

Khrsss...booom....

By now, the sounds of the *Mudskipper* bombardment were virtually inaudible. Far away, a few more muffled detonator charges were heard, and the cacophony of destruction was silenced.

"Keep walking, *y-y-young* one," Jordy ordered, prodding Nathan.

"*Young one?*" Nathan turned. "Thanks for that."

"Certainly, my young *f-f-friend*," came the sarcastic, digital reply.

Adam couldn't help but chuckle at the exchange, pleased that someone was finally poking back at Nathan for all the smart-ass remarks the boy had uttered over the past few weeks.

"Hey, I think I see the end up ahead!" Nathan announced.

"Indeed," Jordy replied. "The *es-c-cape* hatch. We *ma-ma-de* it!"

Adam glanced around Jordy and Nathan, who waddled along a few paces ahead of him. As the tunnel began to narrow, a large rusted hatch remained ahead, blocking the rest of the tunnel. Nathan stopped at its base and tried to open it.

"This thing's gotta be a couple hundred years old. I have no idea how to open this!"

"Utility handle toward the top," Severine directed him. "Pull it out then to the left. Don't tell me I'm so behind the times that I'm the only one who knows how to open an E5 fuel tank latch?"

"Well technically speaking, you are over three hundred years older than us, thanks to the hyper-sleep artificial sleep," Adam pointed out with a smile.

"Didn't they teach you not to point out someone's age in the future," Severine arched her eyebrows. "Step aside, Junior. Let me crack that sucker open or we'll be here all day!"

#

Clicking another detonator in his hand, Delios Deckard chucked the chrome sphere high up into the afternoon sky of the Triassic, where the blue and white clouds began to coalesce with black – the smoke of the burning *Mudskipper* fuselage. The detonator landed perfectly on top of the cockpit, sticking to the remaining glass fragments and imploding the remainder of the roof, sending dark shrapnel raining down on the shrouded interior.

Around the perimeter of the ancient escape pod, he observed the other Exiles engaging in the slaughter, and it made him smile. Some chucked self-made firebombs that splashed over the dome and ignited on impact. Others threw detonators; a rarity in this time period due to limited Federation weaponry, but Deckard didn't care. Just as long as they took out his nemesis, they would be well spent.

Behind him came the crunch of heavy boots, followed by a familiar, stern voice.

Tanner, my loyal second-in-command.

"Sir, what would you like done with these two?" came the gruff voice.

Deckard turned, greeted by Tanner and two other Exiles. In the debris laden sand at their feet, lay the bodies of the two scouts that Severine brought down with her bow. Their faces had glazed over. Death had left its sting.

"They died valiantly," Deckard replied after studying the corpses. "Both followed orders and gave their life for the pursuit of our greatest foe. Have some of the newer recruits bury them down in the marshes. The soil should be easier to dig there. After we survey the wreckage and confirm that she's dead, I intend on vacating this area as soon as possible. The noise might draw up the sauros, and we wouldn't want that."

"Yes, sir," Tanner replied. "You heard the man. Take them and bury them in the marshes. Make sure to erect some form of grave-marker for identification. These two are heroes!"

"Yes, Mr. Tanner," one of the younger Exiles replied as they began to cart away the marred bodies.

"Ah, this has been a long time coming, hasn't it?" Deckard asked him as the *Mudskipper* burned in front of them like a massive funeral pyre.

"It has," Tanner replied. "We finally had her cornered. To think, she thought you were dead!"

Deckard laughed, patting his friend on the shoulder.

"Dead. Could've been. If she would have stuck around to make sure, she might've pulled it off. Her mistake – our victory!"

"Indeed."

The two of them watched in bliss as another round of firebombs and detonators struck the fiery obelisk, now completely ablaze like a massive torch. The small ghastly cemetery down in the trench had been completely scorched, and the entrance inside revealed only the movement of internal residual fires.

"Here she goes!" one of the female Exiles yelled, followed by a swelling cheer of happiness from the surrounding ranks.

With a final metallic screech, the escape pod imploded, collapsing from within and kicking up windy flames that made some of his soldiers jump back in surprise. With the last steel girder to collapse, not even his trio of facial scars could stop Deckard's smile.

At last, revenge!

XII

Delios Deckard watched as twenty of his warriors pillaged the *Mudskipper* rubble. Two hours had passed since the siege. The fires had been extinguished by a flash rainstorm. After an hour of pulling apart the blackened shelter that had once been Severine's domicile, Deckard was beginning to get annoyed with the crew's evident lack of progress.

She should've been found by now! They all should've been found by now...

"Anything yet?" Deckard asked impatiently, pacing back and forth twenty yards above the steaming scrapyard.

"Nothing yet, sir," one of the mercenaries known as Arlo answered, flipping over another shed of debris. "Just a bunch of rusty flakes and old Federation storage bins. Junk mostly."

"Well open the damn bins!" the warlord berated him. "They could've stowed away somewhere!"

"Yes, sir!" the warrior replied, doubling his efforts.

How have they not been found yet? It's impossible! We had them completely surrounded! If they snuck out, someone would've seen them, wouldn't they? This makes no sense!

He glared down at the salvage operation, watching as his soldiers picked apart the Federation storage boxes and lugged them up to the base of the trench where he could observe the results. One by one, the boxes were opened, revealing only ancient water canisters and expired moldy food jars.

Impossible!

In his anger, he turned and spotted a few younger soldiers standing off and leering at the workers below. They would serve as a perfect target for the rage welling inside him.

"*You three!* Get down in that pit and help our team pull apart that scrap! Don't let me catch you standing around again! The sooner we find their bodies, the sooner we can get out of here! I want sentries posted down by the southern hill gap to guard the burial of our fallen comrades. Keep an eye out for sauros!"

"Yes, sir!" came a few replies as various warriors veered off to fulfill Deckard's newest tasks, in fear of a painful retribution if they chose to dissent.

They must be down there in that rubble somewhere!

He stared down hypnotically at his soldiers' progress, expecting any minute one of the debris pieces to be flipped over, revealing several charred corpses.

Nothing! How can this happen? How has she outwitted me?

"Maybe she was never there to begin with," came an agitating female voice behind him.

It was his third-in-command after Tanner. Her name was Arien. She was a tall, alluring brunette with the same murderous lust for payback. If it wasn't for her constant second-guessing of his strategies and tactics, he might have promoted her to be his second. In the last few weeks, she had grated on him all too often – a persistent problem that would have to be dealt with sooner or later.

"What are you talking about?" Deckard turned, immediately furious with his subordinate. "How do you explain the arrows? We lost two loyal soldiers to that bow! There had to be a shooter in that wreckage."

Arien shrugged arrogantly, throwing up her hands that were wound in tight fingerless gloves. Deckard hated when she did that.

"Severine is a smart enemy. Maybe she rigged the place with traps for all we know. We never actually heard her in there. She never responded to any of your threats. I don't think you'll find her in that rubble."

"Arien, we saw her come up from the river through the cavern. If she isn't in that debris, then where the hell did she go?"

"Maybe she gave us the slip somewhere near the river cavern? Can your sources confirm that they actually saw Severine Solens by the river?"

Second guessing me again, I see. Oh, how I'd love to feed you to the sauros, Arien. Soon, my dear. Very soon...

"*You!*" Deckard pointed behind her to a young male Exile. "Get over here!"

"*Sir?*" the young man said, baffled as to why he was about to be chastised.

"What's your name?"

"Mendez, sir."

"Mendez, you saw Severine Solens enter the cavern just north of here, did you not?"

"Yes, sir. It was exactly as I said. She and her two friends crossed the river and entered the mountains through a cave. I signaled to your men to the south with my torch from the hills."

"But you didn't see them come out the other side, isn't that so, Mendez?"

"Well, no. It took me a while just to climb the mountain and signal for help. But where else would they have gone, if not for this escape pod? It only makes logical sens –"

WHAMMM!

Deckard caught Mendez with a swift backhand, sending the young man landing on his back, squealing in pain from the blow and landing on sharpened metal debris.

"Never assume anything in this primitive world, Mendez. That was your first mistake. Your second mistake was that you let me down. And your last mistake is that you aren't down there with the others searching the rubble. Do you know how many precious detonators we wasted on that structure? If she's not in the debris, I'll personally see to it that you're lashed for your negligence!"

The man's teary-eyed face nodded in acknowledgment of his dire circumstances. With a final apology, he turned and crawled down into the trench to help, quickly lugging away ship fragments, hoping to find the scorched remains of Severine and her new allies.

"You're not going to find her down there," Arien remarked. "You must know that by now. We're wasting time here and expending so much manpower so close to sauro territory."

There it is again. Those condescending remarks will be the death of you, Arien.

Deckard looked down at his sword arm, eagerly contemplating running her through with the blade. Second to only Severine Solens herself, Arien was quickly moving her way up Deckard's personal hit list. The problem with killing Arien was simple – she was beloved by much of the crew. She was as beautiful as she was tough. Such a combination, Deckard felt, would eventually threaten to challenge his leadership of the Exiles.

I'll come for you soon enough.

"Are you even listening to me?" Arien whined. "I want her dead as much as you do, but right now it's just not going to happen. She outfoxed us, Delios, and if you can't see that then maybe –"

"Maybe what, Arien?" Deckard asked, with a hint of suppressed wrath.

She took a step back, paying careful attention to his arm sword. Arien knew, despite having a lot of influence over the Exiles, that she was no match for the warlord's unpredictable temper. She had seen him deliver swift punishments without batting an eye – something Deckard used to his advantage to incur fear and respect.

"I think it's high time we pull out of here," Arien said. "We've chased that bitch all over the Triassic map. We were sent out here to scout for food and lost Federation supplies, not waste all our resources on some personal revenge spree."

"Arien, that bitch took my arm! I won't rest until I have her head on a pike! Now get out of my sight before you anger me any further, and take your unwanted opinions with you!"

With a final, spiteful frown, Arien turned and stormed away, barking orders at some of the other Exiles who got in her way. As Deckard turned back to the debris, one of the workers stood out to him – one whom he had become rather appreciative of.

"Eucer, come up here. Take a break, I want to talk with you!"

Eucer raced out of the trench and walked up to the warlord, sweaty and out of breath from the labor. Known for his astounding problem-solving skills and engineering specialties, Eucer Envans wasn't particularly high-ranking in the Exiles, but had earned a reputation of excellence in Deckard's eyes, and thus was highly respected by the rest of the group. From behind his long stringy hair and slightly stocky appearance, his book smarts far outshined his warrior abilities.

"Yes, sir?"

"How's that project coming along?"

"Repairing the XR-90s?"

"No, no. That one I'm not as concerned about. I mean the other, more large-scale project."

"Oh," Eucer laughed uneasily, brushing the hair out of his eyes. "That will be operational as soon as I get an hour or two of free time when we get back to camp. We're lucky we found the field manual. Just a few more bugs to work out, and then you'll have the heaviest artillery in the Triassic!"

Deckard smiled, patting his wise protege on the back.

"Good. I knew you wouldn't let me down. See that it's operational as soon as possible. I'm eager to test it out."

\#

Standing in a wooded area a hundred yards from the *Mudskipper* crash site, Arien Symra threw her knife into a mark in the tree, coming only inches away from the target – the previous knife impression. She had become very skilled at knife-throwing, and used her new passion as a way to funnel her anger from Delios Deckard into a more healthy outlet.

That pompous, one-armed asshole!

She retrieved the blade again and repeated the action, this time catching the first mark within a few centimeters. Her knife-throwing skills were becoming deadly. She yearned for the day that she could use them on someone.

Severine Solens, she thought. *I could stick her in the face with my knife and be the greatest thing that ever happened to the Exiles. Or even better – kill Delios and claim my rightful title as the Exiles leader. But that would mean I'd probably have to kill Tanner too. Tanner is a big son of a bitch. Dealing with him might take a few more people to –*

"What are you doing way out here, beautiful?" called a flirtatious voice, pushing through the branches behind her.

A handsome young man with short cropped hair and ancient Federation armor pushed through the trees, plucking her knife out of the tree and handing it back to her.

"Not now, Juane," Arien grumbled. "What we had was amusing while it lasted, but I promise, I've had better."

"*Ouch*," replied Juane, pretending to be offended. "I'm stung! What's got you so irritated?"

"You know," she shot him a telling look.

"Did that arrogant shithead say something to you again?" Juane pressed. "I told you if he ever said anything to you again, I was going to say something!"

"Yeah, right," Arien replied. "You wouldn't do shit, Juane! No one does, that's just it! We've lived under his tyranny for so long, people just accept whatever he does. In the Exiles, it's 'whatever Deckard says goes'. Something needs to be done about it sooner or later or I'm gonna lose my shit."

"Well, like I've been saying the whole time he was elected warlord," Juane went on, "why don't we just take matters into our own hands?"

Arien turned and looked at him, suspiciously, but interested.

"What are you spouting off about now, Juane?"

"Simple," Juane replied, sitting down on a rotted log. He turned briefly to look at the demolition teams continuing to sort through the *Mudskipper* debris. Once he saw that no one was around, he resumed his presentation.

"With Kaylie and Darin killed, presumably by Severine just an hour or so ago, that means our numbers are officially down to forty-six. I guess if you count the both of us, it's forty-eight. The way I see it, even if we had a third of the force with us, let's just say seventeen of us, we could overthrow Delios Deckard without fear of blow back."

"You're certainly no Eucer at mathematics," Arien said bluntly. "A third of forty-eight would be sixteen."

"Whatever. Seventeen would be better!"

"You think a third of the Exiles would be enough to stop repercussions of doing – what?"

"What do you think?" Juane asked. "Killing Deckard, of course. Obviously, we'll have to dispatch of his loyalists as well. Namely Tanner and Eucer. But realistically, he treats the majority of the soldiers with contempt. I'm sure we'll have no trouble finding people who will turncoat to our side."

"Even if we could pull it off," Arien continued, "and that's a big 'if', how the hell do you intend on approaching these people without them ratting us out to Deckard?"

"I don't know yet," Juane replied. "But this is something I've wanted to do for a long time. We'll just have to keep our eyes and ears open and wait for an opportunity. He often splits us up into scouting parties, right? That may be the best chance. Trust me – there are others who want to see him fall."

With that, Juane started to walk back to the *Mudskipper* ruins.

"Don't stay out here too long," he cautioned. "Deckard's a smart son of a bitch. Don't worry. Our time will come."

#

The sun overhead began to descend farther to the west. Deckard took a seat on a boulder, tired of managing the escape pod demolition. Over half of his force were tired and spent, lugging the last few traces of darkened metal out from the trench, revealing a ring that formed what was left of the *Mudskipper* floor. Tanner remained the only motivated excavator, still looking loyally under every turned piece of debris for any sign of their prey.

Impossible. Completely and utterly impossible!

How had Severine eluded him? It didn't make any sense. Arien's theory of arrow traps didn't make any sense either. There were no traps found in the debris, and there weren't any arrows found either. She had to have been in the *Mudskipper* shortly before the firebombing began. Her disappearance was completely unprecedented.

Deckard mused over the string of events, trying to find the missing piece of the aggravating Severine Solens disappearance act.

First traced her whereabouts a few weeks back. Another sighting of her just north of here a week ago. Same day, realized that she must have a shelter around here. Began a grid search a few days ago. Mendez saw her today, including an adult male with child. Signaled south to where we were. Discovered a hidden valley with a crashed Federation pod. Someone or something in the pod killed two of my soldiers. Firebombed the shit out of the structure, and yet, no corpses were found.

"It doesn't make sense," he said aloud.

Shortly before they closed in on her, Deckard swore that he heard a Federation bot's speakers go off in the shelter. But bots weren't magicians. Did they have radar? Sure, but that doesn't mean they can make people vanish into thin air.

Something about this just isn't right.

And worst of all, that bitch Arien was once again second guessing his command. Her constant criticism would no doubt cause dissension among the soldiers – dissension was not something he looked forward to. This was one of those moments that Deckard wished that Arien would approach him with one of her critiques. He needed to punish someone, and who better than his third-in-command.

"*Dammit*, Mendez!" Tanner yelled from the pit. "I thought you said you hauled out everything! Here's another crate buried in the sand. Help me get this thing out of here."

Deckard rolled his eyes, preparing to order everyone back to their base camp. Mendez shuffled over to Tanner, embarrassed and exhausted. The hidden crate was the last remaining item in the center of the *Mudskipper* floor. Surely Severine and the three others weren't hiding inside it.

What's the point?

"Tanner!" Deckard bellowed out. "Forget about it. I think it's about time that we all –"

"*Holy shit!*" Tanner yelled, interrupting Deckard's command. "Sir, you need to get down and check this out right away. I think we've just found a big clue to Severine's whereabouts!"

"*What?* Tell me, what did you find?"

Deckard raced off his boulder down into the *Mudskipper* trench. He could feel the eyes from his surrounding forces turning toward Tanner and Mendez, who awkwardly removed the crate and were bending down and looking at something buried in the ground. Deckard arrived, smiling at what he saw.

It was a fuel tank hatch – a hatch that shouldn't have been there. Based on the pod's design and schematics, the hatch was in the wrong location.

The soldiers were gathering around now, coming back to the trench and surrounding Deckard who eyed his prize.

"Do you want to do the honors, sir?" Tanner asked respectfully.

"By all means, Tanner. You were the one who uncovered it. Everyone, gather around and arm yourselves. She could be inside. Pry her open, Tanner!"

"Yes, sir."

With a hard tug, Tanner ripped the door off the ground, revealing that it served as nothing more than a cover plate. Deckard stared down at the indent the door left behind on the ground, examining what appeared to be a very elaborate, hidden tunnel. The passage dropped four feet into the earth and then veered to the right, disappearing under the scorched sand.

"Do we send the detonators down?" Tanner asked.

"Negative," Deckard replied. "I don't think this is a shelter. It's an escape tunnel. Tanner, grab six Exiles of your choice. Looks like it heads east. All of you! Pack up your things. We need to double-time it eastbound!"

The Exiles nodded in agreement and quickly gathered their gear, fleeing the trench and beginning the long sprint east.

Deckard turned back to Tanner, delighted at the find.

"If it's a dead end, double back and meet us back at base camp. I have a hunch where this tunnel might lead out."

"Yes, sir," Tanner nodded, preparing to duck into the tunnel.

"Oh, and Tanner?"

"Yes, sir?"

"If you find that bitch, put a pulse round in her head for me, will you?"

"Confirmed. You six, with me! Let's go!"

XIII

"Wow, that tunnel really messed up my back," Severine heard Adam lamenting behind her as she led them through the eastern forest.

"Do all new Federation soldiers from Solis always complain this much?" Severine teased, chopping away at the oncoming vegetation.

"Hey," Adam laughed. "Go easy on me. I'm not battle-hardened like you. Hell, when I got your signal, my whole job consisted of monitoring hologram dashboards and checking on incoming and outgoing spacecraft. I haven't spent three years being hunted by dinosaurs, not to mention psychopaths with swords for their arms!"

"It's not like I had a choice in the matter," she replied. "Stop lagging behind. We have maybe two hours tops ahead of Deckard before he discovers the tunnel and sends a strike team after us. Every second counts, Mr. Ross."

Severine had led them for about an hour after escaping the *Mudskipper* tunnel through the jungle east of her valley where she called home for the past three years. Now, after the attack from the Exiles and the collapse of her shelter, the hope of the fabled portal oscillator was all she had left. Sure enough, as she anticipated, Adam asked the obvious question.

"I think it's about time you told us about this guy," he said. "He damn near almost killed me and my nephew, and we never did anything to him. We don't even know who that asshole is. Who is he to you Severine, and why does he want you dead so badly?"

"I figured you'd ask me sooner or later," Severine said, discovering a trail that led them downhill. "Delios Deckard and I first crossed paths some time ago now. I can't recall how long, but I remember the day like it was yesterday. I was fishing just north of here. At some point, I lost consciousness. I later discovered that I was struck from behind. After some missing time, I woke up tied up in a strange tent by those who I would come to know as 'the Exiles' – Deckard's army."

She grew quiet, letting Jordy and Nathan pass between her as she walked side by side with Adam. She drew her voice to a whisper, choosing not to let the two in the lead hear the darker parts of the tale.

"Forgive me, I don't want your nephew to hear, but I'm sure you can guess what my fate meant to Deckard's army. They... they passed me around to the higher ups, then they let the newer recruits do what they wanted to. This all happening of course after Deckard was done with me."

"Severine, I'm sorry. I didn't know. If I had, I wouldn't have asked."

"Well, now you do," she said sorrowfully. "Now that you know what kind of monsters we're dealing with, you'll have no problem with the second half of the story. As it so happens, after they were all finished with me, I had developed an overwhelming urge to escape – or I would die trying. Deckard ordered them to bring me back to his command tent for another unpleasant experience. But this time, Deckard made two moves he would come to regret. The first – untying me. The second – leaving his sword nearby. I just put two and two together, acted fast and I was gone, slipping into the night before his reinforcements had arrived. I guess now he decided he couldn't part with the sword, so he had it fused to his arm somehow. My guess cauterized the limb with pulse round residue."

"I can't believe this all happened," Adam replied. "It sounds, so... barbaric – so inhumane. This sounds like a tale you would hear about in ancient times."

"We are in ancient times, Adam," Severine replied. "Jordy, watch out for those plants up ahead. They're poisonous. Take us down the smaller trail. That's it. And switch your radar and noise emitters back on. If we're being followed, I want a heads up."

"*Wi-ill* do," Jordy replied, switching their trail.

"You know what I mean," Adam said. "These Exiles are Federation survivors. They were meant to colonize worlds and bring the better part of Earth with them, not the darker parts."

"It's true that they're from the Federation," Severine said. "But we don't know to what extent. For example, take the Neolithic hunters you ran into yesterday. They came from *Supernova* – I can confirm that. But they aren't first generation survivors, nor did they come from the hyper-sleep pods. They are a product of many generations of warped culture and thinking. Until now they have become something else entirely. It's possible that the Exiles are something equivalent to the Neolithics."

"So you don't think Deckard and his band of murderers are actual marooned Federationists?"

"I don't know what they are. I would think that, whatever they are or wherever they came from, that they're no more than second or third generation survivors. They have knowledge of pulse weapons and Federation terminology."

"Do they have a base? Somewhere around here that they call home?"

"All I've ever seen was the camp they held me in. They were just simple tents, not rigid dwellings, which tells me that they travel a lot."

"Well if they didn't come from *Supernova*, where did they come from?"

"I don't know and I wish I did. Because I'd make sure to lead the sauros right to it."

"*Sauros?*"

"It's short for Saurosuchus," Severine replied. "Apex predators of the Triassic. As far as I know, they're unrivaled in size and temperament. They're long four-legged carnivores about twenty to thirty feet long. I've had a few brushes with them over the years and thankfully, I've made it out every time."

"Do you suppose we'll be running into them during our course to the oscillator?" Adam asked nervously.

Flashbacks of the various deaths of his comrades replayed themselves in his mind, and to think there were even larger predators out there made him desperately want to get back to Solis.

"I don't think so," Severine replied. "They tend to keep to more wetland environments like the marshes. They have a small nest where my shelter is, or should I say was, but the sauros rarely traveled into my valley. The *Mudskipper* crash littered the area with shrapnel. Evidently, they don't like sharp objects."

"I think I remember Saurosuchus from my book," Nathan called back. "They don't look too friendly."

"Take my word for it," Severine said, "you'd be better off facing a herrera, a Coelophysis, and a Neolithic at the same time than crossing paths with a sauro."

WHRRR –

"*Aha!*" Jordy remarked, silencing his speakers. "Caught it before it went off. Severine, we have four human signals approaching."

"How far?"

"Fairly close. Downhill, near the river. They don't appear to be coming toward us. Rather, they're walking parallel with us to the southeast."

"*Exiles!*" Severine exclaimed. "It has to be. How have they found us already?"

"I don't think so," Adam said. "I think it may be someone else. Jordy, how far is the river?"

#

Adam watched through the ferns as the river rushed past them. A small rocky coast separated their position from the water. Severine, Jordy and Nathan huddled together behind Adam, waiting nervously for the human signals to come into view and walk past their hideout.

"This is stupid, Adam," Severine pushed his shoulder. "If these are Exiles, and I have to draw my X2 on them, not only are we wasting valuable ammunition and time, but we're alerting other Exiles in the area to our position. My recommendation is to get out of here fast, before more reinforcements arrive."

"I *concur-r-r* with *S-sev,*" Jordy whispered. "Adam, this *id-d-ea* has some serious *r-r-r-amifications* if you're wrong."

"Yeah, Uncle Adam," Nathan added. "What if it's that Deckard guy? We'll never get out of here then."

"Nathan," Adam replied, "if we survived the coelos and the natives, we can survive that asshole. *Ah,* quiet everybody. I think I can hear them coming. Okay, moment of truth."

Slush...Slush...Slush...

Gradually, a series of watery footsteps were heard, cascading over the stone laden coast. Adam surmised that the newcomers were walking around at the base of the water, and at least one of them was splashing through the waves. Finally, the human figures came into view, obscured behind the vegetation they were using for cover.

When he heard Severine draw her bowstring, he quickly put a hand on her wrist and stopped her from loading the arrow.

"It's okay," Adam smiled. "They're with me."

He turned back and watched the faces roll past.

There's Alex Meras, Kara Barnels, Brandy – I think her last name is Dietrich and... oh no! Why on earth would they bring that murderous asshole with them? How did he survive?

Without a second thought, Adam brushed aside the vegetation and approached, vision narrowing on his rival. From outside the tunnel vision, he saw Alex Meras raise his sniper rifle in shock, but relaxed when he saw who it was.

"Oh, Lieutenant! We found you."

Adam ignored the comment, walking toward the bruised man herded in between Kara and Brandy. Wyatt looked up and met with Adam's eyes, igniting a spark.

WHAM!

Handcuffed and defenseless, Wyatt took the blow to the face. The force of the impact was enough to knock him off his feet and send him spinning onto the rocky cove, the back of his head splashing in the water. Adam was on him a second later.

WHAM!

Another blow struck Wyatt in the face, beginning a bloody nose. Adam reached his hands around Wyatt's throat, not suffocating, but holding his opponent in place. Seeing the sergeant struggle in vain but unable to fight back made Adam want to rip his handcuffs off and finally resume their brawl. Finally knocking Wyatt unconscious without the sergeant pulling a pulse pistol on him would be more than satisfying, and long overdue.

"I should drown you right here!" Adam yelled, until he felt Alex and Severine pull him backwards off his captive.

"He tried to kill us," Adam explained as the others blocked off his opponent. "He took Nathan hostage. He was going to just head to the oscillator and leave us here. He deserves to die!"

"He deserves to spend the rest of his life in a military confinement prison on Solis," Alex replied. "Death is too swift for him, Lieutenant."

"We know what happened," Brandy added. "We saw the blast mark impressions in the grassland, and the signs of a scuffle."

"I can't allow you to kill him, Lieutenant," Alex said bluntly. "He needs to go to a maximum lockup penitentiary. It's what he deserves."

Adam took a few steps back, trying to normalize his breathing. When he looked around and saw that the numbers were not on his side, he relaxed. Kara helped Wyatt to his feet unwillingly. To Adam's surprise, the sergeant remained quiet.

"Fine," Adam moaned. "Just as long as you all know who he is. I'll personally see to it that he makes it behind bars if I have to."

"We're all in agreement there," Kara acknowledged. "Glad to see you and Nathan made it out. When we didn't see you at the bottom of the ravine, we assumed you may have been swept downriver. I guess we made the right choice. Who are your friends?"

"I'm Severine Solens. This is Jordy, a Federation logistics bot. We're the only two remaining survivors from the *Supernova* crash. All of the others have died or transcended into jungle hunters, as Adam told me you just ran into."

"You're all that's left from the *Supernova*?" Kara asked. "What about Brett Ambrose – the sender of the distress call?"

"Brett died in an explosion three years ago, right after the signal went out."

"We really should be *g-o-o-ing* now," Jordy urged them. "Seeing as how Deckard's warriors are bound to uncover our tunnel, that only gives us a limited *am-m-mount* of time to *r-r-e-each* your ship, Adam."

"Deckard?" Alex asked. "I thought you said there were no other survivors from the *Supernova*?"

"Trust me, there aren't," Severine said.

"Delios Deckard is a leader of another sect, apart from the hunters," Adam explained. "They're not from the *Supernova*, but nonetheless, they are Federation crash survivors."

"How do you know they're not from the *Supernova*?" Brandy asked.

"Different uniforms," Severine replied. "If they were from my ship, I would've recognized their faces. There's nearly fifty of them, that I know of."

"Why aren't we going back for them?" Alex asked.

"Well, on account that they just tried to kill the four of us," Adam replied. "They're a murderous band of Triassic sociopaths. They have no place in Solis. Actually, Wyatt, you'd fit right in with them."

Wyatt glared up at Adam from his handcuffs, scowling but remaining silent. Finally, he looked down at the handcuffs again, spitting a glob of blood on the coast.

"How far away are they?" asked Kara.

"We don't know for sure," Adam said. "Our guess is at the most three hours, but they could be gaining on us. Severine killed two of their own before they firebombed her shelter. They mean business – I promise. If they catch us, it won't end well, and none of us will be going home."

Adam looked over their faces, unsure of how they felt about the situation. The prospect of leaving potential survivors of the Federation behind, whether they were from the *Supernova* or some other ship, wasn't part of the operation. After seeing the lunacy that the natives had become and the treachery spawned from Deckard's Exiles, Adam realized that Severine and Jordy might be the only ones worthy of being rescued.

"The lieutenant's right," Alex said finally. "We can't bring any of these monsters back to Solis. Although encountering cultures like this wasn't in the scope of the mission, I know that Central Command would decline bringing back anyone or anything that attacked members of our rescue operation."

He turned dramatically to Wyatt.

"You're the only exception."

Wyatt declined to comment.

"So what do we do now?" Kara asked.

"The only thing left to do," Adam said. "Stay together and head to the portal oscillator as fast as we can. If I recall, Sana's last reading was fifteen miles southeast. She said something about two valleys. Severine thinks she knows where that is and can take us there. God willing, the charge crystals will work and the oscillator won't malfunction."

"Okay," Severine said, brushing through them. "We can discuss the specifics on the way. We're wasting time talking here. Keeping a good distance between Deckard and his soldiers is a must. Jordy, how's your radar working?"

"*Go-o-od,* Sev. I can still read all of your signals. As far as I can tell, there's nothing else in our *vac-c-c-inity.*"

"Excellent. Hang near the back of the group. Assuming that they're still behind us, I want your radar closest to their most obvious position. Well, what are we waiting for? Oh, right. You all haven't been shipwrecked here for three years."

"Okay, hotshot," Adam laughed. "You know I'm a lieutenant, that means I outrank you."

Severine shot him a funny look – part witty, part flirtatious.

"I think my three years in unpredictable jungle, numerous near-death experiences from natives, mercenaries and dinosaurs, and the fact that technically speaking I'm three hundred years older than you, all qualify for me outranking you. Not to mention, I'm the only one who knows where these two valleys are."

Adam smiled, defeated.

"I see your point," he admitted.

"Perfect," Severine smiled, brushing into the undergrowth. "Then fall in, soldier. We could be there before nightfall if we hustle."

#

Severine's route took the eight Federation survivors back into the lush jungle. Her chosen path looked like it had only been walked on a handful of times by a small dinosaur, weaving about in an unpredictable manner as it ascended uphill. Adam wasn't sure if she knew exactly the direction she was headed, but a quick glance at his compass confirmed that Severine indeed was heading southeast. The sun was beginning to make its final descent over the distant western peaks, threatening to once again drown them in the uncertainty of the dark primordial world.

After Severine moved to the front of the party, Alex Meras followed alongside Wyatt, followed by Kara and Brandy. Adam stayed behind to help his nephew up the rising slopes, followed by Jordy near the back.

Severine led the party from about ten feet ahead of the rest, using her machete to swat away the crowded foliage. Adam noted her stamina and athleticism as she strode up the slope, barely out of breath while the rest of his party was suffering.

If we both make it back to Solis alive, I just might want to ask her to –

He brushed the thought aside quickly, grabbing a narrow tree trunk to help haul himself up the uneven terrain.

What am I thinking? My own girlfriend's been dead, what, a couple of days? Besides, keep your head focused on the mission, Ross! There're more important things to attend to than falling in love with the badass Triassic heroine – like getting your nephew home safe and sound to Andrew.

CRACK!

Adam turned, just in time to snag his nephew's wrist as his support branch snapped.

"*Augh!* Let go!" Nathan barked, quickly grabbing another branch. "I'm okay! I've got this!"

"I would've caught *yo-o-ou*," Jordy replied, bringing up the rear. The bot was only a few feet below Nathan, staying behind as Severine commanded for optimal radar use.

"Thanks, Jordy," Nathan replied. "But I'm fine."

The boy pushed ahead of Adam, who followed him with a look of irritation.

After all I've done for that kid, you'd think he'd be more grateful, Adam thought knowing that a confrontation would need to happen. At the top of the lush jungle hill, he would get his chance.

"Let's take a five minute rest up here," Severine announced, setting down her longbow and cracking open her canteen.

The exhausted band of survivors pushed through the fern and soaked in the tranquil shade of the overhanging pines. The area on top of the plateau was covered in tall fern-like plants with knotted green tendrils, offering a great view of the wooded landscape around them. Adam was surprised they had encountered no signs of the dinosaurs or other predatory lifeforms.

After he took a long sip of his water canister, Adam spotted Nathan ten feet away from the bulk of the group, trying to glean more information from the dinosaur encyclopedia. He strode over and grabbed him by the arm, tugging him firmly away from the others toward a section where the ferns grew enormous, out of their view.

"*Ow*, let go!" Nathan commanded, ripping his wrist away from his uncle's arm once they were away from the others. "What's your problem?"

"My problem is *you*!" Adam replied sternly, pointing a finger in his nephew's face. "Look, I'm the adult here and your dad's trusting me to look after you. Trust me when I say this, but if I knew that *Harvester One* was going to end up in this crazy backwards world, I would've been a staunch opponent of you coming along. Now all this trip you've been disrespecting me, making all these snide comments. Do you realize what I've sacrificed for you? Do you know what Wyatt was going to do to you back in the fields?"

"I bet it was all a bluff," Nathan replied. "He was just showing off. I'm sure he would've let me go the minute we made it out of the field."

"*Wrong*," Adam fired back, his temper flaring. "Wyatt was gonna kill you and me, if I hadn't stopped him. Anyways, Wyatt is beside the point. I'm tired of you mouthing off to me. I assumed after all that's happened these past two days, you'd start to grow up and respect me more. Do you know how many people died so far so we could complete this mission? Do you even –"

"*All right!*" Nathan whined. "Listen, *Adam*. You're not my dad! I'm aware of my age. I've been trying to help this whole time by reading that book to try to come up with –"

WHHHHISSHHHH!

Adam, felt a sharp, sudden pain in the back of his left shoulder. It started out as a subtle pricking sensation, but soon grew numbing.

What...the...hell...just...

"*Uncle Adam?*" Nathan's voice echoed. "*Hey, what's with you?*"

The numbness began to consume him. Adam felt his knees give out involuntarily. In the distance behind the fern patch, he could here Severine yelling something, followed by two rounds from Alex Meras'

ECSR-20. Through the leaves, he could see blurry forms beginning to enter the plateau, armed with pikes and hatchets.

The natives! They've found us.

"Uncle Adam! Come on, we have to get out of here!"

His nephew's blurry form transformed into colorful wisps as Adam began to lose consciousness. He could feel himself letting go, succumbing to the darkness as the world around him grew void of life. He knew his nephew wasn't sure what was happening to him, oblivious to the ambush that was occurring on the jungle plateau.

It's only a matter of time before they catch him!

"Run, kid –"

With an abrupt fade, it all became black.

XIV

Flashbacks from her capture by the Davenport tribe and later by Delios Deckard and his Exiles came back to haunt Severine as she felt her wrists and ankles bound, the ropes digging into her bruised, sensitive flesh. Her eyes squinted open as she felt her body swaying back and forth, hanging upside-down on a log that two strong Neolithics hauled on their shoulders.

Not again...

That was her only thought as the convoy of jungle hunters lifted her limp body through the trees. She swiveled her head to the back, noticing that her seven other companions had also been apprehended in similar fashion. A look to the oncoming path revealed something even more disturbing.

Ahead, the trail widened into a large clearing in the forest, where a wall of twelve-foot tall sharpened severed trunks formed what looked like an ancient fortress. The natives at the head of the convoy called up to the watchmen on the crudely made ramparts above, who began to operate the entrance into the hidden Neolithic region.

MMRRMMMMRRRMM!

So this is where they relocated to after the Supernova battle years ago, she thought. *I always wondered if they had another colony.*

A massive portion of the trunks swayed away slowly, revealing a hidden gateway that opened. As her captors lugged her toward the entrance, she suddenly noticed the obscene skeletal remains of the original Davenport strung up over the archway, greeting her once again with that sinister, devious grin.

I thought we obliterated you, she cursed, swaying back and forth as she was hauled toward the gate.

The natives carted her and her companions one by one through the massive entrance, revealing the hidden colony awaiting on the adjacent side of the walls. Apart from the horrific cheering and spear poking that awaited her from the onlooking crowds, Severine noticed a heavy contingent of crude huts constructed from mud, rock, and timber. Spread out under the greenery below the shade of the canopy, the village might have looked very scenic, had it not been for the unpredictable barbarians that inhabited it.

Okay, focus! We can get out of here. The twin valleys aren't far past this jungle. There's a lot more of these assholes than I remember from the ship.

SLICE!

Ooof!

Without warning, her bonds were cut. She fell two feet to the ground, moaning as she struck the soil. She had only a few seconds to recover as the sharp spear tips were prodded toward her. Beside her, she could see Adam, Nathan and the others all enduring the same ritual, before they were all shoved off further into the encampment. Adam looked dazed and sluggish, and had to be herded along by two bulky Neolithics. She noticed his eyes had practically rolled back into his head.

Poison darts, Severine assumed. *He'll be feeling that later, I'm sure.*

She might have considered running, if they hadn't been quickly encircled by the hunters.

There has to be a way out of here! I'm so close to escaping this backwards prehistoric nightmare...

The cheering parade led them through a passage that looked to be the main road of the village, eventually emptying out to a large sacrificial area in the center of the fortress. There, an overweight, nearly nude male awaited on a custom-made timber throne. Severine noted that the shaman was adorned in the old garments worn by her rival, Marcus Davenport, before his death at the claws of the alpha Herrerasaur, Gretta, years earlier.

They must have recovered his body and took his clothes. This must be the new leader of the tribe.

With a harsh tap of his wooden cane, the parade stopped and silence saturated the colony.

This doesn't look good, Severine deduced, eyes fixed on the horrific *Supernova* offspring that stared her down.

She could feel the eyes of the crowd on her. Several spears teased her neckline, pricking her skin which resulted in goosebumps. Behind her, several of the natives closed in with knives, eager to pierce her flesh with their jagged blades.

They must remember me...

"*Ee-noff!*" roared the chieftain, rising slowly from his throne.

Enough? Davenport's cult must have learned some of his language...

The obese ruler walked over to the hostages, his footsteps loud and prideful. He finally settled within inches of Severine's face. His hot breath filled her nostrils as she mentally fought off the nauseating aroma, anticipating a punishment if she failed to look away from their feared leader. Finally, after examining her top to bottom, the nearly nude leader spoke again.

"Are yew tis invadar jungole?" the chief asked, his broken language apparent.

"*Yees!*" rang out several cries from his armed spectators.

"Severine, what are they asking?" came a worried female voice behind her.

WHACK!

Kara was immediately silenced by a swift spear shaft to the head. Alex Meras caught her before she fell, picking her up and making sure she stayed conscious.

"Brandy," Severine heard Adam whisper behind her. "You're a translator. Any chance you can help us out here?"

"Oh God," Brandy mumbled, shivering in fright. "I guess it couldn't hurt to try, right?"

She timidly stepped ahead of Adam and stood next to Severine, her body trembling from head to toe. The native chief slowly turned and eyed her, taking a step away from the initial target before standing face to face with Brandy.

"Tis jungole invadar other?" asked the primitive leader.

"Tis Brandy Dietrich," Brandy replied, trying to figure out how their language worked. "Dis jungole good other. No invadar?"

She's not jungole invadar, Severine thought. *It's me. They must want revenge for killing Davenport and Gretta all those years ago. And to think, I came so close! So close to getting home...*

"Tis sound wrong," the obese chief went on. "Tis all other jungole invadars here. Jungole invadar pay tis life. Fire orb vanish. Night come, tis jungole invadars be died! Take invadar tis the huts. Praypar the fire! Tonight, tis jungole invadars punished!"

So long, Solis.

Severine felt a spear-tip prick her back, forcing her forward. At that moment, she knew it wasn't going to be a pleasant evening.

#

The coarse, rough inner walls of the mud hut were beginning to bruise Alex Meras' back. He sat on the uneven ground of the dwelling, his memory struggling to recall the events of what happened in the jungle. The last thing he remembered was hiking up a hill and resting in a wooded clearing with his companions. He remembered something striking him in the neck, shooting his sniper rifle a few times, and then nothing more.

Then the next thing I know, I'm carted through the jungle tied upside-down on a pole into some cannibalistic village...

He yearned for his weapons, but they were nowhere in sight. To his right was Kara Barnels, also tied up and struggling in vain to escape the situation. Across from them sat Wyatt and Brandy. Both were trying the same procedure with no success. The ropes were tied at the wrists and feet, connected by a conjoining rope in the middle. The ropes that bound their feet were tethered to large rocks with a third rope, which made moving around increasingly tedious and limited. Additionally, more ropes joined from latches that were embedded into the sides of the wall, adding additional support. The holding cell was very small and dimly lit, except for the crude torch that burned just out of their reach.

Escape will be problematic. Bound by the hands, knees, feet and they also have us tied to rungs on the wall that they must have collected from the Supernova debris.

"Anyone see where they took our weapons?" Alex asked, trying to use the roughness of the walls to slice through his ropes.

"I did," Kara replied. "Large hut across from the chief's throne in the main clearing. That's where we'll find your rifle and my pistol."

"Good try on the translating, Brandy," Alex commended her. "You did better than I could've done."

"The hell she did," Wyatt cut in. "She said maybe one or two sentences to the guy before they shuffled us in here like sheep to the slaughter. Now we're all probably gonna die in here, thanks to her."

"If I wasn't bound right now, I'd smack you across that ugly face," Brandy replied. "What do you care anyway? When we get you back to Solis, you're going to trial for attempted murder and kidnapping."

"Shut up, bitch!" Wyatt replied angrily. "You've been just about as useless on this operation as Adam's whiny shit-stain little nephew. I did what I had to do to survive. When those dinosaurs attacked in the fields, I did what I thought would get me back to Solis the fastest. You all could've come along, but instead you let Adam Ross call the shots. Now look where we've ended up. The irony of it – we're all in agreement that retreating back to Solis was the right call in the first place."

"We didn't know at the time that there would be two survivors that we'd run into down the road," Alex replied. "That hardly justifies anything you did. And it doesn't validate you wanting to pull out of the mission sooner than expected. The fact that we ran into our objective on the way to the oscillator doesn't mean anything."

"You disgust me, Wyatt," Kara spat at him. "I never thought you were such a pussy while *Harvester One* was in space. Now that you're down in the trenches, we all see you for what you really are; a snake. It's a pity I'll be killed alongside you."

"None of us have to be killed," Wyatt cut in with a dramatic pause. When no one took the bait, the sergeant continued.

"All that has to happen is this. One of us has to get their bonds untied. Whoever that person is can get the torch and burn through the others' ropes. With the four of us together, we can make a run for the hut with the weapons, arm ourselves, and shoot our way out of here. Then we can make for the oscillator."

"What about the others?" Brandy asked.

"There's no way we can save the other four. First of all, the bot's as good as dead – with all that rust, he's slow as molasses. They'll catch him in a heartbeat. The boy will hold us up too."

"Funny, you had no problem taking Nathan as a hostage when it benefited you," Kara remarked. "We're not leaving them behind. Either we're all making it out or none of us will."

"*Fool,*" Wyatt scoffed. "Then go ahead and die here – all because you won't listen. Well, that's fine by me! I'll get out of these ropes and make for the oscillator myself."

"You plan on getting loose from your bonds and getting out of here all by yourself?" Brandy asked. "Haven't you forgotten? You're also wearing Federation steel handcuffs. Good luck cutting your way through those."

"Not to mention finding your way to the oscillator in the dark without being eaten," Kara added.

Although there was no way to see outside, Alex knew by now that it had to be nightfall.

"Sure beats staying here waiting to be killed," Wyatt replied, starting to chew at his ropes with no success. "I can't stand the sight of you people any longer. Had you all listened to me from the beginning, we would've been out of here by now with minimal casualties. Now there's only a handful of us left – and after tonight, I'll be the only one left, because I'm getting out of here!"

Miraculously, Wyatt managed to chew through his wrist ropes and began working the coils that bound his feet.

"You're not going anywhere," Alex said sternly.

"How's that, Corporal Meras?" Wyatt said, looking his former subordinate in the eyes.

WHAMMM!

With an abrupt headbutt, Alex knocked Wyatt out cold, braving the nasty headache that would surely follow.

"He just won't shut the hell up, will he?" Alex laughed, shrugging off the drop of blood that started from his head.

Kara stared wide-eyed at the event and turned to Alex, forgetting about her bonds for the moment.

"That was without a doubt the sexiest thing I've ever seen!" she smiled. "Thanks, Alex."

"Listening to that madman babble on is not how I wanted to spend my last moments. But that asshole stumbled onto something. These ropes must be old if they can fall apart that easily. New plan! Eat our way through the ropes, save the others, and get out of here before we're all that shaman's dinner!"

"What about Wyatt?" Brandy asked, nibbling at her cords.

"I haven't decided yet," Alex answered. "Maybe I'll get lucky and one of the archers will nail him on the way out and make my decision easy."

#

The lights from Jordy's body illuminated the inner hut so brightly that Nathan had to squint. Several of the natives that pushed them into the hut were infatuated with Jordy's lights, so much so that it took them a few minutes to actually shut the door.

"Have they ever seen a Federation bot before?" Nathan asked, unimpressed by the lights

"It *wo-o-ould* appear not," Jordy shot back, examining his constraints.

"Don't you have some kind of hidden pulse gun that can cut the ropes?"

"You must have me *confused-d-d* with the infantry bots of my time. The *m-m-ost* I can do is provide helpful *d-d-data* and give *sa-a-arcastic*, *unwelcomed* remarks. Why are you so *h-h-ostile, young-g* one?"

"It's Nathan," the boy answered harshly. "The name is Nathan."

"I *know-w-w*," Jordy replied. "You see, I *c-can b-be* an asshole too."

Nathan laughed. The bot's hidden humor, language and tomfoolery was starting to earn the machine his respect.

"You know," the boy started, "you're kinda cool, aren't you? Maybe if we ever get out of here alive, we can be friends back at Solis."

"*Th-h-hank* you, you're too kind. We *ca-a-an* be friends *n-n-ow*. We don't have to *wa-ait* until we get *ba-ack*. I *do-on't* think we'll be here awhile."

"What makes you say that?"

"Sev *al-lways* has an escape plan," the bot concluded on a positive note.

"So, why didn't your radar go off when those natives caught us?" Nathan asked, suddenly remembering the bot's hidden alarm capabilities.

"I'm an old *bo-o-t*, Nathan," Jordy replied. "My *ra-a-adar* doesn't work very well, having *be-e-n* exposed to the elements for months on end. I'm fortunate it *work-k-ks* at all, when it does work, *tha-at* is. Now, it's my *tu-u-rn* to ask the questions. Why aren't you and your uncle *ge-e-etting* along?"

Nathan turned and wrinkled his brow.

"Getting awfully personal for someone I just meant, Jordy," Nathan replied.

"*Wha-a-t* else am I going to do to *pas-s-s* time?" the bot replied with a smile. "It's just *me-e* and you in here, *kid-d-d*. Who else are you *goin-g-g* to talk to?"

Nathan laughed. Bots on Solis weren't nearly this comedic and clever with their conversations. Talking with the three-hundred-year-old logistics bot was more fun than talking with kids his own age.

"All right," Nathan conceded. "I guess me and my uncle just got off on the wrong foot. I can't blame him though. I just think he's always treating me like a kid. In front of all these adults, especially the marines – it's just embarrassing. I just wish he'd treat me more like an adult, you know? It's not like he's my father."

"Ah, I *se-e-e*," Jordy nodded. "*Wel-l-l*, think of where you'd be without *hi-i-im*. From what I've *he-ard*, most of your party was wiped out *in-n-n* the first few hours. He's hard on you *beca-a-ause* he loves you! Plus, it's *his-s* job to make sure *you-o-u* get home safe and *so-o-und*."

"I know. Honestly, I don't know why I give him such a hard time. And now I probably won't ever see him or my family again. I'm gonna die here in this... this muddy, crappy hut."

Don't cry in front of the bot! Crying is a dead giveaway that I'm just a kid! And that would defeat the whole point of my argument with Adam.

Nathan found that he couldn't help it. The events of the last few days were catching up with him. He couldn't help but picture the gruesome deaths he witnessed first hand.

Rice Lere. Jonas Carte. Ziven Wyke.

He couldn't handle all the bottled up frustration and anxiety any longer. He couldn't escape the thought that he would be the next to go. The tears began to flow, no matter how hard he tried to choke them back.

"*Dammit!*" Nathan cried, trying to normalize his breathing and heaving chest. "Now I feel like a scared little kid!"

"Hey, *che-e-er* up, *bucko*," Jordy went on, tapping the boy's chin with his metallic, calloused fingers. "Like I've said, I'm *c-c-c-on-fiden-t-t* that Severine will think of *some-thing-g*. And when she does, you better be *re-eady!*"

"Ready how?"

"Well, for starters, don't *fal-l-l* asleep. You want to be ready for when she *kick-k-ks* down that *d-o-or* and cuts your ropes. We'll have only one chance at *battling-g-g* our *way-y* out of this village and getting to your ship."

"How far do you think the ship is from here?" Nathan asked, a glimmer of hope passing over him.

"Not sure. It's *be-e-en* awhile since I've *be-e-en* through these *wo-o-ods*. Severine and I usually choose to keep to the west of the *Mudskipper* valley. We'd rather *ta-ake* our chances with the Coelophysis and the natives than the *sauros*."

The bot shivered at the mere mention of the word. Nathan was starting to understand how fearful the Saurosuchus species was to the Triassic inhabitants. Thinking about the dreaded animal made Nathan, for a brief moment, appreciate his current protection behind the Neolithic fortress.

"I take it the *sauros* aren't your favorite fauna to come across?"

"Not in the *least-t-t*, kid. That's what *has-s* me worried about this mission. Where *your-r-r* ship *cra-a-ashed* is in the same *vicinity* as the *sau-u-ro* territory. It's my sincere hope that *af-ter* we get *out-t-t* of here, we don't encounter any of those monstrous *thi-ings* on the way to your ship."

"As long as you're confident that we're getting out of this mess," Nathan said, blinking away a tear of uncertainty. "I'm glad you seem to think this situation is only temporary. *Ah*, I'm barely holding it together, Jordy. Do me a favor, will you?"

"*Anything-g.*"

"Don't tell any of the adults that I'm crying right now. I don't want them to think I'm a pussy."

"*Colorful-l* language, Nathan," the bot scowled. "*Tisk-tisk*, but *your-r* secret is safe with *me-e.*"

"Thanks, Jordy."

"*No-o* problem. Just *co-o-ool* it with the language, will you?"

With that, Nathan managed to get a hold on his tears, using the pent up frustration as a way to start fiddling with the ropes.

Sitting here waiting for death doesn't sound very productive, Nathan thought. *Might as well do something to pass the time...*

Jordy sat there beside him and cheered him on and encouraged his progress, and at that moment, Nathan knew that he had made a lifelong friend.

#

"What happened?" Adam slurred, starting to finally rouse from his daze.

"The natives captured us," Severine whispered, sitting beside her drowsy companion. "You were probably struck with a poison dart – a common weapon deployed by the Neolithics to induce paralysis. It's basically the primitive equivalent of chloroform. Listen, Adam, you've got to snap out of your funk, and do it now! We're completely bound up in here. They're probably going to kill me – I think I may have angered their chieftain. On top of that, they have the others, including your nephew."

"What?" Adam said, regaining his vocal abilities. "Did you see where they took the others?"

"Your nephew and Jordy are in a hut right across from the chief's throne near the center of the village. I think the others are in a hut directly behind Jordy's hut. And if I remember correctly, our weapons are stashed in another hut right beside Jordy's as well. They must be using the dwellings closest to the chief's throne as prisoner holding cells for the sacrificial ceremony."

"*Sacrificial ceremony!*" Adam shrieked, finally snapping to reality.

"You heard me," Severine said urgently. "They'll probably slit our throats or burn us alive. Trust me, their ceremonies used to be a whole lot worse – I won't even go into it. Just focus on getting out of here!"

BRAWLLLL!

A primitive trumpeting sounded somewhere outside their dwelling.

"Oh *shit!*" Severine yelped. "Native horn calls! It won't be long now. Hurry! Start trying to sever your ropes. Bite them if you have to! At this point, it doesn't matter if they hear us. They're probably on their way to yank us out right now to the courtyard!"

Outside the dwelling, Adam began to hear the faint shuffling of sandals on soil. The horn calls continued, complemented by the faint rustling of a bonfire starting not far outside the hut's walls.

"Please tell me you have some kind of plan besides biting through ropes?" Adam asked.

"Are you kidding me?" Severine turned. "Of course I do! You're talking to the woman who had an escape tunnel ready for Deckard's firebombing. Obviously, I have a plan for escape. I just need my damn hands to make it work. Now do as I say, Ross! Do you want to live or do you want to be cooked for some barbarian's entree?"

"*Live*," Adam replied in shock. "Definitely live."

"Then get to it!"

Suddenly the rickety wooden door to the shack flew open. A pair of armed, rugged natives barged in and severed the prisoners' conjoining ropes and the ropes tied to the rocks. They left the bindings joining their wrists and feet intact as Severine was lifted to her feet. Adam was flung up a second later and together they were prodded back out into the clearing, horrified by what may be awaiting them.

#

Through a pair of ancient digital Federation binoculars that surprisingly still operated at near perfect precision, Delios Deckard watched the primitive ritual unfold from a safe distance.

So, that's where their camp has been hiding, he thought, adjusting his focus to the central pyre that burned in the middle of the fortress.

"Right under our noses," Tanner replied from behind him, hiding behind some large palm fronds. "My scouting party lost track of them just west of here in the jungle when we found traces of many footprints that didn't have the regular Federation boot impression. Thankfully, the rainstorm from earlier made it fairly straightforward to track. Surprised we didn't find this fortress sooner, and so close to our base camp."

"We found it at just the right time," Deckard replied coldly. "We can squash this annoying Neolithic tribe once and for all and conduct my vengeance to Severine all in one powerful blow!"

The Exile warlord smiled as he saw Severine and another male forced out into the clearing, waiting for whatever sacrificial horror awaited them.

"Do you want us to hold off the attack until the natives finish the job for you?" Tanner asked.

"No, I'd like to deal with her personally. Tell the archers to take up their positions around the camp – use firebombs if they have to but no detonators or pulse weapons. No use in wasting valuable pulse rounds on these buffoons. After they're all dead or scattered, we'll move in and capture Severine and her co-conspirator."

"Yes, sir," Tanner replied, trotting away to fulfill the tyrant's tasks.

"*Eucer?*" Deckard beckoned his engineer nearby.

"How can I be of service?" Eucer asked, brushing away strands of greasy hair as he appeared through the vegetation.

"Is our little project ready to go?"

"Yes. All systems operational."

"Good. When I give the order, I want you to send a blast into the village. Nowhere near the middle, I don't want to risk shooting my prize by accident. Perhaps somewhere near the gate. Just enough to show how big our dicks are, got it?"

"It will be done," replied the lackey, walking away briskly to prepare the weapon.

Deckard turned again to the binoculars and continued his espionage, waiting for the opportune moment to make his move. Everything was coming together. He would crush both the Neolithics and his arch nemesis. As he went on, imagining his future unchallenged reign over the Triassic jungle, a final wicked thought fleeted over him.

I've got you now, Severine! You can't rabbit-tunnel your way out of this one!

XV

Ooof!

With a firm thrust, Severine was pushed out into the central clearing of the Neolithic village. The hidden colony in the forest was now aglow with torches and pyres. Hundreds of hateful gazes and arched eyebrows met her stare as she was pushed through the mob. Her vision narrowed on the enormous fiery pyramid in the middle, and she knew where she was being herded.

As the confusion swelled from all sides, she began to continue her struggle subtly with her wrist bindings. A few cord snapping sounds told her that the ropes were very old, and could be cut with ease. Her only problem – if she managed to remove them, she still had the ankle ropes to deal with.

I doubt the natives would let me remove those as well.

BRAWLLL!

A familiar horn call rang out, met with several others as the cheering grew louder. A quick look behind her revealed that Adam was only a few steps away, trying to ward off the many spear tips that were being shoved carelessly at his head.

"Get your hands off me!" he yelled, shoulder-butting one away, providing temporary relief before they clubbed him in the back.

"You prehistoric *fu* –"

WHAM!

Another club caught the back of his head, sending him tumbling submissively to the ground.

Severine chose a different approach. Her silence on the outside portrayed a helpless prisoner scared to die, but on the inside, she searched for an opening – a way out.

Distraction! I need a distraction. Damn, if there weren't so many of them to rescue I could just slip through a gap in the fortress walls. I can't leave them behind! They were going to save me and get me out of this mess!

She gave a quick stare back at Adam, her only hope in helping her with this predicament.

Come on, Adam! Get up! Get up...

Her new found friend remained face down in the moist soil, surrounded by the boisterous cretins. He slowly tried to get up, but the club wound to the back of the head took out the remainder of his reserve energy.

BRAWLLL!

130

More horn calls began to swell in the fortress. Severine could see other members of the tribe, including young children, coming out from their urban dwellings to watch the night execution. Around her, where the huts began to ascend up the slope to the southern fortress wall, she soon realized the entire hillside was crawling with the army.

So many more than I anticipated at Supernova. I thought I killed most of them! It was only the tip of the iceberg...

WHAM!

"*Augh!*" Severine cried as a surprise blow to her back sent an electric painful shockwave up her spine.

One of her captors swatted her with the rod of a spear. She fell forward on her face. As she tried to get up, she felt the points of the spears, and knew they meant for her to remain planted in the ground. A pair of withered sandals appeared at her forefront. The chieftain was standing above her, dressed in ceremonial primitive garments.

"*Upe!*" the shaman yelled angrily.

She was yanked back to her feet, up from her forced bow of respect and shoved forward, again coming face to face with the overweight king of the natives. He was now covered in warpaint, holding a long spear that was almost twice as tall as his own height. Directly behind him, the pyre blazed to a bright orange, wrapping his silhouette in warm, brooding lighting. All around the bonfire, the natives chanted and waved their weapons in anticipation of her fiery death, battling for a front row seat of the action.

BRAWLLL!

"*Ee-noff!*" yelled their impatient leader.

The celebratory chanting ceased, replaced only by the loud crackle of the pyre. The overweight ruler beckoned with his free hand to the grunts on the outskirts of the pyre pyramid.

"Hut opeen' door. Jungole invadar watch!"

Four Neolthics raced around to the other edge of the fire, behind Severine and Adam. Swiftly they opened the doors to an adjacent dwelling, revealing Alex, Kara, Brandy, and Wyatt. Another pair of hunters hurried over to a second hut and opened the entrance, where Jordy and Nathan looked out in horror at the unfolding action.

At the ground a few feet away, Adam tried again to rise up and stop the massacre, only to once again be swatted down. The rod cracked him hard this time, causing him to roar in agony.

"*Run!*" Adam yelled, barely able to breathe as a sandal-covered foot shoved him roughly.

I wish I could, Severine thought, still fiddling with her wrist ropes.

"*Jungole invadar!*" the chieftain went on. "Now tis pay fur killing tis colony! *Moof! Upe!*"

Her movements quickened on the wrist ropes, but she was probably a minute or more away from actually being able to remove them. Then there was the issue of the ankle ropes, but now she was running out of options. Something had to be done – her death awaited her only a few feet ahead.

The chief stepped aside as a kick to Severine's back shot her forward. She landed in the dirt again, inches away from the first flame of the pyramid of burning wood. A trickle of embers shot out in a plume of flame, nipping her cheek and causing her to jump back. The act caught laughter from the crowd, who had once again resumed the death chant, banging their spears together in celebration and calling to the moon somewhere above the canopy.

BRAWL!

DA-DUM! DA-DA-DUM! DA-DUM-DUM!

Drums now joined the grim horn calls. Around her, she could see the sharpened pikes closing in. It was either commit suicide by burning alive or take four javelins to the chest. There was no way she could undo both her wrist bindings and ankle ropes without them noticing and killing her anyway. Behind them, the chieftain awaited, a look of satisfaction coming over his face.

Do I close my eyes for this? Or will I make my last stand like the brave Federation soldier that I am? I suppose it doesn't matter anymore. I won't burn. They'll have to run me through before I endure those flames!

"Get it over with," she said, spreading her arms.

As the warriors closed in, the pikes about to pierce her abdomen, she noticed a bright orange light beginning to envelop her vision. The light appeared small at first, but soon rocketed toward her from above the canopy.

Is this the after life? But I'm not dead yet...

WHOOOSH!! VRRR!

The ray of orange light flashed quickly, and Severine realized that she wasn't the target. The blast crashed into a section of Neolithic dwellings behind her attackers, missing the huts containing her friends but instantly killing many of the unsuspecting natives that loitered nearby.

A Federation artillery blast? Impossible! All the Federation weapons that big were destroyed in the Supernova crash years ago!

Without warning, a hailstorm of arrows began sailing down over the fortress walls, raining down terror and confusion on those trapped inside. The entire clearing around the pyre erupted with frightening chants as the natives scrambled to flee or defend their fortress, abandoning Severine altogether, leaving her standing by the base of the pyre.

Yes!

In a slick, nonchalant motion, she opened her shirt sleeve on her wrist, dropping out a small six-inch knife she smuggled from the *Mudskipper*.

Using the blade with her captors around would have been useless – they would've confiscated the weapon and dealt with her more swiftly. Now with the warriors gone and the village under attack, the time to act had arrived. The blade made quick work of both her wrist ropes and the ankles.

"*Jungole invadars!*" screamed the chieftain, abandoning the ritual sacrifice to command his chaotic, disorganized rabble of followers. "*Tis attecking!*"

It was then that Severine realized that she wasn't who the natives were after.

The Exiles were the '*jungole invaders*'. The Neolothics were at war with Deckard's forces. When the Neolithics captured her, the tribe assumed she was one of the Exile members.

She smiled, reveling in an opportunity for escape.

We're getting out of here!

XVI

Only two of Adam's captors remained in their positions as the barrage of fiery arrows rained down like a storm on the native village. Instinctively, Adam rolled over on his back, just in time to see one of the savages struck through the neck with one of the projectiles, spitting blood over Adam's face as the guard collapsed on his knees.

Against the backdrop of the fiery wave of nonstop arrows landing in the clearing, Adam's last remaining guard looked down at him with an evil grin. Instantly he raised his spear to stab his captive through the chest when Severine appeared behind him, slitting his throat with a small blade and sending him gurgling for life on the ground below.

"*Severine!* What the hell is going on?"

"Deckard's attacking from the outside!" she replied, slicing swiftly through his wrist and ankle ropes.

"*Watch out!*"

She spun around, avoiding a sharp thrust from an advancing Neolithic with a long pike, grabbing hold of it with her free arm. The native yanked her forward, pulling Severine to the ground. Before the brute could deal the killing strike, Adam had retrieved one of his dead captor's spears, throwing it expertly into Severine's assailant. Several onlookers witnessed the spectacle and considered intervening, but were distracted by the oncoming volley of arrows.

Explosions began to rumble throughout the fortress as flaming objects appeared in the air, some catching the overhanging branches ablaze and raining down fire on the village, while others crashed onto the forest floor, igniting the panicking tribesmen.

"Grab a weapon!" Severine ordered, retrieving a fallen club as Adam grabbed a hatchet.

"Let's get my nephew out first!" Adam suggested, gripping the ax tightly in defiance.

"Right! Stay with me!"

Crowds of natives streaked by from both sides as Adam followed Severine toward Nathan's prison dwelling. Structures in the neighboring road behind the crowd were beginning to catch fire. A portion of the outer fortress wall was smoldering near the gate, prompting several natives with primitive buckets to try and hold off the destruction while crowds mobbed the exit.

One Neolithic guard closed the door to Nathan and Jordy's dwelling, failing to notice Severine and Adam rushing behind him.

SPLSHH!

Executing the same motion as before, Severine sliced through his throat and pushed the dying man aside with ease, finishing off the move with a sturdy kick. The door crumpled inward from the force, sending a wave of dust and ash over the two captives inside. Through the dusty air, Adam could see his nephew smile behind a dusty face.

"*Se-e-e*, I told you she'd *c-c-c-ome*," Jordy laughed from his tethered posture.

"Are you okay?" Adam said, hugging his nephew. "They didn't hurt you, did they?"

"I'm fine," Nathan said. "Uncle Adam, I'm sorry about earlier. I guess I just can't be an adult just yet..."

"Hey, it's okay," Adam replied. "I wanted to grow up fast too. Sorry for coming down so hard on you back there. Hang on a second, hold still and – you're free!"

His ax sliced through Nathan's remaining rope knots, just as Severine finished freeing Jordy from his shackles.

"If you two are done with your family reunion we have a burning village we need to escape from," Severine said impatiently, already preparing to flee the hut.

"First we need to free the others! Then we're heading straight for that oscillator! I've had enough of the Triassic for a lifetime."

#

CRACK!

A native entering Alex's holding room was met with surprise as he tripped over Kara's outstretched foot. Having already withered through the ankle and wrist bindings, Alex snapped the native's neck with a skillful twist of his feet by wrapping them around the Neolthic's unprotected head.

"Finally," he sighed, hacking away at Kara and Brandy's ropes with the dead man's hatchet. "I thought I was never going to get an opening!"

"What's the plan now?" Kara asked, peering out the door at the fiery carnage that was laying waste to the village. "Do you see Adam and Severine anywhere?"

"They probably went to free Nathan and her bot," Alex replied. "Our play should be to head for the weapons cache. It should be in one of the neighboring buildings, assuming they haven't all been firebombed to shit by now! After that, we can blast our way out of here and get back to Solis!"

They prepared to flee, but were stopped by a worried voice behind them.

"Hey, wait!" Wyatt yelled, squirming on the floor.

The sergeant struggled frantically with his rope bindings, especially after noticing that the rear of the hut had started to catch fire, spilling thick bursts of smoke into the room as the structure began to deteriorate. Parts of the wall began to melt and crumble onto the floor. The hut wouldn't remain standing for long.

"What do you want?" Brandy turned, enjoying watching him struggle.

"You can't just leave me here!"

"Why not?" Kara asked. "You were going to leave us here! And it wouldn't have been the first time."

More of the dwelling toppled inward. Sparks kicked up from the outside, obscuring the view of Neolithic forms running to and fro to address the ambush. Several figures through the melting structure went down from another round of raining arrow fire, launched from unknown locations outside in the Triassic jungle.

"You can't do this to me, Barnels! I'm a sergeant in the Federation military. And Alex, you've said it before! You want to see me behind bars – not die here under some mongrel's desolate house. Please Meras, let me out! *Please!*"

Alex sighed, turning to the others.

"What do you think? Should I do it?"

"After what that asshole did throughout the past few days?" Brandy remarked. "He's better off dead."

"I think she's right, Alex," Kara added. "He tried to screw us over more times than I can count. He's more of a liability at this point than an asset, but it's your call."

Alex grumbled, walking over to Wyatt and holding out the hatchet to his face.

"Don't screw with me, Wyatt," Alex said sternly, the heavy words foreshadowed by the collapse of another structure just outside. "I've had enough of your shit! If you try to screw us over one more time, I'm putting this hatchet into that thick skull of yours. Believe me, at this point it'd be my pleasure for all the shit you caused us! Do we have an understanding?"

"Yes, yes, of course, Meras," Wyatt nodded swiftly.

Alex chopped away at the rope bindings, freeing Wyatt to stand up.

"What about the Federation cuffs?" Wyatt asked before they could leave the hut.

"Are you kidding me?" Kara blurted out. "The cuffs stay on!"

"There's a war zone out there right now, Barnels!" Wyatt yelled back. "Shit, it's raining arrows and grenades. Cut my cuffs off and I can be useful! I can get a weapon and we can shoot our way to the *Harvester One* crash!"

"Wyatt, *enough!*" Alex ordered. "The cuffs are staying on. I wasn't born yesterday!"

"Meras, please –"

WHAM!

Alex planted a swift backhand to Wyatt's cheek. The sergeant shot a wicked glare at his former corporal, but was powerless to protest any further.

"No more shit from you!" Alex yelled. "Now we're getting out of here, getting the guns, joining up with the others, and getting to the oscillator. Then, as soon as we're back on Solis, I'm making sure you're walked straight up to Central Command for your court-martial."

"Very well," Wyatt replied with a resentful stare, before Alex tugged him by the hand and led them out of the structure, seconds before it collapsed into embers.

#

"Over here!" Adam yelled over the deafening screams and burning debris.

He saw that Alex, Kara, Brandy, and Wyatt had vacated their imprisoned structure and were lost in the shuffle of turmoil that engulfed the village. Dozens of burning and arrow laden corpses lined the marred ground, even as more firebombs and projectiles continued to rain down, slaughtering more of the Neolithics that remained in the center of their micro civilization.

"Lieutenant, what's the plan?" Alex asked as the two groups conjoined together under the sanctuary of a withered pavilion area.

"Our weapons are being held in that hut over there," Adam pointed. "Don't ask me why, but four of those little cocksuckers are still guarding it, even though their village and civilization are completely lost. Half the population has already fled into the jungle."

A short distance away across the road, a surviving hut free of flames was being watched by a squad of Neolithics. Judging by their nervous looks and constant communication, Adam deduced they were probably panicking, and would thus be easy to strike down.

"What's happening?" Brandy asked, eyeing the destruction that surrounded them.

"It's Deckard's forces!" Severine explained. "Remember, I told you about them. This is exactly why they can't be allowed back to Solis! If we don't leave soon, the arrows will kill us all! He won't stop until everyone remaining inside is gunned down."

"Which means we need to get our weapons and hit the road!" Adam deduced. "I suggest that we retrieve whatever weapons we can from the dead. Then we ram them so far up those guards' assholes, take our pulse weapons back and make for the twin valleys!"

WHOOOSH!! VRRR!

Another massive orange blast struck a cluster of dwellings not far from the weapons cache, sending burning splinters shotgunning out in all directions. A passing squad of hunters took the brunt of the splintering house, squealing their last breaths as they perished in the ensuing heatwave.

Deckard has some unreal firepower somewhere out there! Adam thought. *It has to be some kind of Federation anti-aircraft or anti-starship weapon, but what?*

"Are you sure we need those weapons?" Brandy asked, eager to avoid another conflict with the natives.

"If we're heading down to the valleys, there's a good chance we may run into some sauros," Severine replied. "If that's the case, then yeah, we're going to want the comfort of Federation firepower in our hands."

"Sounds like a good plan to me," Alex said, gripping his hatchet. "Ready when you are, boss."

"Okay, everyone, form up behind me," Adam said. "Maybe they'll see how many of us there are and just let us pass. We're gonna have to take them fast – you see what kind of firepower the Exiles have. We're sitting ducks with that cannon around, whatever it is! And those archers aren't letting up from the outside. Let's move!"

WHOOOSH!! VRRR!

Another hut exploded in a fiery blast, shooting splintery embers at the native guards as they watched in jealousy at their tribesmen who ran past without assigned tasks, able to escape the besieged fortress. The distraction served as a useful tool for Adam, who used their disorganization to lead the attack.

WHISHHH!

Adam buried the hatchet into the first native's arm, before turning the weapon back in another hacking pose, swinging the blade into the man's hairy neck, dealing the killing blow. Before the Neolithic squad could prepare an adequate defense, Alex already had his hatchet embedded in the skull of the second defender. After Severine quickly dispatched the third guard, the fourth tumbled backwards, his face washing over in fright before he slipped away into the scorched landscape.

With the squad removed from the entrance, Adam flung the door open, finding their weapons resting on a table unguarded. Ignited roofing fragments began to fall onto the table from the ceiling, spawning small fires. Thankfully, the weapons were left untouched.

He tossed Severine her X2, Alex his ECSR-20 and Kara her ECP-30.

"Jordy, which way out of the fortress is the fastest, safest route?" Severine asked as they exited the weapon storage hut.

"*Impos-s-sible* to tell, *Sev-v*," Jordy answered, looking around nervously for falling debris. "Too *man-n-ny* lifeforms around, both inside and *out-tside* the village. My recommendation: continue, southeast to the *sh-i-i-p.*"

"Good enough for me!" Severine replied.

"If we're going southeast, there's a portion of the wall down near the southern edge," Kara said, pointing ahead. "Looks like no natives are left guarding it. What do you think, Adam?"

"I think it's our best shot," Adam responded, observing the destroyed wall and waving them onward.

Deckard's firebombing had laid waste to most of the Neolithic town. Charred buildings and crumpled shelters were left smoking as the flames smoldered into the soil. Neolithic women herded their children toward numerous openings in the fortress walls that opened up from the siege. The arrow hailstorm had ceased, replaced only by the occasional burning projectile.

Almost there!

The opening that Kara noticed grew close, only another row of houses away. The area that had once been part of the lumber wall collapsed inward minutes earlier, crushing two dwellings on the inside.

"Corporal Alex, watch out!" Adam heard Nathan cry behind them.

"*Augh!*" Alex yelled as a hidden Neolithic jumped out from a nook in a dwelling. Sticking out of Alex's right arm was a small knife, spurting blood from where the grip met flesh. A quick blast from Severine's X2 sent the native spiraling onto the blackened earth, rendering the attacker a lifeless corpse.

"Let me see!" Kara said, pushing aside the others and examining the wound.

"Damn buffoon almost made me drop my rifle," Alex remarked, wincing as Kara looked at the wound.

"Is it bad?" Brandy asked.

"Of course it's bad, dumb bitch," Wyatt snapped.

"*Wyatt!*" Adam yelled. "Kara, can you examine it from the outside? This place is falling apart. Deckard's forces will be moving in here soon!"

"Okay," Kara said. "I'll just use the light from Jordy's external panels. Alex, we're going to leave the blade in for now. I can't tell if an artery's cut or not. I'll look at it again when we're in the jungle."

The sniper nodded, gritting his teeth as he peered at the dagger.

"I won't let a little butter knife like that take me down."

Adam was the first to reach the broken fraction of fortress wall. Beyond the ramparts, the dark jungle stretched in all directions, except for a few external fires that clung to lush vines near the fortress edge. There were no signs of any hidden Neolithics or the Exiles.

"*An-n-n-ything*, Adam?" Jordy asked.

"Nothing," the lieutenant replied. "Alex, let's get you patched up."

#

Streaking greenery surged past Severine as she led them down a serpentine trail into the darkness. The trail gradually widened into a small open area under the dark canopy. Behind, the fires from the Neolithic village had materialized into small orange bokeh circles. Cries from the burning victims were audible, but hard to decipher through the foliage.

"Okay, Kara," Adam said, collapsing on a log from exhaustion. "What can you do about that knife?"

"Alex, sit here," Kara pointed to a large rock. "Jordy, can you shine some light on his knife? Thank you. Okay, let's see what we've got here. *Wow*, yeah. It's in there pretty good."

Kara produced a small, chrome metal medical instrument. A viewing monitor was mounted to one side with a scanner on the other, both of which funneled into a handy grip with an operational trigger. She descended the instrument up and down the sniper's arm one time, focusing on the afflicted area.

"It missed an artery," Kara announced, which was met with some applause and encouraging statements from the audience. "I'm going to pull it out. Are you ready?"

SSSHHHH!

Before Alex could answer, Kara pulled the knife out from the arm. Severine was surprised that the sniper never uttered a single moan. The medical specialist handed him the weapon to examine, before Alex tossed it aside.

"How primitive," came the soldier's blunt remark.

Kara slapped a strip of gauze with adhesive around the wound. The strip reddened, but the blood flow began to slow down.

"He'll be fine?" Brandy asked.

"Should be," Kara said. "We'll be back at Solis soon, he'll get actual help there. How far are these twin valleys?"

"Maybe a few more miles inland," Severine answered. "If we don't run into any sauros, we'll be home-free."

"Don't forget about Exiles," came a sudden voice, the caller camouflaged within the shrouded jungle.

They spun around to see a beautiful woman disperse from the dark vegetation. Initially masked in darkness which kept her concealed, she came forward into the traces of moonlight through the canopy. Her face was attractive yet serious. There was an arrogance to her saunter.

"Arien," Severine leered, leveling her X2 toward her opponent. "I should've known I'd bump into you again."

"Lucky you," Arien smirked.

Fifteen Exile operatives hidden in the darkness made themselves known. Previously unseen, they stepped forward out of the night, relieving Severine of her pistol before snatching the weapons from the others.

"I should've killed you when I thought I killed Deckard," Severine said, begrudgingly handing over her firearm. "I won't make that mistake twice. Still doing his bidding, I presume?"

"My rank and purpose in the Exiles will soon be changing, I assure you," Arien smiled, bringing herself close to Severine's face.

"Why didn't you kill us in the village?" Alex asked.

"And who might you be? There are many more of you than expected. We thought there were just four of you, yet eight I see here."

"Alex Meras," the sniper replied, grabbing his wound in agony.

"Well, Alex," Arien went on, "Deckard specifically requested that you weren't to be harmed. Of course, that's easier said than done when you're hurling firebombs and arrows at a village and have no idea what you're aiming at."

"Did you kill all of them?" Brandy asked.

"That was the intent," Arien replied. "Unfortunately, there were many more than we anticipated. We've been picking them off the map for a while, and just when we think we almost have them all, another colony springs up out of the ashes. Most from today's raid perished from the arrows, but a large group did manage to slip back to the jungle. We'll find them eventually. They're barbarians, and they need to be dealt with."

"So why don't you just kill us?" Adam asked.

"And who might you be?"

"Adam Ross. Lieutenant with the Federation Watch Force and acting commander of this operation."

"I see. Well, Adam Ross, killing you would be my personal pleasure. Alas, our team was told that your capture might be more valuable than your demise, especially pertaining to the events of the last couple of days. Trust me, when we've used up your worth, I'll be glad to put a pulse round in you myself. Consider it an honor – pulse weapons are rare to come by in the Triassic. Your weapons will be put to good use."

"Oh, how *delightful*," Adam glared at her scornfully.

Arien laughed, egged on by her reinforcements as they closed in around their targets.

"I like this one," she laughed. "He's like the male version of Severine. Ball-busting and brave. Deckard will find you amusing as well. Who knows, maybe you and I can have a little fun later – if we let you live long enough, that is. Odds are, we'll kill you with the rest of them."

"I'd rather take my chances with a sauro," Adam replied bluntly.

"You may yet get your wish," Arien said, waving them on. "Anyway, let's get this over with. Deckard has been waiting for you, Severine."

XVII

"Which way, Arien?"

"I don't know, Juane. All your babbling is putting more stress on me than it's worth. Wait, here we go. Everything looks the same in this jungle at night."

The Exiles pushed their hostages through a final patch of ferns, revealing a large game trail nestled in the lowlands area of the forest. Several other Exiles were standing guard in the road, but Deckard and his right-hand men remained unseen.

"Juane, take their weapons to Deckard," Arien ordered one of the gunmen. "Make sure he sees the X2, he'll love having another one of those."

"You got it," replied one of the operatives, hurrying off with the confiscated firearms.

"Well, maybe I'll be seeing you later," Arien said, leering at Severine as she walked past. "But knowing Deckard, your history with him, and what he's got planned for you, I wouldn't count on it."

"Count yourself lucky, bitch," Severine said, staring her down. "Actually, I hope to catch up with you very soon."

"Maybe you'll get your chance," Arien taunted, sending a wave into the adjacent jungle before disappearing into the brush, leaving her squad alone to guard the hostages.

"Friend of yours?" Adam asked her sarcastically, looking around suspiciously, checking to see if he'd be reprimanded for whispering.

"Not quite," Severine replied. "She has a special place in my heart, right behind Deckard himself."

Where is that old bastard, anyway?

CRUNCHHH! VRRSSHHH!

A row of trees on the other side of the clearing swung forward and collapsed to the earth as a colossal mobile battle station crushed over them. Lights from the vehicle clicked on like spotlights as the machine slid through the trees and into the clearing. Several of the Exiles waved hello to the driver several body-lengths above them. More soldiers remained at the top of the vehicle, operating in small one-man gunnery stations with pulse weapons and longbows, shadowed by the massive twin XP-300 pulse cannons. At the center of the orange tinted cockpit, the devious form of Deckard stood amid the artificial overhead lighting, staring down at them with a satisfactory expression.

"Oh my God," Severine said, staring up at the vehicle in awe. "I never thought I'd see one of these again."

"What is it?" Brandy asked from behind her.

"It's an FATR," Nathan replied, looking up at the monstrous machine. "Painted in shades of green and brown for jungle camouflage, I'm assuming."

How on earth that kid knows what an FATR is, I don't know, Severine thought, impressed again by the child's expanded knowledge.

The vehicle continued its imminent lurch forward, pulled along by a pair of enormous treads that churned the earth around them like a meat grinder. The ground beneath them began to tremble. The soldiers ahead stepped past with haste as the FATR lumbered into the open. With a loud squeal of the braking mechanisms, the machine stopped several yards from Severine, exhaust fuming from the riveted underbelly.

Severine noticed that Nathan's observations had been correct. The vehicle was doused in various green shades of coloration. Green FATRs weren't manufactured by the Federation, so she deduced this was clearly an Exile self-painted variant. Severine realized this adjusted paint job explained why the vehicle was practically invisible under the moonlight when it pushed through the tree line.

Above, Deckard gave a wave to Severine before he disappeared from the cockpit view. The rear hatch opened a second later, and Deckard reappeared with Tanner and a pair of armed guards carrying XR-90s.

"Reunited at last," Deckard said as he strode up to his nemesis, his sword glinting from the moon's blue rays.

"Why didn't you just get it over with in the village?" Severine asked.

"That would've been too easy, Severine," the warlord replied. "For all the trouble you caused me, I wasn't going to let my cannon take you down. I had to make sure that I killed you personally this time. We all know how you have a tendency to escape. So, how do you like my new toy?"

He gestured happily to the FATR, an evil smile cracking across his face.

"Impressive," Severine admitted. "You didn't have this the last time we met. You must've found it somewhere in between, but from where? Certainly not the *Supernova*. There was hardly anything left in the cargo bays when I was last there."

"A good magician never reveals his tricks," Deckard replied. "When we found it, it wasn't in working condition. It took some tinkering, but our lead engineer, Eucer, finally got it working earlier this evening. Eucer, give them a wave."

A wiry-haired man from the cockpit returned a single wave before turning back down to the dashboard consoles, adjusting the hologram settings.

"It's a necessary tool to safely travel down in these regions," Deckard went on. "Being that there are so many dangers in the jungles down here, herreras, coelos, sauros and the like, an armored transport is a must. Now, who are these newcomers? They wear Federation suits unlike any I've ever seen."

"They're not of your concer –"

Deckard whipped her across the face with his one hand. As her face settled, he drew close to her.

"Next time it will be the blade," Deckard whispered harshly. "I wasn't talking to you. It's not polite to interrupt people. You there, you look like you might be in charge! Why don't you introduce yourself and your friends?"

"I'm Lieutenant Adam Ross and yes, I'm in charge. This is Alex Meras, Kara Barnels, Brandy Dietrich, Wyatt Brolen, Jordy, and uh –"

"Your son, I'm assuming."

"My nephew, Nathan Ross."

"And what's your purpose being here?" Deckard went on. "Surely, you've come from unknown hyper-sleep pods from some ship."

"We're part of a rescue operation," Adam admitted. "We've been sent here from the future to locate survivors of the *Supernova* and bring them back home with us, to a planet called Solis."

"Strange that you brought such a young boy with you on this mission."

"We didn't exactly know what we were going to be running into. We didn't know about the Triassic."

"I see. And you arrived here from a ship, I presume? One that must have crashed nearby."

"Yes," Adam replied. "Our ship *Harvester One* crashed here days ago. Our pod, *Burrower,* crashed in the northern jungle highlands. We've been headed down south to find the wreck for supplies. We're marooned here."

He must not want them to know about the portal oscillator device, Severine thought. *Smart, Ross. Very smart.*

"I wasn't aware of such a crash," Deckard raised an eyebrow, turning to his guards. "Any of you notice a starship crash nearby over the past few days?"

Several 'no-sir's' followed from his assembled armed loyalists.

"It crashed in the night hours. You may have experienced something of an earthquake. But it's there, I assure you."

"Where?"

"We're not entirely sure. Our communication specialist identified the location as southeast from the *Burrower* position, nestled in between two valleys."

"Two valleys? Yeah, I know the place. Sauro territory. You'd be better off forgetting the supplies and coming to work with me instead. I offered Severine a similar proposition and she shot me down, taking my arm with her as a parting gift. Isn't that right, Sev?"

"False, actually," Severine responded. "After you forced yourself on me, no such offer was made – as if I'd ever join you. Taking your arm with me was just an added bonus."

Severine could feel his wrathful gaze shift over to her as the warlord raised the rusty blade up to her cheek, pressing just hard enough to draw a speck of blood. The scars on his face made him appear more treacherous, although she didn't regret marking him.

"I'd be careful with your words," Deckard went on. "We may find ourselves alone again, you and I."

"I look forward to it," Severine replied, spitting on him. "I'd like that other arm for a souvenir."

Deckard gritted his teeth in anger, drawing back the bladed arm in a display of rage. Severine stood calmly, awaiting her death as the Exile warlord raised the weapon swiftly to end her life, when a young voice broke the tension.

"So, how did you paint it?" Nathan asked.

Adam attempted to silence him, but the words were already out of the boy's lips, drawing the attention from both the armed guards and Deckard.

"Excuse me?" asked Deckard, lowering the blade and temporarily forgetting about Severine.

"Your FATR. How'd you get it to a green shade? I can't believe that you actually had paint with you."

The warlord lowered the sword, leaving Severine and walking over to Nathan. Adam partially stepped in front of the child, but it didn't stop Deckard's advance.

"Interesting question. I guess it isn't really paint at all, actually. If you douse enough swampy goo onto a vehicle, sooner or later you'll get the discoloration you see here. It took a great many buckets of filth and a lot of manpower to produce these results, but it's that effort that kept our vehicle hidden for so long. What was your name again, kid?"

"Nathan."

"Thank you for noticing our hard work, Nathan. Maybe I'll promote you to work in the vehicle someday when you're old enough. Would you like that? Of course, your adult friends probably won't be coming along. I don't think they appreciate my vehicle like you do. So, what do you say? Think you might want to leave the Federation behind and join the Exiles?"

Adam was about to comment, but a voice behind him broke through first.

"Leave him alone, you asshole."

It was Kara Barnels, who was quickly seized by two of the soldiers for her sudden outburst.

"Hey, take your hands off her –"

Alex Meras' rebuttal was quickly met with the end of an XR-90 rifle stock. The blow knocked the back of his head, sending him slamming into the foliage below, grunting in pain.

"I'm sorry, I forgot your name," Deckard admitted as he walked up to her.

"Kara Barnels. Leave him alone."

"Kara, no," Adam whispered, shooting her a warning look. Kara waved him off, diverting her gaze back to the oncoming warlord.

"I don't think you're in any position to be giving orders," Deckard replied. "It's clear that none of you seem to respect me the way you should. In time, after a series of brutal punishments for your repeated offenses that will undoubtedly arise, you'll learn. But before then, I'll leave you with a visual reminder."

Severine turned, eyeing the warlord in a terror-filled gaze.

No!

Deckard raised his arm sword without warning, causing Kara to wince, raising her hands to block the blow. But instead, the warlord turned left, bringing the sword to a stabbing position and surging his weapon forward.

SPLISHH!

"Aughhhh..."

Brandy gasped, looking down at her chest as Deckard's sword arm rammed through her. With a twisted look of satisfaction, Deckard pulled the weapon out in one slick motion, spilling the woman's blood over the ferns at her feet. Brandy gave one last surprised expression as the color drained from her face. Falling to her knees, she breathed her last, tumbling backwards over the forest floor.

"Good strike, sir," Tanner replied from behind him, commending the tyrant's lunge.

"Thank you, Tanner. It needed to be done. The men would've ravished her beyond recognition. Better to be dealt with now than later, I suppose."

"You bastard," Adam managed, choking back his disbelief. With one hand, he pushed Nathan behind him, offering himself up as a shield between Deckard and his nephew.

"You really think you can stop me?" the warlord laughed. "I find your rebellious nature most humorous. Now, Adam Ross, give me one reason why I shouldn't kill you all right here. It'd be ideal – letting you live might cause you to come back for revenge later."

"I – *uh*, there's supplies in the wreck, *but* –"

"Not good enough," Deckard interrupted. "Tanner, kill that one over there, in the handcuffs. He's probably a traitor anyway, and can't be trusted."

"Aye, sir," Tanner replied, drawing a long machete and moving toward Wyatt to deal the sergeant's final blow.

"Wait, *wait!*" Wyatt pleaded, putting his hands out in self-defense. "You don't want to do that. I promise, there's more in the crash than what Ross is telling you. Much more! A device more valuable than pulse weapons or Federation detonators."

"*Wyatt!*" Alex shouted from the ground, unable to prevent the sergeant's remarks. "You filthy snake!"

"Hold up, Tanner," Deckard ordered, realizing the captive was giving up valuable information. "I think we've struck a nerve here. I don't remember your name, but you've got about ten seconds to tell me what you know, otherwise you're gonna be reunited with the woman over there. Now – what's in this ship wreckage that piques your interest so?"

"No, no please," Wyatt went on. "I'll tell you everything. Our ship, *Harvester One*, is equipped with a device that you aren't familiar with, because our society has advanced more than three hundred years since you crashed here – however you crashed here, that is."

"Get to it!" Deckard roared, pointing his sword at Wyatt's throat.

"Right. *Harvester One* is carrying a new device designed by Federation technicians – the portal oscillator. The oscillator is a device that will literally teleport you back to our home world – you can leave all this madness in the Triassic behind and head directly to the present."

"A *portal oscillator?*" Deckard raised an eyebrow. "Now, that's a new one. How does it work?"

"Charge crystals," Wyatt replied. "It almost functions just like pulse weapons do, but obviously the internal parts are designed differently. It emits a large time portal for a few short seconds, suspended on one end in our reality and on the other end in the future, where you'll end up if you walk into the portal aura. Our communication specialist identified that the device is still on the ship as we speak. Supposedly, it has two portal charges left before it's completely useless."

Deckard turned, eyeing the other hostages.

"Judging by the silence of your peers, I'm guessing this is information that was withheld from me on purpose," the warlord went on. "Clearly, you don't want me going back to your precious future world, do you, Mr. Ross?"

Adam remained silent, staring forward, trying to suppress his burning hatred for Wyatt.

"I'll take that as a yes," Deckard scoffed with a chuckle. "Well, Mr. Tanner, I think this changes things. We may yet find ourselves out of the Triassic after all. Get his cuffs off."

"Yes, sir."

Tanner pressed the barrel of his pulse rifle up to the chain connecting Wyatt's wrist cuffs, pressed the trigger, and disintegrated Wyatt's last remaining bondage.

"Thank you, your excellency," Wyatt groveled, relieved to spread his hands again.

"Don't thank me yet," Deckard replied. "If you don't bring that device back to me in an operational status, you'll be the first one I kill! Okay, everyone, change of plans. Looks like a stay of execution is in order, provided that I get what I want – that portal oscillator device, or whatever the hell you call it! And you are all going to retrieve it for me."

"You ignorant asshole," Severine rebuked him. "What makes you think we'll bring you the oscillator? We'll use it ourselves and go forward in time – leaving you here to die with the sauros."

"Well, the sauros are exactly why I won't be coming with you," Deckard smiled. "I'll be here, comfortable in my FATR while you're all out there sneaking around the sauro nests in the valleys to your ship. And to answer your question, Severine, you'll be bringing it back to me for one reason – leverage."

Two of the guards from the rear stepped forward and snatched Nathan by both arms, hauling him away from Adam before he could fight back. A pair of pulse barrels glanced up toward his head, preventing his nephew's rescue.

"*Hey, let go!*" Nathan barked as the soldiers' hands clasped around his arms, tugging him back from the group.

"*Nathan!*" Adam called angrily, weapons forcing him back. "Hang on, buddy! I'll get you back, I promise. I'm gonna get you back!"

"Let him go!" Kara commanded, silenced quickly by a backhand from one of the guards.

"You don't need the boy, Deckard," Severine cut in. "Take me instead. It's me that you want! I'll take you to the oscillator, just let these people go. They haven't done anything to you. Hell, they ended up here by accident!"

"The fact that they interrupted our cat and mouse game is irrelevant," Deckard shot back. "They're here now, and they'll be put to use! Tanner, take the bot too. His radar components will be of use. Put them both in the FATR and seal them in the rear chamber."

"*Ge-e-et* off, you *dir-r-ty cre-e-eps*," Jordy bellowed, trying to swing away from his captors with no success.

"Uncle Adam, don't let them take me!" Nathan yelled.

"I'll be back for you, Nathan! I promise!"

"*Please!* Don't let them take me!"

VRRRRM.

With the final hiss of the FATR rear door, Nathan and Jordy were sealed inside the mobile command rover, cut off from the others. Severine saw Adam sink forward to his knees, trying to get a grasp on reality and channel some unforeseen energy needed to carry forward without confirmation that his nephew would be safe.

"Don't fret," Deckard said, looking down at Adam in disdain. "No harm will come to him if you just bring me the oscillator as Wyatt described. Fail me, and you'll never see your nephew again. And quite frankly, you probably won't see the bot again. I think he'll be of more use to me than you."

"If you hurt them," Severine threatened him.

"You'll do what?" Deckard taunted. "You're in no position to be making threats, Severine. Now *listen up!* The five of you are going to the downed ship and bringing me back that device! You have up until tomorrow, when the sun is highest in the sky. Severine, bring them to the Mountains of Blood. You remember that area, don't you – where you took my arm?"

"The pleasure was all mine," Severine leered at him.

"Well if you're not there tomorrow, I'll be taking your life," Deckard replied. "And the boy will surely die."

"*No!*" Adam blurted out involuntarily.

"Oh yes, Mr. Ross. I'm sorry you and your nephew were dragged into this mess, but this is the way it has to be. Now, Severine, you remember how to get there?"

"I remember," she admitted. "Just east of the twin valleys."

"Correct," Deckard replied. "Don't fail me."

"We're going into sauro territory," Severine said. "You're joking if you think we'll make it through there without weapons."

"You're right," Deckard laughed. "My mistake. Here you go."

With a gentle motion of the wrist, he dropped a concealed small dagger onto the ground by Severine's feet. The blade looked barely over four inches long.

"You must be joking?"

"I never joke, Ms. Solens. Now, if I were all of you, I'd be getting this mission underway. It'll be dawn before you know it, and you know how agitated the sauros can be in the early mornings."

XVIII

The flickering overhead lighting of the rear compartment of Deckard's FATR made Nathan assume the power cells had just recently been activated, taking time to warm up to properly illuminate the interior compartments.

"Hold out your hands," commanded one of Deckard's rugged thugs.

Jordy attempted to struggle. Nathan obeyed without hesitation. After tying a skillful knot with a steel cord, Jordy and Nathan were once again bound. The soldier cuffed them to a central pole in the FATR rear compartment, before exiting into the middle storage room, closing the motorized hatch behind him.

Nathan tried to block out his terror from again being a hostage to an unknown culture by studying the room. He remembered learning about ancient Federation rovers in history class, but never dreamed he'd have the opportunity to be inside one – even as a hostage.

The rear chamber of the rover was lined with metallic marine lockers, crammed full of looted Exile goods, most of which looked like weaponry or supplies to construct firebombs. Steel benches lined the center of the room where Nathan sat with Jordy, tethered to the pole. On the upper side of the wall where the lockers almost ran into the ceiling, narrow tinted windows looked out into the jungle, although from Nathan's perspective, he saw little more than the dark treetops.

"*Oh-h-h*, my," Jordy said finally, fidgeting with the bindings. "How do we *kee-e-ep* getting ourselves into this mess? We really *ha-a-ave* to stop meeting like *this-s-s*, don't we?"

"Jordy, how are we going to get out of this one?" Nathan asked, his voice cracking with uncertainty. "This isn't some flimsy mud hut from the natives. These FATRs are nearly impenetrable."

"I *mus-s-st* admit, these ropes are a tad *bit-t-t* more difficult to rip apart," Jordy replied. "Don't be afraid, Nathan. *They-y-y-y* came for us once *befor-r-re*, they'll *do-o* it again!"

"This isn't as simple as before," Nathan argued. "Do you know what a Saurosuchus is, Jordy?"

"Regrettably, *yes-s-s*," replied the bot.

"Well, aren't they traveling right into their territory?" the boy asked, shifting on the bench.

"Sauros *ten-n-nd* to prefer the marsh *environmen-n-nts* in this region," the bot replied. "My run-ins with *them-m-m* have been brief over the *ye-e-ears*, but *from-m* what I can recall in *m-my* data bank, yes, they are *known-n-n* to inhabit the area in question."

"How on earth do you think they're gonna get through the Saurosuchus territory unarmed?" Nathan asked. "The sauros are much bigger than the herreras and the coelos. They might have had a fighting chance when there were more of us, like right after the *Burrower* crashed, before most of our team was wiped out. Now with only five of them, one of them being that asshole, Wyatt, I doubt they'll be coming back, Jordy."

"What's the *d-d-deal* with that *Wyat-t-t-t* fellow, anyway?"

"I've been trying to figure that out for the past few days," Nathan replied. "It all started before we crashed here. Wyatt and my Uncle Adam butted heads a few times in space. After our escape pod crashed, Adam basically told Wyatt that he would be calling the shots from here on out – that didn't sit well with Wyatt, who basically freaked out, undermining my uncle every chance he could."

"*Oh-h-h-* dear..."

"Anyway, that's just the beginning. After our first battle with the natives, Wyatt left Adam behind for dead, telling everyone that he made it out alive but that Adam had been killed. That night, when my uncle made it back to camp to confront Wyatt about it, he took me hostage, and told them he'd kill me if... if my uncle tried to get me back."

Come on, don't cry again in front of the bot. He's already been through it once!

Nathan managed to continue the story without crying, much to his astonishment.

"And *I'm-m-m* assuming, since when the *firs-st* time I saw Wyatt that he was *handcuf-f-f-ed*, that somehow your uncle got the best of him?"

"Not exactly," Nathan admitted. "He got me back, but before Wyatt could kill my uncle, a herrera sort of – intervened. We ended up falling into a river, thinking Wyatt was dead. When we saw that Alex, Kara, and Brandy had him handcuffed, I was surprised he made it out alive."

"He's like a cockroach – they just *ke-e-ep* coming *bac-c-ck*," the bot said, causing the boy to laugh.

"I guess so, Jordy."

"I *think-k-k* you're very brave, facing the *man-n-n* who took *you-u*," Jordy praised him. "Maybe we'll *all-l-l* get lucky and a sauro will *get-t-t* him, and only the *go-o-od* ones will make *it-t* back."

"I couldn't agree more," Nathan replied. "But suppose they even do make it past the sauros and find the portal oscillator – assuming it still works after the crash. What's stopping Deckard from just shooting them when they get back?"

"You're *full-l-l* of questions, kid, you *know-w-w* that?" the bot chuckled. "I wish I *had-d-d* all the answers. Unfortunately, I *don't-t-t* work that way. All we can do *now-w-w* is bide our time and hope we don't *pis-s-s* any of these ruffians off. But, at least in this-*s-s situation*, we have one potential *mov-v-ve*."

"We do?" Nathan whispered. "What's that?"

"*Well-l-l*, suppose we get *fre-e-e*. And let's also suppose that none of these trigger-happy psychos *dec-ci-ci-cides* to shoot us first. Simple – the firebombs in *the-e-e* storage lockers. We *smash-h-h* them open in here. The *emergenc-c-cy* doors might open if the *insides-s-s* flood with *smok-k-ke*. Best *of-f-f* all, we'll have the satisfaction that we royally *screw-w-wed* up Deckard's ride."

"Jordy," Nathan smiled, "I like the way you think."

#

In the crystal blue rays of the moonlight, Deckard stared down at the murderous blade – the tool he used to replace what Severine left behind after she took his arm. As he stared down at the useful appendage, he caught one last look of Severine and her four unlikely conspirators as they snaked into the trees, heading for the pair of valleys where the fabled *Harvester One* wreckage supposedly rested. Severine's brutal death by his sharpened arm would be postponed once again – but if it meant finally escaping these accursed lands, it would be more than appropriate.

If a sauro gets her instead of me, I'll be fine with that, he thought, laughing to himself under his breath.

The prospect of finally being rid of the prehistoric lifestyle that he and his warriors had come to know brightened his spirits, but the idea of Severine using the oscillator for her own good to escape from his grasps forever made his blood boil.

I must have my revenge. If she makes it past the sauros and escapes to the future – I'll never have my chance!

As he mused over what to do, footsteps from behind Deckard made him turn. It was Brine, one of Deckard's trusted foot soldiers. Despite his loyalty, the soldier was nowhere near being ready to shoulder any serious responsibility.

"You wanted to see me, sir?" Brine said. "They passed out of our range. I'm here to inform you that they are well beyond earshot."

"Good," Deckard replied. "Very good, Brine. You have the makings of a loyal Exile. Please go and fetch Arien for me. She has a new mission that she must be assigned."

"It will be done," Brine replied, rushing off to find Deckard's notorious third-in-command.

After a minute, Arien's slender form materialized out of the trees, heading over to Deckard's position beside the FATR in an area heavily illuminated by the rover's security lights.

"Yes, sir?" Arien said, in a surprisingly subservient tone.

"I'm assuming you've heard everything that transpired from your place in the trees?" Deckard asked.

"Yes, quite clearly. They arrived here on a rescue mission and their ship contains a piece of precious cargo that would serve as more valuable under your possession."

"Correct," Deckard went on. "A portal oscillator – ever heard of it?"

"No, sir. Doesn't ring a bell. Must be a new piece of Federation technology from wherever they came from."

"Evidently, it's what we've been waiting for, after all these years. A device that can transport us out of this hellhole and back to somewhere civilized. At the moment, we have a bit of leverage that tells me our little friends will play by the rules."

"The boy?"

"The boy and the bot," Deckard went on, "but there's no way of telling what will happen on their way to the downed ship. Severine might try to get cute and use the device for herself, and then both my chance of revenge and our chances of escaping will be lost forever with that device. I want you to go after them with a strike team. Make sure to keep an eye on them, and kill them if they try to use the oscillator. It only has a certain number of uses. If they manage to get the device out safely, kill them all and bring the device back to me. Oh, actually, change that slightly. Kill them all – except Severine. Bring her back to me. I'll be waiting at the Mountains of Blood."

"You want me to follow them through sauro territory with only a *small* strike force?" Arien asked. "That's suicide! You'll expend most of our team – myself included. Not to mention how it will be morning when we catch up with them. Sauros are most active in the morning."

"That's not my problem, Arien."

"Why don't you just follow them in the FATR?"

Deckard laughed.

"You must be out of your mind. I'd never send the FATR into the swamps. Water is detrimental for these ancient rovers. You'll have to go in on foot and finish the job."

"I'll need a rather large strike team to carry out the mission," Arien argued. "A small stealth team won't cut it. I'll need at least twenty of our soldiers to properly carry out your objective."

"*Twenty*?" Deckard asked as if she offended him. "That's almost *half* of our remaining force! I'll give you fifteen – fifteen only. Take Brine with you, he's a true loyalist. And Juane, you seem to work well with him. He's more aggravating when he's around anyway. I won't care if a sauro finishes him off."

Arien offered a faint chuckle.

"You really think there's a downed Federation ship in those swamps?"

"We have no reason to doubt their story," Deckard replied. "They certainly come from somewhere other than *Supernova*. Their outfits are different than ours, and their weapons are more advanced. I'll enjoy experimenting with their pulse firearms – especially that sniper rifle."

"And this portal device?" Arien asked. "You think that's real too?"

"Why not?" Deckard answered. "I'm liable to believe anything at this point. When someone tells you about a magical device that can transport you out of the Triassic – you take it as reality, no questions asked."

"Almost sounds *too* good to be true."

"Let's pray that it is true, and that by tomorrow, we'll all be getting on with our lives in a much happier place. Well, besides Severine, that is. Anyways, start forming up your team and begin to tail them. But not too close – I don't want them knowing that they're being followed until they've retrieved the oscillator."

"Yes, sir," Arien smiled, turning and vanishing back into the jungle, ready to gather what warriors she could to follow Severine.

Deckard watched her go, eagerly fantasizing about how the events of the night might play out in his mind.

It's a win win. If Severine and her friends make it back with the oscillator, I'll kill them all anyway. If Severine and her friends die in the sauro territory, that's excellent as well. Maybe I'll get lucky, and the sauros will finish Arien off for me as an added bonus.

He clapped his hands with glee and headed for the FATR rear hatch, ready to depart for the rendezvous point – the Mountains of Blood.

\#

Arien pushed through a Triassic fern patch, stepping into a quiet clearing in the woods that housed a collection of thirty or so small tents, built to look like subtle rocky clusters but serving as the Exiles' temporary sleeping quarters. The beauty of having a mobile encampment was that they could pack up and leave anytime they wanted, moving their sect to various locations across the Triassic jungles.

Where is that asshole at now? Probably set up his tent farther away from the others, hoping for a little late-night nooky from me. Oh Juane, how pathetic are you? Seriously?

After she waved to a pair of armed sentries sitting on a boulder, Arien focused her attention to an isolated tent on the banks of a small creek, situated just beyond the other subtle shelters in the central clearing. A pair of erect torch stands illuminated the tent opening, revealing Juane's snoozing form, right beside his long bow and pulse rifle.

As Arien entered the tent, Juane stirred but failed to wake up. She issued a gentle kick that produced the same result, followed by a swift, rough kick that got the job done.

"*Augh!* Arien, what the hell's the matter with you?" Juane asked, turning in his sleeping bag. "I almost *knifed* you! Don't do that again!"

"Be quiet, Juane!" Arien cut in. "Now, shut up and listen! Deckard captured Severine and the others today. It turns out, there were eight of them all together. Now there's seven – Deckard killed one of the women!"

"Was she pretty?" Juane asked, striving to irritate her further.

"*Quiet!*" Arien rasped. "Before Deckard could kill any more of them, they confessed to something! Something that's just changed everything for you and me. In the valleys near the edge of the jungle, near the swamps, there's a downed ship. In that ship there's a device that acts as a time-jumper of sorts. If we get our hands on it, we're out of this mess for good! Deckard has ordered the newcomers to go and retrieve it for him!"

"What about Deckard and the others?"

"*Forget them!*" Arien went on. "Juane, do you understand what I'm saying? This is a golden opportunity for us to escape! Deckard has assigned me to go after them with a small team of gunmen to watch over the operation to make sure they don't use it to jump back themselves, leaving us in the dust with the sauros."

"How does Deckard expect them to keep their word?" Juane asked, waking up at the excitement of their news.

"He's taken two of their own hostage in the rover."

"I see, and what about the sauros?"

"What about them?"

"Won't they serve as a problem for us when we go and relieve Severine of this device?"

"Not if we blast our way through them. I've been instructed to take up to fifteen warriors with us. That should be enough to handle the sauros long enough for us to snatch and use the device before Deckard knows what's hit him!"

"Is Severine armed?"

"With a little knife, yeah," Arien laughed. "I hope to put a pulse round in her myself before this is over. But in all seriousness, I have no doubt in my mind that the sauros will get to all of them long before they ever reach the wreckage. None of them know the region, with the exception of Severine. Without their bot for radar guidance, I doubt they'll get very far."

"And this ship crashed in the twin valleys?" Juane asked, putting on his armor. "It's a wonder none of us have stumbled on it until now. It's so close by!"

"Well be thankful that we know about it now," Arien went on. "And best of all, Deckard doesn't know about our plans –"

A large, muscular man pushed his way through the tent opening. Juane hid behind his clothes, shielding his naked form from the newcomer, awkwardly using his hands to block his genitals as he slid his armor plated pants on.

"Ever hear of knocking, Tanner?" Juane asked. "Or does being Deckard's bitch give you special privileges?"

Tanner stared him down in an expressionless gaze of impatience, before turning the stare over to Arien. Her last sentence was still jumbled up in her throat. As Deckard's ruthless enforcer eyed them, she wondered if perhaps the big lug heard too much. Finally, the muscle-bound man spoke, ending the stalemate.

"Deckard wanted me to inform you both to keep a careful eye on things down in the swamp," Tanner said. "Sauros have been responsible for many Exile-related deaths in the past years. You'll be going head-first into an area known for its frequent Saurosuchus sightings."

"We'll be careful," Arien acknowledged with a nod, still trying to figure out if he heard too much.

I can't kill him here. Not with all these other tents around. It will arouse too much suspicion.

"Have you picked your team yet?" Tanner went on, shifting back to Juane.

"We were just about to do that," Juane replied, "before you barged in here like an ox. Now, can I get dressed in peace, please?"

"Hurry up," Tanner barked. "Deckard wants your team to depart immediately before Severine and her allies get too far ahead. We don't want to lose them in the jungle."

Tanner shot Arien and Juane a final look of seriousness before slipping through the slit in the tent, the sounds of his Federation boots cracking among the ferns as he headed back to the rover where he was stationed.

"Do you think he heard what you were saying?" Juane asked.

"I don't think so," Arien said when she confirmed he was gone. "He would've said something if he did – or probably would've killed us for treason. Either way, our urgency on this swamp quest just increased tenfold! I'm more anxious than ever to get out of here now."

"What do you want me to do?" Juane said, picking up his pulse rifle and shouldering his hiking gear.

"Go and get some of the usual Deckardian rebels," Arien ordered. "At least fifteen of them, and meet me by the fork in the creek in five minutes. If they give you any trouble, tell them we'll explain it on the hike there. Make sure they're armed with something other than longbows. If we have to fight our way out of there, I'd rather do it with something other than arrows. Understand?"

"Yeah?"

"Good, see you soon."

"Hey, Arien?"

"What?"

"Any chance that before we set out on this potentially deadly situation, we can sneak in a real quick one before we depart? It could be the last time, after all?"

Arien shot him a blunt look, unable to form words for her lover's stupidity.

"Just get the damn soldiers, will you, Juane? There will be time for that when we get out of here!"

"Fine," Juane grumbled, pushing past her into the night.

That is, if I don't leave your sorry ass here instead, Arien thought, stepping back into the moonlight.

XIX

Delios Deckard arrived in the cockpit of his new prize – a three-hundred-year-old operational FATR – greeted by numerous orange status holograms, humming to life over the steel controls. Outside the dimmed windows, several of his Exile recruits stood guard below, patrolling the nearby jungle as they were instructed.

You can never be too careful when there's sauros around, Deckard thought.

He walked up behind one of his subordinates, Eucer, who was still tampering with circuitry to the left of the cockpit. The technician had a steel panel removed, fingering through the bundled wires and searching for an unseen problem.

"How's she working?"

"Other than a constant flickering of lights, which is expected since we've just got the machine operational today, it's running perfectly," replied the technician, maneuvering his hands around the twisted cables.

"Terrific," Deckard replied. "I can live with flickering lights if it means I'm not some sauros' breakfast."

"I have to admit, sir. When we found this FATR in the jungle a few weeks back, this wasn't something I expected to have working. The rover would've been out in the elements for hundreds of years. But once we got past the numerous locked doors and pulled all the cadavers out, it was fairly easy to decipher the controls. Why do you suppose those men died in here?"

"Probably starvation or suicide," Deckard answered. "Something must have had them locked in. This is so close to sauro territory, it's likely that they had the occupants sealed inside."

"You'd think they would've used the cannons or the electrical surges on them," Eucer commented, working through the knotted cables.

"That would be the logical reason," Deckard remarked. "But we aren't thinking about the FATR's power situation at the time. It's possible that they exhausted their energy reserves. You said it yourself that it needed a complete reboot when we got in here. Maybe they overheated their weapons? It's all besides the point – what is the point is that now it's ours! Thanks to you!"

"Thank you, sir," Eucer replied.

"My dear old boy, did you hear the conversation we had with our new friends down there?"

"No, sir. The sound system was being difficult at the time."

"Let's just say that our fate is now no longer loitering in the Triassic," Deckard smiled. "A device has fallen from the heavens, right into our lap. Apparently it's near the twin valleys in the sauro territory, and I'm sending Severine to get it."

"You don't think she'll get cute?"

"Not with our hostages."

"*Hostages?*"

"Oh yes, Eucer. In the rear compartment. We're hauling their boy and their bot. Severine is clever and crafty, but she also has a heart. She'll play by the rules as long as we control those two."

"This must be *some* device then, am I right?"

"It's a portal generator, or something of the like. Apparently, it's a one-way ticket to the future, where the Federation ships have landed and colonized. It's all on a new planet, far away from here. Best of all, I'm sure there's no sauros there."

Eucer's eyes widened.

"Almost sounds too good to be true, sir. I've never heard of such a device."

"Just what I was thinking myself. We'll know soon enough. I'm sending Arien and a stealth operation after them to make sure they don't try anything like bringing back weapons from their downed ship or using the portal device for themselves. But again, I'm sure Severine wouldn't try anything like that. That other fellow who was handcuffed might – I'm not too fond of him."

Wooosh!

The door to the FATR cockpit slid open. Tanner stepped in, offering a respective salute and taking a stance next to Eucer, who gave him a friendly wave as he continued to work on the cables. Deckard surveyed the look on Tanner's face, discovering one unsaid word.

Peril.

"Something amiss, Mr. Tanner?" Deckard asked, turning away from the cockpit glass to his second-in-command.

"Just the same problem as always, sir. Insubordination, plain and simple. Can you guess from who?"

"I don't need to guess," Deckard said with a chuckle. "I already know by the scowl on your face. What did she say?"

"Juane was talking to her in his tent when I walked in on them. I only heard part of the conversation, but from what I got out of it, they're planning on relieving Severine and her allies of the portal oscillator and using it for themselves, cutting you and the rest of us out of the equation."

Deckard's eyes widened in fury.

That opportunistic bitch!

"Has she already left?" he asked, the anger consuming him.

"I believe so, sir," Tanner replied. "With fifteen others."

"You think her team will betray me?"

"She did seem to take the more rebellious ones, sir."

Deckard stopped and thought about the situation, shifting again to the cockpit, staring out at the dark, uncertain wilderness that blanketed the region under the moonlight. He had traveled through the twin valleys a few times, only under protest. Every time, the sauros had driven him out – almost sacrificing his own life on every occasion. Many of his own soldiers had been killed in the marshes of the valleys, and he speculated the monstrous predators would finish the job once again.

"Any thoughts, sir?" Tanner asked. Eucer had stopped working and was watching him as well, anticipating another one of the warlord's surprise outbursts.

"Just one," Deckard said. "We continue to the Mountains of Blood. Hopefully we will reconvene with Severine there and acquire the portal device."

"You don't want to go after them, sir?"

"Negative. The FATR will perish in the swamp if we do. I know Arien, and I know how she thinks. As soon as they encounter the sauros, I'm confident she'll turn back. She has a rough shell, but she's a total pussy when it comes to these creatures. Severine is different. Severine will battle through hell and high water if it means achieving her objective. Now I can't say anything about this Adam Ross or those others that they're with, but I know Severine will make it to the ship and acquire the device. And when she does, I want to make sure we're at the proper place we told her that we'll be, before I put this blade through her heart."

"And when Arien comes back?"

"We'll have to kill her, Tanner, regardless of any uprising that ensues. Honestly, we may have to kill everyone in her group. Arien is very persuasive – her beauty is hypnotic. We have to treat them all as traitors and rebuild the Exiles accordingly. If they make it out of the sauro swamps, we'll do it then. A purge is much needed. It's been needed for some time."

"What are your plans with the bot and the boy, if you don't mind me asking?" Tanner asked.

"The bot will serve as additional radar," Deckard explained. "At the very least, if he begins to show some signs of age, we'll strip him for parts. As far as the boy, I haven't decided yet. After I kill his uncle, he may be more trouble than what he's worth, but time will tell."

"I understand, sir," Tanner replied with a nod.

"Okay, let's set course for the Mountains of Blood," Deckard said, activating the loudspeaker. "All soldiers remaining in the area, prepare to follow the rover toward the Mountains of Blood. We'll test out the FATR's path carving capabilities. Someone wake the rest of the Exiles in the camp – we're moving out. Eucer, start up the engines!"

"Yes, sir," Eucer replied, abandoning the wires and arriving at the controls.

#

VRRRR...

"*Wha-a-at's* happening?" Jordy asked, still struggling with the cord bindings.

"We're moving," Nathan answered. "They're taking us somewhere else..."

The moonlight bouncing off the trees through the tinted windows began to streak sideways as the rover turned, spinning the massive vehicle in a different direction. Two armed guards scrambled up utility ladders on the outside, quickly darting up on the other side of the glass and then vanishing once they reached the roof. Shouting from the outside was heard through the thick reinforced interior as more Exiles began to regroup around their traveling sanctuary.

"Shit, Jordy!" Nathan exclaimed, trying hard to work on his bindings. "This isn't good. Where are we going?"

"I *don-n-n-n't* know," the bot answered. "And I hope we're not here long enough to *fi-i-i-nd* out."

The lockers in the room began to shake and rattle as the massive rover bounced over the uneven earth. Nathan watched as tree trunks and branches began to tumble outside, banging off the glass before falling below, crunched under the FATR's powerful underside.

"Wherever they're headed, it looks like they're in a hurry," Nathan observed, trying to keep his mind occupied with happier thoughts than being kidnapped yet again by another madman.

Wooosh!

The door to the FATR's middle chamber slid open, revealing Delios Deckard sauntering into the room, followed by a pair of armed guards. Nathan gulped at the sinister sight of the warlord's sword arm – hoping not to become better acquainted with the sharpened, serrated edge.

"You two," Deckard started, talking to his armed escort, "I won't need your help here. Head up topside and keep an eye out for sauros or any Exaeretodon. If anything stumbles into the area nearby, I want to know about it."

"Yes, sir," the two soldiers replied, scrambling up the metallic ladder in the next room.

Deckard continued his approach into the room, gliding around the two hostages and taking a seat on the adjacent bench, eyeing them both.

His gaze was cold, Nathan observed. His eyes dark; far more brooding than Wyatt's. Wyatt was an opportunist – a man trapped in a deadly, unpredictable world. A man who wanted out at any cost, having been backed into a corner and forced to take drastic measures. Deckard was the opposite. Nathan sensed that he was a hardened warrior, a man who earned his place at the top of the pecking order, who thrived on chaos. A quick glance down at the metal blade revealed the warlord had yet to remove Brandy's blood.

"*Wha-a-at* do you *plan-n-n* to do with us?" Jordy asked softly.

"I haven't decided yet," Deckard replied. "You both are currently the only bargaining chips I have. If all goes well, I'll have my ticket out of here. When that happens, I'll be in a very good mood. Who knows? Maybe I'll let the two of you come with me."

"You're going after the portal oscillator?" Nathan asked.

"Impressive vocabulary for an eight-year-old," Deckard said, shifting the calculating, cold stare to Nathan. "I didn't expect someone so young to sound so intelligent."

"I'm ten years old actually. On Solis, where we're from, I was actually one of the best spellers in my class. I was one of the top five in my class for vocabulary as well. My dad, Andrew, always said how far ahead of the others I am."

"*Solis?*" Deckard said, taking a sudden interest. "This is the planet where you come from?"

"Yeah."

"Tell me about Solis. What's it like? And why is it called Solis, anyway?"

Nathan was relieved to take his mind off the murderous warlord, trying to visualize the best way to explain the budding metropolis of Solis to someone who probably had never seen a real civilization before.

"Well, it's a lot like a more advanced version of here," Nathan explained. "You still have forests and jungles, but they are more contained and advantageous to the ecology of the planet. There are steel buildings as tall as the mountains, comprising cities that stretch for miles. Travel is done mostly by starships and small hovering land transports. There are no wars. Best of all, there's no Triassic predators."

Deckard laughed, causing Nathan and Jordy to tense up.

"Wow, you do have a good vocabulary, don't you, kid?"

"I guess so."

"So what the hell am I supposed to do with the two of you?" Deckard asked, rising from his seat as if late for an unseen errand. "Plead your case for me. Make me want to keep you around."

"*Wha-a-a-at* do you mean *ke-e-ep* us around?" Jordy replied. "*Onc-c-ce* you *hav-v-ve* the portal oscillator, you'll be *ba-a-ack* on Solis. You won't *ne-e-eed* to be a *murd-er-ous-s-s* Triassic pirate anymore."

"Yes, in theory that's how it'd play out," Deckard replied, with a smile that told Nathan he was flattered by the pirate comment. "But there are a number of unseen problems that may prevent that from happening. For starters, there's the obvious threat of the Saurosuchus colony in the area. The sauros are more than capable of wiping out both Severine, your uncle, your friends and my strike team that I've sent after them. Which brings me to the second dilemma. It appears that there is a little insurrection brewing among my ranks. Do you know what an insurrection is?"

"Isn't that like a rebellion?" Nathan asked.

"Very good," Deckard replied. "Now, had I known about this insurrection, I may have thought twice about sending one of my best assassins, Arien, after Severine. It appears that my protege is planning to steal your uncle's oscillator device and use it for herself, to escape to Solis and leave both me, Severine, and your uncle stranded here. Now you probably at least know me well enough by now to assume that I don't particularly like Arien anymore."

"You're going to kill her?" Nathan asked.

"Correct. It has to be done, I'm afraid."

"What about Severine and Uncle Adam? If they bring you your oscillator device which will allow you to make the time-jump, will you let them go?"

"We'll see," Deckard replied, shooting them a callous look. "Your uncle and his friends from the future may be able to be redeemed. Severine has already made her bed when she cut off my hand and forearm and left me for dead. For all of your sakes, that oscillator better work!"

Wooosh!

Under the flickering lighting of the rear chamber, a tall, skinny man appeared at the entrance to the middle chamber, stepping into the rear compartment.

"Sorry to bother you, sir," the newcomer began. "I believe the faulty wiring may be coming from in here. I want to pop out a few junction boxes to see if I can remedy the problem."

"Very well then," Deckard said, walking toward the exit. "Don't let our hostages bother you. Get done with your work and then report back to the cockpit. I want to test out the twin XP-300 cannon maneuverability."

"Very good, sir."

With a lasting look of suspicion and unpredictability, Deckard flashed them a smile as his scarred visage moved into the middle chamber, the door sliding shut, sealing him off once more.

Wooosh!

The wiry-haired man walked over to a small gray steel panel located on the far side of the wall. He popped it open with a screwdriver, and pressed down on a lever that remained inside.

Who is this guy? Nathan thought, wincing at the man's unkempt appearance.

"There we go," the man started. "That should deactivate the FATR's speakers to the cockpit, although I doubt they still work anyway. I didn't want Deckard listening in to what I'm about to tell you."

"*Who-o-o-o* are you?" Jordy asked, after the newcomer got the pair's attention.

"The name's Eucer Envans. I'm Deckard's jack of all trades, but mainly he just keeps me around because I fix things and can repair the crap that no one else in the Exiles can. Now, what's this I hear about a portal time travel device?"

Nathan looked at Jordy, perplexed by the man's sudden interest.

"It's a portal oscillator," Nathan said finally. "It's apparently still in the wreckage of *Harvester One*, presumably still in the ship's bridge. If it's still operational, it most likely has two uses left. Your boss wants it for himself."

"A portal oscillator?" Eucer smiled. "I'd be interested to know how that works."

"So would I," Nathan replied. "That is, when it actually does work. It's initial field testing proved it can work, but when we went to do a test operation in space, it failed. Then again, before our ship crashed, I saw the blue aura that the device generated. Our captain, Rupert Mason, must have figured out how to get it working before the ship crashed here."

"You're saying this device can literally bypass years of space travel and pluck me right out of this reality and into the future?"

"Basically," Nathan said. "In theory, anyway. I've never actually seen the result."

"I know Deckard," Eucer went on. "I know him all too well. If he gets his grubby hands on that device, he'll use it on himself, and won't take anyone with him. He'll kill us all before he lets anyone go back with him."

"*Why-y-y* do you say that?" Jordy asked. "He *se-e-ems* to like you."

"It's only because I've kept myself valuable," Eucer replied. "As soon as my worth expires, or I screw up one of his gadgets, he'll demote me. We're constantly having to replace people in our outfit. I've been lucky enough that he never wanted me dead – but I've seen him get mad enough to beat the shit out of me before. I knew if I didn't get this FATR working, I'd have been lashed."

"So why won't he let anyone use the portal with him?" Nathan asked. "Seems only reasonable that he'd take his loyal crew members with him."

"And risk everyone in the future knowing what corrupt deeds he's done while marooned in the Triassic?" Eucer shook his head. "He'll die before he sees that happen. Now, listen carefully. This girl that he's after, Severine. If she and her friends don't come back with the device, then

Deckard can't go home. But if she does come back, he'll most likely kill her and her cohorts and use the device. I'm here to tell you I'll not leave you both stranded here if you agree to take me back with you. Do you know how to operate that thing?"

"*As-s-sk* him," Jordy pointed to Nathan. "I've *nev-v-ver* even heard of such a tool."

"Well?" Eucer asked, turning to the boy.

"If you let us go, I'll make my uncle take you with us," Nathan said. "So are you going to let us go?"

"I can't yet," Eucer said, turning back to the door leading to the middle chamber. "Like I said, if Severine doesn't come back with the device, then it's back to the same old grind, and this conversation never happened."

"Which means, if she doesn't come back, then you're gonna let that maniac kill us?"

"*You-u-u* can't just let *us-s* die here!"

"I'm sorry," Eucer said. "It's all dependent on if she returns with the device. That's when everything will change, and the current paradigm will be flipped upside-down. Now I need to get back to the cockpit before Deckard assumes we've been fraternizing."

"*Wa-a-ait!*"

"*What?*" Eucer turned back, annoyed by the bot.

"*How-w-w* do we know we can *trus-s-st* you?" Jordy asked.

The man stopped by the sealed door to the middle compartment to think.

"You can't," Eucer said finally. "We'll just have to wait and see. Now, if Deckard asks, I just came in here to fix the faulty wiring, but couldn't find the problem."

"*Wait!*" Nathan called.

Wooosh!

The door to the middle compartment slid open as Eucer quickly scrambled into the opening and closed the door before Nathan could ask the next question. The boy's eyes refocused on Jordy who turned back, his metallic head tilting with the question.

"*Do-o-o* you think we can trust him?"

"I don't know," Nathan shrugged. "But he's all we've got at the moment."

XX

Severine watched as the Pisanosaurus jumped from its boulder, snapping playfully at an insect before losing interest and bounding off into the trees. When the sounds of the dinosaur first were heard in their vicinity, she was worried it might have been one of the sauros. She relaxed when she noticed it was one of the more docile dinosaurs.

"It's just one of the pisanosaurs," Severine relaxed, waving the others up from their hiding place behind a mossy log.

Thank God it wasn't a saurosuchus, Adam thought, feeling his muscles untense.

"You're the only one who knows what a Saurosuchus really looks like," Wyatt complained. "We're counting on *you* to keep an eye out! That thing was on top of us by the time you picked up on it."

"I don't really know who you are, but you're already on my bad side," Severine glared at him, raising a balled fist. "You don't want to be on my bad side. Got it?"

"Careful," Wyatt warned, his tone ominous. "I'm not above striking a woman."

"Well then you'll have me to deal with," Adam intervened, staring down his rival.

"Put it this way, Wyatt," Kara continued. "We all *equally* loathe you. If you try to as much as harm any of us, it won't end well for you. If I were you, I'd make those degrading comments scarce."

Wyatt turned, pretended to back off, and then with a balled fist, struck Kara across the face, sending the medical specialist into an ancient pine tree, sending needles spiraling over her. Wyatt stood over her triumphantly, wiping his sweaty scalp.

"Serves you right, bitch!"

That does it, asshole!

WHAM!

A surprise punch from Adam crumpled Wyatt to the earth. Before Wyatt could recover, Adam rammed into him as the sergeant attempted to rise to his feet, forcing him through an ancient rotted log and into an adjacent trail in the jungle.

"I've been waiting too long for this," Wyatt beckoned with his hands.

"Likewise," Adam replied, swinging his fist at Wyatt, who blocked it.

Now that I know your fighting style, you cocky prick...

WHAM! PFFT! WHAM! WOOSH!

Oh, fu –

With a surprisingly clean, spin move, Wyatt caught Adam on the side of his head with a kick, spinning the lieutenant backwards and face down into the earth. Wyatt was about to deliver another powerful punch, when a cloaked apparition slid behind him, a small knife pressed to his throat.

"Are you done, shithead?" Severine whispered in his ear, pressing the blade inward gently.

"Yeah," Wyatt shrugged, defeated once again.

"Good," Severine replied, pushing him away and helping Adam to his feet. "You've just volunteered to take the lead. Down that trail, pussy. *Move!*"

Wyatt spat at her boots and continued down the trail, swatting away at the ferns that blocked his vision of the road ahead. Adam helped Kara up, checking over her for permanent damage. She gently waved him off, signifying she could deal with the pain.

"I'm fine," Kara replied, holding her bruise. "He hits like a bitch. Let's hope a sauro gets to him before I do. Hey, Alex. You coming?"

Adam turned, surprised that Alex hadn't interfered with the Wyatt scuffle. Instead, he stood awkwardly, leaning against a tree branch, rubbing his arm.

"Shit, brother," Adam said, observing the sniper's odd posture. "You don't look so good."

As the first rays of the Triassic dawn began to leak through the canopy, Adam could see that the color had drained from his face. The stab wound on his right arm had begun to clot, but a faint bubbling had begun under the gauze, sending small white bubbles rising from where the fissure struggled to seal properly.

"Pus," Kara observed. "This isn't good. Alex, are you still with me?"

"Barely," Alex replied, his voice frail. "Something must have been on that blade – a poison. Severine, what do you... think of it?"

"Neolithics are known to lace their darts with poison," Severine replied, confirming the sniper's suspicion. "Adam, you discovered this first hand. It's possible that the knife could have had some form of mystery potion on it. Alex, how are you feeling?"

"*Uhm*, not good quite frankly," replied the sniper, blinking to stay conscious. "Nauseous, I feel like I'm gonna faint."

"Severine, how far are the twin valleys?" Kara asked. "We need to get to the *Harvester One* crash site as soon as possible. There are better medical supplies there. I should be able to get him the medicine he needs, but not if we don't arrive soon."

"Not far," Severine replied. "Now that the sun's coming up, I can see more clearly. The marshes start right through those trees, down the path that your asshole friend Wyatt just went down. That's unfortunately also where we'll find the sauro nests."

"Okay, we can't afford to wait around," Adam said, putting Alex's arm over his shoulder as a support crutch. "Kara, can you get under his other arm? Severine, lead the way – as quickly and safely as possible. We need to catch up to Wyatt anyway. I don't trust that bastard getting too close to the oscillator without us being there."

The winding trail gradually led them downhill, transitioning soon from sturdy mulch to dampened soil. The environment around began to transition as well, fading from sturdy pines to trees that ascended out of the bog like towering columns. When Severine pushed aside another final fern patch, she revealed the massive swampland that lay ahead of them.

"There it is!" Kara exclaimed.

In the center of the swamp, the colossal ruins of the *Harvester One* lay before them, several hundred yards away. In the ship's wake, dozens of swamp trees had been downed, severed days earlier from the ship's emergency descent as the craft plummeted into the prehistoric atmosphere. Partially submerged in the deeper pools of the bog, Adam noticed the bubbling froth that surged around the crash site.

Finally, we're here!

"It must still be at least somewhat operational," Adam noted, studying the vessel. "Looks like the exterior cooling vents are still emitting pressure. Hopefully that means the bridge doors will open with ease."

"That won't matter," Severine replied. "I can see the bridge from here. The glass is all fractured. Judging by the angle, we might be able to climb right into the bridge from the ship's external ports. They're not underwater like the rest of the ship."

"Any sign of that asshole?" Alex asked, half awake.

"Not yet," Severine said. "It's unlikely he navigated the entire marsh in the short time we let him out of our sights. There's plenty of natural land bridges to choose from – but probably only two or three lead a safe passage to the bridge."

She took an uncertain step onto the first land bridge that formed in front of her feet, appearing only in segments from above the pockets of green swamp water that snaked around them. When her boot failed to sink into the ground, she waved them onward. Adam let Kara move onto the bridge first, followed by Alex who was still being guided between them. As he maneuvered around a patch of long weeds jutting out from the narrow land mass, an impression in the ground revealed itself.

It was a fresh boot print from Wyatt, morphed into the moss laden earth.

"He came through here," Adam pointed out.

"He can't get far," Severine replied. "This place is a maze."

Her words weren't far from the truth. All around them, the swamp continued to reveal more land masses – some obvious ones, others only small patches of rock submerged inches below the surface. To make the route through the marshes even more confusing, the morning sun was beginning to lift a thick fog bank over the marshland, making vision more than thirty feet away a chore to perceive accurately. Already, the jungle was beginning to vanish behind them, replaced by a veil of unforgiving, thick white mist.

"I'm sure glad you know where you're going," Kara said, scooting around a muddy patch.

"I don't," Severine admitted bluntly. "I'm already starting to lose track of the ship."

The *Harvester One* wreck was already slipping away into the foggy world, visible only high in the air where the ship's left wing jutted out to the skies.

As they continued to navigate the cobbled mess of grassy hills that remained afloat from the bog water, a shrill sound cut through the mist, making them spin around in fright.

"RAUGGHHH!"

"Severine?" Kara uttered calmly, freezing in her tracks.

The horrible screech continued to reverberate throughout the region before finally fading away, leaving the group with a palpable sense of dread.

"*Sauros*," the Triassic survivalist replied with a glance around them. "Keep moving – and quietly. It sounded close."

#

Arien scanned the ancient Federation binoculars through the trees, hoping to find any trace of Severine and her four remaining allies. Now that it was morning throughout the lush jungle, movement would be easier to spot, but so far, she found none, save for a few young Pisanosaurs foraging through the undergrowth a quarter of a mile away.

Damn you, Severine!

"I've lost them," she muttered, cursing and roughly passing the binoculars to Juane, hitting him in the chest with the object.

"Well don't take it out on me," Juane replied, trying to mask his anger. "They have to be close. The swamps aren't far from here. I say we just head there and we'll probably link up with them. We already know that's where they're headed!"

Behind them, fifteen other Exiles waited patiently, scattered among the trees hiding behind the trunks, waiting for Arien's command. After waiting there for more than two minutes, they were getting impatient. One of the Exiles, Brine, finally approached Arien and Juane.

"Any sign of them, Arien?"

"*No, Brine!*" Arien snapped. "We've lost them."

Brine backed away at her sudden outburst. Hearing the news that Severine had once again eluded them made some of the Exiles relax and come out from behind their trees. A few soldiers on the outskirts began to fan out, securing the perimeter while Arien and Juane talked out the best course of action in dealing with their missing objective.

"Well, where did you last see them?" Juane asked.

"Ten minutes ago," Arien replied impatiently. "Back at the last ridge. They were right around here, where we are now. I saw them carting off that sniper. He must be injured. I don't understand how they could've vanished so quickly. Okay, let's double time it down that trail."

"Don't you think it's about time we gave them a little motivation?" Juane whispered, getting close to her.

"*Already*?" Arien asked. "And give them time to think about betraying Deckard? I was assuming we'd all have that discussion after we take it from Severine and get rid of her. Keep them busy about taking it from her, and not about repercussions for going against Deckard."

"I say we tell them now," Juane pressed her. "It'll give them inspiration to move faster! They're worn out from the battle last night with the Neolithics. Most have only slept for an hour."

Arien grumbled, realizing that her lover had a point. It was something that didn't happen often.

"Okay, everyone! Gather around. I want everyone here and listening."

As her call drew the warriors around her, she noticed how sluggish some of them were moving, and decided mentally that Juane was right. They needed to be informed of their real mission. It would also prove useful to see if there would be any dissenters among them that may still be loyal to Deckard, and would potentially be problematic down the road.

"*Quiet everyone!*" Juane whistled over the rambling. "Very good. Continue, Arien."

"It comes down to this," Arien started. "Severine and her allies are going to retrieve their portal device that can jettison us out of this shithole by the mere push of a button. Deckard has ordered us to oversee her progress and make sure she doesn't try anything stupid. After which, Deckard plans to use the device for us and transport us out of here, right?"

She observed several nods from around the assembled circle of warriors.

"Well, that's where you're wrong," she went on. "I know how that son of a bitch plays. He has no intention of letting us come back with him. We're only stepping stones to him. You think Deckard wants us to go to this futuristic, perfect world by his side, after all the brutal things he's ordered us to do? Any one of us can reveal what he's instructed us to do here – what atrocities and murderous things we've done, and he knows that! In one way or another, we've all committed crimes against humanity. Therefore, I propose this simple idea: instead of following

Severine and monitoring her, let's just kill her and her team, and use the device for ourselves. Leave Deckard and his loyalists here to die, I say."

She eyed the crew after her speech. Most were nodding in agreement, smiling at the thought of double-crossing their murderous master. Some were hesitant, but seemed willing. Only Brine stepped forward, offering rebuttal.

"Are you seriously suggesting, Arien, that we screw over the man who has given us so much?"

Arien couldn't help but burst out laughing at Brine's cowardice.

"Are you joking, Brine?" Arien asked, part comedic, part threatening. "Listen, as soon as you do something wrong, he'll screw you over too! We've all been subject to his beatings before, haven't we?"

Cheers of agreement roared out from the others. Arien knew that her idea had clearly captivated the audience. They were now hanging onto her every word, raising their pulse weapons in unified agreement.

"And what happens if Severine makes it past you and gets back to Deckard first?" Brine asked. "She already has put some distance between us. If Deckard learns of your plot, he'll *kill* you all! They still outnumber us two to one, plus, they have the FATR to boot. You're no match for those twin XP-300s, Arien – no matter how many people you seduce with your plan."

"Oh really," Arien said with an evil grin. "And who's going to tell him, Brine? Are you?"

Brine backed off. He tried to back out of the circle, but the subsequent Exiles blocked his path, keeping him contained within the center with Arien and Juane. When he put his hands on the first warrior behind him to break through, he was kicked back, spinning back to Arien, terrified at the dramatic turn of events.

"It seems you're on your own, Brine," Arien scoffed. "You know I can't let you leave. I'll give you one last chance to change your mind."

Brine collected himself, rising to his most aggressive stance, staring her down.

"You crazy bitch! Deckard will –"
SPILLLL! SPLAT!
Brine failed to notice that Arien had gently and slowly unsheathed a hidden dagger. With a clean motion, she sliced through Brine's throat. She stared down at him, writhing in agony on the jungle floor as he breathed his last, one hand on his throat, the other giving her a one finger courtesy salute.

"I never liked you, Brine," Arien winked as her foe became still, lifelessly dropping the hand gesture.

"What do we do now, boss?" one of the Exiles asked, proving his loyalty to her as the confrontation with Brine had ended.

"Intercept Severine and her team before they get to the ship," Arien replied. "All we need is one of them to know how to work the device. Personally, I say we kill them all except one of the males. All we need is one person to give us a quick breakdown of how it works. Then we kill him and transport ourselves out of here before Deckard knows what's happened – taking the device with us, of course."

"Sounds like a splendid idea, my dear," Juane replied. "Who's with us?"

A loud, boisterous cheer rang out among them. A pair of soldiers near the back fired off pulse rounds into the air, sending orange beams burning thorough the canopy above, raining severed leaves down on the party. Another man cupped his hands and gave a primitive howl, ringing through the jungle. The party was so loud, that they failed to hear the danger that stalked them through the trees.

"Rauguhuh..."

What was that?

At first she thought it was just Juane's stomach again, but when the odd rumbling continued, she knew it was something else entirely.

Arien raised a hand, immediately annoyed by her team's rowdy celebration. When they failed to shut up, she reprimanded them again, waving her hand distastefully.

"Hey! Will you morons please shut the *fu* –"

Her cursing was again cut off by another prehistoric call, this time on the other side of their location, and noticeably closer and more assertive.

"RAUGGHHH!"

"Dammit, Arien!" Juane screeched, scrambling to get his safety switch off. "Don't tell me that's a –"

"RAUGGHHH!"

The branches behind Arien broke apart, revealing a massive brown reptilian head. The creature spread its gargantuan jaws wide, showing off its dazzling golden yellow teeth as it latched onto the first Exile who failed to recognize the beast's dominant presence.

"Saurosuchus!" yelled one of the frightened soldiers.

"Take that bastard down!" Juane ordered, picking up his XR-90 and firing at the massive carnivore.

A dozen golden beams sailed at the creature, half of which struck the target successfully. With a final whip of the tail, the beast went down, swatting two of the soldiers away with the move. As Arien followed their injured forms sailing through the air, her eyes settled on three more brown beasts lumbering toward them from behind the adjacent tree ferns.

"Behind us!" she yelled, blasting her pulse pistol in their direction.

"RAUGGHHH!"

Arien could feel her heart ready to burst through her faded Federation armor suit. She watched several more of her strike team get taken down by the beasts before she rolled away. Some soldiers slipped through the first wave, only to be greeted by other sauros lying in wait on the outskirts, screaming as they died under the Triassic predators' powerful bite force.

Arien dropped, trying to search for an exit strategy. Profanities looped through her thoughts. Her eyes darted through the vegetation in search of a rotted log or cavernous rock to hide beneath. The sounds of her team being wiped out swelled in her wake. Her heart thumped furiously behind her Exile armor plate.

Shit! Shit! Shitshitshit!

The sauros had herded them into a kill zone.

#

Alex Meras stepped slowly over the swampy moss bridges, his boot teasing the watery edge. He often thought how easy it would be in his current state to drown himself in the swamp and take away the burning sensation that crept up his arm.

Is it deadly? Can Kara fix it? What were those noises in the jungle? Is Deckard following us?

The thoughts continued to flow through him, as he faced the uncertainty of what awaited just a few more minutes away at the *Harvester One* wreckage.

"Hey, keep your chin up, soldier," came the friendly voice from the medical specialist as she supported his one shoulder.

"Kara, is it bad?" Alex asked, his voice bordering on delirium.

"I won't know until I get that gauze off," she replied. "The medicine storage room should have what I need."

"Provided that it's not... filled up with swamp water," Alex said, trying to stay awake. "Damn, Kara. Didn't think that a knife to the arm could do so much damage. Almost would rather take a herrera on than go through this hell again."

"Hang on, brother," Adam replied, guiding the wounded corporal around a bubbling patch of swamp bog. "We're almost there. I can see the ship bridge now. We've covered a lot of ground. Only a few more minutes and we'll be in there."

"I'm counting the seconds," Alex joked, half unsure of what he was speaking about at this point.

As he was helped along through the marsh, something ahead through the gloom caught his eye. A silver shimmering rock, lying low along a patch of other boulders that rose out from the swamp. A close inspection on the stones revealed that one of them was shivering slightly – it had a face.

"I found Wyatt," Alex pointed wearily.

The sergeant was on his hands and knees, trying to make himself appear as small as possible. He cast them a quick look as if ordering them to stop moving forward. His uniform was plagued with swamp muck; he'd fallen into the pools at least once.

What's that jackass doing there?

"You just gonna sit there?" Severine called over angrily to the sergeant. "Actually, never mind, stay there. You only complicate things."

Alex felt movement. In his increasingly delirious state, he could distinguish a large rock gliding slowly through the swamp, directly behind Wyatt's position. The sergeant turned slowly, sighted the monster moving toward him and returned to his crouched fetal position, terrified of the approaching submerged titan.

"Severine," Adam whispered. "Is that what I think it is?"

"It's a Saurosuchus," Severine replied. "An adult. Stay low and move slowly!"

The massive animal ascended from the swampy world, stepping onto a land bridge beside Wyatt's position, letting out a massive daunting roar over the marshland. After shaking itself free of residual droplets, the sauro continued to lumber onto the land bridge, searching for signs of prey.

The path to *Harvester One* suddenly seemed significantly further away.

XXI

Adam and Kara lowered Alex to his knees, crouching behind a large swatch of swamp grass, the only visual barrier between them and the adult male Saurosuchus that rose up from the murky pool and began patrolling the land bridges. A few meters ahead, separated by a pool, Wyatt had vanished once again from his location, using the sauros coming as a distraction to sneak closer to the ship.

"That dick's going for the portal oscillator again," Kara remarked. "We should've capped him. It'd make this whole operation go a lot smoother."

"I agree," Adam replied, keeping his eyes on the massive prehistoric hunter. "Next time, it must be done."

The Saurosuchus was an impressive animal, reptilian in appearance but very different from the herreras or the coelos he experienced days before. For one, the sauro was a four-legged hunter, with jaws as long as a pulse rifle. The fact that the sauros preferred an aquatic territory to hunt made them more horrific – they could be hiding anywhere in the gloomy bog or under the green waves.

"Severine, what do you –"

Just like Wyatt, their mysterious new friend had vanished into the mist as well. The only movement Adam could see came from the Saurosuchus, lumbering slowly away into the fog bank down the monster's respective land bridge. Not knowing where the animal would appear next made Adam cringe.

Hopefully it will find Wyatt instead...

"Where did she go?" Kara asked, spinning around to search the wispy mists of the swamp.

"Never mind her," Adam said, turning back to his two remaining allies, one of which was barely conscious. "She may be trying to lead the sauro away. With any luck, that beast will kill Wyatt and stay busy with his corpse while we make it through to the ship. Alex, are you with me? We can't stay here. The ship is just ahead through the fog. Can you stay with us? We'll have to crawl."

Alex nodded gravely, clutching his arm.

Taking the lead, Adam waved his two friends along. The land bridge ahead began to shrink in width, forcing them to occasionally dip into the bubbling swamp water. A flurry of swift movement under the water by his knee made Adam pause. He relaxed when he saw it was only a school of primitive fish.

"How deep do you think it is?" Kara asked, moving behind Alex to guide him along.

"Deep enough that it can visually hide a super predator like that sauro," Adam muttered. "I can start to see the ship. We're coming up on its rear thrusters..."

Ahead, two massive metallic cylinders covered in slimy plant matter appeared through the wall of fog. The inner shafts had been covered in bramble, probably for nesting material by other dinosaurs. Small four-legged Triassic fauna played in the pools nearby, skittering away as Adam crept slowly toward the downed ship.

Still no sign of Severine or Wyatt, Adam thought. *Would Severine betray us and use the portal herself?*

He shrugged off the idea. He knew Wyatt would do anything to impede the progress and activate the oscillator. Although he'd only known Severine for a few days, he could tell she was different.

Plus, there's no way she'd leave her bot behind. She loves Jordy!

When the trio reached the thrusters, Alex collapsed inside, using the metal rim as a makeshift bed.

"*I need to take... a break... dammit...*"

His voice was faltering again. The sniper sat up, resting his head on the upper thruster, staring in a trance out to the menacing swampland.

Kara rushed to his side.

"Hang on, we're almost there. We just need to get to the front of the cockpit. Hang on for ten more minutes, Alex. *Please!*"

The color in the sniper's face had completely drained. Adam examined the wound, noticing more pus seeping out from the gauze, staining the cloth fibers with red and white. He glanced one time down the ship, noticing that the ship's crash had formed a natural land bridge alongside the metal hull. The bridge, he assumed, would lead directly under the left wing right up to the command bridge.

"Kara, can you wait here with him?" Adam asked. "I'm going to run ahead and see if I can find the safest way through the bog. If my guess is correct, it should be relatively easy from here. I'll be back for you both."

"Okay," Kara replied. "But please hurry. He urgently needs medicine, and I don't want to be alone out here with those sauros if he passes out."

"I won't be long. I promise – I want out of here as much as you do."

With that, he turned and began following the hull of the ship into the mist, leaving his two remaining companions behind him. Soon they materialized into the white aura of the swamps. His last vision was of Kara trying to examine Alex's arm wound without trying to tamper with the gauze. Adam was alone – and he felt it.

Every sound from the swamp made him flinch as he inched quickly along the worn chrome siding of *Harvester One*, trying to hug the metal plating to avoid the rippling waters that teased the front of his boots. Occasionally he saw the swamp fish swimming past, but thankfully, nothing larger.

Slosh...

Adam froze.

Something was moving toward him through the fog – on his same patch of land.

Oh no...

He looked around quickly for somewhere to hide, but there was no refuge anywhere, unless he decided to jump into the putrid swamp water. He quickly rejected the idea, deciding there may be more hidden predatory lifeforms down there than on the surface.

His failure to make a decision culminated in his worst fears imaginable as a colossal beast began to fade up ahead of him on the trail.

Shit. I'm not moving – why am I not moving?

The adult Saurosuchus he had seen just minutes earlier rising from the swamp water had appeared in front of him, lumbering slowly toward him and gradually closing the gap to only a few breathtaking feet. The carnivore was so close that Adam could feel the animal's nauseating breath wafting over his nostrils, so powerful that it blew back his hair.

Oh God. This is it!

Adam stood rooted in his position, unable to run, forced to stare into the sauro's murderous, salivating jaws as the Triassic predator let out a tyrannical growl.

#

Severine's eyes slipped below the gurgling swamp water, blinking at they experienced the murky green slush that enveloped her. She tried to open her eyes underwater, only to be greeted by the cloudy opaque world that many Triassic amphibians called home.

I can't see through this gunk!

She bobbed her head back up to the surface, narrowly avoiding a large spiny fish that slithered past her, bubbling back into the green depths. As she surfaced, she could see the starship's bridge getting closer, materializing through the fog bank. She could see into the windows, noticing several areas where the glass had imploded, creating convenient points of entry.

She had realized in retrospect that diving into the water wasn't her brightest idea. Her reasons for doing so were twofold. The first reason was to avoid sauros on the land bridges, where she knew they preferred to hunt, and the second was to make it to the ship's bridge before Wyatt. With the sniper wounded and slowing them down, she had the best chance of obtaining the oscillator before that maniac grabbed it first and used up the charge crystals.

Ah, it's cold!

She struggled to stay above water as the froth laden liquid enveloped her, paddling slowly as to avoid suspicion from whatever may be lurking below. She felt her body go rigid when something touched her leg.

A fish. It has to be a fish...

Her opinion of the elusive animal changed when it continued to push under her feet, with a strength powerful enough to pull her forward with its muscular back. She regretted looking below when she noticed it was a submerged Saurosuchus, pulling her forward unknowingly, probably assuming that Severine was a fallen tree trunk. She breathed quietly, hoping her saddled voyage would end soon.

Please don't look up! Just keep swimming ahead, you big freak!

Through the thick veil of green goo, she could vaguely see the creature's massive head, turning to and fro as it scanned for prey. With a steady controlled breath, Severine gently retracted her legs into a bent position, relieving the creature of the weight and letting it pass beneath her. It continued traveling without knowing she was hovering above it, soon slipping away into the bog.

This is too much. I have to find a land bridge – now!

She snagged a branch to her left and pulled herself onto a mossy embankment, kneeling as she coughed up some water, grateful to be back on land. When she regained her composure, she glanced around, wondering where the Saurosuchus had pulled her.

She was on a small patch of land that ran on ahead of her, ending up right in front of the bridge. Through the fog, she could clearly see all the outlines of the ship's forefront, noticing that her mossy land patch weaved through a small area of bramble and rotting trees, but was otherwise free of the sauros. She would be in the bridge in less than a minute if she ran.

Crunch! Crunch! Crunch!

What's that? Running? From whe –

A force slammed into her from behind, pushing her forward onto the fungus-covered earth, her face becoming buried in the ground. When she tried to stand back up, the force knocked her back into the marshy soil, trying to suffocate her, using the impression she made with her face as an air trap.

"I'm not going to let you take that oscillator, Severine," Wyatt replied from somewhere above her. "And to think, I came here to rescue all of you. Things have changed. I've tried to kill the lieutenant. Took his nephew as a hostage. Meras wants to send me to military prison when we get back. *Ha*, like I'd allow that!"

Severine could feel the air leaving her lungs, her nostrils consuming decades of decayed organic matter that seeped up from the moistened earth. She struggled with her hands to pull herself up, but Wyatt's weight forced her back into the ground.

"I know you can't respond," Wyatt went on snickering, "so just listen. Obviously, I don't know you very well but I can already tell we aren't on good terms. The knife to the throat sealed your fate. I was going to ask you to join me. Hell, I would've even let you take the bot if that sword-armed maniac hadn't confiscated him first! I'll have to kill you now, because you'll only continue to be a pain in my ass if I let you continue to the bridge. So sad, you came so close to getting out of here, but you were never meant to. Now you'll die. You'll die in the Triassic –"

WHAM!

Severine issued a swift kick by flipping her foot backwards and vertical, catching Wyatt's testicles with an abrupt, powerful shove.

"*Oafff!*" Wyatt moaned, releasing his grip on his opponent and falling backwards, temporarily immobilized. "You... you *bitch!*"

Severine returned to her standing position, briefly wiping her face off from the muck and returning to face her opponent. Wyatt couldn't stand, the kick had taken the fight completely out of him. Instead, he crouched on the verge of tears, holding his crotch through his Federation armor suit. She searched the ground for a murder weapon, finding it in the form of a callous rock lying among the plant life. Snagging up the stone, she stared down at her opponent, ready to deliver the killing blow.

"*Do it!*" Wyatt coughed, writhing in pain. "You – *augh*! You prehistoric, *crazy* bitch!"

Severine glared down at him, feeling no sympathy for the man. Even as her fingers curled around the rock, she let it fall, the stone perishing into the swamp beside her.

"You're not worth it, asshole," Severine replied. "If I see you again, I'll kill you! You have my word. You're a psychopath, and you don't deserve to leave the Triassic. Worst of all, you're a disgrace to the Federation – you put shame to that uniform."

"*Augh!* I'll kill you, you *fu* –"

WHOOSH! WHAM!

A sideways kick knocked him unconscious, spinning the sergeant sideways into the swamp, his face landing in the green veil of murky film. When he failed to get up, Severine made no motion to check on him.

Drown, asshole...

She turned, leaving Wyatt's still form by the side of the land bridge. A brisk sprint down the marsh beds led her right up to the bridge. The giant structure rose above her several stories in height. At the bottom where the metal met glass, the window had collapsed, large enough for her to fit inside comfortably.

She peered through the chasm, happy to see that there were no sauros or dinosaur forms lumbering inside.

Perfect!

But as she was about to climb through the opening, a piercing scream rippled through the marshland. She pinpointed the location – straight down the side of the ship, coming from somewhere in the mist.

#

CRUNCH! SCRAPE! CRUNCH!

Adam watched in horror as the terrifying action replayed itself in an endless loop. Again, the Saurosuchus lunged, chomping once with its insidious jaws and swinging its left front leg forward, hoping to snag the prey with its clawed foot.

Had he not ducked sideways and hid in a cleft in the ship's mangled hull, Adam knew he would've been a goner. The seam in the metal was a result from the impact with the Earth during the ship's crash, creating an opening just big enough for him to snuggle into, but not offering any escape route. The prehistoric hunter had planted itself against the opening, fitting its massive head inside to rip Adam apart, if not for the monster's muscular shoulders which prevented the beast from entering any further.

CRUNCH! SCRAPE! CRUNCH!

The sauro repeated the action once more, reacting in anger with a harsh growl of resentment. With a maniacal stare, Adam knew his opponent wouldn't be leaving until it tasted human bone. With an irritable shake, the sauro swerved its head back and forth, hoping to wiggle further into the crevice.

Adam turned, trying to wedge himself further into the breach, but he had already reached the end of the divide, staring at a steel wall writhed in swamp goop.

Trapped! I'm going to die here.

Without a weapon, he was helpless, forced to stare into the snapping jaws of the sauro.

CRUNCH! SCRAPE! CRUNCH!

"RAUGGHHH!"

"Help!" Adam yelled, unsure if anyone could hear him.

He could feel the cold touch of metal as his hands gripped both sides of the crevice as he tried to force himself further back.

With a monumental push, the sauro managed to wedge its massive shoulders through the gap, bringing its biting distance to within inches of Adam's horrified face. He could feel his shoulders, back, and buttocks touching the far steel wall of the crevice as tightly as the space would allow. The breath and saliva of the animal saturated him with each failed chomp.

Adam's head throbbed, the wound from days earlier returning to torment him in his final moments. He thought he might pass out from the sheer fright of the horrifying spectacle that continued before him. In the back of his mind, he feared for the life of his nephew, and what may become of him when Adam failed to deliver the portal oscillator.

I failed you, Nathan. I'm sorry...

VRRR!

The sauro's eyes bulged, and the beast withdrew from the crevice, a shriek of surprise and sudden terror escaping its jaws. As it backed up from the cleft, Adam noticed an orange halo on the monster's midsection, glowing on the edges and scorched in the middle – a wound from a pulse weapon.

"RAUGGHHH!"

VRRR!

Adam witnessed a second pulse round sail in from the left side of the crevice – the shooter remaining unseen. The blast caught the sauro in the neck, searing through the scales and exiting out the other end, dispersing the fog around it as the bolt vanished into the dreary mists.

The Saurosuchus lunged forward at the attacker, chomping and taking a step forward to decrease the gap. A final blast from the pulse weapon rang through the creature's head, swiftly putting an end to the skirmish. With a final awkward groan, the super predator crashed headfirst into the land bridge, its teeth crunching into its skull from the force of the impact before the monster twisted and splashed into the murky lagoon.

Severine stepped out from behind the cleft, holding an ECP-30 that had been partially covered in swamp grime. Her clothes were filthy, indicative that she had been underwater.

"You know," she smiled, "these pulse weapons of the future are pretty nifty! I like the safety features, but I still prefer a good old fashioned X2-20 from my day."

"What took you so long?" Adam asked, relieved to see her. "Where did you go?"

"Skipped ahead to see what we were going to run into. I found a clear path to the bridge."

"Good. Did you see Wyatt? I think he's going for the oscillator again."

"I took care of Wyatt. He shouldn't be a problem anymore. Where's Alex and Kara?"

"I left them back by the thrusters to run ahead and make sure the path was clear, only to run into the sauro you just gunned down. Thanks for that, Severine. You just saved my life."

"Well we're not out of the shitty situation yet," she replied, yanking him out of the cleft and leading him to the thrusters. "We still need to get your contraption back to Deckard. My pulse blast probably alerted every sauro in the area to our presence. We'll have to get in and get out! I also have a suspicion that Deckard might be having us followed. I thought I heard other pulse blasts coming from the jungle not long ago."

"I heard them too," Adam said, running along the steel hull beside her. "You think he may have had second thoughts? Choosing to kill us before we even obtain the oscillator?"

"It's certainly within the scope of something Deckard would do," Severine acknowledged. "Either way, all it does it give us more motivation to grab that portal contraption and head out."

XXII

Severine hauled herself through the opening into the bridge. Her feet landed on the ground, shattering glass remnants that landed there days earlier when *Harvester One* crash landed into the Triassic era, breaking through the marshland. Adam and Kara came next, helping a wounded Alex Meras through the opening. The sniper's condition had deteriorated quickly; his eyes flickered as he fought to maintain consciousness.

"Finally back where we started," Adam remarked, observing the interior wreckage.

"Looks a little different than I recall," Kara added, helping Alex under one of his shoulders. "I'm going to get him to the medical room down the hall. The damage I can fix easily, provided that the supplies are still there."

"Watch out for sauros," Adam cautioned her.

"Here, take this!" Severine said, tossing Kara her ECP-30. "You need this more than we do."

"Thanks," Kara replied. "We won't be long."

She herded Alex along, skirting around the rubble in the large room and disappearing with the sniper down one of the many connecting hallways that fed deeper into the ruins.

"What's our move here, Adam?" Severine asked, staring around the abandoned command quarters.

"Start rooting through the debris," Adam answered. "The last time I saw this room, it was in top condition, the way Captain Rupert Mason usually liked to keep it. I literally have no idea where to begin."

"How do you even know it's in this room?" Severine asked.

"Shortly before we crashed in the Triassic," Adam started, "an incident obstructed my path to the bridge, forcing me to take an escape pod out of the ship instead. However, before my pod deployed, I noticed a blue aura pulsating from the bridge. That was evidence that the portal oscillator had indeed worked like it was supposed to. After our escape pod, *Burrower,* landed, our communication specialist identified it was still in *Harvester One*. Since Mason was in possession of the oscillator on the bridge, I find it likely that the device is somewhere in the center of this room, where Mason's bridge command port was located. Unfortunately, the crash has made this place a scrapyard. It could be anywhere."

He was right.

The bridge of *Harvester One* had become an entanglement of metallic interwoven elements. Turned over computer terminals sat neglected among steel girders and roofing material that rained down on the bridge like a blizzard. Several sparking wires snaked through the rubble, glowing to life intermittently and flashing signs of fleeting computer life. Occasionally, the subtle glow of terminal screens still beckoned, but no immediate signs of the oscillator were seen.

"So about the center of the room, you say?" Severine asked, climbing over the circuitry by means of an overturned desk.

"About, yeah," Adam acknowledged, stepping after her.

"That would make the location of your device primarily around this region," Severine stated after calculating the room's circumference mentally. "Provided it stayed relatively put even after the crash landing."

She stood on a small heap of metallic roofing support structures that hid what remained below.

"What does this oscillator device look like?" Severine asked, rooting through the debris.

"It resembles a steel wrist gauntlet," Adam explained. "It's a device that the user can choose to wear as a sleeve or operate without wearing it. There are some crystal blue translucent micro pipes running through the device that generate the portal, operational through a digital screen that emits options through holographic projections."

"Should be relatively easy to find," Severine assumed, "as long as you're right, and this device is buried right around this area. Wonder why your captain didn't take the device with him?"

"There are more prototypes being made on Solis," Adam replied, starting to quickly pull apart the material that lay discarded below them. "He probably figured that eventually there would be more people on the ship who would like to use the device, if the ship somehow survived obliteration in the asteroid belt. Thankfully, I'm sure that's what he did. Knowing that each portal will only remain active for so long, he probably saved everyone he could in the first round, and left it behind after stepping in the time warp for himself."

"I sure hope you're right about this," Severine replied, panting as she nearly exhausted herself lugging the rubble away from the middle. "Otherwise, it's both our asses."

"Don't worry," Adam replied, smiling as he moved aside a large pipe. "We've just found exactly what we've been looking for!"

Sitting against the cool white tile of the bridge floor was the chrome gauntlet that Adam had come to know as Captain Mason's first generation portal oscillating device – which up until a few days ago, failed to work properly. Severine smiled as Adam picked it up, eyeing the device to make sure it hadn't been damaged.

"You think it still works?" she asked, studying the gadget.

"Looks like it," Adam smiled with a laugh. "I think some of Rupert's wrist hairs are still lodged in the inner side."

The device hummed and lit up as Adam spun it around. Severine noticed only a small amount of scratches and indentations. Strange hypnotic cybernetic bubbles surged up the small tubes near the screen, disappearing as they traveled back into the device in a seamless loop. She noticed a trio of blue crystals on the back of the device, one of which had lost its luster.

Must have been from the one confirmed portal usage, Severine thought.

Adam pressed a button on the small screen, causing a flurry of digital bleeping as software code began ticking away across the monitor. A blue ray of light shot out from the receiver, displaying a command prompt in 3D holographic space in front of them.

2 Uses Left. Use Portal 2 of 3 – Y or N?

"*Wow,* it's still good after all this!" Adam exclaimed, mesmerized by the dazzling holographic display.

"*Amazing!*" Severine said with a smile, her face illuminated by the blue light show. "What a shame we'll have to hand it over to Deckard."

"We'll have to get it back somehow," Adam nodded.

"Oh, it'll never make it to Deckard," a strange, eerily familiar voice rang out from the corner of the bridge.

VRRR!

An orange pulse blast shot out from the corner of the room toward them. Severine tackled Adam off his feet as the pulse shard sailed past, ricocheting once before scorching the far wall of the bridge. One name remained constant in her mind as she fell over the wreckage, regret forming inside her as she realized her mistake.

Wyatt.

I should've beaten him to death with the damn rock...

#

Kara Barnels continued down the ghostly quiet corridor of the *Harvester One* hallway, shocked by the massive chasm that ran down the ship. Clearly the asteroids and space had taken their toll on the hull. She was surprised the bridge remained connected via a second interior hallway. After a short jog, she was relieved to see that the medical room entrance was also intact just before the hallway dropped off into dark swampland below.

Kara pushed open the entry door with her free shoulder, helping her near unconscious companion with her, setting him against an examination gurney before he tumbled wearily onto the exam table.

"*Ah,* Kara – I feel like shit. Tell me you can fix it."

"I'm gonna do my best, Alex," Kara replied, rummaging through the cabinets that were scattered around the room courtesy of the ship's untimely crash.

"Good. Anything would be better... than... *this*..."

Oh God. Please let it be in here...

She threw open more cabinet doors, greeted with sterilization tools, gurney replacement parts, unused syringes and various medical tablets, but not the exact serum she needed.

"*Anything?*" came a labored voice behind her.

"Not yet, Alex," Kara answered, trying to hold it together as she began hurling objects from the cabinets.

Oh, I hope they haven't taken all of it!

She could feel her heart racing. Her head throbbed, tunnel vision forming around each incorrect object that her eyes latched onto. Finally, in the back of the last cabinet in the medical room, she found what she was looking for.

Serum IC-33.

"*Yes!* Found it."

She reached around the vial, filled with a crystal blue ooze, sealed at the top with an air-tight lid. It was full to the brim, untouched before by any Federation medical specialist or technician. Kara quickly deposited a portion of the mystery potion into one of the available syringes and made sure her needle was prepped.

"What is that shit?" Alex uttered, staring down at the mysterious elixir.

"Serum IC-33," Kara replied, slipping the needle into his veins, injecting him with the medicine.

"Wow, already I'm feeling better..."

Kara watched as the color quickly began to return to the sniper's face. Two minutes later, his body language told her that her patient had made a near complete recovery.

"It was considered a miracle drug a few years ago when it was first discovered. It's a quick antidote for most poisons. This was the last bottle left – I'm assuming they took a lot of the IC-33 serums with them in the pods when *Harvester One* went down. I'll be taking this vial with us, on the off chance we run into any more poison-tipped daggers. Now, let's see how it's healed."

After removing the sniper's gauze wrapping, Kara noticed that the pus that had been escaping the wound had already begun to heal. The blood that had seeped out from the puncture mark now formed the beginnings of a scar.

"Watch this," Kara announced.

She opened the vial and slowly poured it over Alex's dagger wound. The sniper winced as the blue liquid swiftly coated the scar. A fizzling sensation started on the bruise, sending blue wisps up into the air as the scar thinned in scale, effectively sealing the problem permanently.

"*Beautiful!*" Alex exclaimed happily, eyes widened by effects of the miracle potion. "Do you suppose I can drink it?"

"That might not taste so good," Kara laughed. "But maybe in a few years they'll develop a –"

Alex, still coming out of his delirium, reached around her waist and pulled her close – so close that she could feel his muscles all around her, enveloping her tightly.

"Alex," she giggled, trying to maintain a serious face. "You know, we really have only known each other for a few days, you and I. I know the time we've spent together has been rather unpleasant, but –"

"We don't know if we're ever going to make it back alive," Alex replied with a devious smirk. "Sure, they may end up finding the oscillator, but what happens after that? Deckard? The native hunters? The sauros? So many things can pick us off. Can't we just have this one moment of clarity together?"

He pulled her close and kissed her. She stood there returning the kiss, her arms gradually reaching around his shoulders and falling into his embrace. Although it felt amazing, the sensations traveling through her, she couldn't help but wonder about the medicine.

Serum IC-33 has never worked that fast – not in all the time I've spent administering it. I know its results seem to take shape pretty fast... but... wait a minute!

Had it all been a ploy to spend a second alone with her, and not in some sauro-infested Triassic jungle. The sniper had recovered from the Neolithic toxins in record time.

Damn you, Meras...

She didn't care. In the throes of passion, she remembered to gently set the elixir down into her backpack. Then she dashed up on the gurney with him, tearing at his clothes as he kicked the door shut, hoping that Severine and Adam were still busy with their quest for the oscillator.

#

VRRR!

CRASSHHH!

A second pulse blast whizzed over the shelter where Adam lay pinned under Severine. The orange ray plowed through an upright terminal port, destroying the flickering monitor and knocking it onto the floor.

"He must've crept on board and grabbed a pulse pistol from the wreck," Adam deduced as Severine rolled off of him.

"Where do you keep your pulse weapons?" Severine asked. "We can take him if we break off. Flanking him in this mess won't be a challenge."

"There are weapon and ammo depots placed sporadically throughout the bridge," Adam replied. "The nearest ones will be back by the hallway corridor, but they're out in the open – he'll hit us easily. There should be some stashed throughout the terminal ports, but they're mostly buried under all this shit. They look like orange cubes, usually containing a pair of ECP-30s with an extra clip of charge crystals. My guess is that he got lucky and found one free of rubble."

VRRR!

Wyatt approached from behind the debris somewhere near the front of the ship, sending a third blast their way. Adam couldn't directly see him, which told him that the pulse blasts were more for intimidation than for lethal hits.

"We could run down the corridors?" Severine suggested as they took cover further in the room. "We could find weapons in one of the other rooms, then return to take him down."

"We won't get far," Adam said. "There's a large crease in most of the hallways from where the asteroids ripped through. The next weapons cache locations are past it – I guarantee it. We'll have to figure something out in here."

VRRR!

An orange blast fired past Adam's face, forcing his reflexes to fling him behind his concrete obstruction.

"Hold on," Severine said, turning to look for a weapon. "I'll be back."

Have to stash this device somewhere that he won't find it, Adam thought as she darted out of view behind the debris. He ripped off the portal oscillator from his wrist and searched for a location to hide the device, only to be met with more fire from Wyatt, who by now was converging on his position, knowing exactly where Adam was hiding.

"This has been a long time coming, Ross," Wyatt laughed with a rasp in his voice.

By the sound of his footsteps, Adam could tell he was either limping or walking uneasily – unable to increase his acceleration.

"Now, give me the oscillator, and I promise, it will be a pulse blast to the head," laughed the psychopathic sergeant. "As for your little friend, I don't intend to make her suffering fast. I owe her a slow and painful one. Then I'll hop back to Solis, mentioning your treason. *Hah* – you went berserk, killing everyone in the surviving *Burrower* pod. All except me. I had to remove you from the equation if I wanted to get back. It was the only choice, Ross! You must see it that way! You have to. Well, like I care if you do or don't. You'll be dead soon regardless."

Wyatt's footsteps continued to grow closer – too close for Adam. He leaped from his stone barrier, avoiding another pulse blast from Wyatt's gun by inches as he rolled behind another build up of collapsed ceiling material.

"Wyatt!" Adam called out, searching quickly for some kind of range weapon. "Just let us take it to Deckard. With all of us together, we can make it back. All of this can be forgotten – all of our history in the last few days."

"I'm sorry, but it can't end that way," Wyatt laughed arrogantly, still hobbling toward Adam's hiding place.

Where is Severine? Can't she find a weapon deposit?

"I'll try to think of you when I'm living the high life back home," Wyatt laughed. "Who knows, I might even give you a moment's thought from time to time."

Wyatt's footsteps were getting louder. Adam knew he had to move. The cover would be compromised quickly, and he'd never see Solis – or his nephew for that matter – again.

He sprang out of hiding, running swiftly for the far corridor at the back of what remained of the bridge, noticing not far away a weapons cache security box under some fractured ceiling pieces. Suddenly an orange light passed painfully through him, causing him to spin in mid-air, landing with a scream as his back struck the debris laden ground.

"*Aughh!*" Adam cried in agony.

He turned to examine the grisly damage.

Wyatt's blast barely scorched his left arm, leaving a fizzling wound that glowed with orange embers. Ripples of pain jolted through him from the mark and, although not fatal, he knew he was now utterly powerless to defend against Wyatt. Had the blast gone through his muscle tissue, Adam doubted his arm would ever make a full recovery.

A quick look ahead revealed that his enemy approached, stopping once to pick up something on the ground.

The oscillator!

In Adam's frantic spin from failing to avoid the pulse blast, the momentum pushed the device from his wrist, giving Wyatt the coveted prize.

"I thought I'd never see this pretty little thing again," Wyatt smiled devilishly, slipping the oscillator onto his wrist. "Had I been on the bridge when Rupert deployed it, you and I might never have been on this little adventure together. Now, let's see what we've got here."

"*Wyatt!* Don't do it!"

"Go to hell, Ross."

With a quick motion, Wyatt entered a quick code into the screen of the device, which enabled the same holographic command prompt that Adam had seen a few minutes earlier. Wyatt quickly entered the *yes* option.

SHRRRRR!

Instantly, a blue beam of light shot out in front of the device, emitted from a small cylindrical port in the front of the wrist gauntlet. Small polygonal shapes began to materialize in the air, swirling forth slowly as they constructed a massive blue ellipse ten feet in height. The polygons were soon accompanied by additional particles, spinning so fast that they ignited into tiny blue embers, audible by both Wyatt and Adam as they sung happily, generating the rift in time.

Adam couldn't take his eyes off the portal that spun only feet in front of him. With an arrogant smirk, Wyatt stepped around the portal to face Adam, ready to deal the death blow.

"Well, Ross, this is where our story ends," Wyatt snickered, raising the ECP-30 and staring down at his helpless rival.

"This will come back to haunt you, Wyatt," Adam roared over the loud whine of the portal.

"I doubt it," Wyatt smiled. "I can't say it's been fun. But killing you will make for a perfect ending to the last few days. Any last words?"

Adam stared into the barrel of the ECP-30, noticing the orange energy charge glowing inside the barrel that had his name on it. As he was about to offer a final protest, Severine's words cut through their conversation.

"Hey, *asshole!*" Severine's voice came from across the room.

Wyatt turned, trying to trace where her vocals had originated.

"Why don't I give you a souvenir to take back to Solis with you – courtesy of the Triassic."

VRRR!

An orange pulse blast ripped out from the rubble, catching Wyatt between the eyes, disappearing out the other side of his skull into the portal. The sergeant's lifeless corpse dropped the pistol and fell back, sliding into the blue vortex. Adam raced forward and grabbed the cadaver's hand, ripping off the portal oscillator from the cold wrist before letting his dead foe pass through the aura – presumably back to Solis. Ten seconds later, the polygons faded away and the portal ceased to exist, again filling the room with darkness and quiet.

Severine stepped out from behind the debris, helping Adam to his feet as he retrieved Wyatt's pulse pistol.

"Guess he finally got what he wanted," she smirked, helping Adam to his feet.

"Good timing, Severine," Adam replied, developing a new admiration for his rescuer. "My only regret is not being able to pull the trigger on that bastard myself. He got what he deserved."

"Call me *Sev*," she smiled, dusting off his back. "And don't thank me yet. We still have one more shithead to deal with."

XXIII

It was nearing midday when Adam first noticed the red mountainous peaks rising above the tall Triassic pines. The *Mountains of Blood,* as they were called, were a surprisingly short trek from the ruins of the *Harvester One* crash site. After retrieving the portal oscillator and disposing of Wyatt, they reunited with Kara and Alex, escaped the ship through an asteroid damage crater, and left the swamp without encountering any lingering Saurosuchus packs.

Adam had completely forgotten about his small arm wound. The only time he felt pain was when his arm swayed too abruptly. He knew it would heal in a few weeks, save for a small scar that would forever remain. He was thankful that the blast didn't penetrate a muscle and only grazed him. Kara's mystery injection had proved very helpful in aiding the healing process.

"How're you feeling?" Severine called back to Alex, who remained at the rear of the group.

"Like a new man," Alex replied with a smile, nudging Kara playfully.

"Makes me feel better that we're armed again," Adam added.

Among the rubble of the bridge, they managed to find four ECP-30s, each with two additional pulse magazines. Adam was delighted to find an ECSR-20, which he happily collected and delivered to Alex.

"If we stick to the plan, hopefully that bastard won't have time to confiscate them," Severine added. "Of course, it's risky. We'll only have one shot."

"I like those odds," Alex laughed.

"Seriously," Adam stopped, halting the trek and turning to his companions. "I want to thank all of you for sticking by me through all this. Alex, Kara. I realize it hasn't been the smoothest of excursions with me heading up the operation. You both are all that's left from the original *Burrower* crash, apart from my nephew. I cannot thank you enough for helping me rescue him. You have my word. After we kill this son of a bitch and rescue the hostages, we're getting out of this place for good."

"We'll follow you to the end, Lieutenant," Alex grinned.

"Who else is gonna get us out of here?" Kara added, playfully punching Adam's arm.

Her rowdiness made him laugh.

"And Severine," Adam turned. "You're the main reason why we're all here – you're the one that sent that distress call. And now, you're the only person that's helping us get off this planet. You've stuck your neck out for us, and you're helping me get my nephew back. For that – I'll take a pulse shard for you, any day."

"Yeah, yeah," Severine smile, waving off his speech. "Let's keep trudging or we'll never make it in time. With an FATR like that, he's probably already there waiting for us."

Kara and Alex laughed as they passed them up, heading up the trail toward the crimson peaks that awaited two miles inland. As their bodies moved away, Adam could see the deadly Triassic fugitive eyeing him under her low hood with a nonchalant smile – a trace of attraction.

"Come on," she nudged him. "Let's get this over with."

Then she gave him a last once-over before following the others up the path, smiling shyly as she followed the others.

Adam again thought of his recently deceased girlfriend, Jade. Although it had only been a few days since her horrific death in space, it seemed like an eternity of life-changing events had happened that forced Adam to rethink his life. His many near-death experiences in recent days forced him to reshuffle his priorities. If he ever made it out of here alive, he vowed never to go on another rescue operation again, no matter how much Central Command recommended him. Most of all, he felt guilty for thinking affectionately of Severine.

It's only been a couple of days! Adam thought, staring at her shapeliness as she moved in front of him, hacking through the undergrowth ahead with a stalwart log. *What would Jade think? Besides, there's a mission to focus on. You need to concentrate on how to get Nathan back, not ogle over this marooned beauty!*

But no matter how hard he tried, Adam couldn't stop thinking about her. She had spent years fending for her life in a world where death was lurking around every corner. Against insurmountable odds she triumphed, memorizing the landscape in her years in solitude. Her resilience and will to live mixed with her becoming appearance made him yearn to know her more. Another attractive feature she possessed; her deadly mastery of any weapon. It was a trait that had saved him on more than one occasion. He resolved that, if they both made it back to Solis in one piece, he would make an effort to court her.

Cacawww!

A winged creature that Severine identified as a pterosaur called *Carniadactylus* soared high above them, noting their position once with another primordial call before veering left, yawing away into the clouds.

The jungle ahead began to grow less dense. The tightly compacted pine trees now gave way to spacious trails as the forest began a transition into grassy wooded lots. Apart from a few Pisanosaurs grazing among the undergrowth, the area was free from other lifeforms. Through the distant ferns, the base of the first red mountain rose up before them on the other side of a game trail. An adjacent forest across the trail cut through the grassland, signaling that the foliage became thick once more before it ascended the mountain slope.

Traces of broken poles and long extinguished firepits lay shrouded under the lower plants. The grass was matted, trampled by old Federation boot impressions. Adam noticed several of the trees contained pulse blast impressions.

"Where are we?" he asked as the group stopped.

"We're nearing the rendezvous point," Severine replied. "Alex, Kara, make yourselves scarce. Follow from a distance, but not too close. If they find out you're following us, our idea of recapturing the hostages is kaput."

"Right. Watch your backs out there," Kara suggested. "We don't know how many of his Exiles are waiting. They could be spread out through the area."

"We'll be watching over you," Alex added, patting Adam on the shoulder. "Just make sure you draw him out long enough for me to get the shot off. If you keep him talking for a while, it'll make my job a lot easier. After I drop him, you need to get ghosted. His mercenaries will finish the job if you remain in the vicinity."

"Will do, Alex. Let's end this charade and portal oscillate our asses back to Solis."

#

The game trail continued northward, winding along the red bases of the rocky hills. The sun blazed down on them from above, forcing Adam to replenish fluids several times along the trek. He estimated about fifteen minutes had passed before Severine stopped at a fork in the game trail.

"This is it," she stated. "This is where he'll meet us."

"What makes you so sure?" Adam asked.

"Trust me," she replied with a nod. "They've camped here before. It's where they brought me. It's also where I cut off his hand."

She gestured to a bloody slide mark along a nearby boulder. The blood had dried from long ago, but traces still lingered, hugging the surface of the porous stone. A few scattered bone fragments remained from the base of the boulder in the grass; remnants from what the dinosaurs refused to salvage.

"You should have cut off more than his hand," Adam remarked, wincing at the gruesome findings.

"That was my intent," Severine leered. "His guards would've finished me off if I continued. If I had him alone, maybe none of this would've happened."

"You handled Wyatt for me. Maybe I can return the favor."

"I wouldn't mind in the slightest."

An abrupt rustling in the jungle cut the conversation short, causing them both to turn to face the upcoming threat. The ferns on the other side of the game trail stirred as two figures approached, clad in tattered black garbs and blood smeared Federation armor. The first to emerge was a vengeful female face.

Arien.

"I found them, *Juane!*" she called back into the undergrowth as her tired lover lingered after her.

A second man, whom Adam assumed was Juane, stumbled out of the brush. His right arm was completely severed off from what looked like an animal attack. His skin looked pale from the amount of blood lost in the unknown skirmish. In his remaining hand he held a crude Neolithic hatchet, although fighting appeared to be the last thing he wanted to engage in.

"Arien," Severine said, keeping her ECP-30 trained on her female Exile counterpart. "I should've known you'd be the one that Deckard would send. What's the plan now? You kill us and take the portal device to the Exiles right after you kill us?"

"Sort of," Arien smiled, trying to catch her breath. From behind her bloody, saturated face a wicked smile began to crack. "You almost had it, Severine. The only difference – I'm not taking orders from Deckard anymore. I'm in this only for myself and Juane. Now if you don't hand over that dazzling little device on your wrist, I'll put a shard through that pretty little skull of yours."

"The hell you will," Adam laughed. "You kill her, you forget about me. I'll put you down so fast, you won't have time to know what hit you! And at this range, I couldn't miss. Your little stooge with the ax won't be hard to take out either. We've got you outgunned."

"Maybe he's right, Arien..." coughed Juane as he let the hatchet fall from his hands, clattering off the stone below. "They have two guns to our one... I don't think I can really do much here..."

"*Juane!*" she snapped. "Pick up that ax! Stop acting like a whiny bitch and help me! We're this close to getting out of here and you're pussying out on me now? After all we've been through?"

"Pussying out? Arien... the sauros took off my arm... they wiped out our plan... It's over."

Juane collapsed onto his kneecaps, letting another agonizing cough out as he stared hypnotically ahead, accepting of death. Blood continued to drip from his wound, staining the ferns beneath him.

"It changes nothing," Arien hissed coldly.

"Arien... you must... understand..."

"No, Juane. *You* must understand! If you can't help me with this, then you're of no use to me," she turned the gun away from Severine and pointed it at Juane's sweaty brow. "I'm sorry, slick."

"You cold bitch. I... hope you get what's coming to *yo* –"

VRRR! SPLSH!

Adam frowned, disturbed by Arien's cold-blooded nature.

A flash of gold erupted as Juane's body bowled over, eyes bulging open as the greenery of the game trail overtook his body, allowing only his shoulder to be exposed above the leafy swaying tips. Arien turned the pistol back to Severine, a devilish smile on her lips.

"Now, where were we?"

"You really are a heartless bitch, aren't you, Arien?" Adam smirked, keeping her head between his sight, finger teasing the trigger gently.

"It's how I got to be where I'm at," she shrugged with a laugh. "Now, maybe we can work something out here. You see, I'm a little desperate, if you couldn't tell. I can't go back to Deckard. My intuition tells me he already knows what I was planning. He'll kill me rather than take me back into the Exiles. Coming with you is my only choice."

Adam could hear the desperation in her voice. In between sentences she would look around to make sure no one was eavesdropping from the forest. Her speech sounded rushed, as if time was counting down swiftly for her imminent death. Arien may have wanted out of the Triassic more than he did.

"You assuming little bitch," Severine laughed. "What makes you think we'll take you anywhere? You could've helped when they abducted me. Instead you sat by and watched – you left me to die. *Augh!* It's taking everything in me not to blast you right now! Tell me, Arien, if Adam didn't have a second gun on you, would you show the same restraint toward me?"

"You flatter yourself, Severine," Arien thought. "You think I'm not able to kill you both if I wanted to. I'll have you know, I –"

CRRNNNCHHH!!

The conversation was cut short by the sounds of crunching twigs in the jungle behind Arien, followed by haunting laughter. Many figures began to appear inside the thicket, pushing aside the jungle growth as they marched onto the pathway. A second group approached from the game trail, numbering around fifteen, armed with XR-90s. Delios Deckard emerged from the woods, followed by ten additional soldiers. With a wave of his sworded hand, he ordered them to halt a good distance away from the standoff.

"What do we have here?" he taunted Arien with a devious smirk, staring at her behind the facial bruising. "Arien, where are your fellow mercenaries I sent with you? Looks like the only one accounted for is Juane and, well, I see how you treated him in his time of need."

The warlord glanced down at Juane's corpse in disgust, still shrouded among the ferns.

"The sauros got to them," Arien replied bluntly. "Severine and the others led us into an area infested with them. We were ambushed. Most of the crew perished after the initial attack. Juane and I were the only ones to make it out alive. He died from his wounds."

Deckard turned and looked down again at the corpse, kneeling down and pulling apart the ferns near the skull.

"Actually, Arien, it looks like he took a blast from a pulse pistol to the face. Judging by the smoky wisps coming off your pistol, I'd say you killed him – recently."

He rose to his feet again, the inquisitive, humorous demeanor earning laughs among the other Exiles who funneled into the standoff. Arien kept her weapon pointed at Severine, who continued to return the favor. The other Exiles stood away from the engagement, refusing to attack or raise their firearms.

"I had to," Arien lied. "He was planning to betray you. He... he wanted that portal thing for himself! So did the rest of the team that went with us!"

"Seems awfully suspicious that you yourself didn't join in this little plot, no?"

"Delios, I swear – I didn't. I went along with it for the time being, yes. So they wouldn't kill me. They said they would have! I watched Juane kill Brine myself. You have to believe me! I feared for my life. That's the only reason I played along."

Deckard smiled, turning to his armed escorts that now enveloped the area.

"What do you all think?" Deckard asked. "Because you know what I think. I think Arien was going to betray all of us. She handpicked her own strike team to go after Severine – conveniently, her team were more of the rebellious ones that we've dealt with in the past. I'm willing to wager she went in there hoping to kill Severine and take the portal oscillator for herself. If that were the case, we'd all be stuck here forever, wouldn't we?"

A murmur of agreement from the ranks caused Arien to tremble with her hands, although she refused to turn the gun away from Severine. A few chants of 'traitor!' and 'that bitch!' erupted from the guards. Deckard swelled the uproar with a graceful raising of his arm blade.

"Now, now. We all know what Arien really is. I'm confident what we've stumbled upon here is Arien's last step in her master plan to complete what she started. Unfortunately for her, Adam survived as well, and now she's outnumbered."

"Deckard, this is absurd!" Arien cried, sweating profusely. "It's not true – none of it is. Now, why won't you help me get the oscillator from that bitch! She has it! It's right on her wrist!"

#

Stand still, you prick!

Alex stared into the digital scope of the ECSR-20, trying to align the red bead on Deckard's head. There were a few problems with his vantage point. For one, he knew there were several Exiles still remaining in the brush nearby, which committed him to his spot for fear of being noticed. Next, the wind was beginning to pick up moving the leaves frantically ahead of him, frequently obscuring his visual of the warlord. And finally, Deckard was very animated throughout his spiel – refusing to stand still. His movement was becoming increasingly tricky to predict, prolonging his assassination.

Kara, be safe.

The medical specialist had parted ways with the sniper five minutes earlier to locate and infiltrate the FATR, which Alex assumed remained in close proximity to the rendezvous point. There, he speculated, she would find both Nathan and Jordy, hopefully unguarded. If they were guarded, he had no doubt that his new love interest could handle herself in a firefight.

He sat on his makeshift perch – a sturdy branch in a pine tree fifteen feet from the ground, masked behind the canopy from the neighboring crowded branches. When the Exiles passed below him minutes earlier, he was shocked that they hadn't spotted him. But after hearing the commotion generated from Severine and Arien, which ultimately resulted in the wounded Exile's murder, he assumed Deckard's forces were more infatuated with what was happening on the ground than the outlying jungle.

His finger twitched. Alex caught himself before pressing the trigger, breathing and lowering the scope and then re-centering himself, trying to relocate the target. If he had an adequate silencer on the barrel, he might have debated picking off a few mercenaries still lingering in the jungle before choosing to take on the big prize.

Just then, a sudden noise disturbed him, forcing him to look away from the scope. His first thought was that Kara had located the FATR and climbed into a hatch, echoing throughout the woodland. When none of the Exiles ahead in the clearing looked around to investigate, he assumed they hadn't heard it.

As he prepared to lock onto the target a final time, the sound occurred again, this time much closer.

CRUNCH...

He turned away from the scope to decipher the noise.

That's not the FATR or the Exiles. What the hell could it be?

He got his answer when he looked below.

At the base of the trunk, masked in the undergrowth, was an adult Saurosuchus, mouth dripping with saliva and blood of an unknown, prior victim. Alex watched in awe as the beast inched forward slowly, its massive tail swaying and gently rustling the ferns as it moved, eyeing the unsuspecting humans on the trail ahead.

Whoa!

With a closer inspection, Alex noticed that the forest floor was actually crawling with sauros of all sizes, each moving slowly toward their central point of focus – the game trail ahead just beyond the tree line where Deckard continued his lengthy tirade. The Saurosuchus below Alex let out a gentle groan as it continued its silent approach toward the clearing, leading the advance in what would soon be a deadly ambush.

This should be interesting, Alex thought, pressing his eye into the scope once more.

XXIV

"That's enough, Arien!" Deckard went on. "No amount of diverting my attention can change your fate. Take her weapon!"

"How about eat shit and die, Deckard!"

Arien spun fast, her hair a blur as she swiftly raised the pulse pistol at Deckard's forehead. The warlord made no move to escape, instead pointing at her discreetly.

VRRR!

An XR-90 blast streaked out from the closest Exile, catching the tip of Arien's wrist.

"*Augh!*" she screeched, dropping her pistol as it discharged once on the ground.

"Oh, Arien," Deckard smiled. "How predictable."

She cried, falling to her knees and trying to pat the cauterized wound, only to burn her other hand in her efforts, causing her more agony. As Arien made a move for her fallen pistol a few feet away, another blast struck the weapon, exploding the firearm into a hundred sparking metallic scraps.

Adam's forehead pounded as he mentally debated which of the Exiles he should be pointing his weapon at, now that Arien was disarmed.

Come on, Alex, take the shot! They're confused and not paying attention...

"I should've stayed behind," Arien whined. "With the Colony. I should've never joined your operation. That was my mistake. It changed me. You changed me, Deckard!"

The Colony? Adam thought. *Was it another reference to the Exiles? Or something else?*

"I want you to know I'll enjoy this."

"Just do it," the wounded female warrior coughed. "I don't have all day."

"As you wish."

He made a motion with his sworded arm. The Exiles behind him fanned away from her as Deckard backed up. The other clan of Exiles on the game trail did the same, shuffling as far back as the tree line.

"Severine. Adam," Deckard said. "You may want to back away from her. I'd hate to lose the oscillator because you stood too close to the kettle."

What is he talkin –

Severine pushed Adam hurriedly away from the kneeling fugitive.

Arien looked around in bewilderment, trying to figure out why everyone was skirting away from her, and then she saw it – a glowing large orange light, shining through the branches, twenty feet above Deckard's smiling visage. As the light grew to a large orb, she accepted her fate and closed her eyes, spreading her arms in a welcoming, albeit defiant embrace.

"Annoying, even amid death," Deckard scoffed. "Let her have it, Tanner!"

BRRRRR!

The parked FATR fired the massive blast from the twin XP-300 pulse cannons, the orange beam burning through the tree canopy. Chunks of forest debris and body parts sprung up from where Arien was kneeling, soaring upward in a small red shockwave before raining back down, coating the area in her blood. After the tremor settled, Adam stared at the bloody crater left behind, in awe of the FATR's immaculate firepower.

"*Whoo!* Good hit, Tanner!"

Deckard turned and gave a courtesy wave through the foliage. Adam could see the FATR cockpit now as plain as day, fifty yards into the brush. After Tanner returned the wave from the machine's cockpit, Deckard turned back to Severine and Adam.

"Now that she's been dealt with, it's time to conduct the exchange," Deckard began with a wide grin.

He stepped forward with his guards, surrounding them in a semi-circle. Severine lowered her weapon, knowing they were surrounded and outgunned. Adam cursed before also complying and lowering his gun.

"Just as long as you don't plan to double cross us," Severine said, studying Deckard.

"Don't play me for a fool, Severine," the warlord answered, taking a step forward. "I'm nothing to my men if I'm not at least a man of my word. You must know I take my departure from these lands very seriously. Why would I kill you, knowing that the Triassic wilderness that I leave behind will finish the task for me?"

"You're a comedian, aren't you, Deckard?" Severine winced.

"Indeed," the warlord chuckled. "Now, onto business. I take it that your new dazzling bracelet is the device in question? From here, I must say, it hardly looks like a portal generating gadget, although I've never seen one myself to be sure. Now, fork it over!"

Severine took a step back, refusing to submit.

"Might I remind you, Severine, that I have both the boy and the bot in our rover? I'll have no problem executing either of them for the violation of our agreement."

"*No!*" Adam cried, stepping forward to intervene but barred entrance by a pair of Deckard's cronies.

"*Okay!*" Severine cried reluctantly, stripping the device from her wrist and handing it to Deckard who quickly plucked it from her hands.

"Now, that's better," Deckard said, examining the unique contraption. "I'm assuming it works by this small hologram port. I haven't seen a device this ornate in a long time. Just look at how those bubbles flow continuously through those blue circular pipes. Beautiful, isn't it?"

"I'd say so," Severine said calmly. "Now, do we have a deal?"

Crunch...

A gentle snapping of wood rang out through the clearing, causing the guards to turn and survey the jungle behind them.

"What was that?" Deckard asked, lowering the device and turning to his soldiers.

"Might be one of the Pisanosaurs," suggested one of the men near the back.

"Check it out, the three of you!" Deckard snapped. "It might be one of the other three that Severine went into the swamp with. They might be planning something! Find who it is and bring them back here to me at once!"

"We aren't double crossing you, I swear it!" Adam pleaded. "Our three friends died in the sauro swamps. We just want the hostages back. I don't know what made that noise, but I assure you, it wasn't us."

"Well, Adam, deal's off!" Deckard roared. "At least until I can be sure you aren't trying to trick me."

#

Damn bugs!

Kara Barnels crawled on her stomach through the insect-ridden landscape on the Triassic ground. The hovering pests had been plaguing her from the moment she lost sight of Alex in the tree minutes ago. Her terrible decision-making abilities led her down a small gulch in the woods where the bugs had been feeding off a bloated Exaeretodon corpse. Fighting back vomiting, she held her breath and crawled around the dead creature, continuing her slow journey toward the elusive rover.

It must be close! That blast sounded nearby...

She didn't have time to guess, and she knew it. Not knowing whether the FATR blast had killed her friends or if it was only a test firing, Kara realized how urgent her mission was, expediting her progress as she double-timed it through the shrubs.

Oh God! I hope they're still alive. Please let them be alive...

The forest began to drop down, the gully feeding into a spacious wooded area. Kara abandoned her crawl in favor of a crouching run, darting from tree to tree, carefully watching the area for any Exiles that might be left patrolling near the FATR's concealed location.

Then she saw it – a pair of long metallic tubes cutting through the trees some eight feet above her head, aimed to the right, where presumably the rendezvous point remained. She followed the tubes back down, noticing that they connected with a chrome roof, with several external communication ports and antennas. Through the branches, the orange cockpit began to appear amid the green painted camouflage metal. The rest of the vehicle was out of view, tucked below a berm, allowing the vehicle to be parked slightly below her elevation.

Found it!

She looked both ways for more soldiers on patrol and continued to the rover. Slowly, she peered over the edge of the berm down to the base of the muddied treads.

There was only one guard patrolling the base of the vehicle. In the cockpit, Kara noticed two other men, but they weren't paying attention to what was happening on the ground. She exhaled in relief when she turned to her right, peering through the burning hole that scorched the jungle. Through the marred vegetation that formed a leafy frame, she saw that both Severine and Adam were still alive, talking to Deckard. Their body language told her they were outgunned and had surrendered.

Kara looked again at the guard. The male soldier was carrying an ancient Federation pulse rifle, and was walking away from her, toward the front of the rover.

A second observation revealed the rear hatch to the rover was open and unguarded.

Okay, now how do I get down the –

Kara failed to check her footing, cringed when she saw the ground give way, and slid down the slope. The hillside fractured around her, sending her skidding down to a small patch of shrubs less than fifteen feet from the rover's giant treads.

She froze as she looked around again in panic, relaxing when she realized her faux pas went unnoticed.

That was a close one! Now, I assume the rear hatch is the only way I can get in...

As she inched toward the back of the enormous machine, she noticed several ladders leading up to the roof of the FATR. Several weapon ports sat unmanned on the roof – for that she was thankful. Kara debated whether or not to make a break for the ladders, but decided there could be other unseen guards.

Finally, she lurched through enough vegetation to view the back of the FATR, which also remained unguarded. In the back of the enormous mobile battle station, she noticed Nathan and Severine's bot, tethered together in what looked like an ancient military locker room. They were both struggling with the cords, making minimal progress.

She looked both ways again before she stood up briefly from the foliage and waved at them. Nathan wasn't looking in her direction, deep in conversation with the bot. The bot was blocked by Nathan's head, so wasn't visually accessible either.

Dammit! she thought, looking for a break, knowing what had to happen.

I have to run in. I can blast through their bindings and we can take off into the jungle. They'll never find us. It would help if I had some type of distractio –

The sound of a turning pulse rifle pressed against the back of her head made her freeze.

No! The guard at the front of the rover – he must have doubled back and heard me falling down the hill!

"I remember you," came a cruel, demeaning male voice behind her. "You're the medical one. Deckard will commend me for taking you out. Right after he kills the others and takes what is rightfully ours!"

Kara turned to face her killer. It was a young man with reddish short hair, peering down at her six feet away with his pulse rifle, the barrel already glowing with a fresh charge.

"Any last words?" came the wicked question.

She struggled to come up with something witty or an excuse for him not to fire, when a brown object behind the man captured her attention. She thought at first it was a tree falling slowly behind the ferns, but when she saw the rows of jagged, bloody teeth, she recognized what it was.

Saurosuchus!

Crunch!

A twig snapped behind the gunman as the monster drew near.

"The hell was that?" the man asked, turning to see what was coming. Before he had time to utter a useless scream for help, the adult Saurusuchus reared up to its full height, cocked its head to one side and crunched down on the man's skull. The guard's arms flailed up to pry the monster off as he dropped the rifle. With a final crunch the beast broke the man's neck, pulled the corpse to the ground and began to devour it.

The creature shot a cold, reptilian look at Kara before returning to its meal. Terrified that it might attack, she turned to run back to the FATR doors, but halted abruptly before continuing.

Two other sauros were already wandering around the base of the vehicle. They hadn't yet spotted Nathan and Jordy, but continued their approach toward the rear hatch.

Shit! What do I do?

Alex hadn't yet fired a shot, which was supposed to be the signal for her to proceed. If she gunned down the sauros now, Deckard and his thugs would hear the shots – then all of their friends would be killed and the oscillator stolen forever. There was nothing she could do.

Defeated, she slid away into the brush and waited for an opportunity, warily keeping an eye on the feasting sauro.

#

Deckard, you son of a bitch!

Alex cursed mentally, watching helplessly from his perch as a trio of Exiles left the game trail and appeared in the jungle below him. From his spot in the trees, they would easily find him if he didn't move. The only problem in vacating his hiding place; the numerous sauros that lay in wait all around the perimeter, continuously inching closer to the game trail. Several of the specimens had slipped out of his vision, but he still noticed two of them close by, salivating while they observed the action unfolding on the path.

He looked again through the scope. More wind rustled the palm fronds and again barred his view of Deckard, so Alex ruled out taking the shot.

The three Exiles approached from below, fanning out through the shrubbery as they searched for the mysterious source of the noise. Their confident movements told Alex that they were unaware of the many terrors awaiting just ahead of their position.

They'll see me up here – I'm a sitting duck!

He knew what he had to do – descend to the ground. The ground that contained many adult sauros, roaming about for a fresh target.

God help me! Hang on, Adam! Just a little longer. Just have to dispatch these reptilians first!

Silently, Alex positioned himself to the opposite side of the trunk away from the approaching mercenaries and moved down the branches, careful not to step too loudly that it might draw attention from the gunmen or the sauros.

As the tip of his boot touched the mulch floor, he eased off the branches, turning to keep his back to the trunk, and slowly drew a long knife that he obtained from the *Harvester One* ruins.

Where are you, asshole?

A minute later, Alex heard footsteps on the other side of the tree. When none of the crouching sauros in the area made a move for the Exile, Alex knew he'd have to act on the guard himself. A few seconds passed, and a long chrome barrel appeared beside him, coming around the side of the tree as the cautious soldier approached, unaware of the impending danger waiting behind the trunk.

In a clean, discreet move, Alex plunged the knife into the guard's jugular, bringing his palm over the man's mouth to silence his scream. Gradually, Alex eased the body to the forest floor, taking his hand from the mouth after he was sure the man was dead.

After he rose back to his feet, he saw the next Exile approaching just to his left, twenty feet away in the brush, continuing onward and unaware of the murderous encounter that just happened to his teammate. One of the hidden, younger sauros eyed the second guard, stalking the gunman behind a row of tall pines.

Say goodnight, you prick.

The sauro lunged through the trees, breaking the guard's neck with a strong crunch of the jaws, pinning the helpless warrior beneath with its crushing weight. The super predator quickly tore into the feast, tossing up bloody entrails into the air as it ravaged the corpse. Several other younger sauros appeared through the undergrowth, sliding past Alex who froze as they glided past. They ignored the sniper, heading over to partake in the savory feast of the dead man.

Two down, one to go. Now, where did that cocksucker get t –

"*Hey!* You there!" called a harsh voice to Alex's right.

Damn!

"Hey! Asshole! Turn around and meet your maker!"

With pleasure.

Executing a move that he hadn't pulled off since his training on Solis at Central Command combat training camps, Alex spun around and dove ahead, knowing this would draw some of the sauros to his position based on the quick movement. As he lurched forward, he threw the knife with a skillful flick of the wrist, sending the dagger blade first into the skull of the final gunman.

Alex hit the ground and rebounded back to his feet, scampering back up the tree as a large, muscular Saurosuchus lumbered out of the jungle toward him, chomping at his heels, missing only by inches as the sniper arrived at his perch.

Nice try.

Alex relaxed on the high branch as the massive Saurosuchus fell back to the ground, choosing instead to bump away the younger sauros that were feasting on the first human corpse. With the mercenaries down and the monsters distracted with their meals, Alex once again armed the sniper rifle and pressed his eye into the scope.

To his horror, he witnessed at least eight adult sauros at the edge of the jungle, ready to attack the humans on the game trail. If the sauros attacked, it was likely that Deckard would flee, and the mission would be a critical failure.

Dammit! Okay, Deckard, here I come!

#

"Come on, Deckard!" Adam yelled. "We've given you everything you've asked for! You have a one-way ticket back to paradise in the palm of your hand. Now, let my nephew and the bot go. There's no one out in those woods!"

"Quiet, Adam!" Deckard roared. "I don't know you very well, but trust me when I say that you're already wearing out your welcome. Now, until my men come back from the jungle with the report, I won't agree to anything. Damn, they should've been back by now! Where are they?"

"Not sure, sir," replied one of the Exile guards. "Do you want me to go check?"

"No," Deckard replied. "I smell something suspicious brewing, and I don't want any of us walking into a trap."

"There's no trap, Deckard!" Severine yelled. "Just take the device and give us back the hostages!"

He has no intention of honoring the agreement, Adam thought, his hand clenching the pulse pistol at his side, debating on snapping it up and killing the warlord himself. *He'll take the oscillator and kill us all – then probably Nathan and Jordy too. Come on, Alex! Take the shot!*

"I'm not giving you anything, Severine!" yelled Deckard, finally admitting the truth. "Except maybe a sword to choke on!"

"Do it, asshole!" Severine screamed as Deckard approached, raising his sword to strike her down.

#

Finally, Deckard came into view behind the branch barrier, raising his weapon to strike at Severine. Alex followed his head with the bead of the sniper scope, switched off the safety and prepared to fire. Suddenly, below his tree, the sauros took off toward the game trail, presumably egged on by the warlord's deranged screaming.

Make this one count, Meras!

As the prehistoric monsters prepared to crash through the clearing and engage the humans in a life or death struggle, Alex breathed calmly and pressed the trigger, sending a pulse round sailing through the trees at the intended target.

XXV

VRRR!

CLUNK!

An orange blast sailed out from the trees, burning through Deckard's bladed arm and shooting through an adjacent Exile's head, killing the man instantly. By the time the guard's body struck the grassy trail, Deckard spun around, waving his severed blade in the direction of the attack.

"The shooter came from that area! All of you, find out *wh –*"

Deckard's words were cut short as fear gripped the warlord.

"RAUGHHH!"

With a powerful crash, the first sauro that pushed through to the clearing crunched down on the nearest Exile. Lifting up the soldier in its powerful mouth, the creature shook the man to and fro in a horrific display of aggression.

"Saurosuchus!" yelled one of the frightened Exiles, his weapon trembling in his hands.

Adam watched in terror as several more sauros burst through the canopy toward the game trail, gnashing their jaws in anticipation of their dinner.

"Take them down!" Deckard ordered to his men, drawing a pulse pistol and aiming it at Adam's head.

Adam froze as he saw the weapon being lined up with his skull. Chaos enveloped the clearing as the sauros met with the Exiles, quickly tearing into the first wave of mercenaries, but all Adam could focus on was the orange charge building up in Deckard's pistol.

"Sorry, Mr. Ross," he laughed. "Deal's off!"

The orange orb grew and flew toward Adam's face, sailing out of the warlord's barrel. Time seemed to shift and slow down as Adam watched the blast approaching – his life events playing out before his eyes. When the events of the last few days replayed themselves, Adam realized he was having a near-death experience. Had it not been for the sudden impact to his left, the blast would've decapitated him.

VRRR!

Adam watched the golden blast pass over his head as Severine rammed into him, pushing them both behind a set of trees at the edge of the red mountainous base.

Shit! That was a close one!

He crawled behind a tree trunk as Deckard continued to fire away at them from the clearing as more sauros entered the fray. Already the Exile forces had been cut down by a third, choosing to fight off the creatures rather than pursue Severine and Adam.

"I thought Alex would never fire that shot," Adam said, popping off a round from the ECP-30 and tagging one of the Exiles nearest Deckard, killing the guard with a shot to the chest.

"I would've preferred if it hit that asshole rather than decapitate his sword," Severine replied from the trunk next to him, shooting two rounds before ducking back for cover.

The game trail had become a complex web of pulse fire, blood, and death. Sauros continued to pour through the jungle after Deckard's men, lured by the blood of Arien and Juane when they returned from *Harvester One*. Once a mercenary was taken down, the sauros piled onto the corpse, only to be gunned down by the remaining soldiers. Adam noticed it took many pulse rounds to bring one of the animals down – the Exiles wouldn't last long against the primordial onslaught.

Severine tagged one of the men beside Deckard, failing to hit the slinking warlord as he weaved back toward the conflict with the dinosaurs. Adam tried to pick him off as the merciless leader retreated into the fray, missing by a hair and hitting a juvenile Saurosuchus instead.

"*Retreat!*" Deckard yelled to his followers. "We have what we need! We're getting to the rover and activating this bloody thing! Let the sauros finish off Severine and her friend!"

Retreating was easier said than done. Only a few fortunate mercenaries would be able to get through the Saurosuchus pack to the rover, at the cost of other Exiles being mauled to clear the path. Deckard herded himself in the middle of his survivors as they plowed a path back to the jungle, carelessly pushing aside other soldiers into the jaws of the sauros as they gave their lives to get their boss to safety. After the initial sacrifices, six survivors including Deckard streaked away from the battleground, running to the sanctuary. A handful of other Exiles remained in the fray, cut off from their retreating companions and forced to fend for themselves.

PHROOOOOOR!

CRUNCH! CRUNCH!

Adam watched across from the game trail as the FATR pushed through the trees, churning up the trunks beneath the spiked treads to retrieve Deckard and the remaining Exiles that escaped the central conflict. Soon the massive vehicle was completely visible as it pushed into the sunny clearing.

"What do we do now?" Adam asked. "Just stay here until the sauros finish off Deckard's men, and then what? Then they'll be coming for us!"

"We sure as hell can't go through them," Severine replied, holstering her pistol. "Save your ammunition – we'll need it."

#

VRRR!

Alex got off another shot, picking off another retreating Exile, bringing Deckard's retreating party to five and narrowly missing the Exile warlord himself by inches. Deckard turned sideways, looking through the jungle, spotting Alex in a tree.

"It's the sniper!" Deckard yelled. "You two, take him out. You two, follow me! The sauros are still on us!"

"Yes, sir," one of the soldiers replied begrudgingly, knowing that by staying behind and buying time for Deckard, he would most likely lose his life.

The pair of warriors began sending pulse blasts up to the tree, causing Alex to jump to the ground.

"Augh!" the sniper cried in pain, landing on his bruised arm that Kara had only recently healed.

There was no time to recover. Orange blasts sailed up toward him, only now Alex didn't have the sauros to provide help.

The sniper rifle! Where's the bloody sniper rifle?

He looked around frantically, amid several pulse blasts that launched past him.

"He's unarmed! Move in!"

Aw, shit!

As he searched the forest floor for his weapon, quickly pushing away ferns, he calculated their distance as they approached up the hill.

Ten seconds. That's all I've got until they're within striking distance! Ah, there it is!

A patch of chrome glistened among a leafy vine, only a few feet away. Alex went to reach for it, just as a metallic XR-90 barrel popped through the undergrowth above him.

"Aha!" came the first soldier's voice. "I got you *motherfu –*"

Click!

The Exile's weapon jammed, opening up an opportunity for Alex to strike back. The sniper rushed the bewildered guard, slamming the young man into a tree trunk, grabbing onto his opponent's rifle and using it as a ramming device.

A rustling of ferns told Alex the other guard was coming up fast to his right. As he struggled with the first Exile, Alex pushed down on the trigger, sending a blast out and killing the oncoming attacker before the newcomer could strike.

WHAM!

With a swift knee to the groin, Alex finally bested his opponent and snatched the gun away from him. The man begged for mercy, sliding down the back of the tree trunk with his spine before slumping onto the ground, grabbing his genitals in agony. Alex turned the weapon on his opponent.

"*Wait!*" the man cried in desperation, waving a free hand in self-defense. "I can give you information. Information on Deckard and the Colony. You might be stuck here a long time if your portal transmitter fails."

"Portal oscillator," Alex corrected him, training the barrel between the Exile's eyes.

In the background, through the jungle on the game trail, the fighting continued. Cries from Deckard's last remaining forces at the rendezvous point were making their last stand as the sauros ripped into them. A rising swell of machinery told him that the FATR was moving to intercept Deckard just ahead of the tree line. There was no sign of Severine, Adam, or Kara.

"Tell me everything!" Alex said, keeping the weapon on his opponent, wiping his forehead of sweat with his free hand.

"Where would I even start?" the man shook, lowering his hands.

"Start by who you are!" Alex yelled. "Are you first generation hyper-sleep pod Federationists? Or did your people crash here years earlier – like the Neolithics?"

"Second and third generation survivors," replied the wounded man. "Our people crashed here fifty or so years ago. Most of us grew up learning about the Federation from our parents, but few thought we'd ever make contact again with any active Federation starships. We were taught the value of pulse weaponry and Federation technology from the future. But it's dying out. The Exiles search the lands to the south for other wrecked Federation ships that had crashed here over the years, looking for more technology to help supplement our life in the Triassic."

"What's the Colony?" Alex asked. "Where do the Exiles come from? *Tell me!*"

"You should've wasted me when you had the chance," smiled the fallen, smug warrior.

Alex then realized his mistake – letting the man lower his hands. Throughout the back and forth dialogue, the Exile silently made a move for his back, where an X2-20 pulse pistol awaited. With a smile of contentment, Alex watched in terror as his captive swiftly retrieved the weapon and sent a pulse shard into his arm, inches below the healed dagger wound.

VRRR!

"*Augh!*" Alex cried as he fell on his back.

The heat and acidity of the blast was tremendously more painful than the Neolithic's dagger wound. A wave of fiery torment crawled up his arm. But the pain would pass in time – there was something else that needed attending to first.

VRRR!

Returning the favor, Alex shot the Exile through the chest. The man screamed as his body convulsed, dying in agony as the sparks erupted out of his torso like a volcano. Finally, the man dropped the pistol, the gun clattering off the tree root by the corpse's feet, no longer a threat.

Alex dropped his head, letting it touch the moist soil from the back of his scalp as he rolled into a fetal position, trying to tend to his wounds. With his arm marred by a pulse weapon, he was effectively taken out of the fight.

The Colony? The Exiles? Were they the same? What did it all mean?

Darkness overtook his vision as he stared mindlessly up at the Triassic sun shining through the trees, as the sounds of dying soldiers and sauro roars filled the area.

#

PHROOOR!

Kara stared up at the FATR rear entrance through the ferns as exhaust fumed out from the chrome underbelly. The gargantuan machine began to move slowly forward, crushing trees with its powerful approach.

Screw this sneaking around bullshit!

"*Dammit!* Nathan! Hey, I'm coming!"

She stood up from the shrubs and waved her arms, shouting as loud as she could. In the back of the rover, Nathan and Jordy turned and looked, surprised to see her and waving her over to board the vehicle.

"Kara! Help us!" Nathan screamed.

"*We-e-ere* stuck!" the bot added with a digital shout.

"Don't worry!" Kara yelled, streaking out from her vegetation barrier and into the FATR's self-carved road.

Damn! The roof!

Deckard's second-in-command, muscle-bound enforcer appeared on the roof of the rover as it departed. Wielding an XR-90 he fired the weapon down at her in a barrage of orange laser fire. She exchanged shots with the man, but the pulse blasts sailing down at her made the pursuit too perilous. With a dive, she jumped behind a log, with more rounds launched toward her from Deckard's advancing crew on the ground.

This has all gone to shit!

The plan had gone disastrously wrong, as she observed from her vantage point in the shrubs. The sauros moved in to disrupt the deal, causing chaos and confusion during their coordinated attack. Alex missed his shot, leading to Deckard's escape. She caught sight of the warlord and a few others running toward the FATR. After some fire from the jungle,

Deckard dispatched two of them to investigate.

They must be going after Alex!

"There's the other woman!" she heard Deckard yell as he ran toward her, trying to access the rear FATR doors. "Don't let her near our rover! Tanner, prepare to seal the rear hatch!"

"Yes, sir!" Tanner called from the roof of the FATR, disappearing from Kara's view.

They're going to seal up the hatch and trap Nathan inside!

She darted up from the log only to be forced back again by a barrage of pulse fire from Deckard's guards. Avoiding two blasts to her ear, she looked up just in time to see the warlord and his duo of remaining Exile guards jump into the rear hatch.

"Seal her up, Tanner!" called Deckard as he relaxed under the safety of the rover.

Damn!

She stood up from the log as the rear hatch sealed. Deckard turned to her and gave her a mocking salute as he disappeared behind the vaulted door, sealed safely inside the stronghold. The camouflaged rover lumbered away, continuing to carve a new game trail through the foliage with the slicing Carnivore attachment blades.

I have to go after it, she thought, wiping sweat from her forehead as she checked the area for remaining sauros.

VRRR!

A blast from the woods made her pause, followed by a scream and a blast from Alex's sniper rifle.

"Alex!"

She took off running to the left back into the jungle, letting the FATR continue its escape undeterred. The sauros had left the wooded region, their calls echoing down from the game trail as she continued into the shrubs. Several of the Exile's corpses were lying about in the brush, two of which were the victims of knife wounds; their bodies ravaged by the carnivores after their deaths.

Oh, please be alive! Alex, where are you?

Her heart raced as she searched the greenery. The thought of something grim happening to him made Kara nauseous.

There!

Finally, at the base of a tree, she spotted two still forms lying solemnly among the leafy stems. One of the corpses she didn't recognize – his face warped into a death scream and his chest disintegrated via a recent pulse blast. The other face was hidden by a low hanging branch, but she recognized him from the outfit.

"Alex!" she screamed, brushing through the leaves.

She leaned down to examine him. As Kara looked him over, a glowing orange mark on his arm attracted her attention. Small sparking fragments fizzled out from the skin, eating away at the muscle tissue where the blast did its terrible work.

He's been shot by a pulse round! Right through the arm!

"Alex, can you hear me?" she yelled, pounding on his chest.

She could hear the FATR churning foliage somewhere behind her, slashing through tree limbs, followed by a cacophony of pulse blasts from the few remaining Exiles left on the game trail. Soon the sounds of the fray had melted away, as she knelt down on the forest floor trying to revive her unresponsive lover.

#

"*Augh! Auuegh!*"

The last Exile soldier remaining in the clearing was swarmed by the sauro pack. One of the adult monsters latched onto the man's torso while two other juveniles chomped onto his legs. With his final cry, the soldier fell, just as the FATR pushed into the clearing, churning trees into splinters and flinging them into the game trail.

Severine and Adam remained behind the trees at the base of the mountains, watching the action unfold, conserving their ammunition.

"What are we gonna do?" Adam turned to her. "They're getting away with my nephew and our ticket out of here!"

"Calm down," Severine urged him, peering at the rover coming toward them through the brush. "We need to wait for Alex and Kara."

"They're dead!" Adam yelled back, losing his temper. "They would've been here by now, Severine! We have to act on this! It's now or never!"

"You don't know that they're dead!" she shot back. "Use your head! Did you see them die? What do you expect to do? Take on Deckard yourself? He's sealed inside that thing! There's no way in!"

"There has to be! There has to be..."

The sauros turned to watch the FATR approach, growling at its oncoming blades as they scavenged through the first row of animal and human corpses. Someone in the FATR cockpit blared the horn, deterring a few of the juveniles nearest the blades. Roaring in displeasure, they scooted away from the machine and ran off into the jungle, no match for the armored battle station. At the center of the carnage, the alpha male sauro stood up and roared defiantly at the oncoming threat, before giving up and teetering off. Following in their master's footsteps, the remaining sauros followed, leaving the bloody battlefield behind them.

"At least that solves the Saurosuchus problem," Severine observed.

"Severine, they'll ram us!"

"No! They're turning!"

The rover spun to the right, kicking up dirt as the treads turned north. Corpses were rolled out of the way as the ground churned around them.

The rover began to execute a turn up the game trail – a move that slowed the vehicle's progress as the space to perform the maneuver was limited.

"It's getting away, Severine! They're gonna kill Nathan and use the oscillator!"

"They aren't using anything!"

"Yes they will!"

"No they won't!"

"What are you talking about?"

"I removed the damn charge crystals from the rear console!"

"*What?*" Adam stared at her in bewilderment.

She sighed, resting her pistol at her hip as she produced something from a cloak pouch. After unfolding her tattered fingerless gloves, she revealed three charge crystals, two of which had expired.

"I took all three out just in case," she explained. "I figured only the vibrant crystal would work, but better safe than sorry. I couldn't let that maniac escape and leave us here to die. He was going to betray us! Deep down, I knew it! If we didn't make it out from the firefight, it was going to be my last revenge. I'm sorry I kept this from you."

"And what happens when Deckard goes to activate that thing and it doesn't work? Then what, Severine? I'll tell you what happens. He kills your bot – and my nephew!"

"How can you make that assumption?" she argued back. "Deckard will probably keep them to handle a renegotiation. He'll know something is up! He'll probably assume I hot-wired the damn thing and turn the vehicle back around."

"Oh yeah? Well it doesn't look like he's turning anything around."

"What are you gonna do, hot shot?"

"Save my damn nephew, no thanks to you."

Adam cut through the foliage before she could offer a rebuttal, sprinting toward the FATR as it neared completing its ninety degree turn to follow the game trail to the north. To Adam's advantage, the rover's turn put it in a stationary position, allowing him time to catch up to it. Severine watched as the colossal tank spun away, noting that there didn't appear to be anyone guarding the roof.

That crazy son of a bitch might actually pull it off, she thought, watching in awe from the vegetation.

Adam ran up to the right side of the vehicle as it successfully executed the turn, churning aggressively toward the northern path of the Mountains of Blood. With a herculean leap, Adam grabbed onto the sixth rung of the side utility ladder. Severine watched helplessly as his feet dangled inches above the ground as the machine sped up. Finally steadying himself, Adam landed both feet on the bottom rung and began to climb up to the roof, just as the rover climbed over a hill and slipped out from view in the game trail.

Severine darted into the empty clearing, now quiet after the carnage, save for the gentle rustling of the Triassic ferns. Quickly, she foraged through the corpses, grabbing new ammunition for her pulse pistol as well as a long knife from one of the mercenaries before taking off up the trail after the swift armored mobile base.

Hang on, Adam! I know where they're going. And I know a short cut!

XXVI

Gripping the ladder rung with both hands, Adam struggled to hang on as the rover chopped through the jungle. The bumpiness of the journey proved difficult for Adam to maintain his balance, throwing him back and forth, knotting his stomach and generating a painful headache. The faint wound from Wyatt's pulse blast wasn't helpful either, but Kara's medicine did well to alleviate the majority of the burn.

WHAP!

Jungle vegetation began to slam into him from the right as he lowered his neck, trying to hide his eyes from the lashing plant life.

I have to get up this ladder! Won't last long here...

CHOMP!

A familiar gnashing of teeth was heard behind him, followed by a series of swift footsteps over the muddy terrain. A glance down confirmed Adam's worst fears.

A juvenile Herrerasaur was hot on his heels, stamping on the earth and trying to snag onto Adam's left leg as it pursued the fleeing FATR. The dinosaur wasn't big enough to pluck him right off the ladder, but if it latched onto his calf muscle, the weight might drag Adam off the ladder rungs – all the more reason to get to the roof.

CHOMP!

SNAP!

The herrera chomped again, missing as Adam quickly executed a side kick to the creature's jaws, forcing the dinosaur back a few steps and allowing him time to resume his ascent. The carnivore rapidly approached again from below Adam as he climbed higher. After three more failed chomps, the herrera realized its target was too high and abandoned the chase, slinking away into the jungle barrier near the base of the red mountains.

Adam continued his ascent, pausing once to look into the black windows that lined the sides of the rover. The dark glass and chaotic jungle reflections made it impossible to see inside.

Can they see me in there? Are Nathan and Jordy in there? They have to be. How many Exiles does Deckard have left? It can't be many – if he had about forty some soldiers, and most died in the sauro swamp and the remainder were wiped out in the recent attack, it has to be less than ten.

Finally, he reached the top.

Throwing his hand over the upper edge, he pulled himself onto the roof of the vehicle, instantly bombarded by overhanging tree branches that surged past. The rover was so tall that the roof was practically right in line with the upper tree canopy. Below at the treads, he could see several new herreras slowly pursuing the vehicle, although none were large or strong enough to jump onto the roof, eventually giving up the chase like their predecessor did.

Adam searched the roof, trying to understand the vehicle and pinpoint an entrance.

The roof of the FATR was a complex maze of green painted chromatic junction ports and radio equipment cube stations. Several of the components had been rehabilitated to pulse rifle nests, although no guards and weapons were present. A few small geometric obstacles looked like they may have been access hatches, but on closer inspection, Adam realized they were closed circuitry panels.

There must be an access hatch near the front of the rover – there has to be!

Adam resumed his cautious walk down the rumbling machine, careful not to trip on any of the various mechanical components that created the vehicle's roof. Finally, a small circular shape materialized behind one of the junction stations.

The hatch!

VRRR!

Ah, hell!

Adam rolled off to one side, the blast missing his head by accident as his ankle stumbled over an exposed steel pipe. He hit the roof with his shoulder, switching his safety off as he anticipated a firefight.

VRRR!

He looked up from behind cover of a steel cubed ventilation structure, just in time to locate the shooters. A pair of Deckard's lackeys were hiding on the roof behind a crudely constructed gun nest right above the cockpit and directly in front of the access hatch. Entering the vehicle would be impossible without killing both of the roof guards. A two-on-one shootout on the rover wouldn't end well; they had him pinned.

VRRR!

Another blast sailed toward him, scorching into the ventilation structure and fizzling away into sparks. Adam looked over the barrier to return fire, only to be greeted by another blast that narrowly missed his brow.

"Hold your fire!" came a familiar, harsh voice. "Mr. Ross, throw away your weapon and show yourself, immediately."

Deckard.

Adam peered over his cover, half expecting to catch a pulse shard to the head. Instead, he saw that the guards had lowered their weapons. In front of them at the hatch, the warlord popped up through the hole, joined by Nathan's figure in front of him – a pulse pistol aimed at the boy's head.

"Mr. Ross, I must admit this stunt was rather brash. I barely know you and already I'm impressed."

"Nathan, did he hurt you?" Adam called out.

"Not yet," Nathan replied, struggling under his captor's tight grasp.

"Deckard! Let him go! Take me instead, I'm the one you want."

"Of that, I'm sure!" Deckard answered angrily. "But no deal this time. Either you get in here right this second and help me figure out how to work this thing or I'll kill you both! How's that?"

#

"*Ow!* Let go!" Nathan cried, struggling under Deckard's firm grip.

"Be quiet!" Deckard roared back, pushing the child back down through the hatch as the rover streaked through the wilderness. "You two. Kindly make sure Mr. Ross comes down here and doesn't try anything stupid."

Nathan was grateful when his feet touched back down on the internal floor. The thought of his uncle's arrival suddenly lightened his mood. He had doubted that Adam would've survived the sauro swamps and also successfully found the portal oscillator intact. As his uncle stepped off the ladder, he rushed forward and hugged him.

"Man, am I glad to see you!" Adam said, embracing his nephew roughly.

"You came back!" Nathan replied, a hint of emotion in his voice.

"You bet I did."

"Where are the others?"

"It's just us now, kid," Adam replied. "Don't worry, I'm going get you out of here."

"Doubtful, Mr. Ross," Deckard laughed as his two guards descended the ladder. "I might let the kid go. The bot I'm keeping. Your usefulness only goes as far as how well you can troubleshoot the portal device. After that, I'll deal with you as I see fit. I saw plenty of herreras playfully running after the FATR out back. Maybe I'll toss you over to them. That'd be my pleasure to watch."

"You sick bastard." Adam stared him down. "I'll get that portal device working for you. Just don't hurt Nathan. He's already been through enough in this world."

"I'll see how I feel." Deckard smiled.

Adam rushed forward to strike him, but was tackled immediately by the pair of guards that arrived from the roof. As he was body slammed against the cold floor of the rumbling vehicle, a muscular man entered from the cockpit, followed by an additional pair of guards.

"Everything all right in here, sir?" the enforcer asked.

"Perfectly fine, Tanner," Deckard replied. "Mr. Ross has arrived, and by the looks of it, he's already started digging his own grave. Take him to the cockpit and get this contraption working. I want to get out of this hellhole today!"

"Yes, sir," Tanner replied, stepping forward and grabbing Adam by the collar.

With a gruff tug, he pulled Adam to his feet, locking eyes with the new threat.

"Let's go, Mr. Ross!" Tanner ordered, pushing Adam into the room ahead as the metallic doors opened automatically.

"Don't worry, Nathan! I'm coming back for you – I promise!"

"Please, Uncle Adam!" Nathan replied, shouting back. "Get us out of here – I want to go home!"

"I will! Soon!"

Hisss!

The door to the cockpit sealed shut, with Tanner and his pair of guards hauling Adam inside. As the door closed shut, Deckard turned back to Nathan, a scowl on his face.

"If your uncle would've played by the rules, I might've let him live! Instead, he and your friends tried to ambush us – most of our forces are wiped out now, thanks to him. He'll die, along with you, as soon as the oscillator starts working!"

"You can't do this to us!"

"Take him to the rear chamber and seal him in! If he squeals or moans, shoot him!"

#

As the doors to the rover's bridge opened, Adam saw that other than a trio of guards, a pilot, and a scraggly looking scientist, the room was virtually bare. Through the glass, the Triassic jungle streaked past as the FATR picked up speed, pushing swiftly toward an unknown destination. As Adam turned back, he caught a final glimpse of his nephew struggling with a guard as the doors closed behind him.

"I swear if you shoot him," Adam threatened the warlord, before grunting as an abrupt blow to the back of the head sent him tumbling to the ground.

"You need to learn your place," Tanner remarked after striking the new hostage.

"Very intimidating, Mr. Ross," Deckard scoffed, stepping through the frame with Tanner. "But I'm afraid you're out of time and out of bargaining chips. That was some shit you pulled back at the clearing. Looks like your friends weren't dead after all. Well, they probably are now. Those sauros are vicious things. At this point, I'd say I'm the closest thing you have to a friend. Now, tell me how to work this ridiculous contraption!"

"You think I'll agree to help," Adam replied, rubbing his head where Tanner struck him.

"Lest you forget too soon," Deckard went on. "It's not only your life that you're gambling with. Don't think I won't drag him in here and shoot him right in front of you! Or cut him badly and toss him out the rear, and let the sauros or the herreras pick him clean. They have a unique attraction to human blood, as I'm sure you've learned by now. Do you understand?"

Adam nodded grimly.

"Now, stand up and help me fix this piece of shit!"

Adam stood and reached into his pocket for the oscillator charge crystals, when an ominous thought entered his mind.

The charge crystals! I never grabbed them from Severine! For all I know, she's lunch for the sauros or the herreras by now...

Adam scrambled to search for an answer – anything that might buy him some time. His eyes scanned the room as he felt dizzy, certain that death was waiting for him momentarily and, worse, the violent murder of his nephew. His mouth tried to form words, but nothing came out. His head felt itchy, and sweat began to trickle. Deckard stood in front, growing increasingly irritated.

"Ross, don't you know how to operate this thing?"

Adam took the device from Deckard and pretended to examine it, troubleshooting some of the options on the menu, while knowing the true reason the device failed to operate.

I should've snagged those crystals! What was I thinking? Now he'll kill us all!

"Mr. Ross, I'm not a patient man," the warlord went on. "If you can't make that damn thing work, then I might as well toss your ass out back to the carnivores. Eucer, get over here and see if you can make this shitty thing do something!"

The scientist came forward and took the device from Adam's hand, setting it down gently on a utility table near the rear of the bridge. He turned the oscillator on its side, successfully locating the missing charge crystal ports, but failed to assess what they may be or how crucial they were to the device's operations.

"Wow, this really is something. I've never seen anything made quite like –"

"Get on with it!" Deckard bellowed, leaning over Eucer's shoulder. "I want out of here!"

The scientist continued to tinker with the tubing and exterior parts, growing frustrated when the software didn't immediately compute with his wishes. Finally, he gently smacked it with his palm three times, before shrugging to his commander.

"*Uhh*, this device is very elaborate," Eucer lamented, trying to tap the main interface. "I think it might have been damaged in the ship's crash. If Mr. Ross can't operate it, then I doubt that I'll be of *much* –"

WHAM!

Eucer shrieked as Deckard's balled fist slammed into the back of his skull, knocking him down to the cockpit floor. Adam went to help him up but stopped when he felt Tanner's pistol barrel pressing into his cheek.

"Hand it over," Deckard barked as the scientist surrendered the oscillator.

Adam noticed that his rival's demeanor was volatile. His neck muscles were bulging, and his right eye twitched.

"I've had it with these games," the warlord grumbled as the FATR shook momentarily, going over a bump in the road. "Mr. Ross, I think if given some time, I'll figure out the device on my own. Thank you, but your services are no longer needed."

A wicked smile crossed the tyrant's face.

"I don't need you anymore..."

Adam watched in horror as Deckard leveled a pulse pistol toward his head. His eyes locked with his enemy's, and then on the glowing aura of the pistol charge.

"Closing remarks?"

"Just one," Adam replied, his heart rate miraculously calming. "You better hope it kills me. 'Cause if it doesn't, I'll kill you. I'll kill you all!"

#

SHRRK!

Her shoulder striking the coarse edge of the mountain base, Severine skirted through a narrow pathway that snaked between the reddened peaks. From her time spent in captivity under Deckard's careful watch, she gained knowledge of a thin passageway that cut between two of the mountains. It didn't take her long to find the hidden trail, covered in secret by crudely placed sawed off leaves by the Exiles.

She guessed that the FATR, with its wide frame, would be forced to go around the mountains if Deckard wanted to gain access to the easier terrain that sat on the other side of the Mountains of Blood. Once the rover completed its turn a few miles north, Severine assumed the rover should be heading back down the way she was headed. By turning his vehicle around and heading south, Deckard could put distance between his enemies faster once the vehicle arrived at the nearby desert dunes.

Down the terrifyingly narrow road that borders on a cliff, Severine thought, remembering her days spent in captivity. *He's trying to get down to the dunes where he can expedite his getaway.*

With a final push, Severine exited out through the other side of the mountain pass, finding herself standing atop a small gorge that overlooked the road. Beyond, as she remembered, sat the large cliff that emptied out into the sandy dunes. She didn't have time to admire the breathtaking view for long.

EWWRRRRRR!

The FATR! Deckard must be double-timing it if it's here already!

In a matter of seconds, the camouflaged jungle-painted machine appeared to her left, coming up the thin rocky pass below her feet. A pack of hungry carnivores bounded after the machine, which would make missing the roof a deadly consequence.

With the charge crystals to the oscillator fitting snugly in her pocket, she breathed calmly and jumped from the ledge as the powerful vehicle passed below her, praying that she would land on metal and not in the flight path of the Triassic predators.

XXVII

"What was that?" Deckard asked, turning the pistol away from Adam Ross for a second to look up at the ceiling, as if staring at the metallic rivets would reveal the source of the disruption.

A series of hollow bangs continued somewhere above the FATR, as if someone or something was lumbering along the rooftop. To Adam's relief, Deckard turned away from Adam to investigate, peering up at the hatch from the cockpit into the central room.

"Tanner!" Deckard roared. "I think that bitch may have followed us! Go up there and finish the job, once and for all!"

"Why, sir?" Tanner asked. "With all due respect, the hatch is sealed. She can't get in. Just keep the FATR moving, pilot, and she'll fall off."

The pilot nodded, pressing down on the FATR's accelerator controls, pressing the machine ahead at a faster speed. Adam watched in horror as the trees streaked past. The rover turned a rough bend, and the surroundings transitioned from jungle to desert-like rocky outcroppings.

They're heading for the other side of the mountains, but why?

"Because I want that bitch dead!" Deckard replied to Tanner's question. "I can't risk her doing something to jeopardize our getting to the present reality. That woman is cunning; if she wants in here, she's getting in. Now, get up there and wipe her off the Triassic, once and for all. You two, go with him!"

Tanner nodded, annoyed but compliant.

"Come with me," he ordered sternly, heading outside of the cockpit to the hatch. He bumped roughly into Adam on his way out, knocking the Federation lieutenant off balance. The other two guards snickered as they left. Adam winced, pulling himself back up on a handlebar. Deckard and his remaining guard kept their weapons trained on him as he regained his stance. In the background, he could see Eucer watching from the control terminal beside Deckard's pilot.

"Well, Mr. Ross. I must say I'm impressed by your friend's loyalty," Deckard smiled. "If that's her up there, that is."

No sooner than the words left his mouth, the hatch to the roof closed shut, followed by several rounds of muted pulse fire, muffled through the rover's armored shell.

"Oh, it's her," Adam replied. "And when she gets in here, she'll put a round through your ear."

"Not unless we aren't here," Deckard smirked, again raising the gun. "Now, Mr. Ross, fix the damn oscillator!"

"I told you, asshole!" Adam yelled. "I don't know how to repair it!"

"Well you're going to learn," Deckard replied bluntly, a look of irritation passing over his face. "Eucer! Go back to the rear hold and get the boy up here. Mr. Ross here is going to speed up our evacuation process."

Eucer staggered sideways, shocked and unsure how to proceed.

"You're going to kill the child, Deckard?" Eucer asked.

"If our hostage doesn't do as he's told, yes."

"Sir, I really don't think that..."

"Eucer, go and get that damn kid! Or it's you I'll be putting the round into! Why is everyone suddenly questioning me? For shit's sake! Don't you want to get out of *here* –"

WHRRR! WHRRR!

The firefight raged above on the rooftop. The pulse blasts sounded significantly closer, this time almost right above the cockpit.

Severine is winning!

"She's almost here, Deckard! You ready to face her again?"

"Shut up, Ross! Pilot, swerve! Try to throw her off the roof!"

"But Tanner is up *ther* –"

"You think I give a shit? Pilot, spin that damn wheel right now or I'll toss you up there in the firefight!"

The pilot turned back to argue, but after staring at Deckard's pistol, the man turned back and grabbed the wheel hard, preparing to spin the rover into a disastrous turn. Even through the windshield, Adam could see the trail ahead narrowing, approaching a sharp turn to the right, teetering on the edge of a monstrous ravine, exposing endless miles of desert dunes far below.

Adam's heart skipped as the pilot's hands jerked to the side, shifting gravity for everyone on board and those battling on the roof.

Oh, fu –

Adam was thrown off balance once again, this time flipping over a chair in the cockpit and crashing over an unused control console. Behind him, he could hear Deckard, Eucer and the remaining guard falling as well, followed by a cacophony of metallic bangs as they collided with various terminal ports. The FATR turned sharply to avoid the disastrous fall; the pilot choosing instead to ram the vehicle against the edge of the mountain, sending a mess of rocky boulders pounding into the right side of the vehicle and spawning spiderweb cracks up the cockpit glass.

Before Adam could consciously gather his thoughts, he could hear Deckard's faltering voice on the other side of the room.

"Guard! Kill that kid and bring the bot in here, maybe the machine can figure out this futuristic piece of shit after all."

"Yes, sir!"

No!

Adam jumped up to intercept the guard, only to realize that Deckard once again had his weapon at the ready.

"Say goodbye, Mr. Ros –"

WHAM!

Adam was astonished at the speed at which Eucer, Deckard's trusted mechanic, sped across the room and rammed into the warlord's side. Forced momentarily against the wall, his cheek pressed against a bend in the wall, Deckard swung his corroded bladed arm around to decapitate his former lackey. The blade met with air – Eucer was gone, already down the hall to prevent the boy's execution.

"You ungrateful sack of shit, wait till I get my –"

Harnessing all of the aggression welled up inside of him, brought on by Wyatt, the natives, the dinosaurs, and now the Exiles, Adam sailed across the room, leg extended in a powerful sidekick.

With Adam's boot sailing into Deckard's back, the warlord let out an agitated yelp as his pistol discharged once, the bolt zinging toward the front, catching the pilot in the skull.

The lifeless cadaver slumped forward over the controls, jamming the driving mechanism and sending the FATR on a straight shot ahead toward the narrow cliff trail.

#

As Severine's feet left the ledge from the small, mossy ravine, she cringed as Deckard's FATR flew by beneath her. The machine drove past with such ferocity that she feared she'd miss the roof altogether – the alternative being landing an extra thirty feet or so to the rocky floor.

VRABOOM!

She fell ten feet from the cliff onto the edge of the metallic roof, grappling onto an exhaust duct that shot up just beside the rear access ladder. She felt her feet swing past and dangle over the ledge, her footwear hitting off the rear of the vehicle beside the ladder.

"*Augh!*" she cried, grinding her teeth and hanging on to the exhaust vent.

CHOMP!

Severine turned to the ground beneath her, locking eyes with a pair of herreras who chose to give chase to the rover, bounding forward and leaping to snag her feet.

Not today, fellas.

She pulled herself over the roof with a final tug, ignoring the futile attempts of the herreras. Three more appeared above her on the ridge, running alongside through the rocky nooks, searching for the best place to hop onto the Federation machine's roof. One of the dinosaurs paused on the overlook, deciding against risking hopping over and tumbling down to the opposite, more deadly cliff.

"There she is! *Blast her!*"

Deckard's muscular enforcer Tanner was on the roof near the front of the rover, paired with two companions armed with pulse rifles.

Jeez! Does this guy ever run out of henchmen?

She narrowly avoided a blast to her shoulder, tilting clumsily behind another ventilation unit and returned fire, tagging one of Tanner's men squarely in the chest.

"*Aooph!*" the man howled, falling backwards, rolling and disappearing over the edge of the FATR.

"Move in," Tanner ordered. "We need to get closer to take her down!"

Severine traded rounds with Deckard's enforcer, the two of them hopping between the various rooftop obstacles as they advanced toward the center. The other gunman lingered toward the back, cautious to advance too close to the firefight.

"You coward!" Tanner called, shooting off another blast. "It's two on one! Get up here!"

Severine launched a blast toward the subordinate's direction; a move that again affirmed the lad's desire to stay back.

"Are you crazy?" the younger assassin called out. "She's a wicked shot. She'll kill us both! I'm heading back down the hatch!"

"You *fool!*" Tanner replied, again exchanging rounds with Severine. "Do you want Deckard to kill you? It'd be easier if you'd come –"

VERRRRRR! KACHROOM!

The rover turned abruptly, causing Severine to wobble, dropping her firearm. The weapon clattered once over the rooftop before vanishing over the edge. She went to reach for it, missing by inches and helpless to watch as the silver object twinkled away into the desert wasteland far below the narrow road. When she got up, she realized what had happened.

Trying to shake her off the roof, while also trying to avoid a crook in the road, the driver spun the vehicle to the right, which forced the FATR into the side of the rocky hill. Chunks of dirt and earth showered over the front of the vehicle like a sandstorm where the collision occurred, pummeling the cowardly youthful gunman near the front.

You gotta be kidding me!

Before the FATR could clear the debris, three herreras slid down the deteriorating slope and onto the roof, cleverly landing in a way to regain balance. After they grew accustomed to the shifting momentum that the vehicle created, the one nearest the front noticed the isolated gunman, snapping its jaws in anticipation of the meal to follow.

"*No, please! Noooaaaa!*"

With a powerful jab, the first herrera sacked the youth, spreading its jaws over the young man's face before the assassin's hands could reach the dropped weapon. The muted screams rippled through the dinosaur's head as the other two carnivores tore into the convulsing victim.

Well, better him than m –

WHAM!

Severine realized her mistake. In her observation of the attack, she failed to pinpoint Tanner's location. The tall enforcer appeared suddenly in front of her, having stealthily moved through the obstacles to engage her in hand-to-hand combat.

His fist struck her on the cheek, causing her to tumble backwards once again toward the rear ledge. Behind her on the ground, she could hear the herreras chomping and leaping up to pull her down to the trail, salivating at the opportunity to avenge the events that happened at the *Supernova* long ago.

She studied herself before slipping back, knowing that the only way to survive was to challenge Tanner head on. It was a daunting task that she knew would be hard to achieve.

Balling up her fists, she swung once at her opponent's head. Tanner ducked expertly, avoiding the strike and stepping back to the side, returning with a swift kick to her stomach. Severine blocked it quickly, but failed to see his secondary spin kick coming her way.

WHAM!

The kick caught her in the chin. The blow knocked her again onto the roof, her chin smacking off the metal. With a forceful push from Tanner's boot, the fight was over. Her body slipped off the edge. Her reflexes kicking in, she grabbed hold of the vehicle's ledge. The ladder was three feet to her right, just out of reach.

"Augh!"

She looked up to her antagonist, who appeared above her. A wicked smile crossed the enforcer's face as his boot met with her quivering fingertips. Below, the herrera pack continued the chase, grunting with each failed leap. Severine cursed, again finding herself dangling below a hungry Herrerasaur just as she had been while in captivity of the Davenport tribe years earlier.

"You better figure out that oscillator before he does," Severine yelled up at him. "If he figures it out before you do, do you really think he'll take you with him? Of course not. He'll betray you too!"

"*Ha!*" Tanner called down. "I've let him think he's in command long enough. Before long, I'll do away with him and take the oscillator for myself. Just like I'm about to do away with *youuuuaaaaugh!*"

Tanner convulsed as one of the rooftop herreras besieged his back, jumping onto the strongman with a savage leap. Tanner struggled to throw off the beast, shifting on his feet and stepping away from Severine as the dinosaur bit down on his shoulder. With an agonizing amount of effort, Severine again pulled herself onto the roof, rolling onto her back and catching her breath.

"*Get it off!*" Tanner screamed, trying to punch off the animal that had latched onto his back. The weight of the dinosaur was pulling him down. Spinning, he tried to throw the herrera off, shifting again and walking backwards toward the rear edge of the rover.

Unaware that Severine had climbed back up, he unknowingly walked into her trap. Stepping around the exhaust pipe, Severine flung out her leg, tripping her opponent and his primordial attacker, sending them both over the edge of the rover, head first.

"*No!*" Tanner cried, his plea cut short by his skull smashing into the rocky road.

Severine cringed as the herrera pack was on him in seconds, latching onto his limbs. Tanner was too weak to fight back, having been severely wounded from the fall. More herreras appeared from the overlook above, bounding down the narrow trails to join in the feast. The carnivores who were late to the party gave up and resumed chasing after the rover, catching a glimpse of Severine lying on the roof.

These little pecker heads don't give up!

Tired, but aware that the real fight awaited inside the rover, she turned and bounded toward the open hatch ahead. The two herreras near the front turned up from their meal and watched as another human ran toward them. Startled at first and then regaining their boldness, the dinosaurs rose from their dinner and raced to meet her, realizing that if she reached the open hatch she'd be safe – they were too large and bulky to fit through the opening.

RAUGH!

Jumping through the air, the first herrera dove below her. The dinosaur chomped down and bit air, missing Severine's feet narrowly as she launched above the creature. The second herrera spread its jaws with delight, aiming at her head. Severine anticipated the dinosaur's timing perfectly, as gravity pulled her back down below – her feet, legs, waist, body and head vanishing through the open hatch.

#

"We gotta get out of here!" Nathan cried to Jordy beside him, struggling with his bindings.

"*What-t-t's* going on *up-p* there?" Jordy asked.

"Severine's here!" Nathan said. "It has to be her! Or Alex and Kara. Either way, we have to bust out now while we have an opening!"

VRRR.

Suddenly the door to the rear chamber opened. A lone gunman walked in. A look of shame and confusion welled in his face. At his waist was an activated pulse rifle, a round already charging inside the barrel.

"Can we *he-l-l-lp* you?" Jordy asked, confused.

"Sorry, kid," the guard replied, visibly in turmoil. "I don't want to do this. Boss' orders!"

"What?"

Before Nathan could realize what the man meant, he saw the soldier raise the barrel in his direction. The boy's young eyes locked on the charge, its beautiful colors calling him home – to Solis.

VROOM!

An orange bolt of light erupted through the guard's chest, sailing past Nathan and Jordy's eyes in a nanosecond. Sparks and fizzling particles shot through the chest wound. The man tumbled onto his knees, too shocked to breathe. His weapon fell to the side, discharging once into the wall.

VROOM!

The dead man's blast rocketed into the rear hatch access port - a small junction style box mounted to the left wall. In an instant, the rear door began to open, flooding sunlight into the room.

Eucer stepped inside the chamber, serpentine smoke wisps rising from the fired weapon. A look of shock washing over his face, he staggered past the corpse and arrived at the two tethered hostages.

"*You!*" Nathan exclaimed, enthralled to be alive. "Why?"

"Because I couldn't let him kill you," Eucer admitted. "I've listened to his homicidal orders for long enough. Now, hold still. It'll be easier for me to blast through your bindings than for me to try and figure out their knots."

VROOM! VROOM VROOM VROOM!

Eucer exhausted the rounds of the weapon, tossing the gun aside as Jordy and Nathan rose to their feet, free from their shackles.

KACHUNG!

The rear platform had completely extended, landing roughly on the rocky debris as the rover continued onward in its disastrous journey. As Nathan stared out of the exit, realizing he could easily walk off the ramp and be safe from Deckard, he saw that new terrors awaited just outside.

Herreras!

A whole pack of the terrifying reptiles pursued the FATR, eyes narrowing on the three figures standing in the rear chamber of the vehicle. They blinked and maneuvered away from the flying gravel that bounced up toward their snouts, growling in agitation as they planned to scale the ramp.

"Oh *no-o-o-o!*" Jordy bleeped.

"Can you seal the door and bring the ramp back?" Nathan asked.

"No," Eucer lamented, running over to the junction box. "The system's fried!"

Sparks fired out from the wires in a torrent, precisely where the bolt entered the circuitry. Eucer cautiously tangled with the wires with no success.

SHREAAAH!

A herrera hopped onto the ramp, lashing out with its claws as it prepared to board the FATR. Eucer quickly fired off several pulse rounds at the fierce reptile, only to have all blasts pass by and exit into the desert. _

With a growl it jumped another five feet ahead, landing in the center of the room.

Click! Click!

"I'm out!" Eucer yelled, throwing the weapon at the approaching dinosaur.

The rifle slammed into the herrera. With a yelp of surprise, the animal jumped to the side, colliding with a large deep-freeze container. The box shook furiously before teetering off balance – towering over Nathan and pinning him to the ground upon impact.

"*No!*" Nathan yelled, his head, shoulders and arms exposed from beneath the obstacle.

The herrera turned and saw the opportunity, jumping on top of the container and walking ominously toward the boy, seizing the opportunity. Nathan was unable to escape, trapped and forced to watch as the monster approached, crushing him with its weight on top of the box.

"*Aughh*, Jordy, help!" Nathan cried, forced to watch as the herrera approached, saliva dripping from its chomping jaws.

#

Adam ducked as Deckard's blade swung around, just in time to avoid decapitation. Although the warlord's long blade had been severed by Meras' sniper round, what was left resembled a corroded dagger, still dangerous if applied correctly.

WHAAAAA!

The blade sung as it cut through the air, barely audible over the rumble of the rover's treads.

Adam rose back up, just in time to see Deckard's knife coming for another pass.

WHAAAAA!

Backwards somersaulting over the top of a chair and falling over the other side, Adam found himself separated from Deckard by an inoperable Federation mapping table. The distance bought some time to retrieve a weapon – a singular, sturdy pole that must've been used by Tanner for enforcement.

WHAAAAA!

Deckard maneuvered around the table, swinging again. Adam blocked the strike just in time with his chrome pole. The defensive block allowed Adam time to rise back up and challenge the warlord face-to-face, this time driving his opponent backwards, dueling around the cockpit of the unmanned FATR.

Adam tried not to focus on the uncertainty of the situation that had unfolded. No one was driving the rover, which looked as if it had set itself up for a collision course through a narrow cliff trail that bordered a sandy world beside the jungle. The second alarming fact was that the gunfire on the rooftop had ended, meaning that Severine's death may have been possible. He found her demise unlikely; the ancient Federation soldier had been a deadly shot. Finally, he saw what looked like a pack of rabid herreras chasing after the rover, visible through the side windows and trying to board the roof.

WHACK!

Adam smacked the oscillator out of Deckard's hand. The device bounced off the floor and rolled into the middle room, out of view from the combatants.

"You *idiot!*" Deckard roared in rage, stabbing forward with the blade. "You wanna break that thing! It's our only ticket off this vile world!"

The jab missed, launching right past Deckard's opponent. Adam pushed the warlord's arm away, punching his enemy in the face with a sturdy fist.

"*Daugh!*" Deckard shrieked, stumbling backwards against a glass window. He was so distracted by a bloody nose, he didn't see the impressive jump from a herrera behind, which bounded off the other side of the glass before falling back to the trail below.

Adam rushed forward, ready to swing up with the pole and crush Deckard's skull. But the move was a mistake – Adam's weapon banged off a ventilation duct in the ceiling, preventing the strike, allowing Deckard to slice against Adam's shoulder with the damaged bladed arm.

"*Augh!*" Adam cried, remembering the wound from Wyatt's gun.

The injury wasn't severe, but it was enough to make Adam fall backwards, dropping his weapon that rolled over under the pilot's control console. He went to retrieve it, but the rapidly approaching footsteps deterred him.

THUNK!

A sharp, unexpected pain exploded in his abdomen. At first, he thought he'd ruptured an organ, but his eyes soon confirmed the strike was from Deckard's boot tip. The blow bowled him over onto his back, making him forget about the pole, clutching the bruise with both hands as his eyes met again with Deckard's.

Before Adam could rise again, Deckard slammed his boot down once again, connecting with Adam's chest. The attack knocked the wind out of Adam, who lodged both hands under the boot and tried to catch a breath.

The warlord's legs were powerful. The pressure felt like a concrete cinder block was weighing him down.

"Well, Mr. Ross!" Deckard began after a harsh laugh. "I've underestimated your resilience. But you've actually made it easy on me. Instead of having to double-cross my entire team with the oscillator, you've picked them all off for me."

"You'll never figure out how to work that thing," Adam managed a smile, while still wincing under the boot pressure. "You'll die here in the Triassic. Probably today, when the rover rolls off one of these cliffs."

"Sadly, Mr. Ross, you're mistaken. I'm taking the oscillator back to the Colony. There I'll find a way to bring it back to life. I'll just have to do a little more double-crossing to make sure no one else comes back with me. Now, Mr. Ross, prepare to meet you –"

VAROOM!

An orange bolt sailed past the struggle, exploding an overhead exterior monitor and showering them both with glass shards.

"Hey asshole, thought you could get rid of me that easy!" came a familiar female voice from the cockpit doorway. "Took care of your three thugs up there, now it's just you and me."

Severine! She's alive!

VAROOM!

Another orange blast entered the room, barely missing Deckard. The warlord dove to the left, allowing the blast to strike the piloting control console, further adding to the system's failure. Adam relaxed, grateful that the pressure was off his chest and resumed his search for a weapon now that chaos resumed.

VAROOM! VAROOM! Click-

"Oh shit!" Adam heard Severine say.

His friend was out of ammunition. It would become a close quarters fight. He searched frantically for a melee-based weapon. The pole was still out of reach, lodged in a narrow crevice under the table. Adam ruled out that option.

Come on! Give me something here! Anything.

He glanced up once, revealing a fist fight had commenced. Deckard lunged at her toward the entrance. She avoided the deadly move, choosing instead on entering the wide cockpit and having more room to maneuver. A series of grunts and yells proceeded as the two arch rivals moved about in the room.

Adam scurried over the floor. He could feel his stomach growing tighter with each move, adrenaline fueling the quick healing process from where Deckard tried to crunch him. The fight behind him sounded like it took a turn again, back to the central supply room and out of the cockpit doors.

Finally, Adam saw a glimmer of chrome under a chair.

Perfect! I hope it works.

Secured under a chair with tape or some other adhesive, was what looked like an unused X2-20. The activation light on the weapon was still on, revealing potentially a full round of pulse charges. Adam threw his right hand over the weapon, pulled down on the grip with his left and ripped the gun from below the chair, tape still draped over the stock.

Grabbing the top of the chair, Adam pulled himself upright, flicked off the safety and turned toward the cockpit entrance, revealing the worst possible situation that could have awaited him.

Deckard was behind Severine, a knife to her throat.

"I always have a bargaining chip, Mr. Ross," Deckard said, waving the oscillator in his other hand before tucking it under his garbs. "I'll be taking this with me back to the Colony, and you'll be going down with the FATR, I'm afraid."

Deckard gestured to the cockpit glass behind Adam, which revealed another horrific sight. The rover hurried down a trail that grew narrower by the second, toward a steep precipice that dropped off a significant distance. As they approached the ledge, Adam noticed how small the dunes ahead looked from over the cliff. The fall would probably kill them all if they didn't bail out prior to the plunge.

Keeping his cool, he turned back to Deckard.

"Kill him, Adam!" Severine yelled. "Quit peckering around!"

"When I get out of here," Adam began, "I'll hunt you down, Deckard! You and whatever bullshit colony you're talking about. I'll kill you. And if they're with you, I'll kill them too."

Deckard backed up a few steps, pulling his valuable hostage with him. The warlord stopped at the ladder to the upper hatch. He cast a quick look upward, noticing that there were no herreras on top, and took a step on the bottom rung, keeping Severine in front of him. Adam followed into the chamber, pausing six feet away or so before Deckard pressed the blade harder into Severine's throat, drawing a drop of blood.

"That's close enough, Mr. Ross," he smiled.

"Kill him, Adam! Don't let him get away!"

Adam ignored her, instead choosing to study Deckard's eyes, trying to determine his enemy's next move.

What? He's gonna climb up a ladder with a hostage and only one hand?

"It's over, Deckard! Let her go!"

"Uncle Adam!" a voice broke through the fray, calling out from the other room.

Adam turned, looking past the standoff into the last room of the rover. As his eyes focused, he instantly saw the head of his nephew lodged under a massive deep-freeze container. Jordy and Eucer remained not far, dumbfounded on what to do. On top of the crate, an adult herrera proceeded toward the boy, weighing down the cargo with its immense weight, crushing Nathan beneath it. Inch by inch, the creature moved toward the boy's head, jaws agape and ready to strike a death blow. Several other herreras were chasing after the rover, leaping toward the ramp and trying to board.

"Uncle Adam! Please, do something! I'm stuck!"

"Nathan, hold on!" Adam yelled. "I'm coming!"

"Well this is rather unexpected, Mr. Ross," Deckard said after realizing what was happening. "Looks like the rear hatch controls are jammed. Those herreras will be in here momentarily, and you'll be their meal. I, however, have other plans! Here, catch!"

Backing up a step, Deckard fired a kick into Severine's back. Screaming in pain from the force, she shot forward. Adam felt the weapon leave his hand as his friend rammed into him, knocking them both over and tumbling back into the cockpit. By the time Adam looked back up, Deckard had already vanished into the upper hatch, and with him – the coveted portal oscillator device.

SHREAAAA!

The herrera from two rooms ahead cried, taking another step toward Nathan's exposed cranium. Adam realized revenge with Deckard would have to wait. Right now, the only mission was to save his nephew and escape the runaway rover alive.

XXVIII

Adam rushed through the central room, wobbling as the massive vehicle tumbled through the odd terrain. He could feel that old Triassic headache coming on again, brought on by the horror of the thought of losing his nephew.

"Mr. Ross, Nathan *ne-e-e-eds* your –"

Yes Jordy, I can see that!

Adam bumped into the bumbling robot, knocking him into a weapons cache that was strapped against the wall. Through the open door, he could see the herrera trying to chomp down against his nephew's exposed head as the boy convulsed in terror. The weight of the herrera was too strong, pinning the boy below the obstacle as the dinosaur walked on top of the large box. Deckard's stooge, Eucer, remained at the corner of the room, petrified and unable to move.

As Adam stepped over the dead body of the guard, the herrera lifted its head and snarled at Adam, issuing a serpent-like warning with a familiar hiss.

"Uncle Adam!" Nathan cried. "You're alive! Please help me!"

The herrera snapped once at Adam and then back at Nathan, stepping over the box to make its final snap.

With a quick lunge, Adam shoved the bipedal carnivore over, sending the dinosaur tumbling off the box, throughout the room and down the on ramp, crashing onto the earth below. It struggled to get up, turning back toward the departing vehicle and giving a roar of defeat.

Ah, shit! Not this again...

As Severine entered the room and helped him yank the massive crate off Nathan, Adam caught a familiar horrible sight – more herreras. There was a whole pack of the monstrous overgrown lizards chasing after the FATR, running in a full-on sprint along the edge of the ravine. Adam could see the individual dinosaur that he'd just pushed off rejoining the chase, eager for round two to begin.

"I can't move this thing!" Severine yelled. "It's too heavy!"

"Hey you!" Adam called over to Eucer. "Get over here and help us move this scrap!"

Eucer nodded and staggered over, wrapping both of his hands around the crate's edge next to Severine. After a one-two-three count, Adam commanded them to pull as hard as they could. With the combined effort, the deep-freeze container lifted off and rolled over. Adam yanked Nathan up and checked him over for bruises.

"You okay, kid?"

"Yeah, I'm fine!" Nathan yelled, nervous and grateful to be rescued. He threw both arms around Adam and hugged him tightly.

"I thought he was gonna kill you."

"He was."

"Did you kill him?"

"Not exactly, he went –"

"*Wat-t-tch* out!" Jordy bleeped, stepping into the rear room.

Adam turned just in time to see the first herrera leap onto the ramp, shaking uneasily to balance itself. The FATR struck a bump in the road, forcing everything inside the vehicle to rattle. The dinosaur lost balance and fell back onto the road – just as two more herreras leaped back on.

"We have to get out!" Eucer cried, stating the obvious.

The herreras began to climb toward them, now joined by two others who hopped onto the lower ramp. The leader issued a harsh growl as it nudged the others along, instantly spotting the five human targets near the back of the rear chamber.

"Let's fall back to the central room!" Adam said. "We can climb out the hatch!"

They spun in reverse and sprinted through the security door into the armory room, looking up at the hatch, which remained open – greeted by two snapping herrera heads. The dinosaurs glared down the opening at them, shaking from the movement of the vehicle. They were unable to proceed downward; the opening was too small for their reptilian bulky forms to enter through. Nonetheless, they guarded the exit loyally, spitting down strands of oozing saliva at the humans.

Severine quickly fumbled with the lock security panel to seal up the rear room.

"*Ah!*" Severine shrieked, trying to make sense of the toggle switches. "Julius was always so much better at operating these things than I was!"

"Here," Eucer said, hurrying over. "Just hit this!"

Instantly, the door came to life and a door panel shot out toward the other side.

SHREWAA!

The sturdy head of the alpha herrera burst through the opening, only to be met with the oncoming security door. The panel stalled, striking the left side of the dinosaur's snout, preventing the exit to be sealed. The herrera growled in fury as another head moved in below it. The two dinosaurs convulsed and pushed together, trying to force the door open.

"The cockpit!" Nathan yelled. "It's the only safe spot!"

"You said it," Adam returned, shoving the boy and the bot toward the opening ahead. The five humans swarmed into the chamber. Eucer sealed the entrance seconds before the herreras breached into the central room. From behind the security panel, they could feel the dinos ramming their skulls into the barrier, hoping to push through the door with brute force.

"Son of a bitch!" Severine yelled, pointing to the glass.

Adam turned, looking past the deceased corpse of Deckard's pilot to the cracked windshield. Ahead, the FATR plowed through the rocky trail toward the infinite dune lands that stretched beyond – preceded by the massive drop off that approached rapidly.

Shit!

"It's a cliff!" Nathan shrieked.

"Can you stop this thing?" Adam yelled, spinning around to Eucer.

"Probably not," replied the technician, running over to the driver's seat and pushing the cadaver from the chair.

He fumbled through the controls, pushing buttons and switching levers that revealed only faint blips and flickering useless hologram options. The programming had been damaged in the cockpit shootout. Options in the projector displays vanished before Eucer could select them. After he tried a quick reboot, nothing turned on.

WHAM! WHAM!

Behind, Adam could feel the ramming of the herreras against the cockpit door as he braced against it, earning a few more seconds before the dinos could break through the barrier. Through the windshield, the daunting crevice approached, revealing a hundred foot near vertical drop off to the dunes. The ground around the rover began to split asunder, forming small fragments as the road started to crumble.

"We're going over!" Nathan cringed.

"We'll have to jump!" Severine replied, grabbing at a chrome overturned chair. "Adam, help me. We'll chuck it through the glass!"

"*Hurry-y-y,*" the bot gestured toward the oncoming chasm. "The fault is *ahe-e-ad.*"

"*Heaauuuh!*" Adam yelled, lifting the heavy object with Severine.

Eucer raced over to help, and together they launched the projectile through the windshield. The chair shattered the glass with the first try; the barrier having already been weakened by the pulse blast that killed the pilot. The glass splintered off, showering the chair as the seat fell below the cockpit, out of view and crunched by the FATR's powerful treads.

Ahead, the ground continued to split apart as the cliff summit withered away. The vehicle tilted forward, sliding down the deteriorated slope toward the desert wasteland.

WHAM! WHAM!

The pounding behind him continued. Adam heard the gnashing of dinosaur fangs through the metal, followed by a scraping of claws against the other side of the door.

"What are you doing?" Eucer yelled as Severine jumped up on the windshield support over the sparking dashboard.

"Jumping out!" she replied angrily. "Or do you wanna go down with the vehicle? Jordy, get up here!"

"But *Se-v-v-v,* I'm not sure –"

Severine wasted no time in grabbing the bot and throwing the machine out the opening, trying to hurl Jordy toward the side of the rover so the machine wouldn't be crushed by the treads.

"*Whoa!*" Nathan managed.

"He's fine," Severine replied, looking downward as the FATR roared past Jordy's assumed landing position. "Okay, now you, pal."

"Hey, I'm not really –"

"Get out the damn window!" she yelled at Eucer, who waved in submission and leaped toward the same position she threw the bot, vanishing from over the FATR control console.

Warm air flooded into the machine from the dune lands below as the vehicle plummeted forward, and then, everything went vertical. The gravity in the room shifted, sending toppled chairs, glass fragments, and the pilot's body out through the front opening.

Adam pushed Nathan over into a supply closet in the corner of the room, seconds before the door to the central room burst open. Three herreras tumbled into the cockpit only to be pulled by gravity through the windshield. As Adam rushed to avoid the lashing jaws, he saw Severine get smacked by the tail of the alpha male herrera, forcing her to release her grip on the windshield that she had been using as support.

No!

In a flash she was gone, tumbling downward toward the ground below with her three carnivorous foes. Soon the falling debris obscured her location. Showers of rocky mountain fragments skirted past the front of the rover as the vehicle fell toward the desert ground.

"*Uncle Adam!*"

"Don't move, Nathan!" Adam screamed over the carnage, forcing himself into the cockpit utility closet. He reached out to grab hold of the metallic door, casting one last look at the deadly impact that awaited. With a final gruff tug, he managed to pull the door shut as a rhythmic collision rocked the ancient Federation transport vehicle, followed by the torrent of rocks that pelted the exterior plating.

The last thing Adam saw before he lost consciousness was his nephew holding his head for safety in a fetal position and the flickering of the industrial red light above his head. With a spark, the bulb shattered and darkness flooded the chamber.

THE END

Severine Solens and Adam Ross will return.

Don't forget to leave an honest review of this book on Amazon.com and Goodreads.com. Reviews help writers get noticed which will help reach more readers.

ABOUT THE AUTHOR

Joey Kelly (known by his pen name Julian Michael Carver) was born in Pittsburgh in 1992. He graduated from the now defunct Art Institute of Pittsburgh in 2013 with a degree in Visual Effects and Motion Graphics. In addition to writing, Carver is employed as a commercial editor. He uses his skills in multimedia to help market his books. In addition to commercial design work, Carver is also an avid fossil hunter. Carver currently lives north of Pittsburgh with his wife, Cloey.

CHECK OUT OTHER GREAT DINOSAUR BOOKS

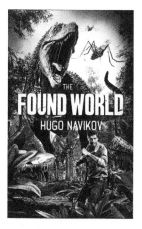

THE FOUND WORLD
by Hugo Navikov

A powerful global cabal wants adventurer Brett Russell to retrieve a superweapon stolen by the scientist who built it. To entice him to travel underneath one of the most dangerous volcanoes on Earth to find the scientist, this shadowy organization will pay him the only thing he cares about: information that will allow him to avenge his family's murder.

But before he can get paid, he and his team must enter an underground hellscape of killer plants, giant insects, terrifying dinosaurs, and an army of other predators never previously seen by man.

At the end of this journey awaits a revelation that could alter the fate of mankind ... if they can make it back from this horrifying found world.

HOUSE OF THE GODS
by Davide Mana

High above the steamy jungle of the Amazon basin, rise the flat plateaus known as the Tepui, the House of the Gods. Lost worlds of unknown beauty, a naturalistic wonder, each an ecology onto itself, shunned by the local tribes for centuries. The House of the Gods was not made for men.

But now, the crew and passengers of a small charter plane are about to find what was hidden for sixty million years.

Lost on an island in the clouds 10.000 feet above the jungle, surrounded by dinosaurs, hunted by mysterious mercenaries, the survivors of Sligo Air flight 001 will quickly learn the only rule of life on Earth: Extinction.

CHECK OUT OTHER GREAT DINOSAUR BOOKS

PRIMORDIA
by **Greig Beck**

Ben Cartwright, former soldier, home to mourn the loss of his father stumbles upon cryptic letters from the past between the author, Arthur Conan Doyle and his great, great grandfather who vanished while exploring the Amazon jungle in 1908.

Amazingly, these letters lead Ben to believe that his ancestor's expedition was the basis for Doyle's fantastical tale of a lost world inhabited by long extinct creatures. As Ben digs some more he finds clues to the whereabouts of a lost notebook that might contain a map to a place that is home to creatures that would rewrite everything known about history, biology and evolution.

But other parties now know about the notebook, and will do anything to obtain it. For Ben and his friends, it becomes a race against time and against ruthless rivals.

In the remotest corners of Venezuela, along winding river trails known only to lost tribes, and through near impenetrable jungle, Ben and his novice team find a forbidden place more terrifying and dangerous than anything they could ever have imagined.

PANGAEA EXILES
by **Jeff Brackett**

Tried and convicted for his crimes, Sean Barrow is sent into temporal exile—banished to a time so far before recorded history that there is no chance that he, or any other criminal sent back, has any chance of altering history.

Now Sean must find a way to survive more than 200 million years in the past, in a world populated by monstrous creatures that would rend him limb from limb if they got the chance. And that's just his fellow prisoners.

The dinosaurs are almost as bad.

CHECK OUT OTHER GREAT DINOSAUR BOOKS

FLIPSIDE
by JAKE BIBLE

The year is 2046 and dinosaurs are real.

Time bubbles across the world, many as large as one hundred square miles, turn like clockwork, revealing prehistoric landscapes from the Cretaceous Period.

They reveal the Flipside.

Now, thirty years after the first Turn, the clockwork is breaking down as one of the world's powers has decided to exploit the phenomenon for their own gain, possibly destroying everything then and now in the process.

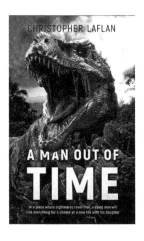

A MAN OUT OF TIME
by Christopher Laflan

Five years after the Chinese Axis detonated an unknown weapon of mass destruction off the southern coast of the United States, Special Ops Sergeant John Crider and the members of Shadow Company have finally captured what they all hope will lead to the end of the war. Unfortunately, the population within the United States is no longer sustainable. In an effort to stabilize the economy, the government enacts the Cryonics Act. One hundred years in suspended animation, all debt forgiven, and a chance at a less crowded future are too good to pass up for John and his young daughter.

Except not everything always goes as planned as Sergeant John Crider finds himself pitted against a land of prehistoric monsters genetically resurrected from the fossil record, murderous inhabitants, and a future he never wanted.